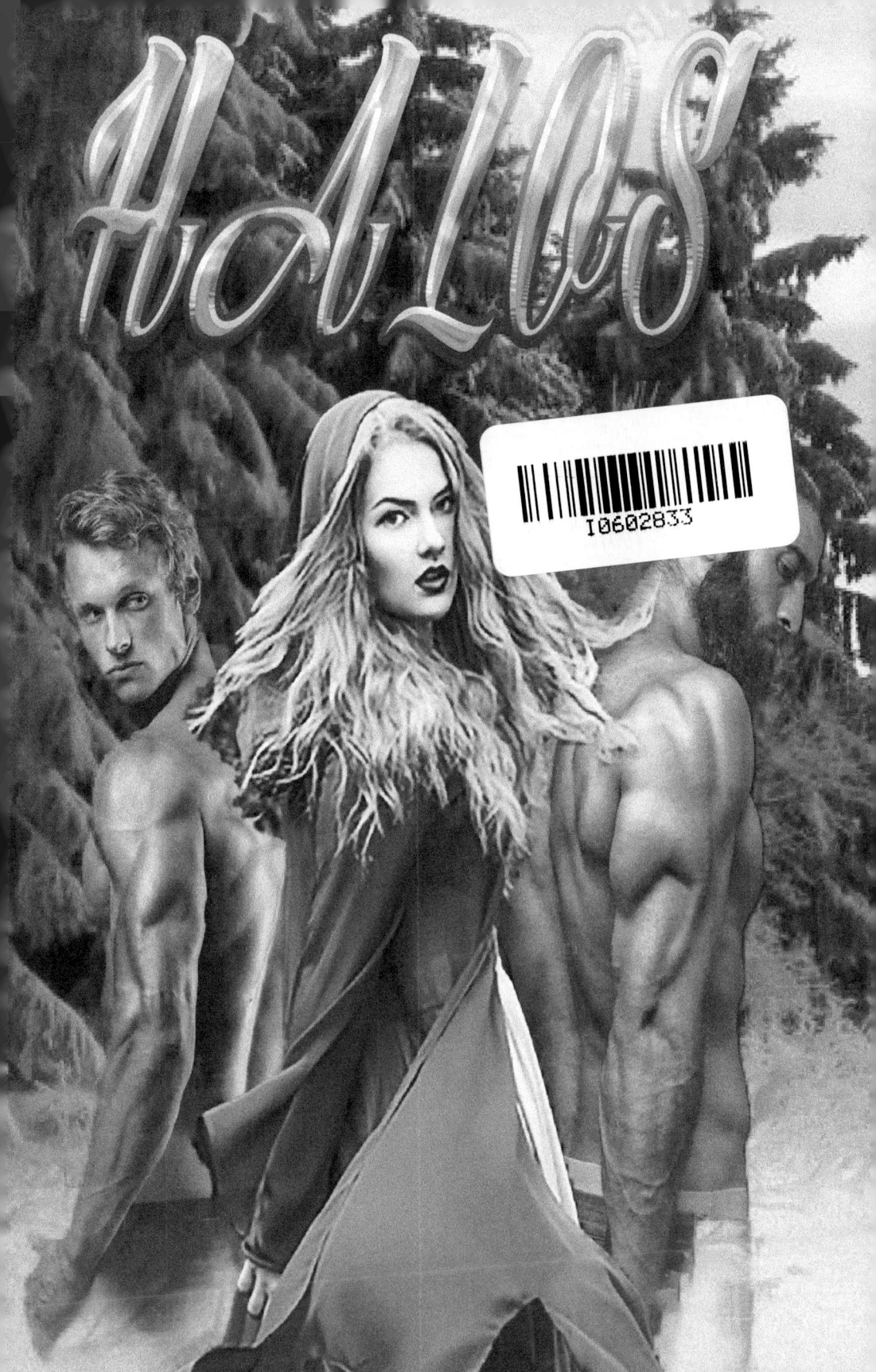

HALOS

HALOS

EBONY OLSON

EBANDMUSE & PUBLICATIONS

EBANDMUSE
PUBLICATIONS

Published 2020 by

Eb&Muse Publications, Sydney, Australia

Copyright © 2019 by **Ebony Olson.**

eBook: 9780648766575

Paperback: 9780648766582

Cover & Title-page by Strange Angel Designs

http://ebonyolson.com/

1

---

*T*he night calls to me as I stare out the window at the
sinking sun. The rising moon sings in my veins, its arrival
like the intimate caress of a lover. It beckons to me because of what I
am, but that's not who I choose to be.

Having turned my back on my birthright so long ago, I sometimes
forget about that life. That I was born a child of the night, and that
my birth burdened me with a title and responsibility. Choosing to
exist in the mundane, and to blend with humans, I walk in sunlight
now, not moonlight. Thanks to the freaks of humanity, my little oddi-
ties seem more a quirk than a worry.

In the past, we were hunted and slaughtered as evil. We've been
called vampires, witches, and every other sort of supernatural being
under the moon, but that's not what we are. Yes, we drink blood, but
we hunt evil humans for our food. Murders and rapists are our
victims.

The only ones of our kind that is undiscerning are the ravenors;
those that have given into their bloodthirst and cannot stop drinking
until they kill. They are nearly undetecatable until they are killing
you, and they are as big as threat to us, as to humans.

Not that humans would notice us amongst them, so few would

care that we exist. They no longer believe in superstition and the supernatural and are too caught up in their political machinations and selfish ideals to notice the world around them.

Only the Halos still hunt us. Enemies for as long as anyone remembers, the Halos vow to make my species extinct, killing us wherever they find us.

It's why my father forced me into the light as a child, and why I decided to remain in that existence over a decade ago. Years of exposure to the sun and avoiding blood gave me a less than extraordinary appearance. Within a few months, my eyes changed from the icy blue of my species to a peridot green. My skin lost its luminous alabaster complexion until I was just a pale human, and my musical voice became ordinary.

When I stepped into the light, I let my transcendence fade to survive and evade. But the night, the glorious night, still hummed through me even an hour from darkening the horizon. More so at the full moon when it played me like a full orchestra. Closing my eyes, I let that symphony of the coming night fill my head, keep time with my heart, and bleed through my veins until arms wrapped around me from behind.

The press of my husband's naked chest to my back startled me from the concert playing within. "Easy, Kat," his melodious voice soothed as his arms tensed to hold me tighter. "You're always so tense when you're cycling."

Freezing in his arms, I turned to let him see the surprise on my face. Chuckling, he kissed my nose as he traped me in the circle of his arms against his formed body. "Come on, Kat, you must know? How often do you call in sick to work, so you can stay home and molest me all day."

"Not as often as I'd like, or I wouldn't have a job." My head fell back as his mouth left a wet path down my neck.

"I've told you before, Love, you don't have to work. I earn enough for us to both live happily." Caressing my back, Yishay pressed me firmly to him as one of his hands tangled in my long platinum hair.

"I like my job." The fire in my belly reignited. He's right, of course.

Every three months, I became insatiable, needing him repeatedly for two days straight. Yishay is my zápalka, my soul's match. I'd known it the first time we'd touched, an innocent introduction that turned our lives upside down.

Lifting me to his waist, Yishay fell back on the bed, catching my mouth with his as I rose to take him inside me. Caressing my hand over the mark on his chest, I shivered. It was the same fear that passed through me the first time I saw it - and every time since.

Months into our relationship, we'd fallen into my apartment hot and heavy, ready to tear each other's clothes off and lose ourselves to the fire between us for the first time. Then Yishay had yanked his shirt off and I'd seen the scar of the triple infinity upright between a crescent and waxing moon over his heart. That mark cooled my lust and had me backing away.

Of course, he'd taken it as a sign of my moral standing and loved me all the more for it. No matter the excuse I gave to end things, Yishay refused to give me up.

Crying out, Yishay filled my body with his again, sating my need for another few hours. Our hands entwined as I fell upon him, and I stared at the silver ring on his left hand, that matched the one on mine. He loved me, adored me, and would die to protect me. I counted on the last when I agreed to be his wife and his mate.

Smiling, I met his pale blue eyes. Kissing his perfect rosy lips first, I followed that with a kiss to the shining white brand on his chest. The one that marked him the leader of my sworn enemies. The King of the Halos.

---

*W*aking after full dark, my sex was needy and wanting to feel my husband inside of me. Of course, it was night, and Yishay 'worked' at night. At least, that's what he would have me believe. For the sake of my sanity, I chose to accept his excuse. The alternative was that at dawn, when he crawled into bed, tired, but hungry for me, I was rewarding him for eradicating my people.

It tore me up terribly when he'd asked me to marry him. For weeks, I weighed the pros and cons carefully. It ultimately came down to take the opportunity to kill my family's nemesis or using his love as another mask and cloak of protection. In the end, I chose life and love over continuing the useless bloodshed. Did that make me a betrayer of my kind? I wasn't sure anymore.

If I knew who the Halos targeted, I would have helped my people, but Yishay never carried on his business in my presence, and never brought it home to the house. Part of me was thankful for that consideration. A long time ago, I'd started believing that other than drinking blood, there was nothing very different between a Halos and a Pâlir. I wasn't the first to think it, or I would never have been born. My grandfather was a Halos. My grandmother, a Pâlir. She returned home to raise her offspring under the protection of the guards when her lover died in the Halos infighting.

For all their righteousness, Halos were considered violent by our kind. Always looking for a Pâlir to maim and torture; if they couldn't kill a Pâlir, they would turn on their own. So far, the only viciousness I'd encountered was from the female Halos, and it was more petty jealousy. Most were resentful of their king having a human mate whom they considered beneath them.

At the thought of my husband, my body coursed with desire. Resting my hand over my womb, I thought on what Yishay revealed at dusk. Of course, I'm sure that subconsciously I was always aware of what my sudden insatiable appetite for him meant. I'd been amongst the humans from when I was thirteen, so it was never explained to me by my parents.

However, I was aware that I required blood to reproduce, and I hadn't tasted the blood of another being in over a decade. Terrified of the hunger rising, I even avoided eating meat. As such, mate as we did, I was never at risk of getting with child, and that saddened me. As a female of my bloodline, it was my sole duty to find a mate and bear healthy, strong children to continue the line.

Yishay and I hadn't spoken about children yet, content to settle into our lives together before we added to our family. But he would want a male heir at some point. I'd already considered it and still couldn't decide what to do about it.

When my stomach growled, I realized that I'd foregone food for the entire day. Groaning, I climbed out of bed, pulling my robe around me as I set out for the kitchen. As I reached the bottom of the stairs, I heard the soft sound of something hitting the floor in Yishay's study. Smiling mischievously, I moved to his door, food quickly forgotten in my desire for him.

In the few years we'd been together, my stealth was the only quirk that ever unnerved Yishay. As I opened the door, he was sitting at his desk looking over his study in deep thought. The sitting area was hidden from my view by the wall of the alcove that housed his bar and TV. Typically, I was much more observant, but at this moment, I wholly focused on Yishay, so I didn't pay attention to the room as I sauntered soundlessly towards the desk.

Reacting to my proximity even before he heard me, Yishay tensed, his eyes glanced down in confusion before he lifted his widened gaze to mine. The bewilderment of that reaction didn't have time to process in my mind. At the same time, our eyes connected, liquid splattered me from the sitting area as a man's pained groan pierced my ears.

Freezing on the spot, the smell of blood became intoxicating. Touching the side of my face, I wiped at the hot liquid now dripping down the side of it. Fresh blood stained my fingers. Hunger of a different kind rose to the surface as I turned my head to take in the rest of the room.

Yishay's best friend, Flick, stood bent over another man on his knees before him. The dagger that sliced the man's cheek still gripped in one large hand, and the other grasped the white-blond hair of a Pâlir. A pitiful cry escaped my throat as my brother's arctic-blue eyes met mine. They were fierce with rebellion as they quickly took in the human in the room before turning with menace toward his predators.

"Kat." Yishay's voice commanded my attention, though, I knew him well enough to hear the edge of worry in it. My ear twitched towards him, but my gaze remained fixed on my brother, Vladimir. Mortified at seeing him here, I wasn't sure whether it was for his safety or mine that I worried. Maybe both.

"Hovno!" Flick's crystal blues took in my presence. The other four Halos in the room suddenly very still as Flick stood to his full six foot eight height and let his broad shoulders slump. "Sorry, Yishay, we shouldn't have bought him here."

'Katarina?' My brother's mind voice called to me, a sinister smile blooming across his mouth. After all this time, I thought he wouldn't recognize me. They forced my leaving, but expected my return years ago to keep our race alive. My presence among the Halos would not be well received. Whimpering, I gave a slight nod of my head as my hand covered my mouth, tears welling up as my mind kicked into survival mode. Kenan would be able to sense it if I communicated with another Pâlir.

"Kat." Yishay turned me to face him, rubbing my upper arms comfortingly.

"We harm no one but those who deserve death, and you know it, Král. We protect innocent humans from those who are just as evil as your kind. You and yours are just a death squad turned corrupt..."

Long black hair arced into the air as Flick struck out quicker than human eyes could follow with the butt of his blade. It struck the side of my brother's jaw. Vladimir fell forward onto one hand, a mouthful of blood and a tooth splattering the floor in front of him, cutting off his retort.

Whimpering again, I tried to pull back from Yishay, but he held my arms firmly, grip tightening to prevent my escape. "Kat, I'll explain later, but I need you to go back upstairs right now, okay?"

Shaking my head in fear, trying to wake up from this nightmare, the tears streamed down my face.

"Just kill the Pâlir and be done with it. Why are we wasting time hearing him?" Lemuel, a squat overly muscular Halos interrupted from the back of the sitting area.

"No!" Pulling free from Yishay's grip, I took a step towards Vladimir protectively.

Getting between us, Flick stopped my approach with one look. When I stumbled back and caught myself on the alcove wall, his face dropped. "Sakra!"

"Indeed!" Saul, one of the older Halos leaning against the bar in the alcove, took another gulp of scotch from the glass in his hand. "I told you not to bring him here."

"He's a prince of the blood who came under a banner of peace to confer with our King. It just happened to be a night the King's husbandly duties to his mate kept him from coming to us." Flick indicated me with his blade. Flinching automatically, I took two retreating steps towards the door. Flick quickly redirected the point of his weapon.

Eyes narrowing in on me, Vladimir studiously took in every inch of me, including the wedding band on my left hand. Vladimir laughed, the sound like bells peeling through the room, startling everyone.

"He's communicating with another Pâlir nearby." Kenan, a tall, lean Halos, and one of the few I liked out of the men in the room stood from where he'd been sitting on the leather lounge and came to stand between Vladimir and Yishay. "And the other Pâlir is close, like outside this house close." Kenan's eyes focused on me from behind his shaggy mane.

Everybody went stiff except Yishay. With a twitch of his head Lemuel and Jabin, the two I liked least, disappeared out the French glass doors that led to the back patio.

"Heya, Kat." Kenan smiled, swiping his pitch-black hair back from his face to give me a good view of his topaz blues and disarming smile.

Barely acknowledging him, I didn't answer. It was taking everything in me not to run to my brother and wrap myself around him protectively — my survival instinct warring with my love for him.

"You won't find them. I've already sent my guard to alert the others."

Stepping forward, Yishay put his back to me. "Alert them of what?"

Vladimir smiled as his eyes flickered to me. "That you do not respect a meeting under the banner of peace. More so, you are mated. To a fascinating woman." Yishay's shoulders tensed, his arm swinging back protectively to push me behind him. "Oh, I hope she's carrying your child when we take her..."

"Kill him!" Yishay ordered fiercely.

"No!" Moving past him, I was within reach of my brother when rough hands hauled me away. Grabbing me, Yishay turned me to him and used his hand at the back of my head to press my face to his chest and hold me there.

Flick moved quickly, the thud and slurp of stabbing someone is not as quiet as you think. Especially not when it is someone you love. The first piercing of his blade into my brother's heart, stabbed deep within my own, forcing the air from my lungs. With each sloshing, sucking sound of the blade ramming home into my brother's chest, my body tensed tighter, my lungs exhaled harder, and my nails dug deeper into Yishay's torso.

Burying his blade one last time, Flick made sure the heart was a ruined mess before my brother's body fell to the ground with a heavy thud. Opening my mouth in a silent scream my knees buckled, then the sobbing racked my body. Only Yishay's arms kept me upright. He lifted me enough to take a few steps backward. Without looking, I knew that he moved to stop the blood from pooling around my bare feet.

"Flick, and I will check around the perimeter. Kenan, take the body out and burn it." Saul decided from somewhere behind me. "Best you soothe your mate and explain who we are."

"Should have done that two years ago." Flick always liked me since he'd seen Yishay's reaction to our first contact. He was a good friend, and his mate, Kira, was the only female friend I'd made within their family.

With a bow of his head, Yishay put his mouth to my ear. "Shh, Kat, shh. I know this is a shock, but we need to talk now. Let's take you up stairs, and you can shower, then I'll explain."

Pushing back forcefully, I took another two steps toward the door, shying away from this side of my husband, from the reality I'd been trying to ignore. When he reached for me, I skidded back and hit the door hard. "Don't!" Taking in the pool of blood on the floor my stomach twisted and knotted painfully doubling me over in agony. "God!"

Yishay moved to me, eyes full of worry.

"Don't touch me!" Closing my eyes, I covered my mouth as the hunger burned down my throat. Turning, I grasped blindly for the door handle, threw it open, and ran from the room.

Slamming the bedroom door behind me, I barely made it to the toilet before my body started trying to expel my heart through my mouth. Dry retching until my throat abraded, I collapsed overwrought with emotion, pain, and a denied hunger, to the bathroom floor.

Worst of all, I couldn't tell which hurt more; the hunger for blood or witnessing my brother's murder at the hands of the man I loved. All I knew is that my world was just pulled out from under me, and I had no idea what to do next.

Protocol insisted I avenge my brother's death, but who do I kill? The one who ordered it or the one who did it? Custom demanded I stand by my mate no matter what. It was my duty to be supportive and to provide him with healthy offspring. That's all women were good for in the Halos culture; keeping house, sex, and breeding. The way of my species was very different. The Pâlir women were equal to the men, if not more valued because women were the only means to a future. We fought side by side with our mates, and as such, taught to defend ourselves from them growing up. It had been so long since I even trained. Flick and Yishay were not only well-practiced but also the strongest of the Halos. I wouldn't stand a chance.

The only option left was to leave. Yishay and I never mated in blood like a Pâlir couple. There was no exchange which held us together no matter what, just a piece of paper and vows. He was my zápalka, which meant more than anything else. It was unheard of to find your true mate and abandon them. Then, there was my vow, my promise, and my oath to my husband. Humans cared nothing for their vows, but Pâlie would prefer to bleed their own heart than to be forsworn. Did I have a choice at all?

When Yishay's arms lifted me from the cold tiled floor, I curled tight into his chest. My body still racked with my sobs, but it was sporadic now. He sat me on the vanity, leaning my head against his chest. "I'm not human, Kat. Close enough so that anatomically you can't tell the difference, but my kind is stronger, faster, and has different practices to humans. For instance, we don't choose our partners." Kissing the top of my head, his hands held me tight, as if he feared I might turn to liquid and disappear down the drain from him.

"It's what your kind call love at first sight, but it's the person made for us, our other half as it were." His fingers were gentle under my chin as he relaxed enough to pull back and lift my face to see his. His face was blurry in my watery vision, but I could see the fear in his blue eyes.

"You're my zápalka, Kat. The moment we first met, I felt it, and I know you felt it too. I should have told you from the start..." Letting go of my chin, Yishay wrapped me tight against him again. "By the gods, Kat. I was terrified of you leaving me. You wouldn't take me to your body until we were married, so I couldn't be sure you wouldn't up and walk away. And once we were married...well, we were so happy, I didn't want to ruin it explaining something no human cares to recognize, let alone know."

"You didn't trust me." The hunger still burned in my throat. It was like the blood was surrounding me, filling my senses, still fresh and calling to that primal side of my being.

Pulling back, Yishay took my shoulders in his hands to look at me properly. "Of course, I trust you. You're my mate, the woman I love, and hopefully one day soon you'll be the mother of my children." I couldn't help my eyes going a little wide at the hope I saw in his eyes. "I just couldn't find a way to tell you after so long, so I didn't."

"I've known for a long time." I don't know why I confessed my knowledge, whether it was to make it easier for him, or the need to be honest about that part of our lives. His jaw fell slack, and he sucked in a harsh breath. "The wives talk when they think I can't hear."

The Halos women quite often discussed their business when they thought my being in the next room made me deaf. Of course, had I been human, that might have been the case. But I wasn't, and I'd heard a lot over the years, most often their disapproval of me. "But it's different to see what you are then just to hear it." Fresh tears poured from my eyes. "I can't ignore this!"

Taking my cheeks in his hands, Yishay forced me to meet his eyes. "This doesn't change who I am, Kat. It doesn't change how I feel about you. I'm still the same person you fell in love with; I just kill a pests to the human race. I'm no different from an exterminator."

Glancing up, I spied the small smirk on my husband's mouth. "You compare them to termites?"

"They're a pest, a curse upon the world."

"They're people! They live, breathe, eat, and feel. They play with their kids, teach them, raise them, and cry for them when they are hurt. You hunt them down and massacre them because they are a little different to you." Standing on my feet, I glared at him. His brows knitted in confusion. "Who made you judge and executioner? What right do you have to kill someone just for being different to you? From what I saw tonight, the only real difference is the hair color?"

Yishay's eyes narrowed as his mind worked, forming a new argument to every one of my accusations before his eyes grew bright, and his usual pouty lips formed a severe straight line. "You know them! You know what they are and you're okay with that."

Stepping back, that wasn't the response I'd anticipated. I'd expected Yishay to argue they were different, to declare himself king and thus he was the judge and executioner, to try and convince me my people were evil. Instead, he looked at me for the first time as if he didn't know me, as if he just discovered I lived a double life, and that look both hurt and terrified me.

"There was a family where I grew up." Withdrawing under the coldness of that gaze, I shied away. "They were nice people. They harm no one but the humans who murder, rape, and abuse. They are a blessing on the human race, not a curse."

"They're evil, Kat." Yishay's growl caused me to back into the bench hard. Wincing, I half turned away from him. When I shifted around him to escape the confines of the bathroom, the growl got louder.

Clearing the walk through robe, I went for the bedroom door again. My feet moving of their own accord, I didn't even realize I was running, trying to escape from my childhood bogeyman. Racing down the steps, Kenan looked up at me from below, worry etched over his face. Out of control and running faster than a human, I couldn't pull up by the time I realized he meant to stop me.

"Kat?" Kenan swung around and caught me at the bottom of the stairs. His arm snaked round my waist and pulled me to him, my back pressed to his chest his mouth at my ear so quickly I'd barely blinked.

"No! Let me go!"

3

"Kat, stop!" Kenan warned as I struggled in his hold. Throwing my elbow hard into his ribs, I forced his body back and his grip to loosen enough that I could twist and thrust my other elbow into the side of his face. He released me. Spinning out of his grasp, I was putting my hand to the handle of the front door when Yishay's palm hit the door hard above my head, stopping me from opening it. His body trapped mine against the door, preventing my escape.

"Stay!" Yishay ordered as if I was one of his people to do his bidding. Not that I was going to argue. Knowing better than to try a fight I had no chance of winning, I whimpered and stilled. Yishay looked over his shoulder. "You okay, Key?"

"Yeah. Sorry, Yishay, I wasn't expecting her to fight."

"Yes, I know." Yishay turned his attention back to my trembling form, pinned between his and the door. "She fights like one of them." Lifting my hair, Yishay let it run through his fingers. "I've never once considered how pale she is..."

"No!" Kenan stepped closer to us quickly. "Don't even think it, Yishay. You know I can sense their kind anywhere near me."

"She grew up around them, fights like them, and bears a resemblance to them..." Stepping back, Yishay turned me to face him, shoving me hard against the door. Wincing at the force, I cringed under his angry gaze and hugged myself, tears streaming down my cheeks.

"Jeez, Yish! She's more Halos than human even. You know that, or you wouldn't be compatible." My eyes shot up to meet Kenan's in surprise. Kenan met my gaze for a moment, a warning to behave evident in them as he tried to soothe his King. "I'm a half-breed, and you've never held it against me as others have. You knew she was human with Halos ancestry when you married her, and it's never bothered you that your children will be half-breed mongrels like me either." Taking another step closer, Kenan had a look I couldn't determine in his eyes.

"She came from the free-territory. More than likely, because of her mixed heritage, she can sense their kind. And because she's a little different to human kids, she probably hung out with other half-breeds or a family of Pâlie growing up. You know there are just as many of them who believe this war is an out-dated dispute between the royal families..." The slight roll of Yishay's eyes told me Kenan was one of the Halos who believed the same. "...Maybe her being a half-breed didn't bother them any more than it bothered you that I was."

Yishay's shoulders relaxed in increments during Kenan's speech, but Kenan watched us warily as if ready to interfere if Yishay got violent. I knew better. None of the Halos would interfere if their king decided to kill me at any point in time. "Maybe." Combing his fingers through my hair again, Yishay rubbed his thumb across the pale strands. When I dared to glance up a sob caught in my throat as I took in the distrust now openly displayed on my husband's face.

"Yishay, you know it. Years you've been together and not once has Kat demonstrated any Pâlir ability or habits. I'd sense it if she were anything more. Your concern right now should be finding the Pâlir who carries her existence on his tongue. We kept your union quiet for a reason. Kat's vulnerable and needs our protection, not our suspicions."

"She defended them." Yishay's eyes unfocused as if he was thinking about something other simultaneously.

"They've never harmed her. She's lived amongst us for years now. Our women are openly hostile towards her at best, and our men are rather scary for an outsider. Did you expect any different a reaction to her walking into that room and watching you kill a man?"

Turning his ear to Kenan, Yishay refocused on me. Nodding his head once in acceptance, Yishay pulled me tight to his chest and kissed my head as I continued trembling in his arms.

"It's time to unite with her fully. For both your good and for her protection. You need to complete the blood rite, and you need to do it tonight." When I tensed in his arms, Yishay tightened his grip around me. The sobs ceased at the mention of a blood rite. My fear of being exposed replaced with a fear of a different kind as the hunger flared again in my throat.

As Yishay's hands rubbed my back, my desire surfaced, adding to the conflicting emotions of fear and thirst already surging through my body. "It's okay, Kotĕ. We just taste a little of each other's blood, and then I will always be able to feel you."

"No!" Trying to escape his hold, my fear of being discovered squashed all my other emotions. If Yishay tasted me, he'd know.

Bracing against me, Yishay used one hand in the arch of my lower back to keep my body pressed to his, and the other gripped the back of my neck.

Remaining close, Kenan stepped into my peripheral view. "Kat, you need to do this. We can't protect you properly unless you fully unite with your husband."

Fingers tangling in my hair, Yishay tugged my head back gently to force my eyes to his. "Kat..."

"No," I returned less forcefully, my breathing already shallow with the proximity of his mouth to mine, his muscular body pressed hard against me.

Peering down at his growing erection, when Yishay's gaze came back to mine, there was a mischievous smile playing across his lips.

As he stepped forward, forcing me back against the door, I shook my head.

"Kat this has to happen..."

"Key! Statues don't talk."

Silence filled the house before my hearing focused in on the pounding of my heart: fear, lust, and hunger spurring my adrenalin into overdrive. Caressing his hand down my back, round the curve of my hip, and back up to find the tie of my dressing gown, Yishay gave it a swift tug. The heavy satin slipped away from the front of my body, exposing me only to Yishay's eyes.

Panicked, I pressed my hand to his chest. Covering it with his reassuringly, Yishay guided my hand a little to the left to his steady heartbeat; my security blanket for two years now. Lowering his nose to my exposed neck, Yishay took a deep breath as his hand slid down my tummy, fingers combing the pale soft hair as his hand curved over my mound.

His middle finger found my already pulsating clit and pressed firmly for a few seconds before sliding further, splitting my folds and finding me damp. A growl rumbled in his throat before his finger pushed into me.

"Yishay..."

Mouth covering mine, Yishay stole any argument before it began. His tongue delved into my mouth forcefully, stroking

My moans echoed off the marble in the entry when his fired touch caressed my thigh, grasped my arse, and lifted me to wrap my legs around his waist. His hot mouth engulfing my nipples was electric, forcing my head and shoulders back as those currents fired down to my womb, preparing me for his thick shaft.

The smooth, hard head of his cock slipped between my moist labia as Yishay's teeth grazed my nipple, stealing my breath. With a harsh growl, Yishay thrust hard and deep, forcing our pelvis's to meet. Crying out, I dug my nails into Yishay's shoulders as he pounded me, hammering my back into the door.

Directing my mouth to his, Yishay used his hand in my hair to hold our mouths hard against each other as he slammed me violently against the door. My body tightened around his in seconds. When I threw my head back to scream my pleasure, I caught a glimpse of Yishay's arm held out to the side of him. Moving quickly, Kenan slashed with a flash of steel, and then red bloomed across my husband's wrist.

Before I could react, my orgasm overtook me. My head hit the door as Yishay covered my mouth with his bleeding wrist. Blood poured down my throat while I was helpless as my body convulsed over his. When I flicked my tongue over the wound, the double pleasure flooded me; both the carnal euphoria, and the relief of starvation. No longer able to resist, I latched onto his arm.

"Mated we are, as husband and wife for all eternity...Oh, Bohovia!" Yishay breathed hard as his own body raced towards the peak of climax. "...My blood in your veins, your blood in mine, we'll hold no secrets. Witness!" Using my vice grip on his wrist to force my head back and to the side, Yishay drove his sharp eye teeth into my jugular. My eyes popped at the new sensation, pain, but not, pleasure and fear. Moaning as he drank me down, Yishay filled me with his life all at the same time.

"I witness this connection." Kenan voiced the requisite words followed by other muttered confirmations. This ceremony was usually part of the wedding ceremony - the blood exchange, not the sex. Yishay was using my current reproductive cycle to force the blood exchange. If I hadn't been pre-occupied, I would have freaked about hearing other people's voices in the room while we were mating. But as it was, I didn't.

Collapsing onto Yishay, I panted trying to catch my breath. The arm I just fed on now braced us against the door while the other held me to him. He was swimming inside me, coursing through my bloodstream. His heart was beating as if it was my own. All our emotions crossed over; both the love he felt for me and the sudden hate.

Lips by my ear, his harsh exhale promised violence. "Pâlir."

Fear surged through me, adrenalin pumping, speeding my heart instead of slowing it in the afterglow. "Zápalka."

"And that is the only reason I'm not ripping your heart out of your deceptive chest right now."

Licking up the side of Yishay's neck, I sucked the lobe of his ear to keep our exchange private. "I'm your food source, aren't I? You're no different to us, you just hide your blood lust in the bedroom and feed off the Pâlie you kill. You're a bunch of hypocrites!"

Pulling back to glare at me with his rage burning in his eyes, but I felt the conflict in his heart — the contrast of what he was raised to believe and what he observed during his time as Král. Glancing over his shoulder towards his study, Yishay gritted his teeth. "Did you find the other Pâlir?"

Hesitating at the ire in Yishay's voice, Flick stepped forward. "No, Yishay. We caught his scent, but he took to the air, and we lost him." Only the males of both species could transvect. Females were stuck on land.

Bringing his focus back to me, Yishay closed down, his features unreadable, but I could feel him now. "Get out and don't come back until you've found him." Placing me back on my shaking legs, Yishay kept his hands at my hips to steady me.

"Yishay, we know you fear for your mate but..."

"Get out, Saul!"

Pressing back against the door to put a little distance between Yishay and myself, I trembled. Yanking my robe closed around me, Yishay retied it to cover me before he bent to collect his pants.

Swallowing hard, Kenan took a step to leave via the study with the others. "Not you, Key. You stay."

Kenan stopped, and we all waited until the others departed, and Yishay buckled his pants. When Yishay caressed my face tenderly, I flinched at his touch, and his eyes softened. "I understand your fear, Kat, but I know marrying me was for love and nothing more. For that reason alone, I'm going to try and overlook what you are. Key is right. If you weren't at least half Halos, we wouldn't be mates. We'll work through this."

Placing a tender kiss to my trembling lips, Yishay turned, so abruptly that I ducked and cringed. Oh, I could feel the truth in his words, feel the love in his heart, but I felt the betrayal just as much. "Have you always known?"

Lowering his head in shame, Kenan took a small step in retreat. "From the moment I laid eyes on her."

"So, you lied to me."

Kenan's head snapped up. "Never! I told you she was a half-breed from the moment she moved in with me."

"You lied just now when you said she wasn't one of them!"

"She's not. I've watched her all this time. This rite is the first time she's tasted blood

There was a polite knock at the door. Not that I could hear it over Yishay's booming, but I felt the rat-a-tat-tat. Probably one of the guys coming back to report and not wanting to enter without permission.

"You could have told me!"

"So you could kill her? You are so sure what your father taught you was right that you would have killed her without hearing me out. Maybe now you will listen to me, and realize it's wrong. What we do is wrong."

Not wanting to draw attention to myself, I kept my voice down. "Yishay, one of your guys is at the door."

Holding up a hand without looking at me, Yishay indicated not to interrupt. So, as the second polite knock sounded, I unlocked the front door and opened it.

"You could have told me after we married..."

My eyes went wide at the man at the door. The ends of his long blond hair swirling around his thighs in the chilly breeze as a smile tilted one side of his sinful mouth. His pale blue eyes sparkled at me over the top of a black carbon crossbow. Glancing back over my shoulder, my panic made my heart skip a beat. Eyes meeting mine, Kenan swore, his pupils dilating as he stepped towards me. In the same moment, Yishay moved toward me, fear pounding in his heart. "Kat!"

Swinging back, I watched the crossbow lift and point over my shoulder as the Pâlir pulled the trigger. The black bolt flew past my ear as I whirled back in amazement, having expected the arrow to pierce my heart. An arm wrapped around my waist as the black carbon sliced through Yishay's right arm. Searing pain burst to life in my upper right arm as I was tugged hard against the body of the Pâlir and dragged into the air. A scream of agony shrieking from my throat as we took to the sky before Yishay or Kenan even made the door.

A few meters' up, a shower of black arrows rained down past me, preventing any of the Halos from exiting the house. Tears fell fast as the house became a distant beacon beneath us. Other Pâlirs fell in behind us to guard our escape. Peering up, I recognized the face of my brother's best friend. It made sense that he'd been close when Yishay caught Vladimir.

Glaring at me, Casimir assessed me. Unable to handle the decreased oxygen at this height, my eyes drifted shut. It had been too long since I'd flown.

"Princess Katiana, you've grown up beautifully."

4

L ying on a cloak with another over me, I woke on the cold hard ground. From a small gap in the fold of the material, I could see a scattering of snow over the earthen forest floor. Moving the coverings from my face, I took in my surroundings.

The thick canopy high overhead caused eerie darkness accentuated by the fog sweeping across the ground. It was quiet. Too quiet. Something was wrong.

Sitting up slowly, I tried to take in my surroundings. Light from the moon illuminated the edges of the gully I was in, but it seemed Casimir had found the darkest trench to hide me. Alone, or at least that's what my eyes told me. My senses told me quite the opposite. Casimir was here; I could feel him, faintly.

"Don't try to run, Princess," the deep voice found me from the shadows of an oak. Even knowing he was there, I couldn't see him. "I'm not going to hurt you."

"Why am I here instead of my family's home then?"

"You want me to take you home and tell your Prince that you are mated, by blood, to the Král of our enemy. That you have been living with our enemy for years? His only sister, a traitor?" Casimir materialized within the shadows, so I could see his face. It was steady, with no hate or loathing, no emotion. "You would have me tell our Prince that his younger sister stood beside her husband and did naught as he murdered her brother?"

The tears were already streaming down my face as I shook my head. Suddenly kneeling on one knee beside me, Casimir licked his thumb and wiped it down the side of my face. "Should I tell your prince how you mated with your husband while your brother's blood dried on your traitorous flesh? Is that what you would have me do?"

"That's not what happened. I couldn't stop them. I tried, but I couldn't without risking..."

"Yourself?"

The guilt crushed my heart in my chest. Nodding once before rising, Casimir turned his back to watch his surroundings again. "I was there, Katiana. I heard what was said and done. You think he is your zápalka?" Casimir said it like he didn't believe it. When I nodded, he sighed and looked back to me. "Your brother understood. He told me to protect you."

"Why did you take me? I was safe there with him..."

"Your husband just killed one of our princes. Do you think that will pass without retaliation, Princess?" It was the first bloom of anger I'd seen in Casimir since he'd taken me.

"You had a shot when you took me. Why didn't you aim for his heart?"

Casimir turned his back on me again. "I missed."

"You never miss. I trained beside you as a child. There was no better shot with the crossbow than you. Why did you choose not to kill the Král while you had the opportunity?"

Turning to consider me a moment, Casimir flicked his head to the left. Suddenly, he was beside me, laying his body over mine as he pressed me back to the ground and pulled the thick cloak over us. When I went to argue at this sudden intimate position, Casimir covered my mouth and put his lips to my ear. "Not a sound, Princess. It may be your mate, or it may be someone who will rip your throat out without a second thought. If it's the first, he'll find us here, if it's not, let's hope they don't."

Shocked to learn we had a new enemy, I wanted to ask Casimir what happened, but he tensed and pressed his hand tighter to my mouth, indicating silence. His anxiety shook my nerves, the beat of his heart against my chest double the average speed. He was worried, not for himself, but for me. He was trying to protect me from an enemy I didn't even know existed.

The forest was silent, and once again, that felt wrong. The wind picked up, a little gust, and Casimir became deathly still, almost as if he'd stopped breathing. Growing up, I'd seen how effectively these cloaks worked. We would blend with the forest floor, foliage, or a tree trunk. Only movement and sound would give us away. Stilling myself, just like I'd been taught to do as a child, I closed my eyes and moved inside myself, leaving only my hearing for surveillance.

My body was on heat. If my mate were nearby, my body would let me know, and it would make him know I was here. The gust of wind moved through the trees until it seemed to be moving over the gully where we hid. Whatever was out there searching, it wasn't my husband. The wind seemed to circle over the area for a good ten minutes before it moved on. Even after I couldn't hear it anymore, I dared not move. Casimir would let me know when it was safe.

He waited what seemed to be an hour or more before he finally took a deep breath and removed his hand from my mouth. "Thank you, Princess, for not putting yourself in danger. I appreciate you not forcing us into the position of having to fight."

Uncomfortably aware of my nakedness beneath my robe, and the growing itch of desire, I hesitantly pressed on his shoulder. "Casimir?" Growing more confused by the minute, I could feel Casimir, not just physically because I felt him before I could see him. Now, my body was reacting to his proximity. Mated Pâlir only responded to their mate. Everything I was feeling was wrong.

"It's not safe to move tonight, Princess. We will wait until the pre-dawn and get you to the safe ground then. Until that time, you should rest."

When Casimir didn't move but stayed staring into my eyes above me, I became even more uncomfortable. When I tried to slide to the side, he dropped his arm to my waist, pinning me in place. "You were meant to be mine. Your father promised us as children."

Swallowing hard, I closed my eyes. All my life I'd know I had a betrothed, but I hadn't known who. Part of me thought the betrothal was the reason my father sent me away, that I'd breached it by getting too close to another.

"We came looking for you when you failed to return home, Vladimir and I. When we couldn't find you, we thought they must have found you first." Casimir's hand drifted from my waist to rest above my womb. "You're in heat, but not with child. Does the Král not want a son?"

"I haven't tasted blood until tonight; until just before you snatched me."

Casimir's head snapped up with worry. "He only blood-bound you tonight?" Taking my chin in his hands to make my eyes stay locked with his, Casimir stared into my eyes, driving the needy itch insane. "Can you feel him? Can you feel his heartbeat, his emotions, anything of your husband?"

Looking at him perplexed by his sudden worry, I shook my head. "I could feel his heart when he first did it, felt his pain when you shot him, but not since I regained consciousness."

"Sakra! My proximity has interfered with the bonding." Throwing the cloak back, Casimir sat up and prepared to stand.

"Why would your proximity affect our bond?"

Casimir touched my cheek with affection. "You wouldn't remember, you were still a child. When they betrothed us, we performed a blood exchange. We completed the entire ritual, except what required we wait to be adults. It's how I recognized you at the Král's house. Your brother couldn't believe it. He was staring straight at you and didn't recognize you; not until I told him I could feel you in the house."

"You recognized me? I didn't even know you were there."

"You were a mated female, on heat, standing in a room with your supposed zápalka, witnessing your brother's murder. I doubt you would have noticed a meteor crashing to earth in the field outside the house."

"But..."

"Your new bond hasn't settled. It's there, don't panic about that, but I'm interfering with it. Like a jammed radio signal."

Brain racing with all the potential possibilities, I lowered my voice. "Is it permanent?"

Smirking, Casimir moved his mouth close to mine. "It can be if you want it to be. We could mate, repeat the blood rite here and now, let our seed decide the victor." As Casimir kissed my lips gently, I jerked away, shocked by his words. He chuckled. "Yeah, I thought that'd be your answer." Rising, Casimir stepped away, assessing the forest around us.

"What do you mean your seed would decide the victor?"

Glancing over his shoulder at me, Casimir gave me a cheeky grin. "Two bindings. Both equally worthy. It would come down to who got you pregnant first. Once the conception was secure, the bond would settle. You would know who the father was because that is who you would be able to feel."

"This has happened before?"

Stooping to inspect the ground, Casimir scanned the forest. "Quite regularly in the royal bloodlines of both Pâlie and the Halos. There have been many occasions where two worthy mates, for the female of the blood, have contested for marriage rights. Unlike humans, who would fight it out and waste blood over it, the female would perform the blood rite with both men. She would take them both to bed, and within a few days, the bond of the successful mate would settle. The other mate would graciously stand aside."

My mouth dropped open. "At the same time?"

Casimir smiled at my obvious disapproval. "Of course. That is nothing new to either lineage. Has the Král never invited one of his First Order to your bed?"

"No!"

"Ah, but of course. The Král thought your parents raised you human. Why else would you walk in the light and look so much like one? Had he known you were Pâlir, or you were Halos, you would have been accepting of his second, at the very least, joining you, or taking his place if he were absent."

My eyebrows disappeared into my hairline.

"The former Král's wife was never left alone. If the Král was not in her bed, one of the First Order was there. Since, he thought you were a half-breed human, Yishay must have been taking his time introducing their ways to you. Obviously, since he waited till tonight to bond with you."

"Casimir..."

"You should rest, Princess."

When I blinked, he was gone. Moving nearby, but I couldn't see or hear him. Understanding then what he meant by our betrothal, I wiped the tears leaking slowly from my cheeks and snuggled back down beneath the cloaks.

Not used to sleeping outdoors, especially not in late autumn, I shivered uncontrollably. The cold seeped up from the ground and found me even within these cloaks designed to keep us warm in the most frigid temperatures. A few hours of shaking and teeth chattering, then the cover lifted as Casimir slid in behind me. Releasing the tie on my robe, Casimir pulled it from my arm and back before he pressed his naked warmth against me. Too cold to care, I snuggled into his warmth. This wasn't about sex, Casimir was trying to stop me from getting a human sickness.

"Stepping into the light for even a year will weaken the strongest warrior. You've been in the light for over ten years, so you're virtually human. You won't have our speed, our strength, our resilience. And, if in the next few days you find yourself with child, you will get even weaker as the babe drains you for what it needs."

"Are you trying to make me feel helpless?"

"I'm telling you the facts, Princess."

"Stop calling me Princess, since when have we stood on ceremony with each other?"

Settling into the warmth, the tremors of my body eased as

Casimir presented his wrist to me. "You're going to have to feed, Kat. Let me provide what you need until you can be safe with your husband again."

"No, it's not blood I need."

There was silence for a moment before Casimir wrapped his arm around me and pulled me tight to him, placing a kiss on my throat. "I can be that for you too."

"Definitely, not!" Driving my elbow back, I put some distance between our lower bodies while he coughed. "I'm mated and married, Casimir, and you're not my husband."

Chuckling, Casimir pulled me back to the warmth of his body. "If you say so, Kat, but you still have another day to go, and that itch is only going to get worse. So, you let me know when you're ready for me to scratch it."

"Not going to happen."

Sniggering, Casimir held me so I would be warm and could sleep.

"Casimir?"

"Kat?"

"Who are these others?"

"Tomorrow, Kitty Kat. I'll tell you everything tomorrow. Sleep." His warm lips kissed my ear, and his body heat lulled me into slumber.

"Kat." A hand ran up and down my arm. When I woke startled, Casimir caught me to him. "It's okay, Kat. Take a breath, and remember last night."

Doing as I was told, trusting his voice, I let the disaster of last night crash into my reality again. Tears created rivers on my cheeks as I remembered my life crumbling around me. Yishay's anger and distrust of me when he realized what I was.

Holding me for a moment, Casimir patted my arm again. "Come on, Katiana. I need to get you to safety before full light."

Moving to collect his clothes, Casimir unwrapped his knee-length blond hair, so it fell around him like a cloak to cover his naked back. The wind picked up, and his hair danced gracefully away from his body, exposing his luminescent paleness to me. My breath caught in my throat. My desire flashed through me like a rush of adrenalin surging through the bloodstream. Biting my lip against the moan of need that balled in my throat, I fell back on the cloak pressing my thighs tight together in an attempt to suppress the wantonness now coursing my body.

Hot lips covered mine as Casimir's body fell upon my writhing form.

"Casimir, no!"

"I know, Kat, but you need sating."

"No."

"You're calling to me with your need to mate."

"No."

His fingers found my heat, and my eyes popped when he pushed his fingers into me. "Trust me." Kissing me deeply, Casimir thrust his fingers into me. Moaning into his mouth as he stole the pants and whimpers from my lips, I forgot everything but my need. His body rubbed against mine, the hardness of him so tempting where it pressed into my thigh. I was mated. I shouldn't react to another man like this, not even while on heat. Casimir was different though; he was my betrothed. My blood recognized Casimir as my rightful mate since our blood-bond settled before I'd even learned to talk.

Digging my nails into Casimir's shoulders, I tried hard to resist letting him possess me. "No."

"Yes." Feeling how close I was, Casimir growled thrusting his fingers harder and faster. "Let go, Kat."

Tears fell faster. "No."

Pressing harder to me, Casimir gripped my narrow throat in his large, steady hand. "We will not be safe if your need is calling to both of us. Let go!"

Fear coursed through me, my back arched away from the ground, and I cried out my release to the watching forest. Casimir's body jerked, a sudden rush of hot liquid against my thigh before he relaxed above me.

Shoving him away from me, I covered myself with my robe as the tears fell faster at the sight of the glistening fluid on my skin. Wiping the offending stain away with the discarded cloak, Casimir sighed, then moved away to get dressed.

"I said no. That word used to mean something in the Pâlie."

"I know, Kat. It still does. I'm sorry, but your desire was calling to me. I need to focus on getting you to safety. I wouldn't have been if I didn't sate your heat first." Returning to me fully dressed, Casimir put out a hand to help me up. Once I was standing, I took my hand back immediately.

Wrapping one of the cloaks around my shivering body, Casimir lifted the hood over my head. Collecting the other one from the ground, Casimir swung into it gracefully like a male ballet dancer performing a pirouette. "Come on, Katiana. Let's get you somewhere safe and out of harm's way."

Sobbing, I didn't move. "Take me back to my husband."

Stopping at the top of the ridge of the gully, Casimir looked back at me sadly. "No, Princess, that would be putting you right in harm's way. The factions have been looking for a reason to start an all-out war. Your brother's death will be the spark. By killing you, they would start an inferno."

"But everyone thinks me just a human half-breed. No one but you knows who I am, and the only two who know I'm a Pâlir at home are my husband and first-order that I would trust with my life. I'm safe there."

Taking a violent leap down the ridge towards me, I recoiled when Casimir grabbed my upper arm in a harsh grip. "That's right, Princess. No one knows who you are but for me. You will be a pawn they kill to incite the Král to war. By the time anyone realizes who you were, it will just serve to add fuel to the out of control fire."

When he released my arm, I stepped back from him rubbing my bicep, sure it would bruise.

"It isn't just vengeful Pâlirs I'm hiding you from, Katiana. There are those of the Kral's people who will kill the half-breed mate of their king if it gives them free-rein to slaughter every last Pâlir alive."

Stunned by his suggestion of treason in both factions, I stared at Casimir.

Stepping closer, Casimir wiped a tear from my cheek with a tenderness that was in opposition to his persona only moments before. "You will not be safe with either race until this war is over."

5

"Why aren't we flying? Wouldn't it be faster?" After an hour of walking, I was exhausted. We'd moved from the forest into pastures, before crossing a fire trail and entering another forest at the base of a mountain range. A range we were now halfway up.

"They'll be watching the skies."

"Why? No one has known where I've been for years. Why would they suddenly be looking for me now?"

"They aren't. The Halos and the Pâlir in league with them will be looking for the Král's human wife to kill in vengeance."

"But I'm with you." The sound of my breathing filled the mountainside as my feet came to a halt. "Only you." Casimir kept climbing. "You sent the others back. You don't trust them. What's going on Casimir?"

Casimir turned and faced me. "I'll tell you, Katiana, but right now, our energy needs to go into getting you to safety before that sun rises." He pointed to the lightening horizon. "And we need to do it quietly."

Swallowing down a small glob of fear, I nodded understanding of the warning in his voice and hurried to catch up.

We trekked up the mountain range for another hour, the sun just peaking above the horizon as we started descending the other side. It was far less steep on this side and we made our way quickly to the bottom. Moving along the base of the ridge, we found another gully with an ice-cold river. Lifting me effortlessly to his back, Casimir transvected across the river, letting the air currents lift him and float him to dry land.

As we reached the bank on the other side, Casimir froze, instantly on alert. Preventing my dismount, he moved at dizzying speed to a thicket around the base of a tree. "Stay here. Don't move. Don't make a sound. No matter what you hear or who you see, not even if it's one of the Král's First Order."

The First Order was Yishay's personal guard, the men who had been in the room for my brother's murder. "Casimir..."

"Not a sound, Kat. You don't move from this spot until I come back for you. Rozuměl?"

"Ano, chápu." Though, I didn't truly understand, but I felt his anxiety like ants under my skin and the caring touch of his hand to my face.

Casimir was gone before the first sob of fear caught in my throat. Huddling down behind the shrubbery, I was scared and cold with hunger cramping my stomach and stirring between my thighs. Once the sun breached the peak of the mountain, I lost track of time. Casimir didn't return. Lying down, I wrapped the cloak tight around me and drifted to sleep.

A bird's call woke me. It scared me with its proximity. Sitting up, I anxiously searched my surroundings, listening for any sounds out of the ordinary in the forest. Nothing. Birds, squirrels, the water in the river, but nothing human or similarly dangerous.

Crawling out from the brush, I stood to stretch. The sun was past its peak in the sky. No Halos or Pâlir would be out and about for a few more hours. Taking a deep breath, I caught the stale smell of blood. Removing Casimir's cloak, I saw the blood splatter over my satin robe. Quiet tears fell remembering how that blood had come to be there and whose it was.

Moving to the river, I stepped in and sunk to my knees. The cold didn't matter as I washed my brother's blood from my face. Sliding out of my robe, I scrubbed at the bloody stains until my crying grew. Clenching the robe in my fists, I wrapped my arms around me, and let my grief go.

It wasn't just the grief; it was the fear of not knowing who I could trust anymore. My heart wanted Yishay. I daydreamed of him appearing out of nowhere, wrapping me in his arms, and flying me home. Just thinking of Yishay sent the butterflies all aflutter in my stomach. The longing for food gone, replaced by my need for my husband.

Remembering this morning, how Casimir had touched me to give me relief, I bit my lip on a strangled sob. Unconsciously, my hand slid between my thighs and mimicked his touch while I thought of Yishay. My breath started coming in gasps as I imagined Yishay kneeling behind me, using his hand to ready me for him. It felt so real, his hand moving over me, his body pressed to mine, the beat of his heart against my back, his breath at my ear, his sleep-filled voice in my head.

'Kat.'

My orgasm came from nowhere as I fell forward, catching myself with my spare hand to kneel on all fours in the river. As the tremors seizing my body subsided, I could still feel Yishay. Sobbing as I sunk my whole body into the icy water, I cried with longing for my husband. "Yishay, I love you."

'Where have they taken you, Kat?'

The reply shocked the hell out of me. Concentrating, I realized I could feel his heartbeat again, like I had after he'd bound me. My stomach curdled as his fear at what had been happening to me through the night churned within me. His dread that he wouldn't find me in time.

'Kat?'

"I'm in a forest. I have no idea where I am."

There was instant distrust choking our bond at my vague answer.

The sensation still fresh from last night when he'd realised I was his blood sworn enemy. *'Did you escape?'*

"No, and yes." Taking a deep breath, I tried to explain in a way that wouldn't make him more distrustful. "The man who took me left me here. He said he was protecting me from...traitors."

'He's a Pâlir, Kat, my sworn enemy. You can't trust him. They will take their revenge for the loss of their prince on you.'

"That's exactly why Casimir said I won't be safe with you either-"

'Casimir?! Casimir is who has you captive?' The sudden rush of fear and rage tapered. Taking a deep breath, Yishay calmed his voice. *'Kat, he is the most dangerous Pâlir there is. He will...'* Yishay swallowed hard as he pictured my lifeless body defiled and drained of blood in a forest. That visual did nothing to ease my fears. *'He was the Prince's best friend and his second. He will want his revenge for personal reasons as well as for their people's loss.'*

"No, he won't..."

'Kat, you have no idea who or what you are dealing with!'

"Yishay...please trust me when I tell you Casimir won't hurt me. He knows killing me will start a war and he said he doesn't want that to happen."

Pleading for Yishay to believe me was pointless, his mind was flipping through plans and strategies while I talked. All the reasons Casimir had kept me alive. He finally settled on the one that seemed the most likely to him, a better revenge than killing the Král's human wife. Using me as bait to get the Král. Sighing long and hard, Yishay decided that could be Casimirs only plan of revenge. *'I love you, Kat.'*

Tears poured forth as I shook my head. "No, Yish. If he wanted you dead, he'd have shot you in the heart when-"

'He took you and abandoned you. His plan is obvious. I can't risk everything I've worked so hard at since becoming Král.

"'But you'll risk me?"

'I'm sorry, Kat.'

"No! I love you. You're my zápalka. You're meant to love me, and to protect me!"

Shaking his head, his anger at discovering my true heritage still lingering as he lay back down in bed to sleep. *'That was before.'*

LEAVING THE RIVER, I WAS NUMB. THE MAN I LOVED, MY HUSBAND, MY mate, wasn't coming for me. He'd already decided I was a lost cause, just another expendable Pâlir. I could still feel the slow steady beat of his sleeping heart, but his mind was closed to me now.

Lost in misery, I absently spread my night robe over the top of a shrub that was bathed in sunlight. Autumn sun at midday would still be warm enough to dry thin material within a short time. Pulling the cloak around my body, I was blue and shivering, but I couldn't feel it. How could Yish have trusted me so little? To have fallen asleep so easily and quickly after he decided I was lost to him? Had I always meant nothing to him, or only since he discovered what I was?

Now that I was just another Pâlir to him, did that make my life forfeit? Casimir was right, I could trust no one, not even the man who had my heart. Sinking to my knees in the sun, the ground was cold beneath my shins, I thought on what Casimir had said about finding me with child in the next few days.

What if that's what Casimir is really waiting for? How much more valuable does the Král's wife become if she's carrying his child and possible heir? Resigned, I curled over my thighs in child's pose. What choice do I have? I have no one left I can trust now. If I run, one of the others could find me after night fall, and they would show no mercy. That's if I had anywhere to run too. Taking a deep breath, I tried to calm my fears. I had to believe Casimir would protect me. If he doesn't...

'I'm dead either way.' I finished in my head.

With the warmth of the sun upon my back, I closed my eyes as a singular tear spilled over my cheek and dripped to the ground. Forcing myself to relax, I concentrated on being empty, empty mind, empty body. Focusing on my breathing, I insisted I find peace because freaking out was not going to find me in a better situation.

When the darkness of sleep left me, I shivered. The sun had moved toward the west and I was huddled in on myself on the ground. Slowly, I eased myself back to sitting, muscles sore from the extended period of stillness. When I was ready, I stood and retrieved my dry, but cold robe from the shrub, slipping back into it before hugging the cloak around me tight again.

It was growing dark, and both the Pâlirs and Halos would be waking up and getting ready to venture out. For a moment, I wondered if the war would begin tonight. Would the morning light reveal a bloody battlefield like in ages past? Or would it be a more subtle beginning? Seeking out and assassinating a few families to start.

Moving back to the hiding spot Casimir had left me in this morning, I doubted being out in the open was a good plan. He'd told me to stay in that spot, so I would. Making sure there were no tracks or traces of my daytime sojourn, I climbed back beneath the shrub pressing my back to the tree beside it.

My stomach growled. Two days without food made it almost roar, but still it wasn't my most pressing hunger. But by morning the need for my mate would abate, so that would be one less thing to stress over at least. Not having Yishay or Casimir anywhere near me definitely made my desire much easier to control.

Listening to the forest, I tried to determine any subtle differences in sounds or air movements like I had been taught as a kid. I was too long out of practice, too far gone from who I should be. Sitting in a darkening forest aware that two races of people are about to start hunting you, gives you a lot of time to think crazy thoughts. I'd moved in with a Halos, dated the king of my blood enemy, and then I'd married him. How could this not be my fault?

If I'd returned to my people when I came of age, resumed my place in my family and married Casimir, I would be safe and protected right now, possibly with a couple of kids underfoot already. I wouldn't have watched my brother die and stood by helplessly, selfishly protecting my own life. I wouldn't be cringing in a darkened forest cold, hungry, horny, and frightened. I wouldn't be bearing the heartache of the man I loved not trusting me. The shame of meaning so little he could abandon me to whatever plans his enemy had designed for me.

Smacking my hand into the ground hard enough that the sting reverberated up my arm, I scolded myself. "Stop it! You are a Pâlir, not some weak Halos woman. You are of the blood. You are stronger than this, so stop it!" Retracting my hand back into the cloak, I hugged myself tightly. "You've been on your own since you were thirteen. This is nothing new for you. If Casimir doesn't come by morning light, you get your ass in gear and you run. You get food and clothing and figure the rest out as you go."

The air shifted and I tensed. It wasn't that I'd heard anything unusual or even that the forest had suddenly gone quiet, I just felt the need to be very still all of a sudden. The sky was dark now, not full night dark, but enough that anything flying became a shadow. I didn't dare look up in case the movement revealed my location, but a sixth sense told me I wasn't alone in this part of the forest anymore.

Two shadows appeared on the opposite side of the river. Barely visible through the foliage, I could just see the knees down of their cloaks. "So, what's her name?" a young voice asked.

"No, idea," a gruff voice answered.

"What does she look like?"

"Human," the gruff voice answered confidently.

"Yeah, that's a great description," the young man answered sarcastically. "Did your Halos informants give you anything useful?" With one leap a sturdy figure jumped the river and stood only meters from my hiding spot.

"All I know is this is where Casimir was seen exiting the forest from last night. So, he's hidden the girl somewhere between here and Halos territory," Gruff announced as he sniffed the air.

"So, basically, we just grab every human female between twenty and thirty that we come across, between here and the Halos boundary?" the other Pâlir returned snidely. "That's not going to get any notice by the humans by morning."

"She's the Král's wife," Gruff snarled back. "She will smell like him. She'll be the only human polluted with a Halos scent between here and there. They only feed on their mates and Pâlirs they kill. That will mark her."

"Except, she's been away from her husband all night, and from what our informant told us, she isn't even bound to him. If she has bathed and changed her clothes his scent will be diminished, if not gone altogether already."

The Pâlir jumped back across the river and grabbed the other by the scruff of the neck. "He feeds." Gruff threw the other Pâlir aside and leapt up into the branches of a nearby tree. "She'll bear his bite still. That will give her away. Now, quit whining and let's get searching!"

The Pâlir still in view collected himself and looked around him. "What if the Halos are lying? Casimir said the girl he took out of there was a young Pâlir they'd taken hostage and were...torturing. What if they are lying about who she was, so that we clean up their mess?"

"We'll know if the girl is human or Pâlir as soon as we find her."

The young Pâlir shook his head. "Well no matter who she is, there is no way Casimir has hidden her in the open. Maybe he took her to the prince to see if she had any inside information. We'd be better off just waiting to see where he goes."

"Did he seem in a hurry to get anywhere this evening? He's not going anywhere near the girl again anytime soon. He's hidden her, so hurry up," Gruff shouted back already a distance away.

"If she is human, and it was me, I'd have hidden her in the free-territory." The lagging Pâlir grumbled to himself as he launched skywards.

Too scared to draw breath, I stayed paralised until I felt the air calm around me. Then, in a rush, I exhaled a sigh of relief. Casimir was protecting me. I just wasn't sure from whom.

6

---

*H*ow many hours I sat there making plans for sunrise, to run, to find clothing, food, and shelter, all before the next nightfall, I couldn't tell you. What I can tell you is that it was the coldest night of autumn, or at least it felt it with only my satin robe and the cloak Casimir left me. Shivering violently, my breath came out in puffs of thick fog to join with the heavy mist that had covered the river and surrounding areas.

The soft thud of feet landing sounded very close to my left, too close. "Kat? It's Kenan, I know you're in there. Come on, we need to get you to safety."

The adrenalin that suddenly surged through me forced me to stillness and to hold my breath.

"Kat, I'm friends with Casimir. He told me where to find you. Come on, let's get you to the cabin."

Diving out of the bushes into Kenan's arms, I hugged him tight. Holding me for a second, Kenan pushed me away, thrusting a bundle of clothes into my arms. "Quickly change, we're in danger here."

Nodding, I turned to pull on the jeans, socks, and shoes under my robe. Releasing the cloak, I dropped my dressing gown to the ground to don the skivvy, jumper, and jacket that was left. A ripping sound caught my attention, and I turned to find Kenan ripping my robe to shreds and throwing it into the river. The temptation to complain about him destroying part of Yishay's first-anniversary gift to me sprang instantly to my lips, but I held my tongue.

Zipping up the jacket as Kenan returned to me, I observed the stress lines around his eyes. Pulling a beanie out of his pocket, Kenan gathered my white hair up on my head then pulled the beanie over it to cover my head and ears before he pulled the hood over my head. "There are gloves in the jacket pocket."

Removing the fur-lined leather gloves, I slipped them over my cold fingers. Gathering up the Pâlie soldier cloak, Kenan bundled it inside his own jacket. Rubbing my hands together to warm them up quicker, I froze when another soft thud landed behind me.

"Kenan, what are you doing here? Yishay had you marked to search the city fringes." Jabin's gruff voice was full of suspicion.

Kenan's eyes narrowed. "And I thought you were meant to be running reconnaissance on the Pâlie stronghold?"

When Jabin stepped to my right, Kenan started circling to my left, but he moved closer to where I stood frozen between them. "I was on my way back. Who's the human?"

"This neck of the Rocky's is nowhere near the path back to Yishay."

"The human?" He was coming up on my right to get a profile view.

Moving quickly, Kenan snatched my arm and swung me around behind him protectively. "An informant. She saw the human girl I was looking for in the field to the north this morning when she was going to school."

The energy of Jabin's excitement filled the air. "She saw Kat? Where? Tell me where she was, now!" For a moment, my fear of Jabin seemed foolish. Yishay trusted him after all, and he was a member of the First Order. Maybe he was just trying to find me to return me to the Král.

'Then why is Kenan hiding you from him? Why is he lying about who you are?'

"As I just said, all she saw was a woman in a satin robe, trudging barefoot through the north field this morning. She was on her school bus and saw her from a distance."

Jabin growled turning to the north. "This would be so much easier if the bonding had taken and Yishay could tell us where to find her. Why the hell wouldn't the bond take?"

"Don't you think it'd look a little suspicious if Yishay told you where to find his wife alive and you bought back her mutilated corpse?"

"She's human and frail. Bad things happen to humans daily. The Pâlie could have located her before we got there, and exacted their revenge. There are various excuses for returning that human dead, and enough of us, who don't want to see our throne polluted with half-breed slush like you, to stand witness for each other."

"She is his zápalka, Jabin! Does that mean nothing to you?"

"Yes. It means that Kat may already be walking around with the heir to our throne growing within her and that she needs to be found and executed sooner rather than later."

A hiss of hate escaped my throat before I could stop it.

Turning back to face us, the smile on Jabin's face grew fearsome. "So, why don't you just step over here, Kat, and let me put you out of our misery?"

Kenan rushed Jabin. "Run, Kat!"

They crashed into one another, the racket like the sound of two trains colliding. If there were any other's out searching for me in this part of the woods, they would be heading this way by now.

I bolted. Not out into the clearing beyond the woods where Casimir had gone just before sunrise and never returned. Turning, I ran into the woods behind me, keeping the stream on my left as I went flat out. My thoughts were racing. For over two days, I hadn't eaten. With very little energy, I had no chance of escaping a hunting party by myself. Currently, I was surviving on adrenalin, and even that would run out quickly.

Entering a small clearing caused by a fallen tree, I took a quick intake of the area. Yanking off my jacket, I posed it over a shrub just below the felled tree trunk. Backstepping into the shadow of a tree a few meters away, I hoped that it would fool whoever was looking for me.

Squatting between the tree and a shrub, I waited. *'What the hell was I thinking?'* As soon as Jabin made a grab for the jacket, he'd know and my being nearby would make me a sitting duck. After ten years in the light, I was only human; a weak, feeble, and defenseless human...except, I wasn't.

Years ago, I'd convinced myself I was human to hide. The best camouflage was to believe. If you walk like a duck and talk like a duck, you're a duck. Humans' didn't drink their lover's blood, they existed in daylight, they worked hard, and they feared the dark for all the right unknown reasons. So, that's what I'd done. In fact, I was so successful at playing human, I'd forgotten who I was, what I was, and of what I was capable. The lie I'd come to believe fed my own feelings of helplessness.

Jabin burst through the trees, snapping my mind back to my present danger. He stopped dead when he spotted the jacket. Laughing, he started taking long strides on his short legs towards it. "Here, Kitty Kitty."

Rising quietly behind him, I moved inaudibly toward him, his own careless noise covering my movement. Stealth, Jabin was not.

Shaking his head at my supposed stupidity, Jabin bent to grab me by the scruff of the neck. As he stood, swearing his annoyance, my jacket in his grasp, I reefed the dagger from his belt and ducked. Spinning around expecting to find someone behind him, Jabin found the area empty. It took him seconds too long to drop his gaze. By the time he spotted me, I was already in motion. Jabin squinted, and his forehead furrowed when I hissed like a feral cat, and with the last rush of adrenalin, launched out of my crouch at him.

Dropping my jacket, Jabin caught me by the throat the same moment the dagger in my hand jammed up and under his ribs into his heart. It was a move I practiced daily as a child since I was only allowed to train with my older brothers. Being smaller never meant weak. Jabin's eyes went wide. Yanking the blade back, I drove it upwards again, then again, and again. His hand at my throat loosened, and with one final thrust, it dropped away as his body fell to the ground, the dagger still protruding from under his ribs.

Standing over him, watching the death spasms overtake his body, I licked my lips as the lingering hunger demanded acknowledgment. Dropping to my knees beside his dying body, I was vaguely aware of the tears on my cheeks, the sobs escaping my throat, and the disgust of hunger wrenching within me. Closing my eyes, I shook away the negative emotions. "I'm not human. This is who I am." Lowering my mouth to one of the gushing gashes in Jabin's chest, I gave up my mask.

The first taste of blood was a contradiction in feelings. The humanized part of me screamed in horror, but the true I, the Pâlir, was only concerned with my hunger, and survival. My throat swallowed convulsively on each mouthful that poured from the dying Halos. The vitality of life filled me. Energy surged into my limbs. Alertness buzzed to life in my head, like a static radio suddenly tuned into the right station after decades of white noise. The sound was pure.

Surrounding me were the animals that scattered from the disturbance. They were standing off to the side a safe distance away, watching larger prey enjoy their meal. Then came the stealthy footsteps of another creature running flat out towards me, but it wasn't enough to force me away from my feed. Jumping a shrub, Kenan landed meters away from me. Skidding to a stop, he swallowed hard and turned his head with a curse upon his lips.

Sitting back on my ankles, I wiped a hand across my mouth. When I looked at it, it was stained dark with the blood on my face. Ripping a piece of cloth from Jabin's shirt, I moved towards the river. Drenching the fabric, I scrubbed at my face with it until it stopped coming away red. The sudden realization I could see color in the dark hit me. Had Jabin's blood been strong enough to revert what was lost to me so long ago?

A shuffle of shoes behind me reminded me I was not alone. Dropping the rag into the river, I turned to face Kenan aware of what he would see.

Meeting my eyes, Kenan bowed his head. "Princess Katiana."

"How long have you known?"

Kenan averted his eyes. "I've always known you were Pâlir, but I'd no idea who you were until Casimir told me tonight."

Moving to collect my jacket, I shrugged into it. "Is he coming?"

While I'd cleaned up, Kenan had taken care of Jabin, removing his heart entirely. He'd leave the body for the carrion, but he'd wrapped the mutilated heart in another strip of Jabin's shirt.

"Probably not far away. He's trying to keep the Pâlie off your trail while I get you to safety." Moving to the river, Kenan started washing his hands.

Struggling to swallow over the large lump that developed in my throat, I averted my gaze. "Then let's go before my conscience turns me into a pathetic lump of hopelessness again."

Returning to me, Kenan stilled my shaking hands and zipped my jacket for me. "You have never been pathetic, Kat."

"Let's not waste Casimir's time."

Nodding, Kenan lifted the hood of my jacket back into place. "We need to move quickly, Kat. Are you okay with transvecting?"

Transvecting was a combination of levitating, catching, and floating on the air currents. "Just don't drop me and I'll be fine."

Smiling, Kenan wrapped his arms around me in a tight hug, my face pressed to his chest. He bent his knees just a touch, then straightened with a jolt, and we lifted off the ground about a meter. Floating for a moment, Kenan adjusted for my weight in his arms, and then, the trees were flashing passed us.

Closing my eyes, I concentrated on feeling Kenan's heartbeat through his jacket. We stayed beneath the forest canopy for quite a while, and then we were in the open for a short time before being amongst trees again. We flew for over two hours through forests for the most part. Occasionally, we'd be in the open for the shortest possible time before we finally arrived deep in the mountains.

Following a path through the forest, Kenan's speed slowed considerably. Half-way up the mountain, he landed in the high bows of a tree, perching us close to the trunk. "I don't want to take you straight in. We need to stop, make sure we weren't followed."

We sat in the tree for near on an hour before a noise drew our attention behind us. Casimir landed on a branch behind me.

"Cas." Kenan sighed with relief.

"You weren't followed." Turning his gaze to me, Casimir brushed my cheek gently with the back of his gloved hands. "You okay?"

"She killed Jabin when he found us and is still in shock by what she did."

Peering more closely at me, Casimir frowned. "Your eyes are blue again...you drank him?"

"I...I was starving. It seemed to make sense not to waste the food."

Kenan tilted his head at Casimir. "She left before her first feed?"

"They all do. The young ones are more likely to assimilate that way."

"So, that was her first kill and her first feed?"

Concern etched Casimir's features. "Let's get her inside before the sun rises, or it will burn out her retinas." Stepping back, Casimir fell from the tree, catching the air currents and disappearing.

Holding me tight to him, Kenan stepped after Casimir. Closing my eyes against the wind that was lashing us up this high, I clung to Kenan tightly. When we landed, we stood on the balcony of an old double brick building high up on the mountain. The ground below was under a few meters of snow. Leading me through the timber-framed double window doors, Kenan turned his attention to Casimir who shut the doors and locked them. "I need to clean up then get back. I was only meant to go as far as the city last night. If I don't show up and neither does Jabin, there will be questions."

"Go get yourself cleaned and changed, so you don't smell like her. I'll get her settled and into bed."

Stepping forward protectively, Kenan lowered his voice. "Cas, I know what she was meant to be for you, but she's married, bonded even. Her mate may be your enemy, but she loves him. Don't force her down a path she won't be able to live."

Looking over Kenan's head, Casimir observed me. "Did you

contact your mate today?" Averting my eyes, I nodded. "He didn't come for you?" Shaking my head, the crying started all over again. "He let you go?" Cuddling myself tightly, I nodded again. "If she was your mate and you located her, would you have just let the night come knowing she would be hunted, without trying to get to her?"

"We have an agreement. We hide Kat until we've dealt with the warmongers, then she goes back to the Král."

Casimir got in Kenan's face. "That only plays out that way if it's safe for her to return. If he wants her back, and if she wants to go back. He's abandoned her because he found out she wasn't human. He was willing to breed with a human, but not one of his own kind. What sort of messed up Král is that?"

"Our Král, Cas. Pâlir or Halos, he is the Král, and she is his wife! Keep your hands off!"

"She'll need to feed, Key, and I'm the only one here. Hands-off isn't an option."

"Guys!" Stepping between them, I refused to look at either of them. "I'm cold, hungry, and tired. Key, you need to get back. Can we argue over who's not going to fuck me later, please?"

They both backed up a step. Giving me a hug, Kenan kissed my forehead. "I'll check on you when I can." Stepping out of the upstairs lounge room, Kenan left me with Casimir.

Draping his arm around my shoulders, Casimir moved us towards the door. "Let's get you in a hot bath while I fix us some dinner. Kenan brought some of your clothes; you'll find them in your wardrobe."

Directing me out of the lounge room, we skirted where the stairs descended to the ground level. Above the void looked to be an old bell tower, but it was sealed off with a thick piece of glass. On the opposite side, we moved into a hall which had a door on each side. Pointing to the door on the left, Casimir then moved to the door on the right. "This is your room. I'm just across the hall."

Opening my bedroom door, Casimir waited for me to enter, then moved to a side door which opened into the ensuite. Leaving me there in the room, he started pouring the water for a bath. The cabin was warm, so I shrugged off my jacket and toed out of my shoes.

When Casimir came back into the room, he knelt in front of me, removing my socks. "Cas, I can undress without help."

"I'll go make dinner then. Come down when you're ready. The kitchen is down the stairs towards the back. Just follow your nose."

Waiting until I was alone, I stripped out of the rest of my clothes and padded into the bathroom. The bath was steaming hot. Lowering myself in slowly, I hissed at the heat on my cold flesh, but once I was in, it was divine. After scrubbing myself clean, I soaked until the water lost its warmth. Sighing with regret of having to move, I pulled myself out of the bath and wrapped a towel around me.

Locating some clothes in the wardrobe, I chose something appropriate to wear around the cabin, hoping I was done with walking around in the snow for a while. Yoga pants, a singlet top, and cardigan would be fine for inside the cabin. There was a week's worth of clothes in the wardrobe, making me wonder how Kenan got them out of the house without Yishay noticing. Who was I kidding, Yishay was probably too busy starting a war to care.

Catching myself pouting in the mirror, I pulled myself up. If Yishay didn't want me, fine. After this was over, we'd end us. He could find an excellent little halos woman or a real human to breed his heir. Heart aching over the idea, I rubbed above my left breast. When my stomach growled, I decided to follow my nose to the kitchen. After all, what else was there, but to survive the war, and learn to be who I was at heart.

7

*A*t the very back of the cabin, I found Casimir in the kitchen. "Where are we?"

Serving up a bowl of vegetable stew with buttered bread, Casimir eyed me. "My mother's place; on the east side of the mountains, in Halos territory. The Pâlie won't look here because they don't know Bronya was my mother."

Gob-smacked, I stared at Casimir. "Bronya? As in Yishay's aunt, Bronya?"

"The same. My father Saber and she were zápalka. They hid it from both the respective factions by coming here. Kenan and I spent our first years in this cabin. When we were of the age that we needed to train, Saber took me to the Pâlie stronghold, since I looked like him, while Bronya took Kenan home to the southeast."

Sitting down, Casimir started eating, but I stood there staring, wanting to know more. Kenan and Casimir were brothers, which explained their friendship. When Casimir raised a brow at me, I sat studying him, trying to find any resemblance between them. Pushing a bowl of stew towards me, Casimir waited until I picked up the spoon to continue.

"Saber and Bronya would come back here to be together. They'd bring us boys, so we'd always remember we are brothers. When the Halos infighting killed Bronya, Saber stopped coming. He died some years later."

"But you and Kenan still come back here?"

"No one knows or cares who my mother is. The Pâlie don't care who bore you, just that you are a good warrior. The Halos are all about bloodlines. When Bronya wouldn't reveal the father of her child, the Halos knew he was half-blood. We'd come here where no matter what, we always belonged."

Finishing my mouthful, I dropped my head. "It's why he's one of the few unmarried. Because he isn't pure."

"Well, Kenan hoped to marry another half-breed, but he made the mistake of introducing her to his best friend." Eyes sparkling, Casimir waited until I met his gaze and quirked a brow. "He planned to let me meet her the following week. When he found out last night that you are my betrothed, Key was angry. He realised no matter what, you were never his."

Stuffing a bite of bread into my mouth, I hoped to avoid having to say anything. I'd liked Kenan a lot, but the moment I'd shaken Yishay's hand, I'd been lost to him. Already blood-bound to Casimir as a toddler, our meeting would have met the same fate. Part of me wished Kenan introduced me to his brother first.

Noting my sudden devotion to keeping my mouth full, Casimir continued. "Most of the Pâlie are over this war. The only Pâlie who support it now, are those so lost in grief and vengeance, they are blind to reason. We've all lost loved ones. It's time to end this nonsense. We are the same species. Just descendant from two different members of the royal family."

"What happens now? Do you let everyone think you killed me?"

Considering me, Casimir chewed his food and swallowed. "You were in heat when Yishay bound you, Kat. The potential is that within two days, your bond with him will settle. Then he will know you live, and he will know you carry his child. Kenan believes that will draw the Král out to find you."

"He was right! You're using me as bait?"

"To make peace, Kat. We won't kill him. We need to get him away from the First Order if we are to make him see reason. The old Král raised his son with the same Pâlir-hate-propaganda as every Halos, but Kenan assures me Yishay questions a lot of it."

Since I'd finished eating, Casimir collected my bowl and took it to the sink where he started cleaning up. "The Král already reduced killing just in his short time as ruler. He no longer endorses hunting parties, and, other than his First Order, which are meant to only scout, he has encouraged his people to assimilate with the human world and take up employment. They are more like Pâlir than they've ever been."

"They still have hunting parties. I've heard the Halos women whispering about it. Some of the Order arranges them. I figured Yishay must have endorsed it?"

Pouring me a glass of water, Casimir sat back down with me. "Kenan assures me Yishay doesn't endorse them, but he doesn't stop them either. The Král believes they will accept the change in time, but while some Pâlir still seek a fight, so do the Halos."

"Plus, it's better to have the Halos kill Pâlie than each other."

Casimir lifted a brow. "There is that. I wonder if it's something in the water on the south side of the mountain range that makes them so violent."

"That, or maybe it's just an asshole gene."

Smiling, Casimir ran a strand of my hair through his fingers. "The sun is rising. We should go to bed. Tonight, I'll take you out hunting, and then I'll need to go check-in and find out what's happening."

"I'm not going to hunt Cas. That's not who I am."

Taking my arm, he led me back upstairs. "You are being hunted. The best way for you to survive is not to hide, but to hunt those who hunt you. They think you are harmless and that works in our favor." Pushing open my bedroom door for me, Casimir winked. "Close the shutters, so the sun doesn't blind you accidentally." Crossing the hall, Casimir slipped into his own already darkened room.

WAKING CONFUSED IN THE DARKNESS OF MY ROOM, I MADE MY WAY TO the bathroom and flinched when I opened the door to the sun-filled room. With my eyes watering, I blinked rapidly, but I didn't go blind. After a moment, my vision cleared, and I was able to walk into the bathroom fully.

The mirror reflected eyes caught between arctic blue and sea green. Washing my face, I checked the time. It was only midday. Stepping back into the bedroom, my bed looked too empty. Out in the hallway, the sunlight filtered down through the sealed off bell tower. Ten years as a daywalker meant sleeping all day was just impossible for me. Packing some more wood in the central fireplace at the bottom of the stairs, I looked around the cabin.

There was another bedroom downstairs. By the photos, it was Kenan's bedroom, so I slipped back out. I wasn't about to invade his privacy. Fixing myself something to eat in the kitchen, I took the sandwich upstairs to the living room, stoked the fireplace in there, and settled down to watch the flames hop around.

"Can't sleep?"

Nearly jumping over the back of the lounge, I glared at Casimir leaning against the doorway. "What are you doing up? Doesn't the light burn your eyes?"

Shrugging, Casimir came to sit next to me, stealing half my sandwich. "That's only a risk for the first decade after you start feeding. As you get older, you can stay out later, so you can be in the light, just not direct sunlight or you stuff your night vision for months. Enough of us have found that out the hard way." Leaning forward, Casimir examined my eyes, lifting the lids and such. "You've already adjusted. Possibly a decade walking around in direct sunlight has built resistance."

With his proximity, I could see that Casimir's iris was also multi-colored. Snow blue mixed with a more ocean blue. "So, you don't sleep all day either?"

"Usually I work all night, so I'll sleep most of it, but not deeply. I heard you coming back up the stairs. When you didn't go back to your room, I thought I better come check on you."

Eyeing him eating the leftover of my sandwich, I pouted. "I was hungry."

Smirking, Casimir lifted his arm and pulled me into his side.

Resting my head on his shoulder, I watched the fire. "My body is used to eating breakfast, lunch, and dinner. I also should be at work right now. I should call my boss."

"Kenan called your work. Told them there was a death in the family, you were quite distraught, and you'd be off for a few weeks."

My eyes went wide. "My boss would never give anyone a few weeks off work."

"I don't think Kenan gave him much choice in the matter. My little brother can be quite persuasive. He'll have you agreeing to something you were totally against before you realize you'd changed your mind."

"Is that how I ended up here?"

"When I realized it was you in the house, I told your brother, then sent Tadeo for backup to get you out. We thought they were holding you. When Vladimir discovered you were married to the Král, I couldn't take you home, not as a traitor."

"But you'd already set things in motion, so..."

"So, while you were upstairs fighting with your husband, Kenan and I were working out how to hide you." Getting up, Casimir started pacing. "The night was already messed up. We were supposedly meeting the Král for peace talks, but that turned out to be a trap. Then we find you, and Vladimir sacrificed himself to protect you."

"They would have killed him anyway..."

"No. Your Král would have released him had he not threatened you. It was stupid of your brother. We thought at first, they'd taken you some years ago, but Vladimir could see you freaking out. When he realised they weren't aware of who you are..."

Hanging my head in shame, I understood. "He thought I was a traitor too? I didn't know what to do, Cas. We met, and then he asked me to marry him. I knew it would hurt my family, but he was my zápalka. We dated, and it wasn't until several months later that I discovered he was the Král. By then, I loved him. I thought if I was married to the Král, I couldn't get any more protected then that."

Casimir didn't look at me, as if he wasn't sure he trusted me. I accepted it. My actions earned their distrust. "When I told Kenan I was going to take you, he ensured the Král bound you. I didn't realize Yishay hadn't bound you yet. It only served to complicate things further. Now, we aren't sure if you carry his heir, I interfere with the bond, and the Král thinks you are a trap, so he isn't coming for you."

"He thinks you are going to turn me against him and have me kill him."

Lifting a brow, Casimir looked at me then. "Is that what he told you?"

"I saw it as one of the possibilities in his mind. He'd rather you kill me than to have to do it himself." The tears came unbidden, and the sobbing started anew.

Dropping down in front of me, Casimir took my shoulders in his grasp. "Katiana, look at me." Lifting my tearing eyes to his, I tried to control my emotions. "The Král thinks I let you escape to draw him out to rescue you. He thinks you are a trap. That when he comes for you, I will kill you both."

"So, by not coming for me, he protects himself, and leaves me to be slaughtered?" I'm not sure that option was any easier to swallow. He was supposed to love me.

Sighing, Casimir cuddled me to him. "The Král does not think like most leaders, Kat. Maybe he has a plan I can't foresee." Urging me to my feet, Casimir wrapped his arm around me as he started walking. "Come on. We both need more sleep." At my bedroom door, Casimir left me and went back to his bed.

Yishay's abandonment became even more crushing the longer I stared at the empty bed. Turning my back on the room, I slipped through Casimir's door. He didn't say anything as I crawled into bed with him. Just held the blanket up as I cuddled in against him. Holding me tight, we both went back to sleep.

8

"So, I'm just meant to stand here and look pretty?" I scowled to no one. The snow was crunching under my boots and the wind was howling through the trees as I was walked through the forest on the west side of the mountains in Pâlir territory

When Casimir left me here, he'd assured me he wouldn't let any harm come to me. He said that I knew how to fight, and that I just needed to remember how.

"Could have at least left me with a fire," I grumbled under my breath as I huddled against the cold.

Unlike my first night after being taken, I was dressed for the cold, but it seemed even colder tonight, or maybe it was the lack of beanie. Casimir insisted I leave my head uncovered and hair braided. This way it was obvious I was female.

My teeth chattering, I found a large boulder and shimmied around it. When I reached the side that was protected from the wind, I shrunk down and huddled there. "Ten times better." My breath fogged instantly.

Sitting there for a while with my eyes closed, I listened to the forest. Despite their stealth, I felt them before they got to me.

"What do you think?" One whispered to the other from several meters away. It was the same mistake the Halos women made, thinking I was human, that I couldn't hear their whispers.

"Right age group. She's alone out here in the dark. Could definitely be her," a gruff voice replied.

The two voices sounded familiar. As they moved closer, I remembered the two men who came near to finding me by the river, and I started hoping Casimir was watching nearby. I could barely take on one guy, let alone two.

'Take the big guy first,' Casimir directed. *'The other is green, so he needs the older to lead.'*

The one benefit Pâlie had over Halos was our telepath ability. We didn't need to be bound to communicate either, unlike the Halos who seemed restricted to telepathy with only their mates.

"Are you lost?" Gruff asked as he got closer.

Gritting my teeth against the cold, I nodded but didn't speak.

"Where are you trying to get too?" He inched closer. His sidekick was closing from the other side, trying to box me in.

Highway Sixteen, east of the Icefields Parkway, and everything south of Highway One was Halos territory. North and west of those same landmarks was Pâlir. If I was the Kral's human wife, I'd be trying to make it south east towards Calgary. Since I was a smart Král's wife, I'd only be trying to make it into Halos territory, especially if I came across anyone not of the Král's First Order.

"Jasper," I shivered. "I'm trying to get to Jasper."

Gruff rubbed his chin considering. "I figured you'd be trying for Calgary?" He smiled when I looked up to meet his eyes. Pushing my back against the boulder, I slowly stood up. "So, you are the Král's wife? Smart to ask for Jasper, closer and on the territorial border. Not that you're safe in either territory anyway." The Pâlir smiled stepping toward me.

"What do you want?"

"You," Gruff answered.

"Dead," the younger chuckled.

"Normally, we only kill criminals," Gruff closed in, "but for you we make a special exception."

"My death will gain you nothing," I spat. "Don't you get it? I'm bait. That's all I'm good for."

"Well, you know what usually happens to the bait?" the young guy smiled.

"I escaped over forty-eight hours ago. Don't you think if my husband gave two shits about me, he'd have sent someone for me by now?"

Gruff smiled, "He doesn't know where you are. The bonding didn't work."

"He knew. He could feel me, can feel me even now. He told me letting you kill me saved him having to do it." That stopped them both as they looked at each other unsure.

'That's not what I said Kat,' Yishay growled in my head.

About an hour after Casimir had left, I'd realised I could feel him, but Yishay only just started paying attention to me.

"It's what you meant," I said aloud, confusing my attackers even further. "I'm not what you wanted. I saw the look on your face, felt your hate when you tasted me. Then you left me to be murdered. I'd have to be really stupid not to put it all together."

'Get ready, Kat,' Casimir instructed.

He was far enough away to not interfere in my bonding, but close enough to know what was happening. Slipping the knife Casimir had given me from inside my sleeve, I focused on my conversation with my husband.

'It's not like that,' Yishay sighed heavily. *'I love you, Kat...'*

'Now, Kat!' Casimir ordered.

"Obviously not enough!" Scowling, I lunged at Gruff full force.

A look of surprise filled Gruff's face as my blade slid home under his ribs and we crashed to the ground. Sinking my teeth into the side of his neck, I ripped out the carotid as I pulled the blade back and slammed it in a second time.

The young one grabbed me from behind. Gaining a squeal my throat as he pulled me from his friend, he threw me away with force. Rolling when I landed, I got to my feet and scurried into the trees.

"Mrdat!" The young guy cursed as he pulled the dagger from

Gruffs chest. He'd heal, but it would take a few hours to repair heart damage and what I'd done to his throat. Until then, the big guy wasn't going anywhere, which left the younger one alone. "Kurva děvko!"

Hiding in the shadow of one of the trees further up the ridge, I waited. I couldn't feel Yishay anymore, which meant Casimir was close. Closing my eyes, I concentrated. Casimir was to my right. Moving towards him, I focused on the feel of him. When I felt like I could almost reach out and touch Casimir, the young guy stepped in front of me. Taking one step back, I watched him.

"You know, I felt bad about killing you earlier. Now, I think I'm going to enjoy it."

"And that right there is the problem. Us Pâlie, we kill criminals for a reason. We aren't meant to enjoy it," I snarled at him. "We do it for food. That's why we pick prey that doesn't deserve to live because they themselves have no respect for life."

"As if the Král would marry a Pâlir," the guy laughed. "You think you can pull that distraction thing on me twice?"

As Casimir stepped up behind him, I smiled. "Yes, I think I can."

Grabbing the Pâlir, Casimir sunk his teeth into his neck holding him in a grip that prevented him fighting back. Ripping out the carotid, he dropped him to the ground.

"Go finish the other one," Casimir instructed. Watching the young Pâlir try to crawl away, I nodded absently. "Kat!" Casimir snapped to get my attention. "Now!"

Running back down the hill to where I'd dropped Gruff, I stared wide-eyed at all the blood in the snow and bit my lip. Despite the injury I'd inflicted, his neck wound had started healing. When I knelt beside him, he thrashed out, slamming me in the side of the head. Scrambling backwards away from him, my hand found my blade from earlier.

Retrieving my dagger, I drove it back into his chest repeatedly. Gruff cried out with each thrust. It wasn't until he stopped making any noise, that I stopped stabbing him. A thump on the other side of his body made me jump.

Dumping the other Pâlie body beside his friend, Casimir looked at me. "Remove the heart, Kat."

My eyes going wide, I shuffled back and shook my head.

Kneeling by the young Pâlir, Casimir shoved his hand up under the Pâlir ribcage. "It's easy. Just put your hand in on the underside. Reach your fingers around to wrap around the aorta and yank it down hard. You have the strength." Pulling his arm free with a sickening sucking sound, Casimir held the young Pâlir heart in his hand.

Throwing up in my mouth, I quickly swallowed it back down. Taking a shallow breath, I slipped my hand into the perforation my blade had already enlarged in the big Pâlie chest. The heart was shredded, smooth, slimy, surrounded by all the blood it had pumped free into the chest cavity.

Moving my hand around, I found the atriums were still somewhat intact. Wrapping my index and middle fingers around the aorta, I took another breath, closed my eyes, and pulled back hard.

This time, the sucking sound did make me vomit, all over the dead Pâlir in front of me. Throwing the heart away, I puked some more.

Chuckling as he retrieved the heart, Casimir set it between the bodies with the other. "You're such a girl!" Helping me stand, he moved me away from the bodies. "At least the temptation to kiss you is gone."

When I elbowed him, Casimir laughed then checked the gash on my head from the big guys punch. "That will heal by morning."

Taking out a small hip flask of lighter fluid, Casimir poured it over the hearts and bodies and then stepped back. "Turn away, Kat."

Turning my back, I heard the strike of a match just before the forest lit up around me.

Casimir wrapped his arms around me from behind. "Let's get you home."

9

Sitting on the lounge drinking hot chocolate, I watched the fire. The shutters were drawn just in case someone wandered by and stopped to stickybeak. Yishay's heartbeat drummed in my chest, and through him, his First Order.

"...killed my brother!"

Leaning against Yishay's desk, Flick crossed his arms. "Which was obviously a message Lemuel."

"Yeah, that they are starting this war whether we step up or not." Methuselah jumped in from further back in the room. "Yishay, they took your wife, have possibly killed her, now they are killing off your First Order."

From where he stood staring out the window, Yishay sighed. "Kat is alive still. They took her into Pâlir territory and dumped her to find her own way back. She's bait for whoever comes near her."

"She must be terrified?"

"At times, Saul. Like tonight, when two Pâlie found her and tried to kill her. Or the night before, when someone she should have been able to trust, tried to kill her." Turning, Yishay glared at Jabin's body on the floor of his study. "Her scent is still on his hand, where he held her throat."

Everyone looked to Lemuel, who shook his head in disbelief. "If she's being attacked, how is she still alive?"

Walking back to his desk, Yishay sat down. "That, I don't know. Our bond isn't set. It's intermittent. Like something interferes with it. I can only feel her when she's truly alone when no other Pâlir or Halos is near her it seems."

Confused faces looked to each other in the room. Stroking his chin, Saul shook his head. "That's unheard of."

"No, it can happen." When everyone stopped to look at Flick, he sighed heavily. "Look, Yishay only bound her moments before the Pâlir snatched her. If for some reason, the Pâlir also tried to bind her, then proximity would be the decider of who can feel her."

The room went silent.

"You're saying you think the Pâlir has bound my wife? Bound a woman he already knew to be married?"

From the back of the room, Yoash stood outraged. "That's sacrilege! No Pâlir or Halos would ever do such a thing."

Omri huffed. "Oh, please, Yoash! We double bind women with multiple suitors all the time. We let their seed chose her mate; as you well know."

"That's quite different." Yoash settled his large frame back in his seat just the same.

Clearing his throat, Flick shrugged his shoulders. "It would be a good move if you think about it. The Pâlir abandons Kat, allowing you to feel her, communicate with her, but at the same time, he can feel her and track her from a veritable distance. In fact, once you are both a certain distance away, you can probably both feel her evenly."

Teeth clenching, Yishay glared at his friend. "You sound impressed, Flick."

"It has a certain amount of strategy to it that I can respect."

"Wasn't your mate on heat when you bound her?"

Eyes wide, Saul shook his head in warning. "Meth!"

"I'm just saying, if Yishay got her with child, the bond would settle within a matter of days. But, if this Pâlir bound her, her...desires would also draw to him until her passion passes."

The room was deathly silent, even longer this time, as Yishay gave Methuselah a hard look. "She is my zápalka, Meth. Are you suggesting she would let this Pâlir have her so easily?"

"No, Yishay, but even we," Methuselah indicated the men in the room, "...are not above taking what we want at times."

"If," Saul butted in, "and that is a big 'if. But, if this Pâlir bound her, and if he forced even worse on her, then he abandoned her to the wilderness where she is continuously attacked, then Kat will be in quite a state by now."

Focus intent on his King, Omri lifted a brow. "You said she's terrified at times. Why only at times?"

Leaning forward, Yishay put his head in his hands on the desk. "Because she thinks I've left her to be slaughtered, that I don't love her, and that I want her dead."

"Why would she even think that?" Flick turned to face Yishay outraged.

Lifting his head, Yishay considered everyone in the room. "I said something out of anger, and she felt everything behind it. When she's not terrified, she's angry, and wishing Kenan had never introduced us."

The silence resounded through the room. Standing, Omri rubbed his grey goatee as he thought. "If what you say is true, Yishay, if your wife believes you want her dead, she will not trust even those in this room. Kat will not trust you."

Licking his lips, Saul sighed. "What is our way forward, Yishay?"

"We killed the Prince, and yet, other than taking Kat, there has been no outward aggression. This doesn't sit right with me. They didn't kill Kat, they took her and dumped her in the wilderness. If she makes it back alive, they've gained nothing..."

Huffing, Methuselah took a sip of his drink. "Other than her hating you."

"...it doesn't make sense they aren't attacking even with stealth assassinations."

Raising a brow, Yoash considered his king. "Maybe they are, and we don't hear about it yet?"

"That is possible." Flick agreed. "We have a lot of individuals who have drifted out of the community."

Nodding, Yishay stood up. "Yoash and Omri, head west, and check Kamloops. Ask around to see if people haven't been heard from. Lemuel and Meth, I want you to go to Jasper and do the same. Ira, when Kenan gets back, I want you to go north to Edmonton. It's likely they'll attack border towns or just outside of them."

"Where is Kenan?" Ira asked politely.

"Informing Jabin's wife, she is now a widow." Sullen eyes drawn back to the traitor's body, Yishay gritted his teeth. He hadn't caught much of the attack. It had been like listening through static. However, he'd felt Kat's fear when she was running, heard Jabin's proclamation that the human needed to be killed to prevent a half-blood on the throne, and felt Jabin's hands around her throat as if it'd been his own.

"It's unusual, isn't it? For them to return a body instead of burning it. They came all the way down here to dump his heartless body on the porch."

"They wanted the message delivered, Omri." Saul noticed Yishay's focus. "They wanted us to know even someone from the First Order hunted the Král's wife. They want Yishay to know even we can't be trusted."

Static silence charged the room. Cracking his knuckles, Flick stood. "Everyone to your duties. Ira, go home. I'll send Kenan to find you when he gets back. Lemuel. Take your brother and lay him to rest."

As everyone left via the porch door, Lemuel heaved his brother's body over his shoulder and followed. As Flick closed the door after him, Saul fixed the three remaining a drink and passed them out.

Dropping into the couch with a sigh, Flick accepted the drink from Saul. "You're right, Yishay. It doesn't make sense if they aren't retaliating."

"Maybe what the Prince said was true. Maybe he did come for peace. Maybe they figured, if he succeeded, things could be great. If he failed, at least they tried."

"That's a hell of a sacrifice for peace, Saul?"

"When it is wanted bad enough, some sacrifices are worth making, Flick."

Templing his fingers, Yishay considered the situation. "Saul, I want you to go to Jasper. I want you to keep watch for Kat."

"You think that's where she is heading?"

"I know it, Flick. She asked the Pâlie directions for Jasper before they attacked. Saul, I don't want anyone to know that's why you are there. You wait for three days. If Kat doesn't show up, come back. If something happens and she's..." Yishay shook his head. "I'll send word if I feel a different direction."

Emptying his glass, Flick shifted forward to lean on his knees while he considered his friend. "If Kat doesn't trust us, why would she come back?"

"Her life has been here since she went to university. Everything Kat has in the world is here."

Shaking his head, Saul leaned against the bar. "Kat's smart. If she thinks both factions are hunting her, she will not believe she is safe here. She will run for the free territory."

"She has to pass through Halos territory to get there. She'll take the risk of running against Halos than Pâlir. That means Yishay is right and Kat will head to Jasper to find transport..."

As the conversation faded from my head, I opened my eyes to find the fire had died right down. Sighing, I unfolded from the lounge and rebuilt it. In the kitchen, I dug around and started cooking some pasta for dinner. I'd been eavesdropping for hours.

"Did you miss me?" Casimir walked into the kitchen.

My heart jumped through my throat. "Could you please make some noise to let me know you're here?"

Considering me, Casimir lifted a brow. "Everything alright, Kat?"

Shaking my head, I started crying.

Enfolding me in his arms, Casimir held me tight. "It's not forever, Katiana."

10

*S*tanding at the open back door, I scanned the cleared area around the back of the cabin. The day was overcast, so there was no direct sunlight. Casimir didn't say if that made a difference, but I was willing to bet it did.

Stepping out into the full light, my eyes didn't sting, and didn't do any more than contract my pupils against the stronger light. Daylight was my sanctuary. I was able to move freely while my predators couldn't.

Clearing a flat bench from snow, I placed down a folded towel and sat down in the middle of the clearing. Breathing deeply, I focused on my breathing as I practiced the meditation we'd learned as children. The clouds split, allowing weak sunlight to spill through. Keeping my eyes closed, I enjoyed the feel of it on my face.

For a week, I'd been in Casimir's custody and killed five men. Three Pâlir, and two Halos. Last night, thankfully, we'd spent nearly the entire night out and not drawn one predator. My injuries were mounting too. From my head wound at Gruff's hands, I'd since added a dislocated finger, which hurt more relocating it, and a deep gash to my upper thigh when the Halos who found me, just on the Pâlir side of Highway Sixteen, cut me. It took a full day to heal.

Each location Casimir dropped me took me closer to Halos territory, leaving a clear trail. Pâlie we burnt. The Halos, we burned their
hearts but left the body to be found. Last night, Casimir left me alone
in Halos territory with directions to Jasper. When I was only a few
kilometers from the town, Casimir picked me up and took a long way
back to the cabin.

*"Something's happening. I've not run across a single Halos all night,
and this is their territory."*

Breathing back to the present, I felt the first drops of snowfall on
my hair. Unfolding myself from my meditation, I moved back inside.
Standing at the kitchen window with a steaming mug in his hands,
Casimir observed me. "You been out there long?"

"Just after midday." Shrugging out of my jacket and boots, I made
for the kettle. When I realized the first day that my moving about
disturbed Casimir, I started using my natural stealth, so as not to
wake him.

"We're only an hour from sunset. I'll report in early tonight, so I
should be back around midnight if nothing is happening. Then, I
think you need some training that doesn't involve killing something."

Sighing with relief, I hugged Casimir. We'd gone out every night
and used me as bait to draw out the warmongers. It was such a relief
last night to come home without someone else's blood on me.

"Kat..." Casimir began pulling away, not meeting my eyes. "It's
been a week. I'm still interfering with your bond, so..."

"I know. No, baby." Pouring some milk in my tea, I averted my
eyes. Casimir was silent as I took my first sip, and the heat radiated
through me. "He's not coming for me, is he?"

Jaw tense, Casimir glared out the window. "No. He'd have moved
by now."

"He sent Saul to Jasper to wait for me. I guess that's something."

"How do you know that?"

"I've been eavesdropping when you aren't around."

Crossing his arms, Casimir lifted a brow. "What else have you
learned?"

"Saul waited three days, and he missed me by one. They've been wondering why there haven't been any attacks to revenge Vladimir. Last night, Yishay ordered everyone to ground. They can carry on their normal lives, but anyone found hunting will be brought before him and reprimanded."

"They found the second Halos body?" When I nodded affirmation, Casimir sat thinking. "That explains how quiet it was last night."

"Halos only kill Pâlie, right?" I'd been building up to this question for days.

"Supposedly."

"So, how do the unmated Halos feed, like Kenan for example?"

"Kenan is one of a few special cases. He was raised to understand our ways. He feeds once a week in the same manner as a Pâlir. It's frowned upon, but for a man without a mate, they turn a blind eye."

"So, he's never killed Pâlie?"

Staring at his coffee, Casimir gritted his teeth. "He is of the First Order, Kat. You don't get there by being a pacifist. He's had reason to kill our kind, just as I have killed his."

"Why are you making me hunt? It's not normal for the women to feed unless they are with child, and even then, it's from their mate for safety reasons."

Caressing my cheek with his knuckles, Casimir sighed. "Firstly, there is nothing normal about you, Kat. There was the potential you may be with child, so I wanted you feeding. Secondly, you are a Princess of the blood. You should know how to hunt and to protect yourself."

When I turned away, Casimir hugged me from behind. "We are predators. However hard you try to ignore that, we are no different than a bear or wolf here in the mountain. We don't always kill. I've taken human lovers and fed from them, so have others. We have to be careful because they don't heal like us, so it takes a certain restraint to pull it off. Those who try without that restraint will kill an innocent woman, or man, in some cases."

Peering over my shoulder, I bit my lip at Casimir's proximity. Tilting his head, he moved his mouth closer.

"Casimir... I'm still married."

Touching his forehead to mine with a sigh, Casimir closed his eyes. "I know, Kat." Casimir's phone rang.

Stepping away, I tried to steady my breathing. "I'm going to shower."

COMING OUT OF THE BATHROOM, I WAS GLAD I WRAPPED THE TOWEL around me when I found Casimir sitting on my bed.

"You're getting a visitor tonight. Kenan wants to check up on you."

"You don't seem happy about it?" Staying where I was, I eyed my clothing laid out on the bed next to Casimir.

"We are in disagreement over using you for bait. He also worries about other aspects of us spending alone time together." Casimir's eyes lingered on my throat. "I haven't told him that you've been hunting, Kat. He thinks I've been the one killing."

Catching on, I sat on the bed beside him. "You'd like me to keep up the pretense?"

"It would be a good idea, in case you do decide to return to your husband when this is over."

There was no arguing with his suggestion that I may not. Chances were that things between Yishay and I could never be repaired now; though, it hurt to think it. "Okay. Will he be staying the night or just until you get back?"

"He didn't say." Turning side on to face me, Casimir cupped my face in his hand. "Kat, if he stays, you'll need to sleep in here. You understand why?" The hunting had made sleeping by myself unbearable.

Closing the space between us, Casimir kissed me. Reacting on instinct, I kissed him back. Tucking me in against his body, Casimir kept control of the kiss, keeping it light and tender. Lifting off the bed enough to lay me back, Casimir pressed his body beside mine, never letting our lips part.

Placing my hand on his chest, I pushed gently, and Casimir pulled back enough to meet my eyes. "Cas..."

"It's okay. I'm not after what you think."

That was reassuring, but his placement and the look in his eyes still told me I was in trouble. "Then what's happening here?"

Brushing his thumb over the pulse in my neck, Casimir met my eyes with the most intense look of desire.

"You want my blood?"

"It's to protect my brother. If I'm not here, Yishay will know he's with you."

"So, you drink my blood, and that blocks him?" Why wasn't I convinced that's all it took?

"A fresh exchange should block him for a few nights."

"Exchange? As in, I also drink?" When Casimir met my gaze, I bit my lip very aware of our bodies pressed against each other with only a towel covering me. "And you're sure it will protect Kenan?"

"I'm sure." Maintaining my gaze, Casimir caressed my hand where it fisted in his shirt. "I won't let us lose control. I know you are new to this, but I've been doing this a long time. I can keep my head about me." Giving Casimir a disbelieving look, he huffed. "I may not want to control myself with you, but I will, for you. I promise nothing more than what occurred our first night together will happen."

"In other words, you expect to get off as well."

"I've been well-behaved in that bed with you all week. Until your bond settles with one or the other, you are still my wife too. The need to touch you is overwhelming. You feel it. It's what brought you into my bed; though, I doubt you realize it." Unclenching my fist from his shirt, Casimir entwined our fingers.

"You promise you'll keep control. We feed, and the most we do is touch."

"I promise." Kissing me before I could rethink my concerns, Casimir turned up the dial on the kiss, leaving me breathless by the time he pulled away. "You're first, Kat."

Squeezing my hand in reassurance, Casimir touched me between my legs as he kissed my shoulder, causing me to gasp.

Positioning my mouth, so it was hovering over his neck, Casimir trembled as he slid his finger between my folds to find my clit. "Now, Kat."

Closing my eyes with a moan, I kissed his neck once, breathing his scent deep into me. He smelled delicious. Opening my mouth, I sliced my teeth into the soft flesh of his neck. His body jerked against mine, and then Casimir's blood rushed into my mouth.

Swallowing mouthful after mouthful, I groaned. Casimir tasted better than any of the kills I'd had all week. The copper mixed with something clean and fruity swam over my taste buds, making me hunger for more. As I licked and sucked his neck, Casimir pressed against me, stroked me, rubbed and flicked me. The room was a lot hotter, but all I could concentrate on was how delicious his blood tasted, and how revitalizing it was.

Using my hair, Casimir tugged my mouth free of his neck and covered my mouth with his. I'd had more than enough, it was just greed that drove the wanting further. Kissing me until my body was bucking against his hand, Casimir urged my hand inside his open fly and encouraged me to grip and stroke him. "It has to go both ways, Princess."

Kissing me until I was gasping, Casimir shifted and found my pulse. As his teeth sliced, my eyes went wide. It hurt, but immediately afterward, the pain faded quickly. What Casimir was doing to my body helped distract from it. His sucking and licking at my neck only heightened the sensation.

At that moment, I understood why the exchange was sexual. The sex distracted you from your hunger, so you didn't take too much. Of course, with our own species, we could take a lot more from each other than we could from a human. We'd heal anything but our hearts removed and burned. It was also an exchange of hunger. Sating one, and distracting from that with the other.

Lost to the heat between us, I didn't know what was happening anymore, I just wanted to feel more of him. Groaning, Casimir kissed me intently. My blood in his mouth tasted different, in that it had me feeding at his mouth like I had at his neck.

Pinning my body with his, Casimir kept control, stopping me from taking things beyond touching as I craved. When I peeked, Casimir imprisoned my mouth and met every cry with his own. Relaxing back to the bed, our kissing slowed, but didn't stop. After righting his clothing without breaking the kiss, Casimir entwined our fingers as we kissed until our breathing was near normal again. Even then, Casimir didn't pull away. He stayed with his face to mine, kissing my eyes, and forehead.

"Please tell me this isn't what it looks like?" Kenan's voice growled from the doorway.

Too relaxed to even feel guilty, I licked my lips and groaned with an aftershock of pleasure.

Casimir smiled at his brother. "I wish you'd walked in on, what you think you did."

"...SHOULDN'T HAVE DONE THAT TO HER."

The guys left me to dress while they talked about what Kenan interrupted. Now they were in the upstairs lounge trying to argue quietly, but as I made my way towards them, I could hear them clear as day.

"I have to go, and when I'm not here, the Král can feel her. We did it to protect you, Key."

"How far have things gone between you two?"

Spying me over Kenan's shoulder, Casimir exhaled. "Kat, everything okay?"

"Nothing is okay anymore. It hasn't been since I watched my husband's men stab my brother to death."

Both of them grimaced on my words. "Why don't you go fix yourself some breakfast? Kenan will be down in a minute."

"You're not joining us?"

"I have to get going."

Seeing me coming before I even knew I moved, Casimir pulled

me into a hug and kissed the top of my head. Observing it all with a frown, Kenan said nothing as I left the room and went downstairs to fix breakfast.

"I'll stay the night. You need time out from each other. I'll babysit."

"I need to spend a full night at the compound before everyone really starts to get suspicious, is more the problem. Any chance you can get a few days free next week. I don't like leaving her by herself overnight."

"Because Yishay can feel her?"

"No, because she frets."

There was silence as I reached the bottom stair. Taking each step as slow as possible so I could eavesdrop.

"Kat prefers sunlight and handles being alone much better during the day."

"Gee, you've used her for bait for a week straight each night. I wonder why she has issues being alone in the dark?"

"You know it has to be done, Key."

"Doesn't mean I have to like it."

Deciding I should try to look like I hadn't been listening, I continued on to the kitchen. By the time Kenan came down, I'd finished scrambling eggs and was serving up the rashers of bacon. Opening the fridge, he poured us both a glass of milk before following me over to the meals table. "Kat, with Casimir..."

Moving the food around my plate, I refused to meet his eyes. "I don't want to talk about it. I don't want you getting in trouble with Yish. That's the only reason it happened. Casimir kept his hands-off me all week; that's the first time he's touched me since you brought me here." Shoving another mouthful of egg into my mouth, I chewed until the food disintegrated in my mouth.

Turning his thoughtful gaze back to his food, Kenan kept glancing sideways at me with those bright blue eyes. "How have you handled being used for bait?"

Stabbing a piece of bacon with more force than necessary, I smushed it into the egg yolk and dragged it through the maple syrup leaking from the pancakes. "Better than I've handled my husband's abandonment."

Studying me, Kenan grimaced. "He's trying to do what he thinks is best for everyone."

My stomach hollowed and vanished, leaving a dark well of sorrow in its place. "Don't do that. Don't give me excuses. I've felt him, spoken to him. I know exactly why I've been left for dead."

"Well, tell me why because I barely believe what he says."

Meeting his eyes, I huffed and took a long draw of the milk before answering. "He knows I'm a Pâlir now." As Kenan went to say something, I held up my hand. "Flick suggested that my captor has bound me, which means they also know I'm one of theirs. Yish thinks Cas went to kill me, realized what I was, and changed tactics. Since Yish is not ready to tell his First Order, some of whom are already looking for an excuse to kill me, that he married a Pâlir, he's keeping up the pretense of me being human, while convincing himself that Cas won't let me get hurt."

"But if he thinks you're the bait, why would he think Cas will protect you?"

"Because I'm Yishay's bait. If Yish doesn't come, then I'm wasted bait, and Pâlie only kill criminals. Yish believes that Cas is moral enough not to break the Pâlir code and kill an innocent."

Brows near his hairline, Kenan spluttered on the mouthful of milk he just took. "He actually thinks Cas will just let you go?"

"It's his most recent theory."

Dropping his head in his hands, Kenan stared at the table. "I'm not sure if that's brilliant or delusional?"

"A huge gamble is my personal opinion. He's not just risking my life, but also my affections for him, and he knows it."

Huffing, Kenan took my hand in his. "Kat, when this is over, and you come home, all of this will just seem like a bad nightmare."

"If I come home."

"He's your zápalka. He'll be able to sense you wherever you go. You're never going to escape him, and you don't really want to either.

Do you know how rare it is for zápalka to find each other? Let alone for a royal bloodline to find their zápalka? You found yours in someone worthy, Kat. Yours is the Král. There is no way Cas or any other guy is ever going to beat that for you."

Collecting the plates, I went to the kitchen to clean up without responding.

Sighing, Kenan followed me over with the glasses. "Okay, so, what do you want to do tonight? Movies, cards, or scrabble?"

"Sex!" When I lifted a brow, Kenan blanched. "There was a time only a few years ago you would have tacked sex on the end of that list for ways to amuse us."

"And then you married my best friend and Král."

"Yeah, well, I took blood, and he still didn't get me with child, so nothing is set in stone yet."

Grabbing my arm as I went to move past him, Kenan scowled. "That's not funny, Kat. You're married..."

"Twice over. And twice bound. What's the usual solution to this situation, Key?"

Dropping my arm, Kenan stared at me with his jaw lax. "You can't be considering giving Cas a chance to win you?"

Shrugging as I headed to the stairs, I glared over my shoulder. "Cas, you, some other guy I take a fancy too..."

"Now, you're just spiteful."

"Are you saying you're not even tempted, Key?" Turning on the bottom step to assess him, I pulled my jumper over my head and dropped my pants to the ground, leaving me naked before him. "It's just sex, Key. It's normal for the Král to share his wife with his best friend, isn't it?"

Eyes wide, Kenan growled. "When Cas warned me you might become hostile to my presence, I thought he meant yelling and maybe crying. Throwing yourself at me was not what even he expected." Stepping up on the step below me, Kenan got in my face. "I'm not Yish, Kat. I'm not responsible for what he does or how he treats people. Fucking me won't undo the hurt he's caused you." Dropping back, Kenan stormed towards his bedroom.

"Nothing can undo the hurt, Key, but being wanted helps endure it!"

When he didn't come out to respond, I grabbed up my clothes and went upstairs to the lounge room.

11

*W*aking suddenly, I blinked up from where I'd fallen asleep on the couch in front of the fire to see Kenan. The tenseness of my body made him withdrew his arm from beneath my knees and back. "I was going to put you to bed."

"I'm fine here." Retrieving the blanket from my ankles, I pulled it up to stay warm. Sighing, Kenan took the lounge opposite me. "Where does Yishay think you are tonight?"

"Home, twiddling my thumbs." Kenan looked at the window, probably wishing that's where he'd stayed. "We're all meant to be staying in right now until Yishay figures out what he wants to do." Sitting back, Kenan met my gaze. "You've always known how to torture me, Kat. Even our first time together, you made me wait hours for any relief."

"Excuse me! You're the one who insisted I come before you'd let yourself go. I think you were the one torturing me!"

Lips tipping up, Kenan met my eyes. "You remember?"

"Of course. It was my first time. There was not a chance in hell I was going to forget you taking advantage of me, let alone you dragging it out for hours."

Kenan's eyes popped. "Wait. You never told me I was your first."

Shrugging a shoulder, I smirked. "Didn't want you getting a big head, did I?"

Kenan sat back exasperated. "Shit, Kat. I was rough with you. I was sick of the way Halos women treated me, and here you were, a half-breed like me, all consoling and beautiful."

"You made up for it plenty in the following months, so don't fret it. Have you been sulking down there all this time, remembering having sex with me?"

Blushing, Kenan turned his face to the fire.

It was so sweet, I chuckled. "How about that game of scrabble?"

The sunrise found us laughing in front of the fireplace. "Time for bed." Noticing the growing light around the window curtain, Kenan stretched then came to the sofa I was occupying to help me up. "How are you handling the time shift?"

"Half and half." As he walked me to my room, I yawned.

Kissing my head, Kenan tucked me into my bed. "I'm downstairs if you need me." Not bothering to try and stay awake, I was asleep before Kenan left my room.

So far, I hadn't managed to sleep past midday, and today was no different. Waking up yawning, I blinked into the darkness of the room. The sound of two distinct heartbeats startled me and made me check to make sure I wasn't in bed with anyone.

When I was sure I was alone, I concentrated and realized one heartbeat belonged to Yishay, but the second belonged to Casimir. Touching my chest where my heart was beating frantically, I swallowed hard. It was the first time I'd felt Casimir from a distance, something I'm sure the fresh exchange of blood caused. Both their hearts were slow with sleep, and their breathing deep and even. Conflicting emotions flooded me, tearing me in different directions. Throwing myself out of bed, I became intent on concentrating on anything else.

After freshening up, I headed outside to meditate again. Movement in the corner of my eye caught my attention as I was getting comfortable. Turning my head, I watched as my brother Vladimir walked out of the woods into the clearing towards me. Breath catching in my chest, I freaked. Speeding through the space between us, Vladimir covered my mouth to stop me screaming, and spoke quietly.

"Relax, Katiana. I'm not here to harm you."

The realization that he was physically here shocked me, my body gasping for breath as he held me restrained.

"Can I let you go?"

Waiting until I whimpered acknowledgment, Vladimir released me, and I wrapped myself around him. "You're alive? But, I heard them kill you?"

Holding me while I sobbed into his neck, Vladimir nodded. "Kenan sent the others off to search for Casimir, then exchanged my body with a Halos Casimir killed earlier. Casimir took me away and hid me until I healed. The Halos don't know I live."

Stepping away, I gathered my composure and frowned. "How are you out in daylight?"

"Did you think being able to day walk after feeding made you unique little sister?" As I stood there with my mouth hanging open, Vladimir urged me to sit beside him. "It's a genetic inheritance. One we keep quiet. Only our mates know, and our children, of course, when the time is right. My wife is quite beside herself right now with our son's tendency to enjoy the daylight."

"I'm an aunt? I've missed so much."

"As it seems, I have with you." Vladimir's shoulder bumped me.

Out of my two older brothers', we'd always been closest. Wenceslas was nearly fifteen years my senior, so he was never around when I was young.

"It appears my baby sister is married to the Král, and somehow, that went unremarked all these years?" When I didn't answer, Vladimir took my hand and squeezed gently. "Tell me how you ended up there. Everything from the time our prince sent you away."

"I..." Taking a deep breath, I worried about how this would sound. "I went to Brentwood until I finished school, then UBC accepted me. I did an undergrad in Arts, then a Masters in Architecture. Those years in the open territory, I'd managed to go unseen or unrecognized by the Halos and Pâlirs there. So, when I got a job offer in Calgary, I took it. There was an ad for a housemate a block from where I would be working, so I arranged to meet the guy and see the place. Kenan didn't even blink when we met, so I assumed, he also didn't think me anything other than human." Stopping on what came next, I bit my lip. Vladimir squeezed my hand to encourage me.

"We lived together for eighteen months, but, it only took a few weeks for me to realize he was heavily involved in the Halos community there. Still, he never brought them home, and I lived in daylight, so our paths only crossed at home. Eventually, we became friends, and then..."

"You were lovers?"

A single tear trickled down my cold cheek. "He was planning on proposing and wanted the Král to approve his choice. He introduced us. As soon as Yishay and I shook hands, I recognized my zápalka. Yishay gave no regard to Kenan and kissed me there and then."

"And you let him, because off the bond between you."

"No, I slapped him actually." Vladimir's mouth fell open as he blinked at me, I smiled. "I cared for Kenan. He was a half-breed who'd been treated poorly by the Halos women. With him, I knew that if he found out what I was, he wouldn't care. Though, in truth, I didn't plan to marry him either. I knew father betrothed me to a Pâlir he deemed worthy, but I thought, for a couple of years we could be good to one another."

"You were young. We all like to experience life a little before we settle down."

"When Kenan realized I was the Král's zápalka, he stepped aside and encouraged us to date. He's a romantic you see, because his parents, as zápalka, defied the divide to be together." Thinking about what came next, I fell quiet.

Vladimir waited a moment. "So, you finally gave in and dated your sworn enemy?"

Facing my brother, I took his hand between both of mine,

pleading for him to understand. "I swear to you it wasn't like that. No one told me who he was because they thought I was human. I knew he was pureblood, but that's all I knew. We dated for three months. One night, while we were out, I...suddenly just, needed him." I struggled to explain how it happened.

"You went on-heat for the first time?" My cheeks flushed with blood, but I nodded. "And when you mated..."

"No, we nearly did, but when I saw the mark on his chest, I freaked out and kicked him out of the apartment." The memory of slamming the door in Yishay's face, leaving him half-dressed in the hall made me smile. "He came back two days later and demanded I marry him. I said no at first."

"I'm not angry with you, Katiana. You married for love. In truth, had I thought about it, it would have been the best maneuver."

Blinking up at my brother, I wasn't sure what to make of his response. It was the opposite of what I expected.

"Katiana, you've married the Král. When you bear his children, you will bear the future Král. As their mother, you will pass on the light walker gene. It will bring the war to an end instantly."

"I'm sorry. How does that work?"

"The divide was caused by the first Král's envy of our great, great, great, grandfathers ability to day walk. It was petty jealousy that caused it, not the difference in lifestyles. If our royal bloodlines join, and the future Král is a light walker..."

"You're sending me back to him, aren't you?" Ignoring everything else, I jumped straight to the point my brother was trying to reach.

"He is your husband."

"So is Casimir!"

Glancing away, Vladimir sighed. "Bearing Casimir's children will not bring about change, Katiana. I know how you feel about what's happened. Casimir filled me in last night. I can't blame you for feeling betrayed and hurt, but when the time comes, you will return to your husband, the Král, and resume your duties as his loving wife."

Rising, Vladimir stepped away. My Prince just ordered me to

return to my husband. If I chose to go against him, I would be cast out as a traitor by my people, and I would destroy Casimir in the process. Tears spilled down my face, freezing in the cold air. "You're here to take me back?"

"Not yet. It's not safe. More than likely, the Král's traitors would have you dead before you got with child. Instead, you will stay here, and Casimir will teach you what you need to stay alive. I will make an excuse to explain his absence at court. That way, Kenan's visit can be few and far between."

Swallowing my emotions, I tried to keep my voice quiet and even. "Then, why did you come today? Why not wait until you were ready to send me back?"

Squatting in front of me, Vladimir took my hands in his. "I remember the way you looked at Casimir as a child. The way you cried when our father told you he was sending you away. You ran straight to Casimir that afternoon and stayed there until our prince found you. I noticed the way Casimir smiled when talking about you last night, and felt the emotion behind his words." Vladimir looked up to meet my eyes. "I came here today to see if it was mutual, and it was instantly apparent. So, I've told you our plans in advance, in hope, you will not make this harder on you both, Katiana. I don't mind the blood exchange; it keeps the Král from knowing too much."

"But don't sleep with him, and don't get attached again?"

Wiping my tears away, Vladimir kissed my cheek. "I think the last would be a futile attempt. You and Casimir always had a bond, even before our Prince betrothed you. After that, it was our father's fault for the drama caused in separating you from each other. It's almost like you are zápalka, Katiana, but everyone knows it's impossible to have two."

Tears rushed down my face; he had no idea how torn I felt.

"Whatever it is between you two, don't make it about sex as well." Vladimir was trying to be stern, but a smile pulled at his mouth. "Well, any more than necessary when feeding on each other."

Unable to look at him, I hung my head.

Vladimir stood patting my hair tenderly. "It must be something unique. To crave one man when you are with him, and another in his absence. It must also be terribly painful for one of our kind."

As Vladimir stepped away, I stayed quiet. "Will you do as I have asked?"

My body shook with the heartache already building inside me. Nodding my head, I started crying, hunching over on the bench.

"I love my wife, but she is not my zápalka. If ever the day came that I did meet mine, I doubt I could let Danica go without much pain, especially since we are bound. Admittedly, after talking to Casimir last night, I fear my wife meeting her zápalka more." Vladimir kissed the top of my head. "I'll see you next when it's time, Katiana."

The wind moving through the trees let me know my brother left. Curled over myself, I cried my heart out while I could. At nightfall, Casimir would return, and I'd need to abandon my heart out here in the cold if I was to survive our time together. Most of all, I needed to find a way to forgive Yishay, so when it was time to go home, I could.

BY THE TIME KENAN CAME INTO THE KITCHEN, I WAS CURLED UP ON THE sofa by the back window. After one look at me, he cuddled me up. "What's wrong?"

"Vladimir stopped by. He wanted to know how I ended up married to the Král."

"Oh!" Kenan dropped into the chair next to me. When I punched him, he fell to the floor. "Jeez, Kat!" He touched his jaw tentatively.

"That's for letting me think my brother was dead. Do you know how much guilt I was carrying? Just wait until Casimir gets back. He'll be chocking on his balls for days!"

What were the stages of grieving again?

"Settle down, Kat. We couldn't tell you because of your link to Yishay."

Assessing how that worked, I frowned.

"What's the matter, Kat?" Kenan's voice was gentle, watching me for any indication of my mood.

"I could feel him this afternoon. He should be able to feel me now if Casimir isn't here, but I can't."

Face relaxing, Kenan exhaled as he sagged into the chair next to me. "That's the blood exchange, Kat. I'm Casimir's blood brother, so my blood activates the bond, but on a much weaker level. Casimir needs to be in the vicinity to shut off your link with Yishay, while I need to be in the room."

"Oh." That kind of made sense.

"What else did Vladimir want?" Observing Kenan, the tightness in his eyes, and the way he was watching me for any tells, it took a moment to realize he thought Vladimir might have been asking me to do something to my husband.

"He told me I'm not to get involved with Casimir. He said it would only cause more hurt when I return to my true husband."

Kenan didn't say anything, which was the only thing stopping me from clocking him again. We sat there in silence until Casimir came into the kitchen a few minutes later. I didn't realize I'd moved until I was wrapped in his arms, sobbing into his chest.

"Kat...What happened?"

"Your prince stopped by before I got out of bed. I think his resurrection was a little too much for his younger sibling. Oh, and Katiana's idea of getting hostile is stripping naked and begging me for sex."

While Casimir was distracted, I lifted my knee hard between his legs and stepped away as he crumbled. "That's for letting me think I'd gotten my brother killed."

Kenan winced then chuckled. "I only got a right hook for that one, luckily."

Leaning on the kitchen bench, Casimir climbed his way back upright, tears shining in his eyes.

"In case you missed the announcement. Vladimir's visit has left our little princess a little unhappy."

Biting his lip while he swore, Casimir took a breath and threw something at his brother. "So, noted! You should head off, Key."

Catching my ruined white jacket, Kenan furrowed his brow.

"It's Kat's jacket from her encounter with the Halos the other night. Tell Yishay you found it at the bus terminal in Jasper. Let him think she's on the move amongst humans. It should keep her safe for now."

Stuffing the blood-stained jacket inside his own as he zipped it up, Kenan pulled his beanie on ready to head outside. "Gives me a cover for not being home last night. What's the plan now?"

With a shrug, Casimir sat down on the sofa where his brother just vacated. "She's not safe yet, Key. She stays with me until she is." Taking a deep breath, Casimir seemed to overcome whatever pain I'd caused. "In a few days, you'll hear a report of her being spotted in Kamloops buying a ticket for Vancouver."

"We're letting him think she's running for the open territory? And I guess you want me to let you know if he sends out a hunting party for her?"

The term made me tense and want to start crying again. Casimir patted my leg reassuringly. "He meant to retrieve you, Kat, not to kill you." Casimir glared at his brother. "That is what you meant, right?"

Inhaling dynamically, Kenan shook his head. "I hope so." Opening the back door, Kenan sniffed the air. "There's a storm blowing over the mountain. You might want to get ready for being snowed in."

"I know." Casimir indicated bags by the kitchen door. "I brought supplies to see us through the week. When you come back in a few days, I'll get you to bring some of Kat's more personal items, since I'm sure you know her brand, etc."

"ah..." Blanching at the insinuation, I did the math in my head and realized Casimir somehow knew my cycle better than I did. "Oh, yeah, I guess that would be handy." Standing up, I hugged Kenan; holding tight and refusing to let go.

"It'll be fine, Kat. You'll see. It will all come together in the end." Kissing my forehead, Kenan left without even a goodbye to his brother.

Appraising Casimir, I shuffled my feet, went to say something, but couldn't find the words.

Standing up, Casimir wiped his thumb across my cheek, catching the tear meandering down the channels left by my previous blubbering. "Why don't you go wash your face while I unpack the groceries? Then we'll get started on your training."

12

"*There* is no way! Transvecting is something only the males of our species can do."

Applying pressure to my shoulders, Casimir forced me to sit on the lounge room floor. "Actually, it's only taught to the males. Remember how sexist our species has always been, Kat? Transvecting allows a freedom that the men did not want their women having."

"Are you sure it's possible?"

"Wenceslas's wife was nearly killed in their first married year because she was trapped to the ground and couldn't outrun the Halos who were after her. Vladimir and I managed to save her, but it pushed the Princes to withdraw the female exclusion to that training. Wenceslas taught his wife, Vladimir taught his, and when Wenceslas's daughter entered training last year, they amended the curriculum to include every female should train exactly as the males do." Casimir dropped down to sit opposite me.

"I thought we already were taught the same?"

Meeting my eyes, Casimir shook his head. "No, Katiana, the males are taught a lot more. We started teaching women to defend themselves after the divide, but we didn't teach them to hunt. That has changed also. For the last year, every Pâlir is taught everything they need to survive. The mortality rate of our young has already halved."

"So, you're to teach me everything that was held back in my training initially?"

"As much as time allows for. You have already learned the basics of hunting, but it will take you longer to learn transvecting than the children whose minds are more open. You've believed for over two decades you could never do it, as such, your mind is going to fight it." When Casimir took up the meditation position, I followed suit. "The way for you to learn is to open your mind to the possibility. That is easiest in a meditative state." Closing his eyes, Casimir took a deep breath. "Go into yourself, Kat. I'll bring you back when you're ready."

Closing my eyes, I concentrated on my breathing. Once it was my sole focus, I dug deeper to find my pulse. There were two, mine and Casimir's. It made me smile to hear his heart nearly in absolute sync with mine. Using our heartbeats as the anchor, I let go into the blackness.

It felt like I'd been floating forever before Casimir reached for me. *'Feel yourself growing lighter like a feather. You are weightless, Kat, you weigh nothing.'*

Silence enveloped me again as I focused on weighing nothing, imagining that I was just bobbing above the ground.

'Open yourself to the air currents. Feel them moving around you, rocking you back and forth, side to side. Feel the air moving your hair...'

That was the easiest. The air stirred my hair even when there wasn't any wind. As soon as I could feel the currents moving individual hair strands, I could feel it jostling me.

'Come back to your body now, Kat.'

Slowly pulling on the anchor of our heartbeats until I was fully present, I opened my eyes to meet Casimir's. The moment our eyes connected, I dropped an inch back to the ground. Jolting, I looked at Casimir shocked.

"Well done, Princess Katiana. You took flight for the first time." Checking his watch, Casimir lifted his eyebrows. "Let's get something to eat, and then we'll try again."

Glancing to the old grandfather clock on the opposite wall, I swallowed. We'd meditated for over four hours. Easing my body out of the position, I felt the soreness of sitting for so long without moving.

While I ate, Casimir set up a lifeline to the woodshed and ensured enough wood was inside to see us through several days of being snowed in. When we went to bed at sunrise, I went to bed in my room. Saying nothing, Casimir merely bid me sweet dreams and closed the door to his room.

In bed, I watched the stray rays of light drift across my ceiling from the open bathroom door. I'd managed to lift myself no more than two inches off the ground each time we tried. On our last attempt, Casimir wanted me to do it without being so deep in meditation. Even though I'd only managed an inch, he assured me that was progress.

As tired as I was going to bed, I thought I might actually sleep past midday. When my eyes opened again, the wind was howling through the trees outside. I glanced at the clock to find it was still early afternoon.

Making my way to the bathroom, I noted how dark it was outside. When I looked out the window, I saw the storm Kenan and Casimir both smelled last night. Just looking at the clouds, I could tell it was going to be a bad one.

By the time the storm finally hit, I was in the kitchen. There was no chance I was going outside with that weather approaching. Checking the central fireplace to make sure the fire was well lit, I then stoked the secondary hearth in the lounge room. Standing at the windows to the balcony, I watched the snow falling.

Casimir wrapped an arm around my shoulder. "Come to bed, Kat. You'll need your energy from now on."

Steering me to his room and into his bed, Casimir cuddled me to him and settled down to sleep.

"I don't know if I have the strength for this again, Cas."

"We've never been given a choice in it, Kat. When you were taken away last time, I threw myself into my training. When you leave this time, I will focus on my duties, and you will be absorbed in your husband."

"Why did they marry us only to separate us?"

"You were a distraction for me, Kat. Your father saw that. He decided you should be the first female royal to join what was becoming a tradition for our women during their teenage years. Keeps them out of trouble, supposedly. That you wouldn't come home after you finished your schooling, was not something your father expected." Casimir let us settle deeper for a few minutes. "Kat, why didn't you come home? The truth this time, don't use uni as an excuse."

My eyes squeezed tight. "I knew I was betrothed, but no one ever told me it was you. When my father sent me away, separated us, I was sure it was someone else. The idea of being forced to marry anyone else tore me apart. I couldn't bear to come back, find you married with a family, and have to see that regularly. I chose exile over that hurt."

Tilting my face to meet his, Casimir kissed me intently. Pulling back, I ducked my head to his chest. "Don't, Cas. It's going to be hard enough as it is." Slipping out of bed, I retreated back to my own room. Curling into bed, I cried for the life I'd given up in stubbornness.

When my father sent me away to school, I'd refused to answer his phone calls. He knew I was still there. The school kept him apprised of my progress. The academic assigned to make sure I adjusted to boarding school life reported of my settling in. Once I'd graduated, and gone to uni, he'd lost track of me.

If I'd done what was asked of me, I'd have returned home after graduation and mated with Casimir. I would never have met Yishay and married him, or be in the situation I am now. No, I'd rebelled once and screwed things up. This time, I'd do what was asked of me, in the hope it'd all work out in the end.

13

The heavy snowfall lasted three days; just long enough for me to get the hang of levitating without having to be entirely within meditation. Another month of three sessions per night, I learned how to ride the air currents inside the cabin.

Now, I was walking alongside Casimir into the woods. After a week of levitating around the house, Casimir decided it was time I tried it outside. Insecure leaving the cabin after so long, I eyed the shadows in the trees like every one of them housed an enemy. "Will we be safe?"

Having left his cloak back at the cabin, Casimir tied his hair up and shoved it under a beanie so that at first glance he'd look Halos from a distance. I'd twisted my hair under a wool hat, stuffed my hands into mittens, and was still shivering in my entire winter garb. Without his blond hair on display, a Pâlir male looked no different to Halos.

"I'll be fine. I've been sneaking around this area for years. You, however, will stand out like a sore thumb once we are airborne. Halos women do not fly." He looked down at my rugged up form. Despite covering my slight curves, the men of our species were taller and twice the width of the women. The one thing I did have on my side was that I didn't look like a Halos woman from a distance either.

Pâlir women tended to be less curvy than Halos, possibly because we did go through some form of training and lived outdoors. Halos women were molly-coddled from birth, and as such, tended to be heavier framed than a Pâlir.

"You need to learn, and unlike you, I haven't spent ten years building resistance to daylight, so we need to do this after dark. After tonight, I'll be okay with you practicing in the woods close to the cabin during daylight, but I need to see your first flight and make sure you don't get hurt in the stronger currents."

Inhaling into my diaphragm to calm my nerves, I tensed as my lungs restricted from the cold air. Winter had set in, and it was freezing walking through the mountains at this elevation.

Taking my mittened hand in his gloved one, Casimir ceased walking. "I'll be right beside you the whole time, Kat. I'd prefer to be doing this on Pâlir territory, the compound would be even better, but we have to work with what we have." He leaned down and kissed my lips lightly. "Keep up!" Lifting off the ground, Casimir smiled at me mischievously then floated away through the trees.

Taking a steadying breath, I closed my eyes and felt the air stir the hair at the nape of my neck. Levitating, I held my balance as the stronger air currents buffered me, then I let them take me in the same direction as Casimir.

During my month of training, Casimir taught me how to change directions, speed, and elevation while transvecting. But all that training happened within the confines of the cabin or backyard. When riding the currents through the trees, it was much more turbulent. Each tree trunk deflected the currents and caused a disturbance.

Swiping my left shoulder on a trunk, I yelped as I lost my control, a branch glanced off the top of my head, and my knee crunched on a felled tree before I landed flat on my face.

Helping me up, Casimir shook his head. "Try again. React faster to the changes you feel."

Brushing myself off, I flexed and straightened my knee a few times, rolled my shoulder, and adjusted my beanie before trying again. This time, I was ready for the turbulence. Darting forward, I shifted my weight to avoid being thrown into a tree by a crosswind, only to be surprised by a crosscurrent and slammed into the opposing trunk. Regaining my breath, I concentrated, and tried again, and again, and again...

When I finally made it five minutes without impacting or glancing off anything, I let out a cry of joy.

Laughing beside me, Casimir grinned. "Faster, superwoman!"

Picking up speed, we swept through the forest, faster than a human's blink.

When I'd gone a fair distance without crashing and falling, Casimir smacked my butt. "You're it!" He took off into the trees.

Laughing, I chased after him. Noting his direction, I glanced off at an angle and crashed into him further up the path. "Gotcha!" I laughed as we tumbled to the ground. My next lot of training instantly began.

Throwing me from him, Casimir launched at me. Sidestepping him, I took off for the canopy. Casimir's hand slapped my ankle hard, throwing my balance, sending me crunching into a tree before landing hard on the forest floor.

Casimir pinned me. "You're dead."

Ramming my knee up between his legs, I threw a punch which caught him in the jaw before throwing him to the side to gain my feet. Making it to the canopy this time, I hid in the branches. The forest became quiet as Casimir hunted me. Closing my eyes, I concentrated on feeling him.

Slowing my heart rate to match Casimir's, I got a flash of the forest through his eyes and saw the back of myself from behind. Opening my eyes, I sprang to the next tree, half floating to make it the distance, as he landed on the branch I'd just occupied.

Surging from beneath the canopy into the open sky, I tried for speed, but Casimir caught me almost instantly.

Tackling me in mid-air, Casimir grabbed my throat tight. "Males are the stronger sex physically, Kat. Our heavier weight will give us an advantage in the open air."

Driving a punch at his abdomen, I hoped to force his release, but he blocked it and swung as he let me go, flinging me across the sky.

Diving for the cover of trees, I raced through the canopy at high speed. Since I was smaller, I could move through confined spaces in a way he couldn't. In the covering of the forest, I held the advantage over the larger men of my species, and I used it.

'*Kat, stop!*'

Freezing on the branch I'd just landed, I turned to survey the forest, my heart racing as it picked up on Casimir's concern.

Landing next to me a second later, Casimir pressed me to the trunk. "Your laughter caught the attention of some passing Halos." Casimir's body pressed firmly to mine as he lowered his mouth and kissed me passionately.

The air stirred as two Halos landed a few trees away. "Pfft, taking a girl flying is no way to court her." One whispered angrily.

The second chuckled. "As if we haven't all done it at one stage. It's how I proposed to Abbie." Casimir's hand drifted under my jacket and down the back of my jeans. "Let's go and let the young have their fun."

The forest returned to normal around us, but we didn't notice. I'll be the first to admit, that if we weren't up a tree in the dead of winter, we'd have probably started losing articles of clothing already. When Casimir went to unzip my jacket, I caught his hands and pulled away. We met each other's eyes for a moment before Casimir stepped back on the branch.

"Race you back to the cabin." Taking another step back, Casimir dropped off the branch.

Inhaling some deep, steadying breaths, I stepped off the branch and raced through the forest to the cabin. We'd been so good trapped in that cabin with each other over the last few months.

As much as I'd wanted to crawl into bed with Casimir each night, I slept in my own. During training, we'd catch ourselves touching unnecessarily and extract ourselves.

The blood exchange was the hardest from which to pull back. Twice now Kenan visited to allow Casimir to make an appearance at the compound. Before Kenan arrived, Casimir came to my bed, and he pinned me down with a hard grip when things went too far.

The last time, Casimir left bruises from how tight he'd held my wrists to keep his control when what he wanted was to lose it. Every day was turning into a test on our self-control. The training became a way to escape our temptation.

Reaching the edge of the clearing near the forest, I stopped. Casimir waited by a tree. "Go inside. I'm going to circle back around and ensure no one followed us."

Going inside, I put more energy than necessary into stoking the fire, before stripping out of my outdoor gear. Casimir was gone for hours. As well as precautionary, I knew his double-back was to put time and space between us until we both cooled down. By the time Casimir returned, I was sitting at the meals table eating dinner. "Yours is on the stove keeping warm."

Fixing his dinner, Casimir sat down at the table with me to eat. After eating quietly, we cleaned up together in the same silence. Afterward, I retired to the lounge room.

A little later, Casimir leaned into the door jam. "I need to go to the compound before sunrise. Kenan is going to come and stay. You've been training all night, every night for months, so you need a break from training tomorrow." Taking my hand, Casimir led me to my bedroom.

"Cas?" Something was going on, I could tell by his tone.

Without responding, he led me to my room and shut the door. When Casimir met my eyes, I knew what he needed. "I can't, Cas."

"I know." He soothed, touching my cheek gently. "My prince has ordered me the same, but I can't resist touching you, and I want so much more than I'm permitted." Removing his shirt, he backed me up to the bed. "I need you in every way." Dropping his jeans to the floor, Casimir stepped out of them.

About to protest, his kiss, the urgency of it, shut any opposition down. Sliding his hands under my top, Casimir pulled it over my head. My jeans joined his on the floor as we fell to the bed. It was the first time we'd been naked together since that first night, and it was exquisite.

Unlike every other time where feeding was the priority, it was now secondary. Touching and bringing each other to pleasure using hands slipped beneath fabric wasn't enough anymore. Our hands and mouths explored naked flesh. Moans echoed through the room, growing louder as the passion increased.

Burying his face in my pleasure, Casimir used his tongue to bring me to orgasm, then turned his head and fed from my upper inner thigh; a feeding only a husband and wife would share. When he finished, Casimir crawled over my body and lowered himself between my trembling legs. Wiping away the tears that slid silently down my cheeks, Casimir closed his eyes in resignation.

"Feed, Kat." Casimir pressed my face to his neck.

Pulling back, I met his eyes. Whatever he saw in mine made Casimir's pupils dilate as his eyes widened, then our mouths locked together. Kissing him until I couldn't breathe, I dropped my mouth to his neck and fed. Rubbing his body against mine, Casimir moaned my name as he moved to enter me.

Then he disappeared. Jolting upright, my body trembled as Kenan's angry voice ricocheted around my room.

"What's wrong with you?"

Rising from the corner where Kenan had thrown him, Casimir gritted his jaw. "You took your sweet ass time!"

Yanking my blanket over me, I blinked at the scene before me, my mind discombobulated by the sudden cessation of pleasure.

"You're prince ordered you to abstain, Cas. He ordered her the same. You are forbidden to each other. You nearly committed treason just now!" Kenan was red with anger. "Have you both fed?"

His eyes full of anger and despair, Casimir shifted his gaze to me. "Yes, just."

Snatching up Casimir's clothes from the floor, Kenan flung them at him. "Good. Get out. I'll clean up your mess."

Casimir went to leave.

"Cas, don't do this to yourself. If nothing else, get yourself under control for her sake. Don't come back until you are sure you can restrain yourself. If it takes a few days, then take it. I'll make do on my end if that's what's needed."

Nodding to his brother, Casimir glanced at me then stormed out of the room.

Relaxing a little, Kenan turned back to face me. "Oh, Kat!" Beside me instantly, Kenan held me as I trembled and sobbed in his arms.

"He called you to stop him?"

"Yeah. Casimir told me he'd spent hours out in the cold trying to cool off, but as soon as he came back, he knew he wouldn't last the night without taking you." Kenan sighed heavily. "I told him to feed, knowing it would slow him down and give me time to get here."

"I can't choose between them, Key. I love them both, need them both, want them both."

"Well, luckily, you don't have to choose. Your brother, your Prince, has made the choice for you."

As that statement broke me, Kenan bundled me up tighter. At sunrise, when I still cried, he slid beneath the blanket with me and cuddled me as I cried in my sleep.

14

---

*S*tanding in the kitchen, drinking a cup of tea, I sighed. The sky was clear for the first time in weeks, but the woods didn't seem inviting. Three afternoons I'd practiced transvecting through the trees around the cabin while Kenan slept. Three evenings I'd played scrabble or curled up to watch movies with Kenan. Four sunrises I'd gone to bed, heart heavy that Casimir hadn't returned.

The afternoon of the fourth day was clear with pale sunlight reflecting off the heavy snow cover on the ground. However, I wasn't content with just flitting around the cabin. The boredom was getting to me, so I needed books to read, and I wanted more of my stuff with me. Placing the tea on the bench, I pulled on my coat and boots and slipped out the back door.

Trying to walk on the ground would have left my jeans wet up to my knees, so I levitated from the back step. Staying below the canopy, I made my way south to Ghost Lake. It's incredible how to drive there would take hours, probably longer since you'd have to hike from the cabin to the road, but transvecting took just over an hour. If it was night, and I was able to fly above the treetops and over the mountains, it wouldn't even take that.

Landing a few trees back from the clearing around the house Yishay and I moved into after we married, I observed the house for any signs of movement. The acreage was clear for over a hundred meters from the house, more from the south, which Yishay loved for security. I'd liked it because of the view of the lake.

The house was quiet and shut up, as was normal during the day. For a moment, I considered turning around. If the wrong member of the First Order was on watch duty, I could get myself killed. There was always a member of the first order sleeping in the downstairs guest room during the day.

Trying to remember the roster, I cursed annoyed. It was months since Casimir abducted me, so I had no idea which rotation it was up too.

"You're here now, Kat. Just get in there, get your stuff, and get out before Yishay wakes up."

Taking a deep breath, I flew to my office window. The spare room upstairs was my drawing-room. Trying the handle, I smiled when it opened with only the tiniest click. Sneaking in, I shut the door quietly. Slipping out of my boots and jacket so I could move soundlessly, I collected a few things, drawing pad, pencils, and a book I'd been keen to read but never got to. Shoving them into my shoulder bag, I left them by my boots.

The next part was the trickiest. Despite it being daylight, I knew to move around the house risked alerting someone to my presence. Going into the room where Yishay was sleeping would be hard. Not only in my effort not to wake him, but to see him and have him within reach again.

Creeping my office door open, I tiptoed lightly across the upstairs landing. The house was still quiet, almost as if it was empty. Waiting a minute to see if the watch heard me, I held my breath. When no sound came from downstairs, I moved down the hall to our bedroom.

Opening the door, I peaked through the gap. Yishay was asleep cuddling my pillow. Holding back the sob that nearly crashed over me at the sight of him, I leaned on the wall outside the room and composed myself before tiptoeing into the room and the wardrobe.

Grabbing my old university backpack, I opened my drawer and started shoving some of my warmer and comfier clothes into it. In the bathroom, I collected a few other items I'd been doing without and moved out to the bedroom. There was a photo of Yishay and me on our bedside table from our wedding. Creeping forward, I picked it up and tucked it away in the bag. Turning away from my heartbreak, I made it to the door before Yishay woke.

"Kat?"

Pausing, I glanced over to see him sitting up in bed, watching me with confusion. Facing him, I lowered the bag behind me and settled it on the floor. Swallowing hard, I nodded in answer to his question. Terrified that if I opened my mouth, I'd choke on my fear, I clenched my jaw shut.

Yishay reached out a hand to me. "Come back to bed; work can wait."

Realizing Yishay thought he was dreaming, I swallowed again and took his hand, letting him pull me onto the bed. Rolling me onto my back, Yishay moved over me with a naughty smile. My breath caught as his fingers shifted my jumper upwards.

"It's too warm in here for this." Shifting it over my head, Yishay left it over my arms, so it effectively bound me. Kissing across my abdomen, Yishay made easy work of the fly on my jeans.

Wrestling out of my jumper and singlet, I put a hand on Yishay's chest to stop him. The moment I touched him, that impulse died. Despite the pain he caused me, I wanted him to touch me, and to feel wanted again. Wandering my hand up to his chest to his neck, I pulled his mouth to mine.

Soughing into my mouth, Yishay reefed my jeans off and threw them across the floor. Pushing up, I rolled him onto his back and straddled his hips while we kissed. As he slid into me, I moaned; I'd missed this so much.

In our two years of marriage, we'd barely gone a day without sex. Only ever if one of us went away, and we always made up for that absence on return. Now, I'd gone months, and in that time, the sexual tension between Casimir and I grew full to bursting. It didn't help that the love I never doubted between Yishay and me became so clouded in suspicion, I wasn't sure what it would be like coming home.

None of that mattered at this moment. There is nothing more definite in overcoming grief and hurt than sex. Being touched, kissed, held, and passionately taken. It was like therapy without words. Sex possessed healing powers all of its own.

Of course, it changed nothing, really. Yishay thought he was dreaming, and I could very much believe, at this moment, I was too. His hands gripping my hips as I moved over him, our tongues wrestling while kissing him, it was all so surreal after our time apart.

When we finished, I kissed him and rolled away. "Where are you going?" Yishay smiled as I pulled my singlet and jumper back on. "Come back to bed. I want to hold you."

"I have to go." Blowing Yishay a kiss, I held back the tears that threatened to spill forth. "I love you, Yish." Pulling on my jeans, I kept my face turned away.

Falling back to the bed, Yishay got comfortable. "Fine, but I'm waiting for you to get home tonight, and I'll be having you again before I go to work." Closing his eyes, Yishay sighed, his breathing was already growing heavy by the time I picked up the bag and slipped from the room. Grabbing my jacket, shoes, and shoulder bag from the study, I moved downstairs to the front door. We hadn't exactly been quiet upstairs, so whoever was on duty more than likely knew someone was upstairs with their King.

"Kat?"

Glancing over my shoulder, I started pulling my boots on. Thank the gods for it being Saul on duty.

"What are you doing? How did you get in without me hearing you?"

"I just came to get some of my stuff, Saul." Yanking my jacket on, I was slipping into the straps of the backpack when Saul grabbed my arm.

"You can't leave again, Kat. You need to stay here where you are safe."

My restraint broke, and the tears fell down my face. "But I'm not. Two Halos tried to kill me, Saul. One of them was Jabin, a member of the First Order."

Saul's face dropped. "We know, Kat. I'm sorry for what you've been through, but Yishay will keep you safe."

Shaking my head, I stepped out of his grasp. "He left me for dead, Saul. The Halos want their king to mate with one of his kind. I won't ever be safe here again."

Opening the door, I ran out into the daylight, knowing Saul couldn't follow. Halfway to the tree line to the east, I looked back. Yishay and Saul stood watching me from my office window. Tears fell harder as I blew him a kiss goodbye.

Running into the trees, I put several hundred meters between myself and the house before I levitated. Catching the currents, I headed east until I hit the Ghost River, then followed it north. Purposefully leaving a trail following the river until it branched north and west, I was careful to touch nothing as I turned north and took a long way back to the cabin.

By the time I landed in the clearing out the back, the sky had grown dark with a new storm and snow was starting to fall again. Stepping inside, I dumped my jacket and boots and took my bags up to my room.

Kenan's phone rang just before sunset. He found me sitting in the bath, knees to my chest, as silent tears cascaded down my pale cheeks.

"You went home? How did you get there and back so quickly?"

Ignoring his question, I shared the grief in my heart instead. "I can't go back, Kenan. I'm like you. They'll never accept me, and they will always plot my death."

"Yishay won't let that happen, Kat." Kenan stroked my damp hair reassuringly.

Resting my chin on my shoulder, I met his eyes. "But he already did when he abandoned me."

When I emerged from the bathroom, Kenan sat on my bed holding the photo I'd taken from the house. "It was the first thing Yishay noticed missing." He continued staring at the picture while I dressed. "I wanted to hate him for taking you, but in my heart, I knew you belonged together. I still believe that, Kat." Kenan put the photograph back on the bedside table.

"He thought you were a dream until Saul woke him. He would have thought it a lie, but Saul dragged him to the window. Yishay said he'd never seen you look as miserable as before you ran into the forest. He thinks you've chosen to leave for good. I couldn't fathom why you'd go home only to leave until I saw this picture." Kenan looked up at me. "You wanted the memory with you."

"I wanted a lot of things, Key." Pulling my jumper on over my singlet, I walked down to the kitchen and started cooking breakfast.

Kenan came in and helped me, but it wasn't until we sat down that he finally broke the silence. "Yishay thought I was in Vancouver searching for you these past few days. I made up a sighting report and sent him a message I'd gone to check it out. He's called me back to try and intercept you. Saul told him what you said. They both feel I'm the only person you'll trust." Staring out the window, Kenan contemplated the weather. "I'll have to leave soon. Will you be alright here alone?"

"Cas isn't coming back, is he?"

Stopping with food halfway to his mouth, Kenan put it down and reached out to take my hand. "He will come back once he's had his fill."

Unsure what he meant, I blinked at Kenan.

"Other women, Kat. He can't have the one he wants, so he's trying to rut you out of his system."

"Oh!" Swallowing the ball of spit trying to suffocate me, I studied my plate. "Will that work?"

"It didn't work for me, and I wasn't betrothed to you, but it helped me to cope with losing you better."

"Did he....how come...I mean, if he thought I was dead?"

Kenan's eyebrows nearly jumped off his face. "Cas never thought you were dead, Kat. He could always feel you, just not enough to find you. The best he could figure was you were in Halos territory. It's why he thought you were being kept hostage." He scrutinized my expression. "Yes, there have been other women in his life, but they weren't you."

When I didn't answer, Kenan started eating again. "He used to talk about you when we were younger before your father shipped you away." Kenan smiled, his eyes in the past. "We'd come here to hang out, and he'd tell me all about his beautiful princess, how wild and impulsive you were." The smile died on Kenan's face suddenly. "When you went away, he'd go to your school to watch you without your father's knowing. When you disappeared he..."

Shaking his head, Kenan took another mouthful before continuing. "Suffice to say, if he'd ever told me your name, shown me a picture, the moment you turned up on my doorstep, I would have returned you to him just to see a smile on his face again."

Finishing his breakfast, Kenan stood. "I would give anything to save you both from what you must be going through, Kat, but Vladimir is right. You belong with Yishay. Not only because he's your true mate, but because of the peace your children can bring the factions. Whatever is between Casimir and yourself, you need to let it go."

My eyes stayed glued to the table listening to Kenan's footsteps as he prepared to leave. Did no one understand? I couldn't let Casimir go any more than I could Yishay. If what Vladimir said was true, then my connection to Casimir existed before my father bound us in betrothal. Maybe it was possible to have more than one zápalka.

Coming back into the kitchen, ready to leave, Kenan touched my shoulder gently. "If I can make it back before dawn, I will. Stay inside and keep the place locked up. I'll be back as soon as I can."

15

"*K*at?" A familiar and worried voice called to me across the street. Turning around, I found Keira running to catch up with me. "Bohovia, Kat! What on earth is going on? Flick said that the Pâlie took you and here you are..." Keira looked down, confused at the grocery bags in my hands, "shopping?"

Keira, who was a half-breed Halos, was raised human, and as such, still wandered around in the hours just after sunrise and just before dusk. Something I'd forgotten when I figured a quick shop in the early hours of the morning would be safe. After three days alone in the cabin, the food situation had grown dire enough for me to need to risk it.

"Keira...I have to go." Walking quickly down the street, I bit my lip.

Grabbing my arm, Keira pulled me to the side, so we didn't draw attention. "No, Kat! Flick told me some of what's happened. If you are here, why haven't you gone to Yishay?" Keira's bore all the physical resemblance to the Halos, black hair and pale skin, but she lacked the luminosity that the pure breeds possessed.

"Because it's not safe, Keira. It's not the Pâlie trying to kill me; it's the Halos."

Closing her eyes, Keira looked away, but there was no surprise. "I've heard whispers amongst some of the more vocal wives that the Pâlir did them a favor by taking you. That once you were dead, Yishay would be free to marry a pure woman." Keira looked at me with tears in her eyes. "I thought they were spitting their usual venom. I didn't realize anyone would have the balls to....it explains why everyone's on warning, but surely the First Order?"

"Jabin was the first to try and kill me. I should go. Keira, for your own sake, you shouldn't tell anyone you saw me or that we talked."

Biting her lip, Keira blinked a tear from her blue eyes. "I'm sorry, Kat. When I saw you, I unconsciously yelled to Flick. He's on the phone to Yishay, and they want me to bring you home."

Shaking my head, I stepped away as Keira went to take one of my bags. "Keira, if you try to force me, I will scream and have you arrested. I'm not going back to be murdered." Backing away, I noted the way Keira's mouth fell open, and her eyes were darting between mine.

"You're leaving Yishay?"

"Like I could if I wanted to."

Making my way to the bus stop, I cursed under my breath. I'd thought going to Red Deer would be safe, but I'd forgotten about Keira. Flick's call to Yishay had him awake and purposefully in my consciousness.

You need to trust me, Kat. I won't let anything happen to you. Trust Keira to bring you home safe to me.'

His insistence only made my heart hurt even more because I couldn't trust anyone anymore.

Getting off the bus halfway to Calgary, I walked into the woods and closed my eyes pained by Yishay's persistence and the awareness he was tracking me.

Focusing my thoughts, I used the Pâlie way of communicating to reach out to the only person I trusted.

'Casimir, I can't block Yishay. I can't get back to the cabin if he's in my head.'

Pale blue eyes flashed open in my head, cranky and half-asleep, Casimir fumed. *'What are you doing away from the cabin?'*

'I needed food.'

'You should have waited for Kenan to wake.' The bark in his mind-voice made it evident he wasn't happy to hear from me.

'Cas...Kenan left days ago. How long did you want me to wait?' The resulting confusion didn't put me at ease. *'Great! He didn't even tell you he'd left. Now, I can quite honestly claim everyone I ever cared about has abandoned me.'* The silence that followed was deafening. Sucking in a deep breath, I tried to breathe through the pain in my chest. "If that's how it is."

Angry now, I gritted my teeth as the air currents at the base of my neck stirred my hair. Levitating before I realized, I swept through the forest, taking four different directions and rounding back before I reached the back door of the cabin. Both bags of shopping got shoved into the fridge. I didn't care that there were pantry and bathroom items in there. I'd made up my mind.

Storming upstairs to Casimir's room, I located his crossbow and bolts. Back outside, I set up a shooting range. As a child, I'd been a good shot, nowhere near Casimir's proficiency, but I hit the target every time. Knocking the first arrow, I aimed and fired. The bolt made contact but was far from the bullseye. Reloading, I kept going. By mid-afternoon, I was hitting dead-center every second shot from varying distances.

Forgetting about food or any other requirements, I moved around the backyard firing arrow, after arrow, until every single bolt I loosed hit the bullseye. As the sun descended, I packed away my days training, went inside, and locked up ready for another night alone.

INITIALLY, I THOUGHT IT WAS THE WIND THAT WOKE ME, STARTLING ME into sitting upright in bed and listening intently. When the noise came again, I froze. Someone was walking across the roof. Another quieter sound informed me another was on the balcony outside the living room trying the door handle. Slipping out of bed, I levitated across the room to my bedroom door.

Remaining inside the room, I pressed my back against the wall next to the open door, but their voices traveled down through the bell tower despite the massive plate of glass insulate.

"...all locked up. Chimney indicates the fire is burning, but it hasn't been attended for hours."

"There are footprints outback from during the day, but nothing coming or going from the cabin." Omri's voice boomed even in his version of a whisper. "Let's move on. I suspect it is a human dwelling."

"I don't get why she'd run from Keira? They were friends," Ira murmured.

A third voice from a person I didn't even realize was there spoke quietly. "You watched your husband murder a man, and then your husband forces you to drink blood moments before you're kidnapped, taken into the mountains, fed on, forced to drink a strangers blood, plus bohovia knows what else. Your kidnapper releases you, Jabin finds you and instead of bringing you home tries to kill you, who knows what else happened in that encounter? At some stage in that first twenty-four hours of your world being destroyed, your husband tells you your life is expendable."

Flick seemed to jump across the roof to stand with the other men. "That was only the first day, Ira. We know through Yishay's connection that over the following week, Kat was attacked nightly, sometimes by numerous assailants. It's been nearly months, and in all that time, not once has Yishay, her zápalka, gone out to try and find her himself, and Kat knows it. Would you trust anyone, Ira? Put yourself in Kat's shoes. She's gone to ground, and she isn't going to trust a single one of us." Flick's voice lifted as if he'd taken to the air. "But, thanks to Keira, we now know she's in Halos territory. She's also scared, alone, and heartbroken."

There was a moment's silence as if the others waited for Flick to go ahead. "Do you think the rumor is true, Omri?"

"Which one?"

"The one that suggests the Král didn't go after his wife, in hope, he'd be free to take a Halos woman as his mate instead?" Ira choked on his last word.

"She is his zápalka! No Halos worth a damn, not even a Pâlir would conspire to have his zápalka killed. It is this youthful ignorance of what it is to lose your true mate that leads to these hovadina rumors. If any of you knew the dark empty pit of pain that losing your zápalka opens inside of someone..."

There was a thump like a body landing heavily on the roof. "I'm sorry, Omri, I forgot..."

"You're young, so let me spell it out for you. Yishay was sure Casimir would be noble enough not to kill Kat. By all accounts, she was bait, and when it didn't work, it would seem he's let her go. Our sources tell us he's been at the Pâlir compound for over a week now. So this isn't about the Pâlir or their revenge anymore. Yishay's distrust is about Jabin and the others who hunted and still hunt, the Král's zápalka. Or did you think we were sent out in groups of three now to stop us getting lonely? If Yishay can't trust his people, why in pecklo would Kat?"

The noise of them leaving relaxed me slightly, but then Omri's words penetrated my tired brain. Sinking to the floor beside the door, I curled into a ball. Kenan told me about Omri one night while trying to convince me to marry Yishay. Omri found his zápalka, but he recognized her as his hand gripped her heart and ripped it from her chest. In confusion, Omri tried to revive her, to put her heart back. Fifty years ago, under the rule of the former Král, a Pâlir was a Pâlir.

The Halos Omri was hunting with, threw him away, and burnt the girl's body and heart while Omri looked on in horror. They say his hair turned grey the instant his zápalka burned to ash.

The incident turned Omri feral. First, he killed the halos that killed his zápalka, then he left and roamed the earth living like a Pâlir, feeding only on murderers, especially if they were Halos. It wasn't until Yishay took the throne and turned his back on the old ways, urging his people to assimilate with the humans that Omri returned to be part of the change.

Crawling back to my bed, I sheltered beneath the blankets, as if that could stop all the hurt stabbing at my heart. If the Halos hated me this much just thinking I was human, imagine how they would react when it finally came out that I was Pâlir royalty.

Morning light found me setting up targets through the woods around the house. The day was spent learning to shoot on the fly. It was difficult. You were continually adjusting for air currents as you moved through the trees and simultaneously trying to aim and shoot while moving at breakneck speed. At lunchtime, I sat down bruised and battered from connecting with the trees and wondering how on earth Casimir ever got good at this let alone perfected it.

'Persistence and practice, Katiana.'

Ignoring Casimir's little chuckle at my frustration, I returned to the practice course I'd set up. My focus was entirely on surviving, which meant hitting bullseyes every time I fired a bolt.

By sundown on the third day of practice, I was hitting the targets, but only occasionally getting the bullseye I needed. Carbon arrows would only slow one of my kind down if it were a direct hit to the heart. I needed to get better. Slumping into the upstairs lounge with the sandwich I'd made for dinner, I barely had the energy to stand, let alone cook.

Dozing, I was startled awake by someone trying the door handle. Sitting frozen still, I hoped if it were another patrol, they'd pass by, but then I heard a key enter the tumbler and unlock the door. Instantly, I was on my feet with the crossbow pointed at the still closed curtain. Kenan darted inside, shaking the snow from his hair as he closed the door and curtain behind him. Turning into the room, Kenan hesitated, his smile faltering at the sight of the crossbow shaking in my hand.

"Kat?" Rushing forward, Kenan knocked the crossbow aside and pulled me into a tight hug. "What's happened? You're terrified."

Sobbing into Kenan's shoulder, I gripped his jacket. "I didn't think you were coming back. You shouldn't have. He's busy now, but if he pays attention, he'll know you're here. Casimir is too far away and..."

Keeping my face pressed to his chest, Kenan rubbed my back. "While I'm this close I'll be fine. I'm not staying. I was passing through to report back to Yish and managed to slip my team for a short time. We've been out searching the Halos territory every night since you went to Red Deer. They know you're still here somewhere, so Yish has all of the First Order out trying to find you. I suspect the others are out looking for you too."

"I've had a few visitors trying the doors over the last week."

Relieving my hand of the weapon, Kenan tossed it to the couch as he held me tighter. "That explains the bow. I needed to let you know, Casimir called. He's furious I left you alone. Vladimir forbade Casimir returning after he found out where things nearly went. Cas is not even to communicate with you. Vladimir is hoping the distance and silence will free your emotions to your husband again."

Taking a deep breath, Kenan slowed his speech and softened his inflections, as if he may scare away a rabbit he was stalking.

"Cas wanted you to know he didn't abandon you by choice. He said it was important you know that. That neither he nor I am staying away by choice."

Without any warning, Kenan grabbed my jaw, forcing my head back and to the side as his teeth sunk into my neck. Only managing a weak whimper, my knees buckled. Following my body to the floor, Kenan sealed his mouth to my neck as he drank his thirst. Without sex to distract, it was painful. The draining sensation was like an uncatchable itch crawling beneath your skin. At that moment, I discovered that it was impossible to scream or even make more than a pitiful whimper while being fed on because you can barely breathe.

Finally, Kenan broke away. He touched my face tenderly wiping away the silent tears. "I'm so sorry, Kat. I haven't fed all week and likely wouldn't get another chance."

Limp and barely coherent, I understood that Kenan hadn't returned to warn me or make sure I was safe. He came to an easy meal, one he could do more than snack on and not risk killing. Betrayal quaked through my body, like a volcano edging eruption.

Picking me up, Kenan carried me already semi-unconscious to my bed. "You'll recover by morning, but get a good breakfast. I'll stoke the fires and lock up when I leave."

Kissing my forehead, Kenan turned out the light as my eyes fluttered closed on darkness.

16

*A*fter Kenan's visit, I woke in the morning more focused than ever. It took another two days of non-stop practice before I felt confident that I could hit a target in the heart on the fly. The nights quieted again, and I wondered if they'd stopped searching for me or just moved to a new area. Eventually, curiosity got the better of me.

As the first rays of dawn lightened the sky, I landed in the trees to the west of our house. They looked over Yishay's study and our bedroom above. Stilling when I felt the air currents behind me change, I huddled against the trunk and observed as a Halos flew overhead carrying a woman. Saul landed on the porch outside the study, and when the woman turned to look around, I recognized Batyah, Saul's daughter.

Batyah was pretty for her forty years. Widowed before I even came to Calgary, her son was the same age as me. Curious as to why Batyah was here at sunrise, I pulled the binoculars I'd found in Kenan's room from my pocket. Yishay greeted Batyah in the usual Halos manner and then stepped back to his desk while Batyah and Saul moved into the house.

Yishay continued speaking to someone I couldn't see. After a few minutes, I watched him switch off his desk lamp and move into the house, followed by Kenan. Since Saul was on day watch duty only the other week, I assumed it was Kenan's watch currently. Movement upstairs caught my attention. Shifting the binoculars, I focused on our bedroom window where Batyah stood looking out.

Acid burned in the pit of my stomach, the contents growing more fetid as I watched her disrobe. Swallowing the bitter taste creeping into my mouth as Yishay closed the bedroom door, I forced myself to watch Batyah join him at the foot of our bed. When Yishay started to remove his clothes, I accidentally dropped the binoculars and clung to the tree trunk to stop from falling off the branch myself.

Tears streamed down my face as I clung there, eyes squeezed tight on the images already flooding my mind. Steadying my breathing, I argued through the pain. *'See it, Kat. See it happen, or your imagination will run away from you.'*

Floating to the ground, I collected the binoculars and returned to the trees. Jumping to a limb closer to the clearing for a better view of the room, I took another deep breath and promised my self assurances that I needed to see it with my own eyes before I raised the binoculars.

Swallowing the first cry that rippled up my throat at the sight of Batyah in Yishays arms, his mouth feeding at her neck, I clamped my teeth together when they fell onto our bed, and all I could see was Yishay's naked shoulders as he lay upon another woman. A purebred Halos woman old enough to be my mother.

Ira's words burned through my brain. *'The Král didn't go after his wife in the hope he'd be free to take a Halos woman as his mate instead.'*

As the agony of betrayal burst into an inferno in my heart, I couldn't restrain the hurt any longer. Screaming, I fell from the tree and landed with a loud thump. A secondary scream of pain escaped, I clutched my injured left arm to my stomach as I scrambled to my feet. Doors flew open at the house - Yishay at the bedroom balcony, Kenan and Saul at the study.

Glaring at Yishay, still naked, licking Batyah's blood from his lips, I wished I'd never met him.

"Kat?" Kenan called taking a step off the porch. Wincing from the sunlight, Kenan stepped back beneath the protection of the porch.

As the sunlight breached the tree line on the east side, Yishay stepped back and shut the doors.

"Kat, what..." Kenan's eyes followed mine to the balcony above his head and back.

Holding up the binoculars for them to see, I dropped them as I turned and, limping from the fall, started back into the forest.

Kenan cursed. "Kat, come back! I can explain."

Ignoring someone I once considered a friend, I kept walking. Once I was deep enough to go unseen, I levitated and flew back to the cabin.

'Kat, what's happened?' Casimir felt my pain by the time I got back to the cabin. When I refused to answer him, he returned to being quiet.

While I still felt Casimir during his absence, the pull to Yishay was stronger. When I slept, I dreamed of Yishay calling me home, trying to convince me in my sleep that I'd be safe with him. The problem was, I dreamed of Casimir too, and those dreams continued from where I'd last seen him. Now, as I crawled into bed, tired and hurting both physically and emotionally, I didn't want either of them.

17

Soaking in the bath, I examined the hardened calluses on my fingers and hands from five days of constant training. A strong gust of wind buffeted against me. Frowning, I checked the window to make sure it wasn't open. It took me longer than it should have to realize it was my awareness of Yishay moving through trees, closing in on my location.

Splashing half the tub of water across the room, I jumped out grabbing a towel. After months, Yishay was coming for me himself. Typical that when you don't want a guy, they finally find courage. Or, maybe it was knowing I was in his territory, which meant he wouldn't be walking into a trap. No, I knew what triggered this action. Yishay knew what I'd witnessed this morning, and now he needed to finish what the Pâlir started.

Quickly dressing, I ran downstairs to gather the things I'd packed earlier. Pausing long enough to pull on the beanie and grab up the map I'd been studying at dinner time, I flew out the kitchen door. Casimir warned me to stay beneath the canopy when training me, but I wanted to get clear of the cabin without leaving a trail. Taking to the sky, I headed North West for Jasper.

Spying smoke curling above the tree line, I dived for it. Landing in the trees just back from the cabin, I checked the coast was clear. No lights were on, and there were footprints in the snow leading to the woodshed. While the prints themselves meant nothing, it was more likely that they belonged to a human.

Transecting to the back door, I made sure to touch the door frame and allow Yishay to see me standing there. Tuning Yishay out, I trudged away from the cabin, west towards the ridgeline, making sure to leave a trail on the trees. At the top of the peak, I stopped for a break. Removing a sandwich I'd packed away before dinner, I ate it quietly.

I planned to try for the free territory tonight, but Yishay's surprise movement changed my direction. Thinking about Yishay brought him to mind. He was standing at the back door of the cabin I'd walked away from taking a deep breath. 'She was here within the last two hours.'

Packing up my bag, I slung it onto my back as I checked the map for bearings. If I could make it to the Icefields Parkway several hours away on foot, once I crossed the road, I'd be in Pâlie territory.

Crouching down, Flick studied my imprints in the snow. 'The footprints lead away from the cabin. She's carrying weight, probably a backpack. She's on the move again.'

Rubbing his chin, Methuselah considered Yishay. 'Maybe that's why no one has found her. She's not staying put anywhere.'

'Well, she'll be slow-moving after falling out of that tree today. Shall we...' Saul indicated my steps led into the trees.

Cutting into my eavesdropping, Yishay reached out to me. *'Kat, where are you going?'*

'As if I'd tell you!'

Levitating, I transected across the mountain tops, eyes tearing in the freezing temperatures. If they were only a few hours behind me, I was running out of time. Tracking me would force them to keep amongst the trees, which would hopefully buy me enough time to reach the territorial border.

Moving quickly, I stayed alert. Large objects moving through air creates an enormous shift in the currents, so their approach reached me with plenty of warning. Stopping, I ducked behind a tree, heart in my mouth as two shadows flew overhead. Yishay had sent scouts ahead. The top of the mountains was reasonably barren except along the Dowling Ford. Relying on my small size, I'd moved through the snow-laden forests of the Ford quickly, but I couldn't risk getting lost, so stayed close to the bank of the river.

Once the scouts were out of sight, I began to transvect again. I didn't want to go higher, which would make me more visible, but staying to the trees was slow going. In comparison to the men, I was slight, so I wouldn't affect the air currents anywhere near what the men did. That was all I had on my side.

Yishay reached the sight I'd stopped to eat only a half-hour ago while I was only halfway to the road.

"Hovno!" Taking a deep breath, I focused on my brother. *'Vladimir, I need safe passage into Pâlir territory.'*

'Katiana, what's wrong? Why'd you leave the cabin?'

'They found me. Yishay is tracking me. It's true what they were saying; he wants me gone, and he's already replaced me.' I didn't mean to pass my hurt to my brother, but even my mind voice broke on the admission.

There was a moment's hesitation. *'Where are you?'*

'About thirty minutes away from the ninety-three, north of Panther Falls, where the river passes through at the south end of Nigel Peak. I'm honestly not sure I'll make it.'

'You'll have safe passage if you make it across the road. Run the river, Kat, it's below the peaks, but will be like flying open air.'

Swiping at the tears stinging my cheeks in the ice-cold wind, I pushed through the trees to the river. Vladimir was right. Flying the river was like flying open-air and not having to deal with the reflecting air currents off the trees. Picking up speed, I raced for a safe harbor. Rounding the last bend in the river before the road, I felt the air currents change. Swinging to shore, I slammed into the nearest tree, catching myself on a branch before dropping to the ground at a run.

They may not have seen me in the air, but they'd heard me hit the tree. There was no need to look behind to check; I was sure of it. The road was in view when Omri landed in front of me. My first reaction was to cry in frustration of having made it so close. The second was a more primal instinct. Pulling out the crossbow, I knocked a bolt and aimed it at Omri's chest.

Mouth falling open, Omri stared at me. "Relax, Kat, I'm not here to hurt you."

"Liar!" As Omri stepped towards me, I stepped to the side. If I could get him to circle, I could break for the road. "You're one of them, and Yishay is your Král. You will do as he asks and it won't even dint your conscience."

"That's right, Kat. I'm one of the good guys. The Král wants you safe and unharmed, and that's exactly how I intend to see you stay." Omri's right eye flickered.

Spinning around as Methuselah closed on me, nearly in arms reach, I aimed and fired, quickly reloading as I turned back to face Omri again.

Stopping dead, Omri stared wide-eyed at his companion. "Kat, you don't know what you are doing! We are your allies."

"I stopped knowing who my allies were the moment Jabin's stubby fingers wrapped around my throat. I stopped trusting a single word out of any Halos mouth when my husband, the man who promised to love me, to protect me, abandoned me to his enemy and took another woman to our bed..."

"Kat, that wasn't what you think. Batyah and Yishay made that arrangement before you married..."

The pain of his words nearly caused me to drop the bow. Circling me to get to Methuselah to remove the bolt from his heart, Omri stopped when he saw my reaction to his admission, and he instinctively took a step towards me. Recovering, I raised the bow back to his chest. Omri froze. He looked at me then, really looked at me for the first time since he'd found me.

"Your skin is luminescent, your eyes, your voice...does Yishay know?"

Eyes filling with tears, I didn't try to hide the pain in my heart. "When he bound me. It's why he didn't even try to stop Casimir taking me."

"Kat, you have every right to be scared, but you know my history, I will do you no harm. Put the bow down, let me remove the bolt from Methuselah, and I'll explain everything."

Lowering the bow slightly, but not enough that I wouldn't be able to shoot if he rushed me, I inclined my head towards Methuselah. Moving quickly, Omri removed the bolt.

"You must have been feeding to get your color back, Kat. It's no different to what Yishay was doing..."

"They thought I was carrying the Kral's son. They wanted to make sure the child got the sustenance it needed." While Omri saved Methuselah, I kept backing to the road. "I don't want to fight you, Omri. I want to walk away, to be left alone, and not be hurt anymore. Tell Yishay he doesn't have to kill me. I'll give him a divorce and-"

"Divorce is a human thing, Kat. It doesn't exist in our species."

"Then I'll go live in the free territory, or leave altogether. With distance and time, our bond will fade, and he'll be free to breed with whomever he chooses. I won't stand in his way, Omri. That should appease the others."

"Kat, you're upset, scared, and hurt. Things have happened to you that never should have happened, and there is no undoing it. Just let me explain.-"

"Put the crossbow down, Kat," Yishay's voice ordered from the river as he walked towards us with nearly all his First Order at his side. Swallowing hard, I instantly trained the bolt on him. Everyone paused but Yishay. "You're not going to shoot me, Kotě, you remember how much it hurt when the Pâlir shot me."

Blinking back tears, I backed closer to the road.

Not taking his eyes off me, Omri tried to stop Yishay's approach. "Yishay, you're cornering her, and she's terrified."

Ignoring Omri, Yishay kept coming. "Put the bow down, Kotě, and I will explain what you saw this morn-"

"Stop calling me that! I'm not your kitten or anything else anymore. I know what I saw, and thanks to Omri, I now know how long it's been happening. What was I? A game? A way of slumming it until you were ready to breed?"

Kenan stepped up next to Yishay. "Kat, you're getting hysterical-"

"Don't you talk to me! You knew all along, and you played me just as much as he did." I pointedly aimed the crossbow at Yishay. "I can still feel your teeth in my neck as you fed on me. Do you know how much that hurts? I couldn't breathe."

Everyone was looking at Kenan now, Yishay glaring.

"I'm not like all the rest. I don't have a mate, and you were working us from sunrise to sundown with no chance for me to feed. I was starving and lost control. Every single man here has done it at some point."

"Not with the Král's wife, and especially not when she's already scared stiff of us all," Flick scolded

Still backing towards the road, my heart was hammering in my chest as Yishay matched every one of my steps. Giving up, Omri shook his head in regret. Sad, regretful eyes coming to focus on me.

"She used to be mine! If you think that I stopped loving her because the Král walked in and took her from me, you must be delusional!"

Blinking and mouth falling open, Flick glared at Kenan. "You knew where she was. You found her after she escaped, brought her back, and hid her?"

"Someone had to do something, Flick. Yishay sure as hell wasn't going to save her!"

"Enough!" Yishay yelled before Flick, or any other of the First Order could respond. "Kat, put the crossbow down now! I will take you home and explain everything there, in private."

Backing into the guard rail, I shook my head. "I am not going anywhere with you ever again. You have lied to me from the very beginning, and you're lying to me now. I've heard your plan, Yish. Let the enemy kill your wife so you can marry a pure Halos."

"Bohiva! Kat, that's a nasty rumor started by hopeful purists."

Throwing one leg over the railing, I glared at my husband. "Yet, it was a full-blooded Halos woman in our bed this morning, and how many other mornings, for the past two years?"

Growling, Yishay rushed forward to grab me. I squeezed the trigger. For a moment, utter silence fell upon us as Yishay froze, his hands clutching the bolt in his heart. Screaming, I doubled over the pain in my chest, the loss of balance plunging me over the railing and onto the road. As Yishay hit the ground, I pushed off the ground below me, pure agony pulsing throughout my entire body.

The first to react was Ira. "Mrdat! She just shot her Zápalka."

"He's not my zápalka." Staggering across the road, I made it to the middle before my father appeared on the other side of the guard rail, his white hair blowing out behind him from the wind. Freezing in the middle of the road, I stopped and stared. He was too young to be my father, but he was the spitting image of him. "Wenceslas?"

My eldest brother nodded slightly, his stern features taking in the chaos on the other side of the road. There was no need to look back to see Saul pulling the bolt from Yishay's chest. The searing pain buckled my knees, and I half collapsed on the road.

Stepping to the rail, Wenceslas let the wind carry his voice. "You need to cross the road entirely, Katiana."

Getting back to my feet as Omri and Kenan made the guard rail on their side of the road, I stumbled towards my brother.

"Kat, stop!" Kenan begged.

"Sakra, it's the Prince."

Glancing over my shoulder, I spied Kenan about to jump the guardrail.

"If you place your body over that rail, Halos, you will start the war you and your Král have been trying to avoid." Behind Wenceslas, over fifty Pâlie emerged from the darkness. "Let the girl go. She's been hurt enough. Come, Katiana."

Tripping the rest of the way to the guard rail where Wenceslas stood, I fell into his arms.

Lifting me ready to carry me, Wenceslas frowned as he met my eyes. "Hello again, Princess. Still shooting yourself in the heart, I see." Cuddling me tightly, he went to turn away.

"Wenceslas!" Yishay's voice rang out across the road. Wenceslas turned to see Yishay supported by Saul as the hole in his chest still bled. In contrast, Methuselah was still unconscious on the ground. "That is my wife, my zápalka. You will put her back on the road and walk away."

There was no please or thank you. Even to Pâlie, the Král still held the authority.

"My brother came to you under a peace banner, and you killed him."

"He threatened my wife and unborn child."

"So, you love her?"

Gritting his teeth, Yishay refused to give his enemy ammunition.

"It is a simple question, Král. Do you love your wife? If not, and what she believes is true, I can end her existence right here for you, and we can all go on our merry way?" Grabbing my throat, Wenceslas let me drop. Hanging from his hand, I gasped for breath over a meter off the ground.

Choking down our connection, Yishay croaked. "Don't!"

Relaxing his grip, Wenceslas lifted me back into his arms. "You do love her."

"She is my zápalka, of course, I do."

"And you want her back; not to kill but as your wife?"

"Yes."

"Then she will be our hostage to ensure the next time we talk to you of peace, you listen."

"She is my wife!"

Allowing the smallest smirk to lift the side of his mouth, Wenceslas raised an eyebrow. "She will be treated like a Princess. As if she were my sister. I swear an oath."

Scowling, Flick swore next to Yishay. "Your sister? The one you sent away, and when she went missing, had the nerve to accuse us of holding hostage."

"The same. As it turns out, we were not so greatly mistaken." The

Halos exchanged confused glances, everyone but Kenan, who stared painfully at me. Wenceslas gave a short bow. "Good evening, Král. We will be in touch."

A moment later, we were airborne, a string of profanities following us into the sky from the Halos territory.

18

*S*taring at my shaking hands, I looked around the room. This wasn't in my childhood bedroom like I'd expected. When we arrived last night, Wenceslas carried me to the extended family wing of the royal family's residence in the compound. It was the bedroom I would have moved to when I took a husband.

The door opened as Wenceslas stepped into my room, followed by an over-privileged woman with a fabric laid over her arm.

"Did you get any sleep, Katiana?"

"Some. It's weird to be here."

"I imagine you hoped never to find yourself in this building again. You will remember my wife, Jarka. She has appropriate clothing for you. After you dress, you will join your family for snídaně." Wenceslas turned to leave.

"Will Otec be there?"

Nearly tripping, Wenceslas blinked wide eyes back at me a moment. "I guess it didn't occur to Vladimir to tell you. Our Otec died a few years back at the hands of the Halos Lemuel. I rule this family now."

My eyes itched as I shrunk back. Observing my sorrow for our father, Wenceslas walked out, leaving his wife to close the door after him. Jarka laid out the traditional style dress on the bed next to me. It was much the same as the one she wore, but where hers was baby pink, the one on the bed was sapphire blue.

Peering at me through heavy lashes, Jarka all but sneered at me. "We still hold to tradition within the compound."

"I remember."

"Really? I'm surprised you remember anything of us after you turned on your people."

Expecting this perception, I didn't let it upset me. Casimir warned my people might see my marriage as an act of treason, so I ignored the jab and stood to change. If it was one of my brothers or childhood friends treating me like a traitor, I might have felt reticent, but my brother's wife never liked me, nor I, her, so when Jarka got in my face, I wasn't going to back down.

"The only reason you are welcome here is because of your traitorous marriage."

"Listen here you narcissistic otrava. I was sent away from my home and people before I'd even had my first bleed. My family never bothered to visit me or write to me for the years they knew where I was. I owed them nothing!"

"They are the royal family. You cannot expect them to enter the free territory for the sake of a lovesick girl?"

"They are my brothers! That makes me royal too, you self-important fena. They didn't think I was in danger when they dumped my ass in the free territory."

"Maybe they could already see what a disappointment you were?"

"Well, this disappointment zmařený so badly she may be the answer to ending a feud that has spanned centuries. I may have married your enemy, but he wasn't mine, and out of the two women in this room, at least I can truthfully claim to have married for love, not for position."

The hate in Jarka's eyes was pure and clear. The murderous intent flashing across her face made me almost laugh; Jarka had always been hateful to me, but now she had a good reason.

"I see. You're one of the others. The ones who want war and want me dead to get it. Are you going to try and kill me now, Sestra?"

Taking a step forward, Jarka pulled a knife out of the folds of her dress. The side of my mouth tempted a smile.

A pretty Pâlir, a little older than me, threw open the door and entered the room. Her mouth dropped open, and her feet stopped short before her eyes narrowed. "Is Wenceslas insane leaving you alone here with his sister? Get out!"

Giving the new arrival a contemptuous look, Jarka stormed out of the room. The slim-waisted woman closed the door, then threw a pale green material at me. "I'm Danica. I brought you a dress." She ripped the blue dress Jarka had given me off the bed and threw it at the wastebasket. "I wouldn't wear anything that běs gives you. It's probably been dipped in acid first."

"Vladimir's wife?"

My awareness of her made Danica smile. "So, he told you about me? Vlad told me about you too. The sister he grew up with, and now that you have turned up again, the wife of the Král. Jarka probably hates you because she didn't think of seducing the Král herself." Pushing me towards the bathroom, Danica chuckled. "Hurry up, before the boys eat all the food, and we get left with bread and butter for snídaně."

Changing into the traditional winter dress for our women, I sighed. The sleeves buttoned tight from wrist to elbow before relaxing around the upper arm, and a boat neck cut shoulder to shoulder to leave our necks and shoulders free to our mates kiss. Admiring how the loose fit dress pinched at my waist, I felt comfortable for the first time in over a decade. These are the clothes I grew up wearing. Human clothes were utterly foreign to my body before I left; just another addition to the list of things I hated about my father sending me away.

When I came out, Danica was standing placidly by the window. "Danica."

Jumping and placing her hand to her chest, Danica assessed me.

"My god, you're quiet! I was talking to your brother. He wants me to warn you that Casimir eats with us."

Sinking onto the bed, I folded my hands in my lap and hung my head. "I'm not hungry anymore."

Giving me a sympathetic look, Danica took my arm and led me to the window. "Your Prince demanded your attendance to snídaně. It will not do to be a guest in his house, already suspected of treason, and refuse your Prince. He will already be angry about his wife's behavior."

"He knows what she is?"

"A feral she-bitch? Yes, he is quite aware that the traitor is not his blood, but his bedmate."

"And he hasn't killed her because?"

"Because I walked into the room before she planted that knife in your heart."

"Tried to put that knife in my heart, you mean."

My words making Danica smirk. Glancing out the window, I saw my family gathered around the meals table in the interior royal court- yard. Two young boys ran around the table playing while a teenage girl scowled at them from next to Jarka. My brothers and Casimir sat eating without exchanging a word.

"So, Wenceslas has no physical proof of her treason and was hoping that leaving her alone with me would solve that for him."

Shrugging a shoulder, Danica walked to the door. "We should go down."

"Did Vladimir tell you about Casimir and me?"

"Yes."

"I can't go down there if he wants me to obey him still. It was hard enough before, but now that I know..." Now I knew of Yishay's betrayal, how could I resist Casimir?

Returning to stand next to me, Danica looked down at her husband as Vladimir's eyes lifted to my window. Turning his focus to Wenceslas, Vladimir's lips moved. Wenceslas' fist thumped the table making everyone stop as he growled a response. Shaking his head, Vladimir started eating again.

"I'm sorry, Katiana. Wenceslas insists, and, as you just saw, he is not in a negotiating mood."

Taking my hand, Danica led me downstairs to join my family for breakfast. There was a guard outside my door, and more scattered along every exit passageway. The room may not be a prison, but my brother may as well have put me in shackles for the number of men posted to make sure I didn't try and leave. When we entered the courtyard of the grey stone building, all the men stood while we approached the table.

"Sit, I'll get you a plate." Letting go of my hand, Danica ventured to the steam table on the sideboard where all the breakfast foods were keeping warm. The two boys instantly went to Danica's side and started talking animatedly with their mother. Jarka only produced a daughter for Wenceslas, that made Vladimir's sons the future Princes of our people. A fact, I'm sure, that contributed to her seething hate.

With my brothers situated next to their wives, and their children beside them, I sat next to Casimir. Luckily, Casimir was furious and glaring between Wenceslas and Jarka. Placing a plate in front of me, Danica took her seat on the other side of me, instructing her boys to sit between her and Vladimir. Everyone returned to sitting after Danica sat down.

Eyeing the huge pile of scrambled eggs, rashes of ham, bacon, sausages, and the pancake smothered in butter, I pressed my lips closed to withhold the moan of disgust.

Lifting my plate away, Casimir scraped all the meat to his plate before setting it back in front of me with a smile for Danica. "Thanks for the seconds, Danica, but your husband will catch on to your favoritism if you keep that up." Danica, who had been looking at me in shock, recovered enough to wink at Casimir then became very attentive of her food.

Sitting back and crossing his arms, Wenceslas considered me. "You don't eat meat?" Biting my lip, I shook my head. "Even now after you've fed?"

Stopping myself from glancing at Casimir, I shook my head again.

Rolling up the pancake, I waited for the excess butter to drain off before I started eating.

Cracking his jaw, Wenceslas placed his elbows on the table. "I see. Tell us about your husband, Katiana."

"Which one?"

Casimir smirked into his next mouthful.

"Kat..." Vladimir sent me the same warning he did as children when I was trying my father's patience.

"There's not much to tell that you don't already know."

"Is he a good lover?" Jarka jumped in.

"Why? You want a ride?" Raising a brow at the traitor, I then flitted my eyes by my brother's before focusing on my plate. "He's a man. He's a king, and he's a...husband. Up until a few months ago, he was good at all those things. Now...I couldn't tell you certainty in anything about the Kral."

"Does he seek peace?"

Lifting that brow again, I met Wenceslas's eyes. "It seemed he did. More so than your wife does anyway. Why did you leave her in the room with me? Hoping I'd kill the fena for you?"

Laughing at the absurd idea I might be able to take her on, Jarka soon realized no one else thought the possibility so ludicrous. "As if a Halos woman could ever best me."

"She is a Pâlir," Wenceslas responded dryly.

"Born a Pâlir, lived as a human, pampered like a Halos. She couldn't even..."

Cutting her off, Casimir didn't even lookup. "If you tried for Kat's heart, your daughter would be morning the loss of her mother this moment, Jarka. Kat protected herself against Jabin of the First Order when she was tired, cold, and starving. Since then, she has learned to survive quite skillfully."

Jarka's hate seemed to grow exponentially. Her daughter, who I expected to emulate her mother, started watching me with interest.

Smirking, Danica mock whispered to me. "Jarka has always thought herself the best fighter of the women here. Really, it is that her hate drives her beyond what morals restrain the rest of us from doing. I quite often wonder if her need to hate everything is why she failed to produce a male heir. Since she most certainly hates too much to enjoy the pleasure of creating a life with her mate."

"Shut your face."

"I'm sorry, am I wrong?" Danica's face a mask of sincerity. "Have you and Wenceslas had sex sometime this decade?"

When Wenceslas gave a sarcastic huff, Jarka stood and stormed away from the table.

"You really shouldn't goad her, Teta. You know Matka is not quick to forgive."

"Your mother is many things, Velika. Forgiving is something she is purely incapable of for even the smallest slights. Your matka has hated me since the day I gave birth to a son." Danica turned her attention to me. "How much she will hate the Princess Katiana when she births the future Král?"

"She needs to live long enough to see it first," Casimir muttered.

Unsure if he meant Jarka's time was ticking, or if he was referring to my chance of conceiving the Kral's child, I lowered my head. Either one wasn't a good thing.

Touching my hand reassuringly, Casimir gave it a gentle squeeze. "You will do your duty, Kat. You may have sought your own way in life, but you have always attended your Prince when he has asked it of you."

Staring intently at where Casimir's hand still lingered over mine, Vladimir cleared his throat. "Speaking of which, after we've eaten, I think we should adjourn to your study, Wenceslas, and discuss how we move from here. Yishay will not be happy we have taken his wife."

"He surely is not. I have directed our people to be alert for retribution."

Having eaten the pancake, I pushed my plate away. "Yishay won't attack. You didn't seek reprisal for Vladimir's murder. He will see taking me as a hostage as something to be wary of, since you may still choose to take your vengeance out on me. If..."

Frowning, Vladimir narrowed his gaze. "If?"

Taking my hand, Danica patted it. "If he still loves you. That's what you were going to say, correct?"

"If that's the case, you should move me away from Casimir, for Yishay to see that I am safe. Then contact him for negotiations."

"And where would you have us remove you too?" Wenceslas asked with a raised brow.

"Take me to the free territory."

"Why would I send my hostage to the free territory, when I can send a soldier and achieve the same result?" Wenceslas stood, smiling at me. "It is good to see you again, Katiana. We have missed you." Wenceslas left the table. "Vladimir, Casimir, when you finish, bring Katiana to my study and we will plan, but make sure she eats something decent first." He went through the arched doorway that led into the Prince's residence. Casimir procured an apple from the side table and handed it to me.

Rising from the table, Vladimir took his youngest son's hand. "I will settle my family and join you both momentarily."

Taking the hint, Danika ushered their sons towards their part of the compound. Waiting to be alone, I looked up to meet Casimir's eyes. As he sat back down, I bit into the apple to stop from talking. My family was anything but subtle.

"I was forbidden to return, Kat, and for a good reason. I would not have resisted you any longer. You do not wish that on your conscience, as well as what has already occurred between us."

"Well, thank Vladimir for looking out for my conscience for me. Next time, try using your own words instead of regurgitating my brothers at me."

Standing up, I walked off towards Wenceslas study, taking the guess he took over my father's.

19

"We should wait until Kat is říje připraven again. That way, she will most likely be with child before the others can form a plan." Ignoring the sudden flush to my cheeks, Vladimir proposed the timeline.

My brothers discussed my life as if I was absent from the room. Templing his hands, Wenceslas considered Vladimir. "Do we know Kat's cycle? Our species is not known for regularity."

"Every three months." My brothers looked at Casimir. "My brother Kenan was her housemate and lover for twelve months. Kat was last říje připraven when I took her, and again just after you refused to let me return to her, it's why I nearly lost control with her. We have about two months."

All three men sat back in their chairs, thinking.

Silent during the first hour of discussions and plans for negotiations, I was happy for them to thrash out their demands without my input, but now the conversation turned towards me. "How can you be sure Yishay won't kill me? He may have been lying last night, Wenceslas. He couldn't very well order my death in front of all his First Order, especially Kenan."

With a shrug, Wenceslas didn't even look at me. "All he need do was tell his men you were Pâlir and they'd have supported him."

"No, not all of them. Not the important ones. Kenan and Flick are his best friends. Kenan was in love with me, and Flick mated a half-breed. Omri lost his zápalka who was Pâlir, and Saul seems equally as peaceable."

"Yet, it is Saul's daughter who is in your husband's bed. Surely, the chance to have your daughter breed the future Král is worth turning a blind eye."

The absolute acceptance of this on my brother's face left me gritting my teeth. "So, you will risk my life in the hope that the Král will take me to bed one more time before he tries to kill me?"

Leaning forward intently, Wenceslas finally met my eyes. "You will be říje připraven. Yishay will not stop taking you for at least two days. After that, if he attacks you, I do not doubt by what Casimir has told me of your fighting ability, that you could defend enough to escape. You are my sestra, and you have daylight to protect you."

"And if I fall pregnant, the bond will settle, trapping me for life married to a man who hates me."

Huffing, Wenceslas sat back. "Welcome to my life."

"She is not your zápalka. You could send her away and not feel her missing from your life as if someone tore the heart from your chest. Having had it done to me twice now, I can assure you that you would not speak so easily of this if you understood the real loss."

Dropping his arms to the armrests of his chair, Wenceslas sighed. "Katiana, I grieve that you feel used in this matter, but humans have wielded their daughters as pawns for centuries. What we plan is nothing new to history, even ours. If you get with child and Yishay spoke the truth, you will most likely live out a happy life with your husband. If you are forced to return home and find yourself with child, I will kill the Král the moment your son is born and rule as Prince until his time comes." Wenceslas paused, looking to Vladimir before continuing. "And if you should find yourself a widow, you will, of course, have your Prince's blessing to renew your bond with Casimir."

Dropping his face, Casimir tried to hide his smile, but it was there.

"In the meantime, Casimir, I think a few days in the free territory will make for good reconnaissance. When you return, you will continue Katiana's training."

Vladimir sat forward, anxious. "I do not think that is wise, Bratr."

Wenceslas sat back. "Emotions are unimportant in this matter, bratr. Our sestra will not be at risk of conceiving. If she takes Casimir to her for a few weeks, I care not. They are both fully aware and mature enough to understand, that when she is říje připraven again, Katiana will return to her husband, the Král, and do her duty to conceive a son. Now, that we have that sorted, Katiana will be confined to the residence until Casimir returns and is free to train her."

Standing, Casimir opened the door. "I will see Katiana to her room, then pack for my sojourn."

Wenceslas smirked. "Casimir, take care. If you think Jakra will not be reporting every breath, Katiana takes while hostage here to her Halos allies, you are wrong. Do not jeopardize Katiana's safety by handing the Král ammunition. Keep what happens between you both in the trees."

"Even the trees have ears and whisper," I repeated our father's constant warning about gossip and secrets. It made the three men in the room smile.

"Oh, how it has been boring here without you, Katiana," Wenceslas beamed before shooing me out of his office.

AS SOON AS I WAS IN MY ROOM, CASIMIR CLOSED THE DOOR, PULLED ME back to him, and pressed me to the wall kissing me ardently. Gripping his shirt, I couldn't push him away, but I was fighting my desire to let go as well. A few moments later, a knock at the door pulled Casimir back. Taking a steadying breath, I moved further into the room, keeping my back to the door.

"It's Vladimir," my brother called through the closed door.

Opening the door, Casimir closed it again after my brother entered the room.

"I thought...well, Kat is still your wife at this point, Casimir. If you wish to feed before you leave, I believe, it would be best that I supervise. To stop things getting out of hand and to prevent the wrong sort of gossip getting out."

"What gossip would you prefer?" I turned to glare at my brother.

"I'd prefer none, but if tongues are to whisper, I'd prefer it to be of inquisition, not love."

"Because it hurts to be fed on without sex?"

Vladimir's eyebrows rose. "No, because blood holds thoughts. If I were to ask you questions while Cas bled you, he would know your true answer." Vladimir glanced at Casimir. "Did it hurt when Cas fed on you?"

"No, we've never just fed from each other, there's always been...It was just a question."

Studying me for a moment, Vladimir frowned as he turned to Casimir. "Make it quick."

"Don't I get a say in this?"

Vladimir quirked a brow. "Would you refuse your husband?"

"Never. It just feels awkward having an audience."

"Honestly, Kat! The Král fucked you to bind you in front of several of his First Order." My mouth fell open as I stared at Casimir, but he just smiled. "As I hear it, it was quite a spectacle for those who got to watch."

Slapping Casimir hard, I hoped to wipe the leer off his face, but he just growled and pulled me to him, kissing me before I could protest. We fell to the bed, hands tugging at the clothing between us so we could touch skin to skin. When Casimir's hand delved between my thighs, I gasped for air, and he took my proffered neck. It was amazing at how different the feeding experience is by adding sex to the mix. The pain of his bite instantly overpowered by the pleasure his hand was building.

Once he'd taken his fill, Casimir concentrated on what his

body was doing to mine. Kissing down his neck, I found his pulse and opened my mouth, ready to feed. Pain in the back of my head blinded me momentarily. Crying out, my hands reached up to find a hand gripping my hair hard. Blinking through tears, I found Vladimir's angry eyes focused on Casimir.

"Have you always fed on each other like this?"

"She knows no other way, and, since I am not to keep her, I didn't feel the need to teach her otherwise." Snarling, Casimir removed himself. Vladimir destroyed the moment, so we wouldn't be finding any release with each other now.

"She feeds on you like prey? Damn it, Cas!" Releasing my hair, Vladimir turned his back. "You were meant to be training her in every way. She will feed on the Král, and he will think she intends to kill him and react on instinct."

Casimir got in Vladimir's face. "If I trained her to do to me what a wife does to her husband, there is no way it would have stopped until we both condemned ourselves. You forbade us to be with each other. I did the best I could. You want her to learn how to please the Král; then you let her sit and watch you and Danika together while I'm in the free territory." Storming from my room, Casimir slammed the door behind him.

Standing with his mouth hanging open for a moment, Vladimir blinked and his eyes fell where I'd curled into a ball and watched him over the top of my knees. "It's impossible to have two zápalka, Katiana. Everything about you and Casimir has screamed zápalka since you were kids. Are you sure about Yishay?"

"Four months ago, I was certain. Every touch, every kiss, the way his body reacts to mine. But I thought he loved me and was faithful to me too. If the last is a lie, can't it all be?"

Face morphing and falling, Vladimir dropped on the bed next to me and cuddled me into him.

"I love Cas. I was away from him so long, I thought he'd forgotten about me and moved on, so I did too. I didn't expect Yish, but I was happy with him. Now...I'm not sure it could ever be the same. I'm not sure I can leave Cas behind again. I'm not sure about anything anymore, and I hate it."

Holding me, Vladimir rocked me while my tears soaked through his shirt until a knock sounded at the door. "Come."

Danica stepped in, her face turning sympathetic when she saw me huddled in my brother's arms. "Your Prince wishes you to join him, Vlad. The Král has sent a messenger."

"What here? He sent a messenger to the compound?" Vladimir asked while his brows hit his hairline.

"He approached the border just after nightfall and called for an escort. He announced he was carrying a personal message from the Král for our Prince." Danica fell silent, but her eyes stayed intent on her husband, and I felt sure, she said something that she did not wish me to hear.

Kissing my forehead, Vladimir stood up and kissed his wife. "Stay with Katiana in case." He left the room quickly.

Sinking on the bed beside me, Danica collected a brush from the dresser. "I love having my hair brushed when I feel terrible." She started brushing my hair.

"Does Wenceslas think the Halos are going to stage a jailbreak here?" Keeping my gaze lowered, I picked at a thread in my dress.

"No. Wenceslas is sure the Král will not endanger your safety by risking a rescue from the Pâlir compound."

"Then why are you babysitting?"

"What makes you think it's for anything more than comfort, Katiana? You've been left alone for months, and you are distressed by what those months have entailed. We wish to be your family."

"Vladimir knows I can handle being by myself, Danica. I've been alone since my father sent me away from here ten years ago. They didn't worry then. He left you here because you can speak to him through your bond. You're the silent alarm."

"I see you paid attention to your father's ways just as closely as your brothers did." Putting the brush down, Danica leaned back on the overabundance of pillows. "Do your brother's know just how cunning you think?"

"They put a guard on the door, didn't they?"

Laughing, Danica ran her fingers through my hair again. "Tell me about your husband. The one I don't know. Is he caring and considerate? Does he make you happy?"

"He was perfect, or I thought he was. We had issues, of course, every couple does, but we seemed to move past them and be happy. Now, I know differently. He has a lover who he's used for feeding all these years that I never knew. His idea of a peaceful meeting with my Prince was to have him on his knees while his First Order beat him for information." Lowering my voice, I curled in on myself again. "He would have killed me for what I am the night he bound me, despite our years together and my being his zápalka, if not for Kenan."

"Casimir's brother? Was he your lover once? And he is the Kral's best friend?"

"No, that's Flick. Key and Yish are more like brothers. They disagree a lot but care for each other. Whereas, Flick is always a soldier first and foremost, a friend second. Flick wouldn't question an order Yish gave, Key would."

Danica blew out a breath. "Brothers and best friends. You do know how to form one hell of a love triangle. Granted, you didn't realize the connections, but still. Could you imagine how it would have gone down if you married Casimir's brother?"

"I never intended to marry Key. He is a great guy, but I wasn't willing to marry for anything but the connection I felt with Cas."

"Then why didn't you come back for him?"

"Why didn't he come to find me?"

Danica nodded understanding. "Men always think us women will come begging if we want them bad enough."

As my door opened, Danica was instantly on alert. Wenceslas entered, followed by Saul. "There you have it. You see that the Král's wife is housed as a guest and is well."

Saul stepped closer. "Kat, could you stand and come closer, please? Yishay wants me to see that you are being taken care of before I release his message."

Standing, I moved forward, stopping a few meters away, so that Saul could see I moved freely, I turned slowly.

"Could you remove your dress please?"

"No!" Stepping back, I found Danica right behind me. Taking my hand, she held it securely.

"Kat, clothing can hide bruises and other signs of mistreatment."

Wenceslas growled. "You dare to insinuate we would beat the Kral's wife for fun?"

"The Král is aware that a Pâlir has already forced himself on her. As such, you are all to held suspect of such treatment." Saul took a step closer. "Kat, please? Yishay asked for a full physical." Saul was a doctor, that's why Yishay sent him.

"I haven't had sex with anyone but Yishay since we met, forced or otherwise."

Eyebrows drawing together, Saul took a step closer. "Kat, we know another bonded with you, and that he used your vulnerability at the time to force that on you. You don't have to protect them."

"No! He relieved my need that first night despite my protests, but Casimir and I have never had sex."

"But he united with you? You drank his blood, and he drank yours?"

Unsure how to answer, I looked to Wenceslas.

"Don't look at him! You answer me, Kat, you answer your husband and Král. Did Casimir lepeni you against your will?"

"No." Closing my eyes, I couldn't prevent the tears that started to fall.

"I don't believe you. All the evidence points to a lepeni. Please, do as I ask and permit me to inspect you, Kat?"

Stepping between us, Wenceslas backed Saul up with his presence. "That's enough! She has been through enough these past months without you calling her a liar. The Král's wife has answered your questions and refused your request. I confirm that Casimir also claims he has never penetrated her body. Give me the Král's message or leave now."

Wanting to die of embarrassment, I squeezed Danica's hand and met Saul's glare with my own. Retrieving a letter from his coat pocket, Saul handed it to Wenceslas.

"Thank you. I will have the guards escort you back to the border safely."

"Read the letter first, Prince Wenceslas. I am not to leave this room until the Král's questions are answered."

Scowling, Wenceslas walked to the window before reading the letter. When he finished, my brother folded the letter and looked out the window for a long minute. Releasing my hand, Danica stepped away as if she knew what was about to happen. We waited a few more minutes in silence before Vladimir entered the room and shut the door after him. He walked to the window where Wenceslas handed him the letter to read.

Saul's mouth fell open. "But he's dead. I saw him killed!"

"Yes, and now he lives." Wenceslas couldn't hide his pleasure at Saul's surprise.

Vladimir glared at the letter. "This is ridiculous!"

"We either give him what he wants, or we give over an excellent reason why." Turning to assess me, Wenceslas sighed. "She will fight it."

Vladimir handed the letter back to our eldest brother. "This is wrong. I would believe Danica's word."

"I wouldn't believe Jarka's." Wenceslas lifted his brows humored by the comparison.

"Which says a lot about the state of the Král's marriage, does it not?"

Heckle's raising, Saul fumed. "You know nothing about the Král or his wife."

"I know he let his enemy take her, and that he abandoned her to the will of her abductor. I know that whatever passed between them in her months lost was enough to make her fear him, to run from him, and to beg for refuge with his enemy." Crossing his arms, Wenceslas glared at Saul. "I watched a terrified woman shoot her husband in the heart, knowing it would cause her extreme agony, rather than let him touch her. I heard her plea for protection that she believes her husband will kill her."

"She is scared and confused. The Král understands her fear."

"So, he should since he caused it. Tell me, Saul, how long has your daughter been fucking the Král?" Quirking a brow at Saul's grimace, Vladimir stepped closer until he was even with Saul's shoulder. "You know that was the nail in the coffin, don't you? That no matter what transpires here today, or in the near future, Katiana is never going to forget your daughter, a pure Halos woman, naked in the arms of her husband." Gazing over his shoulder, Vladimir looked at Danica. "No woman worth loving could ever forgive that depth of a betrayal. But that is for another day. Today, the Král wants to know if his wife has betrayed him."

Following Vladimir's gaze, I watched Danica's eyebrows lift in surprise and then furrow in anger. "I will not be a party to this!"

"You will stay and do as your husband tells you." Moving away from the window, Wenceslas stopped in front of me. My brother looked down at me with regret already in his eyes. "Take off your clothes and lay on the bed. You will let the doctor inspect you, and you will not fight this in any way. Jsem pochopil?"

Shaking my head as tears poured down my cheeks, I didn't understand. "Please?"

Taking my face in his hands, gently, Wenceslas forced me to meet his eyes as he spoke to my mind so only I could hear. *You will do as your Prince instructs, Katiana. Your husband wants to be sure that we are not trying to put our sons in his place.* My eyebrows shot into my hairline. *'Exactly. We can't explain that away without giving away your station from birth, which thus far, the Král is unaware. Will you do as I ask?"*

Closing my eyes, I let the tears ran faster.

Dropping his gaze to the side, Wenceslas backed away from me. "You have fifteen minutes, doctor." Opening the door, Wenceslas walked out, but Vladimir and Danica stayed.

Danica went to step towards me, but I shook my head, so she

went to join her husband, and both turned their backs to give me privacy.

"I'll turn while you undress, Kat. Lie across your bed, and you can cover yourself with a sheet, but I will need to examine all of you for abuse and feeding."

My eyes went wide as I looked at Vladimir. He didn't turn around, but his shoulders tensed.

"I see. They've fed on you."

"Not the Princes', but I was questioned earlier."

The tension leaked out of Vladimir's shoulders; I'd given a plausible excuse.

"Rather archaic, Prince Vladimir. I thought you believed her?"

"I said if she were my wife, I would believe her word. Katiana is not my wife."

Accepting the answer, Saul indicated I should get ready. Crying quietly, I moved around to the side of the bed and pulled the quilt back. Following Saul's directions, I let him know when I was ready. Closing my eyes, I pressed them tight when he lifted the quilt from my legs and whimpered when he touched me to spread my thighs.

"I know you've been through enough, Kat. I'll make this as quick and unobtrusive as possible."

The bed dipped under his weight, and I fought not to slam my legs closed. When Saul touched me, I jumped and pulled away as I wrapped the quilt around me. "Please don't. I swear to you that I've only had two lovers in my life. Kenan was my first, and I've only been with Yishay since we met. Please, I can't bear anyone but my husband touching me." Covering my face with the quilt, I sobbed. "Why is he doing this to me? Is killing me not enough, he has to humiliate me first?"

Arms wrapped around me; the scent of Danica's light perfume surrounded me as she pulled me to her. "That's enough! I don't care what the Král wants or that the Prince ordered her to accede. Katiana spent the last four months scared and heartbroken. This visit is only going to make it harder for her if negotiations are successful. You realize that, right?"

"It's okay. I saw what I needed. There are no indications of inter-course having taken place recently. I still need to check Kat over for injury."

Turning me into her, Danica started to lift the quilt. Wailing, I gripped it tighter. "It's okay. He wants to see we haven't beaten you and that no one has fed on you where a lover would."

Pressing my face to Danica's shoulder, I let her pull the quilt away. Rolling me forward to expose my back, Danica then moved my shoulder, so Saul could see my breasts. When the quilt was covering me again, I eased my grip on Danica.

"Okay, it's nearly over. The doctor is just going to check your neck to confirm what you told him about this morning." Hand caressing the side of my face, Danica turned my head away.

Holding a colored light, Saul shone it on my skin, then shifted my head to check the other side. "This light shows old scars as well as recent. It wasn't just this morning, Kat." Shutting off the lamp, Saul sighed as he looked at me intently. "Casimir fed on you several times while he held you?"

Pulling the quilt tighter, I stared at the floor.

"Okay, Kat. I've seen what I've needed to see. Now, it's your turn to listen. Yishay loves you. He wants you back healthy and happy and wants you to carry his children. Batyah and Yishay made an agreement when you married. He didn't want to feed off you until you knew, and as time passed, he couldn't find a way to tell you, but it's just food."

"Liar!"

"Okay, a little bit more than food, but as you have experienced, feeding without pleasure is painful. I promise you, Yishay only touches my daughter to feed. If he could do it without, he would have. He wants me to assure you that once you return, now that you know, you will be the only woman in his bed and the only person he feeds from."

Fresh tears ran free. I wanted to believe Saul, but I saw what I saw, and it's hard to ignore what you see with your own eyes. There was too much evidence to the contrary. When Saul went to take my hand in comfort, I flinched away.

Sighing, Saul stood up. "Yishay made a full recovery from the physical damage that bolt caused, but he is hurting that his zápalka feared him enough to shoot him in the heart, Kat. He raged half the night that you took that shot."

Stepping back into the room, Wenceslas observed me. "I hope you have what you need, Saul. Your escort is waiting for you. You can take this as a reply to the Král's demands." He handed Saul a sealed letter.

Accepting it, Saul tucked it away before leaving the room.

Wenceslas stopped by Vladimir. "Is she okay?"

"No, Bratr. Our sestra is on the verge of falling apart, and this just pushed her to the edge."

20

'*K*at.'
        Rolling over in my bed, I ignored Yishay for the third time since sunrise. So far, he begged to explain his side of things. Now, he settled for something far more straightforward.

'Kat, I love you.'

Blinking back tears, I closed my eyes. '*I hate you. You've had another woman in our bed our entire marriage, and you have the nerve to insinuate I betrayed you. I was angry you abandoned me. I was heartbroken when I saw Batyah in your arms, but today you made me hate you. Be glad I fell into the arms of your enemy, Yish. They are going to hand me back to you for the easy price of peace. If I were free, I'd be long gone with no intention of coming back after what you have done. I hate you with all my soul.*'

'I have explained my decisions, Kat. You are my *zápalka,* when you come home to me, you will find your love for me again. Things will be different this time. I know you're not human now, I won't have to hold back and be careful with the fear of killing you.'

Yish sounded so sure of himself. Throwing back the blankets, I moved to the window that overlooked the courtyard. The compound was built into the mountain, so the only windows overlooked the inner courtyard. '*You have to get me back first.*'

Without thinking, I struck the window with all my strength. Breaking glass reverberated through the deserted courtyard. Picking up a dangerous looking triangle, I thrust hard at the same time the guard in the corridor burst through my door. Eyes and mouth opening wide at the agony burning in my chest, my knees crumpled to the floor. In the recesses of my mind, I heard two men screaming in joint pain.

"Call for the Prince!" Kneeling beside me, the guard pulled the shard free of my heart.

Heavy footfalls announced Wenceslas' arrival. "What happened here?" Dropping beside me, his eyes were bright with anger.

"She did it to herself, my Prince. Doesn't she know we can't kill ourselves?"

Frowning at the guard, Wenceslas blinked and dropped his gaze to mine, his tender fingers wiping at my tear-streaked cheek.

"Tell him..." I struggled to breathe through the pain, "every time he tries to talk to me. If he doesn't hear my hurt, I will make him feel it."

Eyes closing, face and voice full of compassion, Wenceslas heaved under the weight of my words. "Oh, Katiana..." Whatever Wenceslas was about to say, was wiped away by the arrival of Jarka.

"Such passion! While I admire your tenacity, Katiana, it is not a trait desired in a princess or a Kral's wife."

Wenceslas wasn't looking at Jarka, so he didn't see the tiniest hint of emotion that flit through her eyes when she looked at me. Not the hate I recognized last time. No, this was something softer, something more profound to her bone.

"Make yourself useful, Jarka. Send a guard for the Doctor and then return to your beauty sleep. Mayhap, it will sink beyond your skin one day." Lifting me, Wenceslas carried me back to the bed. Going to the bathroom, he wet a face towel before coming back to wipe my brow. "Remember, Sestra, when you hurt yourself to punish one husband, you punish the other by default. Does Casimir deserve your pain?"

"Do I?"

Blinking at my spite, Wenceslas turned as the door opened to admit the Doctor. "Check her over, then knock her out, so the Král cannot incite any more tortures on his wife."

Closing my eyes on Wenceslas' retreating back, I felt the prick of a needle in my arm. Shadows fell around me, then I fell through the floor and into an abyss of nothingness.

"KAT?" HESITANT AS HE APPROACHED WHERE I SAT IN THE WINTER-FRUIT orchard, Saul stopped at the far end of the bench.

In spring it would just be leaves. Right now, it held rows of fruit laden trees with the gullies between carpeted white. It was dark and peaceful and quiet. It was the only time out of the compound I was permitted each evening. Saul's intrusion was unwelcome.

Sitting tentatively at the furthest end of the bench, Saul remained quiet for a moment. The two guards appointed to watch my every move, casually stepped closer, having previously given me my space. The guards who accompanied Saul out to the gardens stayed quietly behind us, but close enough to eavesdrop.

"How are they treating you, Kat?"

The silence fell between us like a dead weight.

Turning to face me, Saul sighed. "Kat, you haven't said a word to me the last two times I visited. I'm sure Prince Wenceslas has made it clear that negotiations are based on your return to your husband. You are going to have to start talking to me." When I didn't respond, Saul looked me over. "I see you are still wearing the traditional style clothing. Were you not happy with the clothes I left on my last visit?"

"Women wear traditional dresses here." One of my guards cut in. "Pâlir or not, it does not matter." Saul gave the guard a hard look. With a shrug, the guard turned his attention to me. "Your time is up, we must return inside."

"My time isn't up yet!"

Undeterred by Saul's snap, the guard gave another shrug. "Then best you talk while we walk, Doctor."

Standing, I started walking back to the compound gate, the guards falling in behind me. Rushing forward, Saul grabbed my arm, stopping me. One of his guards stepped between us and backed him up. "You were told not to touch her."

"Then get her to answer me. The Král wants his questions answered."

"A sound has not passed her lips during her wake since she returned from the drugged sleep six days ago. On every visit, you were told this. Nothing has changed."

"Then tell me what she says in her sleep?"

At that, the four guards became uneasy and closed themselves around me almost protectively.

"We must return to the compound for oběd. The Prince has invited you to join the royal meal table, Doctor, before returning to your territory." One of Saul's guards responded before turning and heading towards the gate, keeping a protective barrier around me.

At the gates, we entered the compound and made our way to the royal quarters and the courtyard where the family took their meals. We were the first in the yard, so I moved to the side bench and grabbed an apple, placing it in the pocket of my dress, before taking my seat at the table.

Darka and the boys were the first to join us, Darka taking the seat next to me. She eyed Saul before placing a hand on my wrist gently. "Are you well?"

When I nodded, Darka returned her attention to the boys who were practicing their training on each other. When Vladimir and Wenceslas entered the courtyard, they were deep in conversation, possibly a slight disagreement. As soon as they spotted Saul, the discussion stopped, and Vladimir herded his sons to the table in a playful manner.

Wenceslas held out a sealed letter for Saul. "Will you join us, or do you need to return to the Král immediately?"

"I'd welcome some more time with Kat." Tucking the letter away in his jacket, Saul followed Wenceslas to the table.

"You can sit by me, Saul, my wife, and daughter will not be joining us tonight." Taking his seat at the head of the table at the far end from me, Wenceslas eyed me.

Meeting his eyes for a moment, I turned them back to the courtyard.

"Did you manage to get the Král's wife to talk to you? She has said naught to us since the Král incited her to attempt suicide."

"It was never his intention to hurt her," Saul responded politely as our meals were placed in front of us by the kitchen staff. "But, it does concern the Král that the woman he is resting these negotiations on is no longer the woman he married."

"He should have thought about that before abandoning her." Wenceslas picked up his fork but paused. "The Král surely understood that his wife's abduction would, at the very least, leave her traumatized. Everything that has happened since, however, is on his head. He failed to seek her, protect her, and in essence, betrayed her."

"I was referring more to the physical changes."

Brows drawing together, Wenceslas looked me over. "I admit, I have not noticed any changes during Katiana's stay here."

Saul bowed his head. "Of course, you did not meet Kat until a week ago. You would not have noticed the subtle differences that the first order did when you took her." Saul returned his eyes to me. "We thought her human with Halos ancestry until that night, and, while it has been agreed that her blood must still be mostly Halos for her to be the Král's zápalka, her current physical similarity to the Pâlie has also been noted."

Wenceslas studied me with genuine interest. "You are right, Saul. Her paleness does in itself lend itself to Pâlir ancestry, but the green of her eyes is a very human trait, no Pâlir or Halos purebred or half breed I've ever met, has anything but pure blue eyes."

Saul nodded. "I admit, her eyes seemed bluer on the Icefields parkway, but here I can see enough green swimming in them to agree with your observation."

"From what I hear, the chaos that happened before Katiana's departure that night would have everyone unsure of minor details such as eye color," Vladimir interjected casually. "Perhaps, it could have been a result of Katiana being fed Pâlir blood or even a change that occurred after her bond with the Král. None of us were there the days after her bonding to know how it affected her."

"Casimir could clear the confusion." Saul sounded like he was trying to speak around grit in his mouth. "Though, I've noted Casimir's absence from the compound since my first visit."

"We felt it best for Katiana's comfort that Casimir take some leave for the duration of Katiana's visit." Wenceslas turned concerned eyes to me. "You have barely eaten a thing, Katiana. Are you not hungry?"

Shaking my head, I stood, a question without talking.

Wenceslas sighed. "Very well, your guard will escort you to your rooms."

"Wait. I want to know what happens when Kat sleeps. I've been told nothing passes her lips when awake, hinting that something is said when she sleeps. The Král wants to know."

"She screams for her husband to save her. Kat talks of Jabin and what he said and did to her." Keeping his eyes downcast, Vladimir shook his head. "Other times, she just cries." Picking up his glass of wine, Vladimir looked into its depths before meeting Saul's eyes. "The nights you visit are the worst. Tonight her nightmares will be so painful, she will curse ever meeting the Král."

The tears in my eyes threatened to spill over as I took in the silence of everyone around me. While aware of the nightmares, I hadn't realized I'd been so vocal. The first night I'd woken from the dream, I'd found my guard in my room, weapon drawn, but sympathy covered his face. Now, that sympathy was mirrored on the faces of all the Pâlie in the courtyard.

Swallowing, Saul took one step towards me to draw my attention. "Is there anything you need, Kat? Anything you might give me for Yishay..."

Glaring at Saul, I walked towards my quarters without a backward glance. Inside, I ran up the stairs to my bedroom, threw open the door and fell on my bed, smothering my sobs in a pillow.

A hand brushed gently down my back. Jumping back, I blinked at the intruder. The man standing on the other side of my bed was entirely unexpected.

"Kat, shh, I didn't mean to scare you." Yishay soothed.

Torn between throwing myself into his arms and running from the room, screaming, I swallowed the ball of spit blocking my airway. What was Yishay doing here? Did peace mean so little to him he was willing to destroy any chance of it?

'Vlad. Yishay is here.'

'Here, where?' Vladamir sent back sounding suddenly alert.

Stepping around the bed to me, Yishay reached for me, but I jostled back out of reach. Moving quickly, Yishay grabbed my arms, pulling me against him. "You are my zápalka, the woman I love. Do you know how much it hurt me that you could shoot me?"

'In my room.' My fear echoing through to my brother.

Lowering his mouth, Yishay brushed his lips against mine. A sob caught in my throat; I was torn up in my feelings for this man. I both loved and hated him in equal measures.

"I have missed you so much, Kat. I dream of you every night, to the point I can't tell what's real and what's not in my contact with you." He hovered over my lips. "Perhaps this is a dream now. Are you a dream, Kotě?"

Inhaling and exhaling, I shook my head. "No." His face so close to mine, I felt his smile more than saw it.

Pressing his mouth hard against mine, Yishay wrapped his arms around me to hold me to him. Swooning in his arms, a buzz passed through me to my toes, until every muscle in my body relaxed, so I could melt into his hold. It didn't matter my brain was screaming at me, my body, my heart, both knew his arms were where I belonged.

One of Yishay's hands caressed my neck, down to grope my breast causing me to gasp and arch into him. When his hand descended and left me, I hesitated. Something was wrong. Never before had Yishay and I been passionate like this and his erection not pressed like a stone rod against my tummy. "Yish?"

"I'm sorry, Kat."

Sharp pain bloomed in my abdomen before piercing up into my

chest. Breath escaping me, I stared at my husband who cringed as he too felt my pain. Lowering my eyes as Yishay pulled his blade free from underneath my ribs, I tried to scream, to plead with him. He hadn't gone for the heart directly, it would have been a kindness to do it that way. Yishay wanted to make me suffer.

Trying to pull back from him as he dropped the dagger, I struggled to get free, but his other arm still held me, his strength and power preventing my retreat. With a grimace, Yishay pushed his hand into the hole his blade just made. Finally finding my voice, I screamed as he moved his hand into my chest cavity.

"Why couldn't you be human, Kat? Or full-blood Halos?" Cringing with his own pain, Yishay slid his fingers around my rapid beating heart. "Anything but Pâlie. Anything but my enemy."

Gripping his chest so hard blood bloomed around my fingernails, my scream broke on a sob, my heart hammering against the palm of his hand.

"Look at me, Kat."

Lifting my eyes to Yishay's, I noted the tears spilling down his chiseled cheeks, but it didn't soften the betrayal.

"You are my zápalka. I will spend the rest of my life in agony, knowing I will never love another, but it's better to live a life full of regret than see a Pâlir child on my throne."

As his hand squeezed my heart, I screamed anew. The yell was short-lived this time. Wrenching his arm back, Yishay ripped my heart out of my chest. Excruciating pain burst through my body, and then blackness enfolded me.

21

---

*S*itting up in bed, I clasped my chest. Vladimir and four guards stood in my room, faces full of worry. Blinking away tears in the dim lighting of my room, I realized I dreamed of Yishay again. Opening his mouth, Vladimir hesitated, closed it, and shook his head. Sitting by me on the bed, Wenceslas rubbed my back. As my body started to shake anew, he pulled me into his arms and held me. Dismissing his men, Vladimir closed my door.

Holding me like my father did when I was a child, Wenceslas sounded just like him. "It's time to tell us what you're dreaming, Katiana."

Opening my mouth, I spilled the essence of my nightmares. Sobbing and crying into my brother's chest, I relived Yishay killing me over and over again. When I'd finished, Wenceslas held me tighter. "Call the doctor, Vladimir. Then call Casimir home. Their bond should protect her."

"You think she's seeing the Král's plans for her?"

"No. I believe her being able to feel him heightens her fear. The Král can feel Kat's anxiety, which is why he has been sending the doctor every other day to check on her."

"We should send her away, Bratr. Let Casimir take her somewhere she'll feel safe. If Saul comes while Casimir is here, he will know for certain they are bound, and the Král will ask for Casimir's heart."

"He already has as part of the negotiations. I've refused. I reminded the Král that once Katiana carries his child, their bond will settle, and he will be the only person in his wife's heart. Our people have seen enough bloodshed. I refuse to bargain for peace with more." The door opened as the doctor came into the room, needle already in hand. "Sedate her. She's barely sleeping or eating because of the nightmares."

"Bratr!" Vladimir warned.

"We need to keep her healthy, Vlad. If that means knocking her out so she can get a decent rest and her appetite back, then that is what will happen." Tilting my face up to meet his eyes, Wenceslas blinked glassy blue ice at me as the doctor took my arm. "Get some rest, Katiana."

The needle pricked my arm, and I fell through the bed into an abyss of darkness.

FEELING LIKE MY HEAD WAS FULL OF COTTON WOOL, I TRIED TO OPEN MY eyes but gave up after a few moments. Dropping my head back on the pillow, I went back to sleep.

STRETCHING, I HUDDLED BACK AGAINST THE BODY BEHIND ME. THE ARM around my waist firmed a moment, indicating my movement woke them, and then released. Freezing, I focused. The second heartbeat synced with mine. In my head, Casimir smiled as his hand pulled back across my waist to my hip. From there, his hand slid to the gully between my thighs, and rubbed me gently, coaxing me to open my legs for him.

"Cas?"

"The bar is lifted, Kat. Your Princes' want me to teach you everything, including how you should feed on your husband." Kissing across my shoulder, Casimir bunched my dress so he could slip his hand between my bare thighs.

Grabbing his wrist, I stopped his movement as I exhaled roughly. "Not yet. Not here. Too many eyes and ears."

Inhaling my neck, Casimir rubbed his nose along it. "I've missed you. Have a shower and dress. When the sun rises, we will head to the free territory."

Frowning as he slipped from the bed behind me, I sat up to face him. "How? You can't be out in full sun."

Quirking his brow, Casimir gave me a cheeky smile. "No. I can, however, sit inside a heavily tinted car, wear sunglasses, and drive to the free territory."

Never having considered that way of getting there, I smiled. Picking up his shirt off the end of the bed, Casimir pulled it over his head.

"Come on, Princess. You need to eat a decent meal. Then we will pack ready for our excursion."

After eating with the family, I returned to my room alone to pack a few things. Casimir told me to expect to never return to the compound, so I prioritized the more personal items. Not that I had many.

Just before sunrise, my brothers came to my room to wish me a safe trip and remind me I would be returned to my husband when the time was right.

"Casimir will train you in everything you need to know. Everything, Katiana."

Looking into my brother's pale blue eyes, I chewed my lip. "How will you explain my absence?" After the last dream, Saul would most likely return sooner than later.

Crossing his arms, Wenceslas exhaled. "We are sending you away for your own protection. A Halos tried to assassinate you last night. He broke into the compound while our guards were busy escorting the doctor out, and made it as far as your bedroom door. It would appear he received instruction on exactly how to locate you and when you would be alone. As such, we have moved you for your own safety."

Blinking at my brother, I forced my mouth closed and swallowed. "Did that really happen?"

Huffing through his nose, Wenceslas snickered. "Of course not! As if any of those pissants could get into our compound unnoticed. However, a Halos was discovered trying to follow the doctor to the compound, captured, and killed. So, we have a body to show for our accusations."

A knock at the door brought Danika and Casimir into the room together. Dropping a heavy duffle to the floor, Casimir eyed my brothers. "I'm ready."

Stepping into me, Vladimir hugged me tightly. "Train well, Katiana. We'll see you again when it's time."

"I'll miss you."

In response, Vladimir kissed the top of my head.

Giving me the traditional Pâlir farewell, Wenceslas captured my face in his large hands, moved me close, and kissed me on the brow above each eye. "May the stars guide your way safely, Katiana. I'll miss your spirit every day." His thumb wiped away the single tear that escaped down my cheek. He'd never said anything so emotional to me before.

Sweeping me up into her arms, Danika hugged me tight, before pulling away to do the traditional farewell. She kissed me - the older always farewelled the younger. There were no words; her tears said it all. The likelihood of us ever seeing each other again was low.

When she released me, Casimir held open the door. The guards escorted us down to the garage to the heavily tinted SUV that Casimir would use to drive us west to the free territory. The same place my father expelled me to at age thirteen. Driving through the underground car park, we entered the tunnel.

"I forgot about the underside of the compound. My father never allowed me down here, so I never saw it until the day I left for school. I remember it seemed to take forever to exit.

"The tunnel runs for ten kilometers to the boundary of the

compound property. It is heavily monitored with cameras. There are emergency stairs every five hundred meters which allow for infiltration should an enemy enter the tunnel in daylight." The gate started to lift as we approached. "Access is controlled from security, so you need clearance to leave as well as enter." Casimir looked across at my lap, something I considered quite dangerous since he was driving at high speed. Reaching over, Casimir placed his hand over mine, which was grasping my skirt until my knuckles were white.

"Why the fear, Princess? Do you think they'll ambush us?"

"No. I'm worried I won't survive having my heart broken twice."

Squeezing my hand, Casimir put both of his hands back on the wheel. Speeding through the gate, we started the ascent. The ramp curling upon itself like a snake as we launched to the surface. We escaped into the predawn, Casimir sliding his glasses into place, then turned off the gravel track onto the faux driveway and headed for the main gate.

"Have you been okay?"

"The fact you are here should answer that."

"Vladimir told me about the nightmares, and that you've hurt yourself to spite the Král."

"He had to tell you?"

"About the nightmares, yes. The self-harm I got to feel first hand, though, I thought..." Licking his lips, Casimir stayed focused on the road.

Bugs chewed on my insides as I closed my eyes. "I'm sorry, it wasn't my intention to hurt you, Yish just wouldn't listen to me."

The main gate came into view as the sun breached the horizon. The metal filigree hinted to a wealthy estate, but most of it was woodlands of wild fauna, the sprawling manor was underground. Pressing down on the accelerator, Casimir sped through the gate. The first time Casimir slowed was to turn out onto the main road, but even then, with everything cut back to allow a clear view in both directions, the wheels skidded as we turned south.

It would be hours before we got to the free territory, and to get there, we would need to drive the border of the Halos territory. It was daylight now; I wasn't nervous about being found. We would be well and truly clear of either area before the sunset. Overcast as it was, daylight to Halos was still daylight. For the Pâlir, there was room to move as long as their eyes could be protected.

Being alone with Casimir when his intentions were obvious was gnawing at my nerves. While I wanted to be with him, I also remembered what it was like to be taken from him. The emotional upheaval of the last near five months was already wearing on me. My cycle was regular as clockwork. That gave me just more than a month to learn to protect myself, to root out as many of my enemies as we could before I would be handed over in the name of peace.

The idea of being in the same room as Yishay again sent shivers up my spine, both of fear and longing. Yes, I missed him, but I also feared him, loved him, and loathed his very existence. My emotions when it came to Yishay were absolutely conflicted. Brain, heart, and soul warring over his right to be my zápalka, my mate, my forever after. Thinking about Yishay left me torn apart. The one person who should have always protected and cared for me betrayed me.

The more I examined what happened, the more conflicted I became. What grated most was that I had no choice. When I was říje připraven again, I would have to forgive and do my best to make this pain go away. One month, and it would all change. My fear was finding out just how deep his betrayal went. To return home with Yishay and not live out the day.

"We have something important to negotiate," Casimir broke my attention from the snow, waiting until I met his frosty gaze. "Music." Smirking, Casimir hit the power on the radio. "Linkin Park, okay?"

Recognizing the song instantly, I nodded. "From the Inside. Fitting." Turning my eyes back to the scenery, I sang along quietly, letting the tears of fear, anger, and betrayal flow freely.

22

A striking two-level, three-bedroom apartment on the water's edge was our destination. It had views over False Creek and the park next door. The location made the park a certifiable feeding ground at night. Muggings, rapes, all those sorts of activities that you don't see in broad daylight. A Pâlir could stand at the window and just wait for its prey.

The apartment held some lovely designer touches, including dramatic eleven feet ceilings, crown moldings, and marble finishes throughout. The seamless cherry wood-paneled kitchen with its high-end appliances and granite counters opened to a family room that connected via glass fold back doors to the private sunny patio. It was a luxury I'd never expected.

We parked in one of the three designated car parks for our place, then Casimir took me for a tour of the downstairs gym and pool before taking me to the apartment. "You still live by the day, so I'm going to expect you to train if I'm not awake. Use the facilities to run faster and get a little stronger. You've already taken on Jabin alone, but we don't know who will come after you once you go back, or if they would be alone."

"Reassuring," I muttered, looking around the apartment.

"I have a friend nearby who is going to help me train you for multiple attacker defense. For now, though, we've been awake a long time. Let's sleep for the rest of the day, and then we can start the training.

There was a look in Casimir's eyes as he led me to the king bed in the upstairs master bedroom. "Cas, I don't know..."

"Just sleep right now, Kat. Training will begin at sundown." Releasing my hand, Casimir undressed and dropped the blackout blind as he crawled into the bed.

Feeling exhausted, I joined him. He pulled me tight against him, my head resting on his chest, his heartbeat echoing in my head as we slept. It was the best sleep I'd had in weeks. Waking refreshed, I opened my eyes to watch Casimir sleep. He looked peaceful.

Bound to Casimir, I could feel him, and I knew him. Casimir had always felt like he was a part of me, so how could Yishay be my Zápalka? Here in Casimir's arms, he felt just as thoroughly the other half of my soul as Yishay. Casimir's eyes opened. He watched me watching him.

"Is it possible to have two zápalka?"

Casimir traced my brow with a firm finger. "Many times in history, the impossible has been proved possible. Man flying, man going into space."

"If it's true, one of you have to lose your zápalka in favor of the other," I mourned because we knew it would be Casimir who lost.

"If it's true, then there might be another out there for me."

Meeting his eyes, I knew he didn't believe that for a second. I didn't think that. "I'm a freak of nature!" Groaning, I hid my face in his armpit. His scent encasing me, stale from sleep, but warm and masculine. Pine and musk.

Threading his fingers into my hair, Casimir massaged the back of my skull. "You are a princess of your people, and the queen of your race. You will breed the future Král, and you will bring peace to our people after centuries of hate. You are what you need to be, Katiana, and we will both do what needs to be done for our people to have peace."

I lifted my watering eyes to assess Casimir.

When Casimir stroked my face, a tear broke free. "Don't cry for me, Princess, we are pawns to fate's hand, and we move where she places us."

"Pawns are for sacrifice."

"And the Queen is the most powerful piece in play." Casimir moved my face closer. "She protects the king; the rest protect the queen. All our hopes lie with you, Katiana."

"Cas..."

His mouth crushed against mine, tongue pressing hungrily between my lips, demanding me to submit. Refusing surrender, I fought back. Opening my mouth to his, I thrust my tongue into the fray as I moved my body over his. Grabbing my hips, Casimir pushed me down slightly, so I was sitting over his eager pelvis, then he caressed up and molded his hands to my breasts. Thumbs brushing my nipples, Casimir circled and flicked, causing my thighs to tighten either side of his.

Kissing down his neck, I arched my back, so I could nibble across his chest, flicking my tongue over his nipple. "Teach me."

A shiver passed through Casimir as he moaned. "Elbow or groin. A wife feeds from the elbow or groin, a husband from the neck or groin."

Nodding, I took his hand from my breast and threaded his fingers with mine as I placed it to his side. Kissing across his shoulder and down his arms, I licked across his inner elbow.

"Here?"

Closing his eyes, Casimir pulsed against my inner thigh. "There."

Tasting the skin again, I then twisted to capture his nipple between my teeth. Squirming down his body, I adjusted to lie between his thighs. Spreading his legs wider, I took his swollen sacks in hand and moved them aside. Licking over the femoral artery, I nibbled playfully with my teeth. "Here?"

"Yes!" Casimir moaned.

Turning my head, I licked up his length, tracing the largest vein in the male body with my tongue. "But not here?"

"Not if you plan to use it." Sounding tortured, Casimir fisted my hair and forced me up. "Kat..."

Placing a finger to his lips, I met his eyes. "I know how to feed, Cas. Now, I know where. Consider me taught, but I'm not going to feed until I need the heir because if I look Pâlir when Yishay takes me back, I won't survive the first hour I'm there."

Swallowing with effort, Casimir stared into my eyes as I took his length in my hand and circled the head with my tongue. There was absolute desire in his gaze and the pain of losing someone you love. Sure my eyes reflected the same, I felt our time together was tainted; a clock ticking our time away, reminding us with every touch, kiss, and breath, that we would never truly have each other.

Circling his swollen gland again, I gazed up at him, waiting. Closing his eyes, Casimir dropped his head and released his grip on my hair. Taking him into my mouth, I fed on him like I was starving. Casimir pumped his hips up, and as he swelled, his hand gripped my hair again to encourage my tempo.

"I need to feed, Kat." Pulling my head away, Casimir rolled us, slipped between my thighs, and nestled his dripping glands between my folds. "Be mine, Kat. For this short time, be my wife?"

Running my thumb over his lips, I peered into his agony and felt it as my own. "I'll always be yours."

Casimir moved into me, gently and controlled. Gasping, I opened my legs wider to allow for his hips and pelvis to press deeper. Capturing my mouth, Casimir kissed me intently, taking his time, like he was memorizing the feel of me. My breath caught in my throat; the feeling of Casimir inside me was like coming home. His touch, his smell, his kisses, everything about Casimir was where I belonged. It was the most real sense of belonging. Taking my hands with his, Casimir swept them above my head and held me down as he rocked his body over mine.

"Look at me, Kat."

Our vision met, my heart leaped into my mouth, and the world disappeared. All that existed was us; our body's pressed together, allowing the souls within our bodies to meld as best they could at this moment. Another consciousness brushed over mine, followed by a tug. Something inside of me stretched and pulled in opposite directions. Casimir was joined to one half; Yishay the other.

Caressing over my heart, Casimir tilted his head as he peered through his lashes at me. "Does it hurt?"

Shaking my head, I panted as the third heartbeat felt so close it could be pressed against my back. "How can this be?"

Eyes still wide in awe, Casimir dropped his mouth to mine and kissed me deeply. Whether he liked it or not, Yishay was pulled along with our passion. Taken by it, I could picture him in my head, lying in bed with his erection in hand. Opening his eyes, Yishay breathed my name, his pupils wide with lust and dread.

Dropping his mouth to my neck as my breathing became erratic, Casimir pierced my throat gently. Fisting my hands in his long hair, I cried out his name as he fed. Yishay cried out in pain and desire, and as I found climax with Casimir, Yishay came with me, Casimir, a heartbeat after us.

Licking my neck clean, Casimir kissed me deeply. The salty copper of my blood coating his mouth made me hunger for blood. When I demanded air, Casimir moved his mouth to my ear. "He knows now, Kat. The Král will feel me feed, and feel it every time I'm with you like this. He'll know you're mine as much as his."

Tears filled my eyes. "He'll kill you. Then I'll never be able to forgive him."

Lips sipping my tears from my skin, Casimir used his tongue to trace their path until his mouth placed light kisses over my eyes. "Fate lights our path, Katiana. We just walk where we are told."

"I can't accept that. I won't accept that. I've loved you my entire life; you're my zápalka too. If he kills you, he'll lose me."

A deafening roar of anguish and anger ripped through my mind. Cringing, I covered my ears, helplessly trying to mute the torturous sound, but it was inside me, and I couldn't block Yishay out. I didn't know he was still there, that he could hear what was said. In my mind's eye, I watched him rip our bedroom apart in his rage. His violence suffocated me like volcanic ash spewing from an angry volcano.

"Katiana!" Panicking when I started suffocating beneath him, Casimir withdrew from my body. As soon as he did, the connection with Yishay was lost.

Able to breathe again, I clung to Casimir as my fear drowned me. Yishay was beyond angry; he was beyond reason in his hatred for Casimir and me. "I think we just destroyed any chance of peace."

Nodding, Casimir caressed my cheek in comfort and closed his eyes. The rapid movement of his eyes behind his eyelids indicated he was communicating with another. At a guess, he was reporting what transpired to my brothers. Way to have your sex life outed to the family. Rolling off the bed, I meandered to the bathroom. My reflection showed me more pale than usual. The shadows under my eyes made me look dead, and my irises were no longer green, but not blue either. The reflection was a Pâlir who had been tortured and starved.

Blinking at my appearance, I sat down on the closed toilet. My body was cold, shivering, and despite the connection being severed, I could still feel Yishay's anger like molten lava in the pit of my belly. It took a minute of sitting there to absorb Yishay's last thoughts before the connection severed. My eyes sprang wide, my bottom lip trembled as fear shot through my bloodstream. When Casimir walked into the bathroom, I lifted my eyes to meet the arctic storm in his.

"He's going to kill me."

23

"*D*uck and spin."

Tucking my body, I started to turn to face my other opponent. A hard hit struck my lower back, another collided with my shoulder, and a third struck my abdomen and sent me sprawling. Huddled in a ball, I coughed over the pain.

"Don't look at me like that," Ilaja muttered, "you know if this were real, she'd be heartless by now."

Shaking his head, Casimir helped me up. "Do you need a break?"

"No, Ilaja is right. Let's keep going." Turning to face Ilaja, his blue eyes peeked out at me from beneath the unkempt mess of his dark hair. He looked modern, and when he first walked in, I'd nearly put a bolt through his heart. A Halos helping me learn how to fight Halos was not what I expected.

Ilaja and Casimir faced me, looked at each other, and in unison, lunged for me. As I ducked and swerved, blocking punches and grabs, I thought back on the last few weeks since Yishay connected through me with Casimir.

The fact my two husbands could feel each other now worried Casimir when bringing Ilaja over to help train me four weeks ago. Ilaja used to be one of the first order, and one of their best next to

Flick. He left before I met Yishay, for reasons he wasn't willing to share with me. Casimir knew. That knowledge between them was there in the way they looked at each other. Ilaja helping us could go badly for him if Yishay found out. That's what unsettled Casimir with this new three-way connection. He didn't want to put a Halos, or at least this Halos, in danger.

Feinting, I ducked right, came up on the inside of Ilaja, and jabbed my fingers in his solar plexus as I swung my elbow into Casimir's nose. They both let out grunts, but I went straight back into my attack on Ilaja. Jabbing my fingers in his windpipe next, I grabbed Ilaja's nose and twisted as he fell to his knees. Stepping around behind him, I put the bolt I had up my sleeve to his neck with one hand, jamming it in, and raised the crossbow with the other, aiming it at Casimir's heart.

I fired. If I thought about it before I did it, I wouldn't. I'd learned the lesson of hesitating too many times over the weeks. Stepping back, ready for the pain, I closed my eyes. But it never came.

Peeking through my lids, I saw Casimir had caught the bolt right in front of his chest. Smiling at me, Casimir shifted his nose back into place. Yanking the arrow from his neck with a grunt, Ilaja stood slowly, rubbing his throat. While they looked at each other, I took another step back.

Nodding once at Casimir, Ilaja turned to me, holding out the bolt to me.

"You're a Královna I could get behind. Live long enough, and I will swear my allegiance as your first order." With a bow of his head, Ilaja grabbed his jacket and left.

"That's it?"

Collecting the weapons back into his bag, Casimir exhaled. "That's it."

"I don't understand."

Throwing my jacket to me, Casimir slipped into his and grabbed up the bag. "This was never about your skill as a fighter, Kat. You have always been strong and brave. You're only weakness is that you always hesitate to go for the kill." Casimir met my eyes.

"You know I only took that shot because I blocked out it was you."

Casimir stepped towards me. "You cringed immediately after. You didn't hesitate even though you knew it would cause yourself excruciating pain."

"I've experienced it before and survived."

"Even more reason to hesitate. You know how bad it is now." Casimir touched my face gently. "You can never hesitate when your life is on the line, Kat. Never. Not even if it's going to rip you to pieces afterward. Fight to survive first, and deal with the agony when you are safe."

Blinking tears from my eyes, I stared into Casimir's eyes. "You're not training me to survive the others; you're training me to survive..."

Placing a finger to my mouth, Casimir prevented me from saying Yishay's name. "Names are always power, Kat. When you are bonded, speaking someone's name can draw them to you." Stepping back, Casimir wiped the blood still on his face onto his black t-shirt. "Let's not give him the satisfaction of seeing me like this."

Smirking at Casimir's cheeky wink, I took the bag from him. "Clean up, then let's go home."

THE APARTMENT WAS DARK AS WE APPROACHED FROM THE OTHER SIDE of the park. Walking with his arm around me, Casimir tucked me into his chest. He was watching the area around us for danger. Since I was keen to get out of the cold, I focused on the windows of our apartment. That's the only reason I saw the shadows moving around inside.

'*There are people in the apartment.*'

Lifting his head, Casimir noticed what I did. Lowering his face again, Casimir stared at the ground, and I saw the rapid movement of his eyelashes. Cuddling me closer, Casimir kissed my head. '*Not our people.*' Looking to the east, he searched the sky for the coming daylight. '*We'll go straight to the garage, get the car, and get out of here.*'

Instead of going to the courtyard doors, we adjusted our direction to the main entrance of the apartment building and took the stairs to the underground car park. Opening the bag as we skipped down the stairs, Casimir handed me one of the full quivers and a crossbow.

Tying the quiver to my belt, I held the bow across my body under my jacket. Casimir already had his in place, and his long hair hid the quiver at his back. Those pants didn't hide the bulge at the front.

"Are you turned on by possible danger?"

Casimir shrugged. "Blood and adrenalin are pumping. I'm not hard, but I'm not sitting easy either."

Shouldering open the door, Casimir pulled me back into his body to walk to the car. We needed to cross to the middle of the car park, something unnerving at this time of night, or morning, as it was.

Casimir squeezed my shoulder to hold me tighter. *'Two are following behind; three others are closing in from the sides.'*

Keeping my eyes on the car ahead, I didn't look for the enemy. If we made it to the car, we stood a chance of getting out of here unscathed. *'How did they find us?'*

'Focus on surviving first, wonder about the betrayal later.'

Good advice as it was, I still swallowed the word betrayal with difficulty. Releasing me suddenly, Casimir turned to his right. His bow was in his hand before he'd finished turning and the bolt flying towards one of our pursuers a second later.

Dropping to my knee as I turned to my left, I shot the only pursuer in my line of sight. A car blocked a heart shot, but the bolt pierced the Pâlir's right eye and brain. He dropped to the ground, fitting.

"Get them!" a loud voice boomed. Recognizing the voice of one of the ranked Halos, I swallowed. Abraham wasn't one of the first order, but he was someone.

While I noted the two behind us that Casimir had already dropped, he grabbed my arm and yanked me into a huddled run forward, so we were covered by the cars. One was Halos, the other Pâlir. This was a joint operation by the others.

'Keep behind the tires so they can't shoot your legs.' Reloading his bow,

we listened for the next approach. *'We need to get to the car, so we are going to alternate until we get there.'*

After Casimir pointed to multiple locations, I nodded. We had another five still coming. With a glimpse of dark hair, I readied my bow.

'You move first, I'll cover you from behind. Shoot forward. Go!'

Running in a crouch, I aimed and fired as I did, stopping by the next wheel. Casimir moved. Clear for a second, I relocated behind a pillar. A moment later, I heard a whistle. Ducking, I rolled out into the open, came straight up out of the roll and into a one-handed cartwheel to change the target, then ran to the other side. Bolt after bolt followed me across the open space and thudded into the two cars protecting me.

'Go again.'

Taking a breath, I ran through the next row of cars. Bolts marked my path, lodging into the metal and smashing windows. Without him needing to tell me, I understood why Casimir had me keep going. Their focus on me and the barrage of firing gave the snipers position away. As I made it to a safe place to cover, Casimir stood, aimed, and the Pâlir fell from where he was nested in the pipes along the roof.

A Halos yelled as his heavy footfalls hammered the bonnet of a car then launched himself at Casimir. Aiming, I fired, getting him in the neck. It didn't stop him, but it would slow him down.

The air currents shift around me. Throwing myself forward seconds before another Halos crashed down in the space I'd been crouching. Running out into the open, he followed and attacked.

Heart beating fast, I dodged and blocked his first grab and shifted straight into defense mode. Abraham stepped back, extending to his full height and bulk. "She said they trained you. It was bad enough when you were human, to know you are Pâlir." He spat at me. When I dodged that too, he looked me over. "Don't look like no princess to me."

Well, fuck! They knew. "Only one person would have revealed that." Checking the periphery, I could feel the air currents shifting. Wenceslas' wife came into view a second later. Moving quickly, so she couldn't get at my back, I aimed the bow and fired. The bitch dodged, but not enough. Screaming as the bolt caught her shoulder, Jarka dropped to the ground.

Using the distraction, Abraham rushed me again. He may be significant in the Halos, but if he'd ever been a good fighter, he'd let a life of indulgence and laziness erase it. Using the bow to block the dagger he thrust, I spun, taking his blade and arm out to the side, then came up right in front of him.

Closing my mouth around his throat, I sank my teeth deep to grab his esophagus. Yanking my head back, I took his trachea with me. Blood spurted everywhere as he stumbled, suffocating. Spitting out the cartilage, I turned in time for Jarka to take her first swing at me.

As I defended against her attack, I admitted that in hand to hand, yes, she had strength and skill. If she was the best female Pâlir fighter like she claimed, she should have shot me with a bolt while I was distracted. She was fast, but I was just microseconds faster and able to block everything she threw at me.

Glancing to the side, I grabbed the wrist of the attacking arm, used her momentum to pull her forward, passed me, turned her as my hand grabbed the back of her head, and shoved her face hard into a car window.

The window shattered; Jarka screamed. Tripping her feet, I let her own weight impale her throat on the broken shards still held by the door.

Stepping back, I looked around for the movement I'd just felt and came face to face with Saul. My breath rushed from my body as his presence hit me like a fist to the stomach. "Not you? I know you should, but please, don't let you be one of them."

Peering around at the bodies, Saul didn't make a move against me. While he assessed my enemy - none truly dead while their hearts remained encased in their bodies - Casimir came to my side, yanking me back several steps.

"No, not I." Disgust clouded Saul's features as he looked upon Abraham. "We followed him. We knew he was one of them, but for him to mobilize his men, meant they had found you."

"And you waited until they were all dead to show up?" Casimir didn't trust Saul, not that I could blame him.

Others were approaching. Too numerous for us to fight our way free. Grabbing Casimir's jacket, I moved him back. "Cas, you have to go. There are too many. You need to go, or Yish will kill you."

Folding his hands in front of him, Saul eyed Casimir up. "I would listen to Kat if I were you. We are here for her, and we won't harm her, but the Král will kill you."

"Cas, please?" I begged.

Studying my eyes, Casimir was hesitant.

"Don't hesitate, remember?"

Giving my cheek one quick caress, Casimir pressed his lips to mine. *'I'll always love you.'* Floating off the ground, Casimir transvected to one of the fire exits.

Once Casimir was out of sight, I turned my focus back to Saul. Members of the first order marched down the car ramp behind him, and behind them, the one who held the angry heart I felt thumping in my own chest. The one who made my heart race with fear and desire. The one who had betrayed me, so thoroughly.

Stepping into my line of sight, Saul held his hand out. "Princess Katiana, I need you to relinquish your weapons."

Gulping, I closed eyes for a moment on that title, my fear rising exponentially. "You know?"

Carefully removing the bow from my hand, Saul met my eyes. "We know."

24

"For your own sake, act like you missed him."

Handing over the last of my weapons, I ignored the silent tears gliding down my cheeks. "I did. Even when I learned to hate him, something I never thought I'd do, I missed him."

Studying my eyes, Saul bowed his head slightly then moved me out into the open.

"Take their hearts and dispose of the bodies," Yishay ordered as he approached. "Clean this place up. Kenan, make sure there is no security footage."

Bowing, everyone broke off to do their duty. Only Flick was beside Yishay when he stepped up to me. The tension was like a fluid wall of magma between us.

"You betrayed me."

"Batyah," I replied coolly.

Yishay moved forward, an intimidating step. "You bonded with another. I would never have done that to you."

"No, you just left me for dead. Everything I have suffered these last six months has been at your hands, Yish. You have betrayed me since before we married, so don't you dare act like our vows were sacred. Everything I have done has been to survive because you abandoned me."

Eyes squinting, Yishay advanced a warning step. "Really, Princess? How did fucking your kidnapper work into that equation?"

"I don't have to answer that because you can feel the answer. You know."

Yishay grabbed for my throat, but I disengaged before he could find purchase and stepped out of reach. "So, now I see the real Katiana."

Shaking my head, I took another step back as he stepped forward. "You've always seen the real me. I never hid who I was. That was the result of months of being hunted, and of not knowing who to trust anymore. I had to change to survive. I had to fight, had to kill..." My voice cracked on the acknowledgment. "You were meant to love me as much as I loved you."

When Yishay took another step forward, I stepped back. Yishay advanced again, and I retreated. "Stand still, Kat. Don't make this worse than it needs to be."

This time when he stepped forward, I held my ground, trembling as his body stopped inches from mine.

"If you resist me or harm me, I will flatten the Pâlir compound and be rid of your kind for good. Peace rests in your hands, Katiana."

Glaring at him, I hated him for threatening my people when he caused all of this. But when he lowered his face, I couldn't stop even my lips trembling. Rage, love, and so much fear for the man standing before me.

Using his nose to trace a tear along my cheek, Yishay moved his face to the side. "God, being near you, is like standing in a cyclone of emotions." His hands brushed up my arms as he placed one tender kiss just below my ear.

The contact caused me to shiver. The same thrill of his affection was there, but it was overwhelmed by a new dread. For the first time, I was apprehensive about him having his mouth near my neck; something, I was aware, was caused by Kenan.

My instinct was to shove him away, but I stilled my hands, gripping the bottom of my jacket to prevent protecting myself. 'Peace,' I repeated over and over in my head. 'He promised peace.' My brother's had shackled me as the sacrificial goat on the altar of amity. I needed to play my part.

Wrapping me in his arms, Yishay restrained me as his mouth found the sweet spot on my neck. My heart thudded manically in my chest. The pain was searing as he sank his teeth into me and drank me. Gripping his shirt, I couldn't scream or breathe. My only satisfaction was that instead of moans of pleasure, Yishay whimpered.

He felt every second of my agony, but it didn't stop him. He took more than would kill a human, and still, he drank. He was searching, looking for an answer in every mouthful of my blood, seeking something he could feel, but not locate.

"Yish," Flick murmured gently. "Much more, and her heart will stop."

Relinquishing me entirely, Yishay pulled back and let me go simultaneously. Falling into Flick's waiting arms, I was lethargic and weak, almost entirely drained. Unable to fight or escape.

"Put her in the car, she's not going to be a problem tonight." Yishay directed, avoiding looking at me. After watching Flick lift me into his arms, Yishay turned and walked away.

"How did you get access?" I wheezed as Flick opened the back door of Yishay's car

"One of ours lives here." Face softening, Flick tucked my hair behind my ear. "Are you okay, Kat?"

Blinking, I wasn't sure how to answer that. His kindness wasn't expected.

Applying the seatbelt, Flick sighed. "You went through a lot, Kat. I kept imagining Keira in that situation and questioning Yish's reasoning." Flick shook his head. "He didn't know you were their Princess when he abandoned you, so he couldn't be sure they wouldn't harm you. I could never have done that to her."

"The only person who knew was Casimir. Even when he came to take me that night, no one knew I was the missing Princess. Cas thought I was a traitor when he first took me, that I turned on my people to be with Yishay. Until that night, my family didn't know where I was."

Frowning, Flick observed my eyes.

"You see. Everyone was willing to sacrifice me. Yishay because he knew I was Pâlir, my people because my zápalka is their enemy." The tears fell freely. "My only sin was falling in love, and everyone has condemned me for it."

"Why did you let Casimir bind you?"

"You don't understand, I was a child when our parents bound us. I wasn't even aware until he took me." Closing my eyes, I felt as helpless as I was. "I don't know how, but he is my zápalka too. It is the only reason why Casimir protected me."

"That is impossible."

"No, it isn't," Omri, who was behind the wheel, chimed in. Swiveling his head, he observed me, then Flick. "It's happened before, and if Yishay kills the Pâlir, he will kill her and himself in the process. Their bond is secured now. They will live or die as one."

Looking between us, Flick's eyes went wide. Slamming the door, Flick transvected to Yishay's side, speaking frantically.

"You just lied."

Omri shrugged. "I omitted some truth. Your men are protected from each other via their bond with you. If one kills the other, they will die too. You would survive it, you're strong enough."

"I wouldn't want too."

Omri bowed his head. "No, you wouldn't want to."

"I'm sorry you lost your zápalka."

"I reckon you and Flick are about the only ones who truly understand it. Yish could, but he's not as empathetic as Flick."

Letting my head roll to observe Yishay and Flick, I recognized Ilaja and felt a trickle of betrayal.

'Your friend is here talking to the Král.'

'I know,' Casimir answered almost immediately. *'He let them into the underground carpark. Are you okay?'*

'You know I'm not.'

'I'm sorry, Princess. I've let your brothers know, both that you are in the Král's custody, and about Jarka.'

'They should be overjoyed with the news,' I sighed sarcastically. *'Will you be safe?'*

'Yes.'

The car door opened before Yishay dropped into the seat beside me and Flick in the front seat. "Let's go, Omri."

Starting the engine, Omri drove out of the underground carpark. It was still dark, but the horizon was lightening. Yishay held his phone out to me. "Call your Prince and tell him what happened."

"They know."

Putting his phone away, Yishay slid his sunglasses on and sat back for the ride. "Your boss rang the week after you were taken. It put me in a predicament. Normally, we are informing employers the member of their staff is deceased, not abducted." Taking my hand in his, Yishay fluttered his eyelids at the contact. The ache in my chest, like constant heartburn I suffered whenever I wasn't touching either of my husbands, eased.

"I told your boss you were abducted. He worried about you and was very supportive. Last month, he called to enquire how I was and if I'd heard anything. He explained that while he mourned what I was going through, he couldn't continue to hold a position for someone who, after so long, is more than likely not returning."

That sounded like my asshole boss. It also allowed Yishay to do anything he wanted with me. No one was going to be looking for me. Yishay was subtly letting me know, to the humans, I was as good as dead. He could lock me in the basement and keep me there; no one was going to be looking for me.

The sun came over the horizon. Closing my eyes on the light, I exhaled. When I opened them next, my irises would be the in-between color that marked me a daywalker. The tinting was heavy on the windows, so despite the brightness outside, the car stayed relatively dark.

With my eyes closed, I let my mind slip from my surroundings and into the darkness of sleep.

"CASIMIR," I BREATHED HIS NAME AS HIS LIPS BRUSHED MINE. WE KISSED passionately, hands caressing, enjoying the calm that our touch brought each other.

Suddenly, I was snatched away from his grasp, both of us restrained from one another. We fought to reunite, but our captors held us easily. The ache in my chest returned as the room we were in faded, and I was taken by faceless men to an open grave. Wrapping me in heavy chains to restrain me, they left me on the ground beside the hole.

Looking up, I found Yishay standing over me. "Yish, please, help me."

"I can't kill you. That doesn't mean I have to sit back and accept you being with him." With a heavy boot, he kicked my body into the deep hole.

Landing heavily and uncomfortably, pain searing me, I was sure I'd just fractured several ribs.

Spitting out a mouthful of dirt, I pleaded with my husband. "Don't do this. You'll suffer too."

"Not as much as you," Yishay mourned. "Do it."

Dirt fell upon me. Unable to lift my arms to create an air pocket around my face, I struggled to breathe. Soil filled my mouth and nose, was sucked deep into my airways. The pain of suffocation, of being buried alive was mine, but I did not die. Minute after minute, day after day. Dead, but alive.

Then the bugs came, the insects and bacteria that eat buried animals, return our nutrients to the earth, and free our souls from our tormented bodies. A new agony filled me. The pain of every single bite was nothing to the awareness of being eaten alive.

25

*S*truggling to breathe, I sat up on the bed panting. Observing the bedroom I'd shared with Yishay for the last two years, I was alone on the bed, but not alone in the room.

"You talk in your sleep," Yishay informed me quietly from the reading chair. "You never used to do that."

Tears falling quietly down my face from the dream, I stayed quiet.

"I know you've been having nightmares, and that they are very detailed and real for you. I've felt your fear all these weeks. I even caught glimpses of some of your dreams at times. So, I understand why you fear me, and why your mind is adding to it with such horrible imaginations."

Remembering the last dream, I shivered and pulled my legs up to my chest to hug.

"I would never bury you alive, Kat. Nor will I take your heart. I promise you that." When I stayed quiet, Yishay stood. "You might want to have a shower and freshen up."

Slipping off the bed, I went to the wardrobe, collecting fresh clothes. Yishay was undressing as I stepped into the bathroom. Watching him hesitantly, I tried to work out his angle. "So, that's it, we just go back to how it was?"

Sitting on the bed in a huff, Yishay met my eyes. "No, Princess Katiana, that is impossible."

At least we agreed on that.

"Abraham's wife spent the night informing my people I was bound to the missing Pâlir Princess. That contaminating my bloodline with a human was bad enough, but to do it with one of the pale ones."

"Maybe you should educate your people about their own history. Remind them that we are all the same species, and the divide was caused by our Král's jealousy of his younger brother."

Yishay looked at me, bizarrely. "What are you on about?"

"It shouldn't surprise me that you are ignorant of the true history. The Halos were never ones for letting the truth mean anything to them anyway." Shutting the door to the bathroom, I nearly screamed when I looked in the mirror. My hair, face, and clothes were covered in dried blood. Turning the water on hot, I threw my stained garments to the side - there was no saving them - and scrubbed the night from my skin and hair.

Once I was dressed in a pair of pajama bottoms and singlet, I returned to the bedroom. Yishay wasn't there, but Saul was. "He's making a phone call."

"I'm guessing I'm not to be left unsupervised?"

"It's for your own safety, Princess."

"I'm pretty sure I'm bound to a Král."

Saul nodded. "Right now, giving you that title would ruffle more feathers. We need to ease our people into this development."

Annoyed with this, I sighed. "Try telling them it was fated. Say that the gods wanted the royal bloodlines to reunite, or else, the Král wouldn't be my zápalka."

Lifting a humored brow, Saul relaxed a little. "That is a very optimistic viewpoint, Princess. However, the moment the existence of your other zápalka becomes known, the legitimacy of that argument will be lost."

He had a valid point. "Omri said this has happened before."

"Omri is a history buff. He spends his free time in the Halos archives reading. That is who Yish is talking to currently."

"To determine if there is truth to my claim?"

"Yes."

Moving to sit on the bed, I eyed Saul. "Why don't you hate me? Your daughter could take my place."

Saul shook his head. "My daughter loved her husband. Batyah is good friends with the Král, but they do not love each other that way, and she has no design on the crown. Batyah has her children, and at the age she is, she doesn't wish to have more. Their arrangement was one of convenience. Blood for sex. She never drank from him." Standing up, Saul moved towards me. "As for why I don't hate you. It is because I know you, Katiana. I saw a girl who accepted Kenan for who he was, a girl who resisted her zápalka when she realized how it would hurt her friend. A girl who didn't let blood or status determine how she thought of someone." He smiled gently, taking my hand and examining my fingers. "A little known fact about Pâlir girls, when they reach maturity, they bleed into their fingernails." His thumb ran around the tips of one of my pink nails. "Not enough to make it obvious, but enough to give the nails a rose hue that looks like translucent lacquer."

My breath caught in my chest. "You've always known?"

"Always, what you are." Using his other hand to turn to my face, Saul caressed the birthmark behind my ear. "And always who you are. But I was there when you met Yish, Katiana, you did not plan this, and you did not enter this arrangement with an agenda." He removed his hands. "Who else could be more worthy of our Král than a Princess?"

Noise by the door drew our attention to Yishay, who openly glared at Saul. "I'm starting to wonder if I was the only one ignorant of my mates' species," Yishay grumbled, coming into the room. "Kenan knew, you knew, should I convene a vote to see who else in the first order recognized her as Pâlir from the word go?"

"You were blinded by love," Saul offered. "You saw it, you just weren't willing to admit it to yourself."

Yishay placed his phone beside the bed. "Meaning...?"

"Flick, Omri, and Methuselah have all suspected for some time. Had her eyes been blue when we met her, it would have been obvious. The green pigment in her eyes threw them. They'd never met one of our kind who abstained from drinking blood, let alone eating red meat."

Yishay shook his head. "Go away; I'm tired and over this shit today."

Bowing his head, Saul left shutting the door.

"Did you want me to go?" I asked, standing up.

Raising a brow at me, Yishay dropped his tracksuit pants to the floor. "Get into bed, Princess. I think we both need a good rest before this blows up in our face."

Climbing into the bed, Yishay patted the bed next to him. Swallowing my trepidation, I slipped into bed, pulling the covers up. A moment later, I was moving through the air and found myself sitting on Yishay's lap, meeting him eye to eye.

We sat there, staring at each other. Placing his hands on my hips, Yishay slowly lifted my singlet top over my head. Taking the weight of my breasts, his thumbs teased my nipples. "I dare you to tell me to stop."

I knew better. From the first time we slept together, I'd never been able to resist Yishay. After that, his touch, kisses, and sex were addictive. He knew it because that's how he felt about me.

Giving me a moment longer to object, Yishay dropped his mouth to my hardened nipple and sucked it hard. Gripping his head, I arched into his mouth and whimpered at his roughness.

My heart thundered in my chest, breath short and raspy, blood pumping to the sensual areas of my body, increasing sensitivity. The pressure of Yishay's growing erection against my pelvic bone made it impossible to sit still. Yishay guided my hips against him with his free hand. Lifting his face, Yishay took me in with his lust-glazed blue eyes burning with need. "It's only you now, Kotê. I don't have to hide what I am from you, and you don't have to hide who you are from me." Caressing my cheek, Yishay asked if I understood what he was saying with his eyes.

Nodding a little fearfully, and yet, the fear of discovery I'd always harbored had sailed. That cat was so far out of the bag; it was a god damn lion.

"He taught you how to feed?" The question was more clarification than a query.

Biting my lip, I nodded. "I never did; not how a wife does a husband, but he told me where."

Yishay studied me. "When they fed you in case you carried my child?"

When I touched his neck gently, Yishay's eyes popped. By how his brows nearly touched his hairline, I gathered he was stunned, and I think relieved. Lifting my body, so I stood on the bed above him, Yishay dragged my pajama pants down and helped me step out of them. Then guiding my body forward until I stood over his face, he lavished his attention to his place of worship. Using the wall behind the bed to stop me from falling, I bit my lip while my breathing became ragged, and tears escaped at how much I'd missed being with Yishay.

When my legs were shaking, barely able to stay standing, Yishay lowered me to rest over him. As he slid home, he captured my mouth and kissed me deeply. We both felt it when Casimir became aware of us.

Laying back on the bed, Yishay looked up at me with curiosity as he placed his arm out on the bed. "Feed, Kotê, it's time we were truly open with one another."

Hesitating, I lifted my watering eyes to the ceiling. Threading his fingers into the hair at the back of my head, Yishay guided my mouth to his prone elbow. The angle that gave him was deep and glorious. Moaning, I licked his elbow. When I scraped my teeth along the tender flesh, Yishay physically shivered in excitement, all the way to the tip of his...

"Please, Kotê, we need this."

Maybe he was right. Perhaps being real with each other would help mend the rift. I doubted it, but it was a start. Plus, I'd really missed having regular sex.

Sliding my teeth into his flesh, the flashback when I hit the vein filled my mouth, and I started drinking. Yishay's hand was in my hair, gripping me, holding me tight to his arm. His passion grew harder, his hips thrusting upwards eagerly, his moans and grunts growing in intensity.

Taking very little, I drank enough to cap that hunger, then I licked the bite clean. Using my hair to bring my mouth to his, Yishay kissed me deeper than he ever had before.

Rolling us quickly, his kisses echoing his body's depth in mine, Yishay drifted to my neck, turning my head to give him the right approach. My eyes widened as his teeth sunk into me. The angle of his pelvis found that spot, and suddenly I was climaxing.

Stopping drinking while I came, Yishay took very little, even less than me. Sealing the bite, Yishay kissed me, then gave me his release, pumping his hips until his body trembled, and his breath rushed out with relief.

Rolling to the side, Yishay pulled me close just like he always had after sex, and kissed me passionately. Without saying a word, he snuggled into me and closed his eyes.

Caressing over the brand on his chest that marked him the King, I ignored my tears pooling on the pillow beneath my cheek. "I've always loved and feared you. Half a year ago, I loved you more than I feared because I was sure you loved me enough to protect me. Now, doubt has fed my fear and turned it into an animal with sharp teeth and no trust. I don't know how to tame it."

Lifting to watch Yishay sleep, I was surprised to see his eyes staring back at me. Caressing my cheek, Yishay wiped away my tears. "I earned your distrust, Kotê, but you need to listen to what your heart tells you. You need to hear what it's always known."

Kissing the tip of my nose, Yishay pulled me closer until my ear pressed to his chest, so I could hear and feel his heart for real, and not just the ghost of it that had haunted me in his absence.

Now, another heart haunted me. "What about, Casimir?"

Yishay tensed beneath me. "One mess at a time, Kat."

"Did Omri explain-?"

"Yes. What he said makes sense. I hate it, but I must accept it."

"Explain it to me?"

"Tonight, Kat. I'm exhausted."

Closing my eyes as his body relaxed next to mine, for the first time in months, barring the nights I slept with Casimir, I didn't wake from a nightmare screaming.

———————

26

*T*he light was blinding outside, but I stood out on our balcony, absorbing it. Yishay was fast asleep, and, apparently, it didn't occur to anyone that I might escape via the daylight.

Methuselah sat cross-legged outside our bedroom door, sleeping with his back to the wall. When I opened it earlier, he woke and watched me. "I'm hungry." I didn't try to leave the room.

"You can wait until sunset to eat like the rest of your kind." I guess he was still miffed about me shooting him. Not wanting to push my luck, I endured this for the first few weeks being home. Today, I'd had enough playing prisoner.

Standing on the balcony, I listened for any other sounds of movement in the house. Smiling to myself, I levitated, transvecting over the roof and down to the kitchen door.

Checking there was nobody nearby, I quietly opened the door. Touching down as I stepped inside, I calmly collected a bowl, cereal, milk, and spoon, stepped back outside, and returned to the balcony. After setting my breakfast down, I closed the door and sat down to eat.

Just for the satisfaction, I ate two bowls before going to shower, then I curled up in the corner and started reading one of the books

I'd left on my bedside table before I'd been abducted. As the sun began to set, I became antsy, squirming in my seat, hot and, well, I had an overwhelming need to be fucked, hard, and fast.

Groaning in his sleep, Yishay woke, sitting up suddenly to assess me. With a small smile, he threw back the sheets and took his massive erection in hand as he lay back on the bed. "Come on, Kotê; I'll give you what you need."

Standing before I caught myself, I closed my eyes and bit my lip on the need riding my body. "Yish? We both know what will happen."

"I've waited long enough, Kotê."

"But, with everything that has happened? With everything that is about to happen?" Crawling onto the bed anyway, my mind and body were not on the same page.

"Peace will come from uniting the royal family, Kat." He guided me to straddle his hips. "The best way to do that is with a child born of both our bloodlines."

"It could create an entirely different war."

Caressing my face, Yishay's thumb brushed my lips. Opening my mouth, I took his thumb into my mouth and sucked it like I would his hardness. Groaning, Yishay fed the tip of his cock into my heat, causing me to moan loudly as I pressed over him. There were no words for how good it felt to have him sink into me.

Unlike last time, I understood this need now. I was říje připraven, or 'on heat.' Circling my hips, I wanted more of him deeper, and faster. Casimir was right there with us like he was pressed against my back, thrusting into me from behind. *Feed, Kat.*

As if guided by an invisible force, my body tilted towards Yishay's arm. Grabbing Yishay's hand from my hip, I pinned it to the bed and curled over myself to bite his inner elbow. Yishay cried out as his blood flowed into my mouth, hunger for his blood waring with my body's longing for his seed.

Moaning loudly, Yishay threw me off him, rolling and pinning my chest to the bed, he pulled my hips into the air and thrust deep into me. As Yishay fucked me harder and faster than ever before, I clawed the bed. He grew larger as he strained against my need for my zápalka.

Fisting my hair, Yishay yanked my head up at the same moment he drove his body forward, forcing me to lie beneath him. Maneuvering my head to the side, he drove his teeth into my neck, his cock pulsing in time with my blood pumping into his mouth.

"Yish!" My body seized beneath him.

Breaking from my neck, Yishay yelled as his body responded to my call, and he spilled his seed inside my welcoming body. Milking him for every last drop, I cried out again and again as life was herded towards my womb.

'Good girl, Kat. I'll let your brothers know it is done. You will always be my wife in my heart.'

Reacting, my body and mind splintered by the orgasm, leaving nothing to hold my heart together, I burst into tears. Cuddling me too him, Yishay held me while I mourned the all too soon loss of my connection with Casimir. It had to happen, I was Yishay's now, his seed the victor of my body, but that wouldn't erase Casimir from my heart.

When I calmed, Yishay withdrew and showered. Noting the breakfast cereal, he frowned but didn't say anything to me. Hugging the pillow in bed, I cried silently. My emotions and reaction to this moment hurt Yishay. He wanted to celebrate us finally conceiving, and I was crying my heart out for another. My connection with Yishay demanded I share his joy that I make him feel better about this situation, but how could I do that when my happiness was also dependent on the heartache of another.

"I have to go deal with this mess, Kat. I need to admit you are the Pâlir princess, and that we are going to bring peace to our people. I need to convince my people that I haven't betrayed them and that this was fate's hand." When I remained with my face buried in the pillow, Yishay kept his distance. "Methuselah will remain here with you along with a guard of my first order."

"You know they are going to come for me."

"The first order will keep you safe. You are my zápalka, and you carry my child, the heir to my throne inside you; they will do their duty."

"Jabin thought his duty was to kill me, and that's when he thought I was human."

"You will be safe. I will be back before midnight. If anyone attacks, stay in this room and let the first order do their job."

Finally, turning my head, I assessed my husband, blinking tears from my vision until it cleared. "If they can't protect me?"

Gritting his teeth, Yishay folded his arms, looking every bit the ruling king. "The only reason they would fail is if you get in the way, Kat. Stay in our room, keep the doors locked, rest, and recover. Perhaps, you could work on being happy about carrying my child by the time I get back."

Sitting up, I considered him. "Do you want this child? Do you even want me anymore? Am I just a pawn in this game for everyone?"

Scoffing, Yishay opened the bedroom door. "You are a Královna and soon to be the mother of the future král. Get your head around it and start acting like the zápalka I loved."

"Fuck you! You abandoned me. I'll be whoever the hell I need to be to survive, but it will be my choice. You don't control me."

Cheeks lifting, Yishay glanced over me. "I've missed my fierce Kotê." He left before I could respond.

Realizing he'd managed to get me to stop mourning Casimir and start fighting for my life, I sighed. The shine in his eyes as he left was pride, to see the strong woman he fell in love with, not just because I was his zápalka, but because I'd made him win me over. Rolling my eyes, I fell back on the bed, annoyed, but it didn't stop the small smile that twisted my lips. "Oh, stop! So, he loves you for more than fate demanding it. He still abandoned you, threatened, and hurt you. Then he has you back for less than twenty-four hours and knocks you up."

Peering down my body, I moved my hand to cover my flat tummy. We'd just put a baby in there, and now Yishay was having to fight his own people to give his child and me a chance of surviving the next week. He was going to have to fight for peace. Frowning, I looked at the night outside the window. Getting out of bed, I checked that all the windows and doors were locked. After showering, I dressed before opening the bedroom door. Methuselah stood there looking every bit the bodyguard.

"Dinner is being made, Kat. I will let you know when it is here," his voice a little warmer than earlier.

"Do I need to get a taste-tester, make sure it's not poisoned?"

Methuselah chuckled. "Omri is cooking. You will be fine."

"You know I prefer to cook for myself."

"Not tonight, Kat. Everyone is keyed up, too much has happened, there are unsettling rumors," Methuselah shook his head. "Yishay needs to know you are safe so he can deal with the others."

It bothered me, and it made me worry for an entirely different reason. "What rumors?"

"Go back to bed, Kat. You are říje připraven and will want your husband again shortly. Go rest, so you have the energy to take his mind off it when he returns."

Annoyed by the instruction, I rolled my eyes. "Halos and their perception of women. Seriously, I put a bolt in my husband's heart and still managed to cross the boundary. How weak do you think I am?"

Taking a step forward, Methuselah leaned on the door frame as he grabbed the door handle. "Oh, I don't mistake you for weak, Kat. You are exactly the fierce little kitten the Král names you for, and you become something ferocious when you are cornered." He rubbed his chest as if he still felt the bolt in his heart. "We want you to stay in your room, so our Král can be focused, so he does not have to worry about you as well as the so-called loyalists."

Nodding understanding, I stepped back, allowing Methuselah to close the bedroom door. Instinct was demanding I keep everyone out tonight, so I locked the door. The only person I was letting through that door before sunrise was my husband. Either of them. If Yishay came home without issue, then everything would be okay. If Casimir showed up, we were in for a whole world of trouble. He wouldn't unless my life depended on it, but part of me worried if he'd make it in time.

Unlocking the door, I bit my lip as I looked at a frustrated Methuselah. "Are you all connected?" Methuselah nodded, his brows bunching. "Ask Omri, if Yishay gets hurt, will that disable both myself and my Pâlir Zápalka?"

Taking out his phone, Methuselah hit the press to talk. "Omri, pop quiz as a personal request for the Královna. If one of her zápalka is injured, would the other be disabled by the pain, or just her?"

"Neither. While they would both feel it, Kat's connection with the second zápalka would protect her from being disabled by the pain."

Methuselah and I were staring at the phone in awe.

"A blessing in disguise, really. It would be the only time our zápalka doesn't become our weakness."

Swallowing the lump in my throat, I had to know. "Omri, what has caused this?"

Silence filled the space for a long moment. "The last time, and I'm guessing it would be the same this time, but you may need to check your birth records, the woman was a twin in the womb, but born a normal child."

Blinking, Methuselah, and I stared at the phone. "What the hell does that mean?" Methuselah growled, annoyed.

"I believe the princess was a twin, that her sibling died in the womb, and the princess absorbed her twin into her, taking her twin's connection and zápalka also."

We both stood there, quiet for a moment. I didn't buy his excuse. Zápalka was a connection of the soul, not the body. Again, Methuselah broke the silence. "Well, damn! If your twin had been a brother, the Král might not have been so objectionable to letting your other zápalka join you."

Something dropped in the kitchen. "Meth!" Omri scolded.

"Who's to say it wasn't a brother?" I asked a little shell shocked. "Zápalka is not restricted to heterosexual encounters. We have many same-sex zápalka."

"Not in the Halos we don't," Methuselah murmured. "At least, none that declare it openly."

"Just very close friends who choose to live together and not bother with taking a partner." I'd seen the way specific Halos acted occasionally; it just took me a few years to realize that the Halos were as uptight about same-sex zápalka as they were about a Pâlir Královna.

"Very close friends," Methuselah murmured with a controlled nod.

"Omri, stop breaking stuff in my kitchen."

Shutting and locking the door again, I went back to my bed. While I didn't believe the theory Omri was trying to sell me, it didn't hurt to do some fact checking.

'Wenceslas, was I born alone?'

27

The car lights came up the drive just before midnight. Standing in the dark by the window, I waited patiently for it to come into the open, so I could confirm it was Yishay's car, then I relaxed. While I wanted to rush downstairs and into his arms like I used to, I stayed in my room.

As I sat waiting on the bed, my need for Yishay grew stronger. It was an itch under the skin you can't quite reach, and that itch just happened to be between my legs and in a place that only Yishay could scratch. The yearning grew with every passing moment he was in the house and not in this room.

Just because we knew he'd put his child in me, didn't mean my body was acknowledging that yet. It could take days before a female who was říje připraven to confirm pregnancy, or for her body to recognize her state. Our kind could tell when we conceived ninety percent of the time, that was part of the bond. The ten percent who conceived and were unaware were those that are unbound.

Pulling my top off, I dropped my pants to the ground and lay on the bed. With my hands exploring my body, I gasped and moaned as I tried to relieve that insane need.

'*Kind of busy, Kat,*' Casimir muttered in my head, the need calling him across the distance. A flash of him fighting two Halos behind my eyes.

'*You think I want this?*' I grumbled back. My fingers found heaven on the front wall and stroked lovingly. Heavy footsteps thumped up the stairs. If it weren't for me knowing it was Yishay, I wouldn't have been able to force myself to stop.

Scrambling off the bed as he marched up the hall, I had the door unlocked and open by the time he reached it, Methuselah watching wide-eyed as Yishay caught me up in his arms, lifted me, and pressed me to the wall. Within seconds, I had Yishay's fly open, and his throbbing hardness inside of me. "Goodness, Kat," Yishay breathed as he hammered me into the wall. "I've missed you so much."

Using his hair to give me his mouth, I kissed him hungrily as he buried himself repeatedly. "Deeper. I need you deeper."

Dropping us to the floor, Yishay pinned my knees over his elbows and gave me what I needed. Another hunger rose in me as I neared climax. Letting my legs fall wide, I pulled Yishay down to me, and without warning him, buried my teeth in his neck. Tensing above me, Yishay gripped my hair hard in his fists as he growled. Drinking, I mewled desperately, needing him to sate both pangs of hunger.

"She's with child," I heard Saul soothe someone, "she's reacting to the instinct to feed her needs and his."

Slowly, with more control then I wanted him to have, Yishay pumped his hips hard into me, going as deep as he could then circling them, grinding his pelvis into mine. My head fell back, my physical hunger sated, I moaned long and loud as Yishay repeated his slow, hard, grinding fuck.

Picking up speed, slowly, each pump and grind collecting momentum until it was one fluid movement that had me grasping his biceps and crying out my euphoria. Dropping his mouth to my neck, Yishay fed while he circled his hips, continuing my pleasure. Taking very little, Yishay threw his head back and let the entire house know he was satisfied.

Collapsing on me, Yishay kissed me fiercely. "God, I've missed this," he whispered, breathing hard with exertion. Hand traveling down to my abdomen, Yishay caressed my womb tenderly as he kissed me with the same emotion. "Can I get back to work now, Kat?" Chuckling as I near purred with happiness beneath him, Yishay showered me with kisses.

Smiling up at the ceiling, I mumbled permission. It was about then, I realized we weren't in the bedroom. As Yishay pulled away, I noticed Methuselah still watching, and Saul standing a little further away, decently averting his eyes.

"Go have a shower, Kat, then come downstairs and hear what happened tonight."

"Okay." Throwing myself over to my stomach, I got onto all fours and crawled back in the room, swinging my ass at him.

"Kat. Behave!"

Reaching between my thighs, I collected some of the sticky residue leaking from me and sucked my finger in my mouth.

Methuselah chocked on a moan. Yishay growled hungrily. "Saul, tell everyone to take a fifteen-minute break. My mate needs help showering."

"Of course." Bowing his head, Saul grinned as he walked back downstairs.

"Come on, Kotê," Yishay laughed, picking me up and swinging me over his shoulder. "Let's make sure you are sated and clean." Smacking my bum for good measure. Yishay carried me into the bedroom. Shaking his head, Methuselah smiled as he shut the door.

"THEY WERE SHOCKED BY THE REVELATION, BUT EVEN MORE SO, BY THE evidence, Omri provided from the archive," Yishay informed.

"Do you think it will make a difference?" Omri asked skeptically.

"Most were satisfied no great crime was committed, and that it is the fates will that has brought the two houses back together."

"Most, but not all?" Kenan added.

Yishay nodded. "Saul...?"

Saul stood up. "There are those who feel that just because we were once the same species, does not mean we should be again. In their mind, the divide happened for a reason, and it shouldn't be messed with."

"Is it enough to cause a consequence?" Everyone looked to me, unprepared for me being involved in this sort of thing. A handful didn't look happy with my inclusion.

"Enough with large influence and power enough to cause an issue," Saul confirmed. We all turned to Yishay to await his sage decision.

"Princess Katiana is my Zápalka. We are not the first Pâlir-Halos pairing, in fact, over the years, the lack of Halos finding their zápalka may be attributed to the fates wishing to unite us as one again. Perhaps, those who have failed to find their zápalka might do so amongst the Pâlir."

"That's a far-fetched theory," Lemuel argued. "If you try and sell that, and you're wrong, the people will turn on you harder than they already are."

"The people fighting peace are those who already have their zápalka," Kenan grouched, "and the people who gain financially from the war. They don't care for peace because they aren't the ones fighting this war except for their pocketbooks."

"Don't forget the bloodthirsty," Flick offered, eyeing Lemuel.

The argument went back and forth amongst the first order. Yishay, Saul, Omri, and I sat listening as some defended against the uniting of the two houses, and others argued for. The fact that my presence didn't stop them voicing their dissent, albeit phrasing it to be the views of others, let me know these members of the first order were potential threats to me and my child's welfare.

"What was said about the split?" I eventually stopped the heated argument by asking. "How much detail about what caused it was given?"

Tilting his head towards me, Yishay drew his brows together. "Only that it was petty jealousy on the Král's part. Was there more to it?"

"There is always more to it. Though, details tend to get lost in history, especially when the victor wrote it. Which explains why the Halos were in the dark about the truth of your own origins."

"I liked her better when she was just an unimportant human," Lemuel grumbled, "at least she kept her trap shut then."

Striding forward, I grabbed his balls, forcing him to walk back into the wall, so quickly he didn't have time to react. When he raised his arm to hit me, I smiled. "Do it! Strike your Královna."

Snarling, Lemuel opened his mouth to reject that I was anything to him, but his eyes flicked to take in the room, and he shut his mouth.

"That's better, now we all know who is truly unimportant out of the two of us because even human, as the Královna, I still outrank you." Releasing his balls, I stepped back as he curled over his injured jewels, then I turned to meet the eyes of every one of the first order.

"The only reason I am here is that your Král is my zápalka. Be sure, I would never have chosen this life, and I would never have wanted to be part of Halos society. Your women are weak and self-important fenas, and the majority of your men are arrogant chauvinists. That is why I rejected the Král once I knew who he was. A nobody Halos for a zápalka?" I shrugged, "I could live with that. One of the first order? Challenging, but I could have probably handled that. The Král? I cried for three days straight when I realized how cruel the fates game would be played."

Yishay's eyes were hard and angry at my words, but I needed to be honest and remind these men this was not something I wanted any more than them. It also didn't mean I would lay down and die for them.

"I would have preferred any other man on this planet be my zápalka than the Král of my enemy, but that is the cards fate dealt me."

Taking a breath, I closed my eyes and softened my voice on the next admission. "I have spent so many nights wishing Yishay was just the average man because once I let him have me, I let him have all of me. None of you will ever know the courage it takes to give your heart to the one person in the world who could destroy you in one word.

"Even if you found your zápalka in a Pâlir, you still wouldn't understand what I sacrificed in loving him. None of you will ever experience the fear of standing in a room of your enemy, pretending to be unaware of their murderous intentions against your own kind because of love. You will never understand the heartache of watching your most beloved brother have his heart shredded, and you being defenseless but to witness and beg his forgiveness."

With my heart falling open in the silence of the room, I lifted my eyes to each of them. "I was sure Yishay would kill me if he ever found out who I was. I was sure you all would support my cold-blooded murder. I was terrified my own family would have me killed for treason when they realized I'd accepted the Král as my zápalka. So, it didn't take much for me to accept that was the case when I was abducted, and my zápalka determined I wasn't worth coming after.

"So, before the next one of you judges my worth on my looks or my gender, I want you to imagine the one person you love most in the world turning on you. I want you to think about every person you've ever cared about treating you like a bargaining chip, disregarding your emotions, and fears. Even then, you would only have an inkling of what it has been like for me these past years, of what it takes for me to stand in this room with my zápalka and admit I still love him, despite how much I hate him."

My eyes rested on Yishay, allowing him to see every bit of truth in my words. The room was deathly silent as I stepped towards him. "The Halos are your people and your problem until peace is found. The Pâlir have already come to the table. Do what you need to, Yishay, to bring your people around because if they turn on you, and if they threaten the life of the future Král within me, the Pâlie will rise like a tidal wave and wipe the Halos from the world."

"The blood is united," Yishay murmured, his eyes dropping to my womb as the recognition finally hit. "The Pâlie will defend their future king."

"I warned you, Yish. It was your choice, as it always has been."

Going to the door, I left the room, shocked silence shaking the Halos and their ideals behind me. It was their move; the final game was about to begin.

28

"ow long?"

Yishay tucked my hair back behind my ear. "A few hours at most."

Rolling off his chest, we both lay looking up at the ceiling, my fingers lightly caressing my abdomen. "I don't want you to go."

"I need to convince my people I haven't betrayed them. Once I get them on our side, as soon as they have accepted our bond, then we can start working towards peace."

"I have to put his life first. Anything that threatens me threatens him. I need to deal with that, no matter what that means for you."

Adjusting to face me, Yishay caressed his hand over my abdomen. "Just try and discuss it with me first. That is all I'm asking."

We spent the early hours of today fighting over the threat I'd made downstairs. Telling your husband his life was unimportant once your child was born never went down well. Saying that to a King...yeah, he wasn't happy. Add wiping out his people if need be to ensure the safety of the future Pâlir King, and that was an argument waiting to happen.

We never really settled the fight. My hormones kicked in halfway through, and we started an angry fuck that involved several walls, possibly needing repair and at least one broken chair. By the time we were both done, we were too exhausted to keep fighting. We curled into bed in each other's arms and decided not to discuss it anymore.

"I told the truth last night. I hate that I still love you after you abandoned me. Casimir and I would never have formed this unnatural bond, had you come for me when you should have. All of this is your fault."

Grunting, Yishay climbed out of bed. "It happened, get over it. I am Král, you carry my child, there is nothing to be done about it." Yishay turned at the bathroom door and glared at me. "I'm sick of being forced to feel how you miss him, so you need to deal with this shit quickly because I'm not going to keep putting up with it."

"If you harm him or get someone else to kill him, I will never forgive you."

"A small price to pay for getting rid of an inconvenience."

I was off the bed in seconds. "You would have let any of your first order tend me in your absence, Yish. I know the tradition, that first-order were rewarded with nights with their Královna. The only man I will let in my bed is my zápalka, either of them, so think very hard about that idea of yours before you carry through. A mother can teach their child to hate someone as much as they do."

Yishay stepped forward threateningly, but I didn't back down. "Be careful, Kotê. I am the ruler. You may carry a title, but you will always only ever be my wife."

"I don't want your crown. I have my own, and it weighs more than enough. I have never cared for your title and position; if anything, it's what I despise about you most."

"Lemuel was right about one thing," Yishay snarled on his way to the shower, "I liked you better when you were a nobody."

The vase from the table in the corner smashed against the bathroom door as he slammed it. Kenan came through the door, looking worried. "What was that?"

Swiping the tears from my eyes, I pulled my robe around me quickly. "Yish threatened Casimir and said some other hurtful things. I'm going to make breakfast."

"You're not going to clean that up?" Kenan looked at the smashed bits of the vase on the ground. "Was that his mother's favorite vase?"

Shrugging, I shouldered past Kenan. Fifteen minutes later, I was sitting at the breakfast table, being watched sympathetically by Omri when Yishay came out of the bathroom upstairs. My name was yelled along with some very impolite terms for my character.

"What did you break?" Omri asked.

"Rosetta's favorite vase."

"Ouch. You know that's a family heirloom, right?"

"He best get used to it. If he threatens what matters to me, I'll break what matters to him."

"You matter to him."

"Not enough. Plus, he already broke me." Rising, I took my bowl back to the sink.

Storming down the steps and into the kitchen, Yishay glared at me as he fixed himself something to eat. Ignoring him, I stamped my way back upstairs and into the shower. I took my time, aware that Yishay would be gone before I finished. Tonight, he was meeting with his people again, answering any questions they might have, and trying to convince them peace and a merge of the bloodlines was the way forward. Dread filling my heart, I hadn't wanted him to go, but Yishay put his people before me, always.

Once I was dressed, I went into my drafts room and started drawing up plans to turn it into a nursery. My job was gone, my career more than likely over, I may as well put my skills to some use. My guard was moving around downstairs, and a game of monopoly was in progress. As I was finishing the layout, heavy footsteps raced up the stairs. Stepping into my office space, Omri placed a finger to his lips. He gestured I move towards him and stand behind the door, then he turned the light off. That's when I realized all the lights in the house were already turned off.

Rushing across the room warily, I slipped in behind the door. "What is going on?"

"The others attacked the meeting," Omri informed quietly. "They are keeping Yish, and his men pinned down, but not going for a kill."

"Distraction while they deal with the problem?"

"I believe so."

We waited quietly. It took a few moments before there a crashing sound, and a grunt echoed from downstairs. Omri stiffened. The sound of a door opening, and then numerous boots rushing across the timber floors. Cursing reached us, along with many other grunts and yells. "There's too many," a voice called, and then another door burst open, and more people were moving into the house.

Boots came running up the stairs. "It's Lemuel. We have to get her out, the guard downstairs is overrun. Where is she?"

Omri positioned himself to look like he was guarding the top of the stairs. "She is hiding. I will call her out once we have a safe path to leave. You check the bedroom balcony; I'll check her studio and see which way looks best."

Boots walked off towards my bedroom as Omri came into the studio and walked to the balcony doors opening them. A bolt struck him in the back of his left chest. Omri jolted, then fell unconscious to the floor. Covering my mouth to prevent from making a sound, I sunk into a crouch. Rushing back down the hall into the studio, Lemuel looked around. "I know you, Omri, you would never expose or abandon your charge."

The crossbow was hanging from Lemuel's hand as he stood over Omri. Anger gripped my insides at his disloyalty, but I had to move, or when Lemuel turned back to the door, he would see me. The balcony doors were open, I could make a run for it, but it was clear land for a hundred meters. Lemuel would be on me before I made the tree line.

Another pair of boots rushed up the stairs, and Lemuel stepped into the wardrobe out of sight. "Omri?" Kenan called from the top of the stairs. Rushing into the room, he spied Omri prone on the floor. Cursing, he pulled the bolt from Omri's chest. "Kat?" Kenan quickly stood searching the room. "Sakra! Please tell me they didn't get her," Kenan mumbled as he stepped towards the wardrobe to look for me.

"No," I called, standing up to warn him. "Lemuel is..."

Kenan turned his head as a bolt impaled his chest. With eyes wide, Kenan gaped at me while his knees buckled. He turned his head back in time to watch Lemuel walk out of the wardrobe and aim his crossbow at me.

Letting the air currents lift me, I transvected quickly across the room, Lemuel hesitating a moment at seeing a female fly. He recovered just as I reached him, and his finger twitched on the trigger. Spinning mid-flight to change his target, I dodged, he followed, and the bolt flew past me and shattered the glass on the open balcony door.

Lemuel tried to follow, but I was smaller and faster and already behind him, landing on his back like a monkey.

"Hovno!" Dropping the bow to the floor, Lemuel tried to stop me grabbing the blade at his waist. "Give it up, Kat." My arm around his throat was restricting his breath, chocking, Lemuel rammed back into the wall behind us. The impact was hard, but that just made me tighten my grip. Lemuel was busy trying to reef my arm free of his neck while stopping me from getting hold of his blade and trying to get it himself, so I used one leg to block his attempt, the position giving me effectively four limbs to work with against him.

Glancing over his shoulder, Lemuel changed direction and rammed back into a door frame. Jolting from that hit that caused the wood behind my spine to splinter, I tightened my grip around his throat, gave up on the dagger, and used my hand and feet to hoist myself up further on his shoulder.

Lemuel roared victory as he grasped his hilt, but it was short-lived. Gouging my fingers into the inside corner of his eye, I pushed in until the first knuckle felt liquid, then I scooped my finger in behind his eyeball and pulled, causing a sickening pop.

Screaming, Lemuel stumbled forward, cursing my very existence as he fell to hands and knees. Jumping from him, I rolled on the floor and collected the crossbow. Checking it was still loaded as Lemuel got back to his feet, I aimed as he turned, eyeball hanging by the nerves and veins from its socket. With his dagger was in hand, Lemuel used his good eye and hearing to locate my heavy breathing.

He rushed me as I fired. The bolt found his heart, but Lemuel didn't drop.

With only a moment to panic, I threw the crossbow aside and moved my hands to a defensive position as his body slammed into mine. My breath rushed out of me, the cold press of steel and blood, hot and gushing across my chest.

$\mathcal{W}$e stared into one another's eyes, mine wide with fear, his unfocused, not here. With both the bolt and the dagger buried in his heart, Lemuel would hold in limbo until they were either removed, and he healed, or his heart was destroyed, and he died.

Bending my knee up, I gritted my teeth and rolled, pushing the lump of traitorous shit from me. Crawling to Kenan, I yanked the bolt from his chest, him having already done the same for Omri.

The fighting was still happening downstairs. Looking to the balcony doors, I considered that I could run, but that wasn't going to solve the immediate problem, and there could be more of them out in the dark. Collecting the crossbow from the floor, I found the rest of my bolts on Lemuel. It was the one Saul took from me when I was captured. Loading it, I walked out to the stairs and witnessed the fighting on the ground floor level. Yishay left me six of the first order. Three of those were unconscious in my studio. Lemuel had been a traitor, but the others were fighting for me.

Lowering myself to the floor, so only my head was peeking through the rails, and to stop my heart being a target, I aimed the crossbow at the three Halos attacking Saul. I knew he was on my side, and I needed as many of them as I could get. Taking them out, one after the other, in a matter of seconds, I turned my attention to the other Halos traitors as Saul looked up at me, his eyes as far open as his mouth.

Within a matter of minutes, the fighting downstairs was nearly nonexistent. There another group still in Yishay's study, but I couldn't see that from here. While Saul and Somie rushed into the office to assist Methuselah in dispatching the last of the traitors, I sat up, pushing back to the far side of the walkway, crossbow still at the ready.

"Close the doors," Saul ordered. "Secure the downstairs area, I'll check upstairs."

"We should secure the perimeter," Methuselah debated.

"We don't have enough men. They could pick us off out there. We stay inside protected. When the Král returns, his men can secure the boundary." Footsteps echoed up the stairs, Saul taking them two at a time. When he spotted me, his face fell. "Are you hurt?"

"Lemuel shot Omri and Kenan," I informed him, my voice surprisingly calm.

Peering into the studio, Saul marched forward, observing the broken glass on the door. Slamming the shutters into place, he closed the balcony door. As Saul came back into the hallway, he looked downstairs. "Pull the shutters into place. It will give us a better defense until the rest of our men are here." Continuing into the bedroom, Saul opened the balcony door and closed the shutters before locking the glass door. When he came back out, Saul helped me stand. "You need to shower, Kat."

When he tried to relieve me of the crossbow, I flinched out of his grasp. "I'm keeping it. It's the only weapon I have against them."

"No offense, Královna, but you and the Král have been fighting, you're emotional, and you've already broken something very dear to him today."

"No offense, Saul, but one of your first order just tried to use this crossbow to put a bolt in my heart. Until this situation is resolved, I'm keeping this within easy reach."

Studying my eyes, Saul bowed his head in acceptance. "I'll check on Omri and Kenan, then report to the Král."

"Are they on their way back yet?"

"The last report said they were still under attack."

Swallowing my fear, I moved into the bedroom and took that suggested shower. Once I was clean, I tried scrubbing Lemuel's blood from my clothes, but I didn't like my chances. With a huff, I picked up the clothes and took them down the laundry. It was close to dawn, Yishay still wasn't back, and we hadn't heard anything further. They were under siege, and we were told to lock up and stay safe.

Placing the crossbow on the bench with the clothes next to it, I collected a bucket from beneath the counter and started filling it. Closing my eyes, I could feel Yishay. He was safe but tired and angry. Sighing, I turned off the water and dumped my clothes in the bucket with the stain remover.

"It's me," Somie reported outside the door. "The intruders failed. Lemuel is upstairs with a bolt and knife in his chest. Kenan and Omri were shot and are both still unconscious. The princess is still very much alive, and the sun is almost up."

At first, I didn't really pay any attention to Somie reporting to who I guessed was Yishay, but then I hesitated at the way he phrased it.

"No, but they are three down now, only two left to guard her. You won't get another chance like this."

Was he stupid enough to conspire while I was in the room next door? Glancing up, I realized the light was off.

"She's upstairs in her room, but Saul has ordered Meth and me to stay on guard down here. If I go up the stairs, it will be instantly suspicious..."

Not waiting to hear any more, I collected the crossbow and opened the laundry door. Glancing up suddenly, Somie's mouth fell open, and his face drained of blood as he realized I'd heard it all. Squeezing the trigger, I moved quickly and caught the phone as he fell to the ground, putting it to my ear.

"...care, just kill the Pâlir already," the familiar female voice demanded as Saul and Meth rushed into the kitchen and stared at the sight before them.

Lifting a brow, I placed the phone on the speaker.

"Somie? Are you hearing me? I said to kill the princess now. If you have to kill the other two to get to her, do it."

Throat convulsing, Saul took the phone from my hand. "Message received, Carlotta," Saul murmured to Abraham's wife.

"Good. Call me back when it's done." She hung up.

Slipping the phone in his pocket, Saul stepped forward and pressed his foot down on the end of the bolt, ensuring it was rooted in the heart. "Put him with Lemuel, Meth. Yishay can cut their hearts out himself."

"Make sure he gets the names of all the other traitors before he does," I grumbled, walking to the laundry door.

"Kat, where are you going?" Saul worried as I opened the door.

"You can't protect me here." Flinging the door open, I stepped out into the morning light.

"Kat, wait!"

Squinting against the light, I dashed for the tree line. None of the Halos knew I could transvect yet, so it was best to keep it secret for now. Once in the trees, I let the air currents pick me up and steal me away.

Leaving a false trail, I was halfway to the Pâlir border when I felt something approaching. Stopping amongst the branches of a tree to focus, I closed my eyes and felt the movement through the trees. It passed me by, despite my heart thudding like a war drum.

Quiet settled on the forest again. Taking a deep breath, I relaxed, opened my eyes, and covered my hammering heart. My brows furrowed, my heart was beating steadily, so why did it feel like it was racing?

The air currents shifted out of nowhere. There was no time to react before a body landed on the branch before me. Lifting the crossbow, I aimed as Casimir dropped the hood of his cloak. Relief flooded me, tears poured down my face in a moment, and suddenly, the night was too much to take.

"Kat," Casimir breathed my name, then I was wrapped in his arms. "Kenan contacted me, told me you fled. I've been tracking you for two hours."

Stopping, I stepped back. "You can go out in daylight? It doesn't affect your vision?"

Casimir sighed. "Your great, great uncle was my great, great grandfather. There are several who have the ability. It is no longer restricted just to the royal bloodline."

"Do my brothers know?"

Casimir cringed. That was no. Taking my hand, Casimir pulled his hood back up. "Let's go. You need to rest."

"Are we going to the compound?"

"No. We're going to my place. It's on Pâlir territory, but close enough to the border that we can meet Yishay quickly."

I didn't argue. Yishay would demand I be returned, but I was going to put my own condition on that this time.

"Kat," Casimir touched my cheek, "are you okay?"

"Yes, I've just made a decision, and my brothers are going to need to hear."

Casimir nodded. "Vladimir will meet us at my place."

Stepping into him, I took Casimir's face in my hands and kissed him. "I've missed you."

"I know. I could feel it. I've missed you too." He kissed me deeply, wrapping me tight within his arms. We spent the better part of five minutes kissing before Casimir pulled back. "When we get to my place, you need to contact Yishay, let him know you are safe."

"I will. I need to tell Yish my demands as well."

30

The itch was getting worse. Having Casimir close and not acting on the need of our bond was skin tearing, literally, I was starting to scratch myself badly. Grabbing my wrist, Casimir gently replaced my hand with his, slipping his hand beneath my top to touch my needy flesh.

"I can't. Not until I know Yish is safe."

Lips pinching my neck, Casimir held me tight. "I know. I'm going to stand here, touch you, and watch that treeline with you until he arrives. I'm just giving your body enough to hold you over."

As his hand groped my breast, I sighed, my head falling back on his shoulder. "He could betray us and bring the first order to kill us."

"You carry his child, Kat. He won't harm you, and he won't kill me while you're present. He knows he would lose you doing that."

"Will the others be ready to go by morning?" Squirming in his grasp, I arched into his hands, trying to distract myself with strategy.

"They will be. Once we have the list, we will make the last of the preparations. I already have one of the daywalkers scouting the address of the Halos you gave me this morning." Casimir's thumb circling my nipple slowly, causing me to pant a little.

"Okay."

When his phone rang, we both jumped, then Casimir handed it to me.

"Hello?"

"I'm at the agreed location," Yishay answered. "Where are you?"

"Did you come alone?"

"If you mean did I come with Kenan and Flick only, yes."

"Kenan knows the way in."

"How?" Yishay asked suspiciously.

"It's where he brought me when he found me after you abandoned me." Hanging up the phone, I handed it back to Casimir and stepped away from him. "How am I going to do this when all I want is to get naked with you two?"

Smirking, Casimir caressed my cheek. "You'll manage."

Casimir was over the moon with my idea, and my brothers agreed it was an excellent solution to our unique problem, but all of us accepted Yishay was going to have a fit. Jealousy would be the most significant issue now. It wasn't just a man's ego I was dealing with, but a kings.

Taking my hand, Casimir gave it a squeeze. "Let's go downstairs. They'll be here in a few minutes."

After initially going to Casimir's house past Jasper to see my brothers, we'd come to the cabin I'd spent months hiding in to meet with Yishay. He wouldn't come into Pâlir territory, and this wasn't a conversation for the public domain. The cabin was determined to be the best option. The idea was that if it went wrong, only Casimir would be lost. Of course, while Yishay thought he was coming in three-strong to only Casimir, we knew he was wrong.

"I'm terrified."

"He won't harm you, Kat."

"It's not me I'm worried about."

Stopping on the bottom step, Casimir turned to face me. "Pawns and kings, Kat. Your duty is to him; my duty is to you."

Taking his face in my hands, I pressed our foreheads together. "You are not a pawn to me. You are my rook."

"A queen and a rook together outrank any bishop or knight." Grin dimming, Casimir stepped away. "But, not the King. Let's put the kettle on."

In the kitchen, I set out cups, making the brews according to how I knew they all liked their tea or coffee. While the kettle boiled, I went to the window and watched the yard. The snow was still heavy on the ground. "If this goes bad, you'll never be able to come here again."

"This is Kenan's retreat. You know where to find me if he rejects the idea. We can meet at my place."

As optimistic as Casimir was, I knew, that if Yishay rejected my idea, I'd have to give Casimir up for good. He knew it too, I could see it in his eyes, but it was sweet that he tried to distract me with the possibility of an affair.

As the kettle whistled, Yishay and Kenan floated out of the trees. Flick would be watching for a trap. Relief flooded my insides, and before I knew what I was doing, I threw the door open and rushed outside, throwing myself into Yishay's arms.

Wrapping me in his warmth, Yishay put his face into my hair. "Kenan, check out inside." Clinging to him, purely enjoying the sound of his heart next to mine, I sobbed a little trying to hold back the tears. "Kôte!" Yishay murmured, his hand fisting in the back of my hair.

"I didn't want to leave, but I couldn't take anymore, not knowing who to trust. I needed to feel safe."

"I know, Kat," Yishay soothed, an undercurrent of anger reverberating in the depth of his tenor. "I felt your anxiety, your fear, your relief when you made it to safety. I know why you left, but you can never do that again."

Swallowing, I peered up to meet his eyes. Yishay stroked my cheek lovingly, but I could see his brain working behind his concern. He was a king, and after last night, something would need to happen.

Inhaling deeply, I took Yishay's hand and urged him to follow me inside. "Come inside. I need to know where you are, to see if peace is still on the cards."

Tensing beside me, Yishay held me above the snow and transvected to the kitchen door, placing me on the top step and looking around.

"All clear, Yish," Kenan called.

Turning, Yishay whistled. Flick descended from above, landing on the back step as Yishay stepped inside where Kenan was pouring the hot water into everyone's cups. Yishay and Casimir squared off. They were of a height, but Halos were built sturdy, the Pâlie was lean and fast.

"Casimir. A lifetime of hearing your name whispered in terror and awe, I expected you to be more."

The thinly veiled insult made Casimir smirk. "Looking less is why Halos have always thought themselves more, right up until I was ripping their hearts from their chests."

Nodding, Yishay, took a chair at the table. We all followed suit, Yishay ensuring I sat by him. "Last night, the others attacked a general meeting with my people," Yishay explained. "I talked of peace, but they brought war. They hurt innocents and did nothing to help their cause. Of course, we know that attack was merely to distract and prevent us from reaching Kat while they went after her. As soon as daylight came, they retreated, possibly hoping their comrades had dealt with the perceived problem."

"When they find out I am still alive?"

Yishay's fists clenched on the table. "They will try it again."

"Do you want peace, Král?" Casimir asked straight out.

"I do."

"Do you love my princess? Will you fight for her, protect her, and fight for this peace?"

Yishay gritted his teeth. "You question my commitment to my zápalka?"

"You abandoned her once..."

"You took her from me!" Yelling, Yishay stood up. "I have a duty to my people, and I have no heir. If it had been a trap, I would have died and left no král to rule. The Halos hierarchy would never have recognized the Pâlir princess. They would have gone to war with each other to claim the throne and killed innocents in the process. I had to make a choice, possibly the hardest I've ever made in my life, and I chose to believe you would not harm an innocent woman then to sacrifice my people to the warmongering aristocracy."

Blinking, I reached out and wrapped my hand around his white-knuckled fist. Yishay flinched, but then his hand slowly opened and encased mine in his.

"I sacrificed the woman I love for my people because you took her from me. She carries my son; I won't lose her again," Yishay seethed.

"The aristocracy, the others," Casimir replied neutrally, "they were already planning to kill Kat before I took her."

Silence swept through the room in a breath as Casimir placed some folded papers on the table. "The night our prince came to talk peace, he was bringing you these communications we intercepted. We didn't know you were married. We only knew they were planning to kill a woman they knew would incite you to war. When Vladimir saw our princess at your house, he realized two things. His sister was a traitor, and that is who they planned to kill. He instantly ordered me to protect her and use her to draw you out to discuss peace."

"Why did they think Kat was a traitor?" Flick asked. "Your people thought we kidnapped her years ago."

Nodding once, Casimir flicked his eyes to me. "We thought you kidnapped her, and that somewhere along the line, you seduced her. I knew Kat better than that, so I took her to safety and heard her out. I already knew Kat was my zápalka, so to hear her recognize another as hers hurt."

"So, you renewed your bond and tried to steal her from me?" Yishay accused, reading the communications Casimir had tabled.

"I refreshed our bond to keep her safe. I didn't realize your bond was fresh. But, yes, I hoped she would realize I was her true zápalka, and whatever she had with you was not real." Sitting back, Casimir wrapped his legs under the table around my ankles, so we were physically connected. "I was wrong. Kat is equally our zápalka, but as you are King, and I am merely a soldier, I must accede to the better man."

"We will come back to this," I interrupted the intense stare between my men. "What will you do now? The others have made their intentions clear, so what will you do to protect me?"

Exhaling, Yishay took his seat beside me. "If I turn on my people, on the aristocracy, they will turn on me. As we have already discovered, they have people even in my first order who could use their proximity to me to assassinate me."

"Did you bring the list of names?"

Yishay took a sheet of paper from his pocket. "I need to know what you plan?"

Putting his hand out for the piece of paper, Casimir lifted a brow at the King. "A counter-attack. The others attacked the Pâlir princess, they struck at our Královna. You may be willing to let that go, but we will not."

"War will not give us the peace we seek."

Taking the sheet of names and addresses, Casimir snapped a photo with his phone before sending it to his men. "No, but a few quiet assassinations can definitely lend a hand."

"The others will demand I seek revenge."

Inhaling, I cleared my throat. "Which brings us to the rest of the condition of my return. I am the Pâlir princess, I am on enemy territory, and guarded by men of whom I can trust only a few. I have decided to create my own first order from a mixture of Pâlir and Halos to protect me, and Casimir is going to be my first guard."

Flick blinked, Kenan held his breath, but Yishay glared. Taking my hand, Yishay near crushed mine in his vice grip. "Can everyone excuse us for a moment?"

"They stay. This involves them. It is why I ensured Flick came with you. He is your first guard, so Casimir will report to him, but otherwise, the rest of my first order will report to Cas."

"This will make things worse, Kat. Your Pâlie will need to move within our territory, and I am not even going to ask where you expect Casimir to sleep."

"It would be a good start to showing you mean peace. Peace means the territories no longer need to exist, and having my guard be the first to live here makes sense."

"Everyone will see it for what it is, Kat," Yishay argued. "Your moving your lover in with us."

"So, what? Everyone knows already. What they also know is that Casimir is the best warrior from the Pâlie guard. Everyone is scared of him, and rightfully so. Who better to protect your wife and son, Yish, than a good warrior with a personal interest in keeping me alive?" The only sound in the room was my angered inhalation.

"What she says makes sense, Yish," Flick broke the silence.

"Don't start," Yishay warned.

"If he wasn't her zápalka, would you see the sense of it?"

"But he is!"

"Take your ego out of the equation," I challenged. "I love you equally, but what I need is people around me I don't fear."

"You fear me!"

"Can you blame me?"

Meeting my eyes, anger, and hurt flashing in his sapphire gaze, Yishay turned and walked away from the table, looking out the window as he processed my demand.

Tapping his phone in his hand, Casimir stood. "I'm going to go upstairs and speak to my prince."

Flick stood too. "Kenan and I will run a sweep around the perimeter again."

They left, leaving me waiting at the table for Yishay to demand I let Casimir go.

"I do not trust his intentions," Yishay finally explained.

"Do you trust me?"

Turning his head slowly, Yishay appraised me angrily.

Let down by that one look, I exhaled and averted my eyes. "I see."

"How do I know this is not a ploy? You bring him in, then once my son is born, kill me in my sleep and crown him as the King?" His voice was low, calm, too calm.

"Because the people would never allow that. Because the crown is something, Casimir does not seek. He only wants me, and if he has to share me to have me, he is willing to do that."

"You do not love us equally, Kôte. You hate me as much as you love me."

"He abandoned me too! When our prince ordered him to give me up, Casimir left me here, stranded. I was heartbroken and resented him for it."

"You forgave him, but you haven't forgiven me."

"I haven't forgiven a god damned thing! Trust me, he suffered long and hard for not fighting for me. He felt me stab that glass into my heart as much as you did. None of us remain unmarred by what has happened."

Huffing, Yishay shoved his hands in his pockets. Rising out of my seat, I moved to him, wrapping my arms around him to ease our need for physical contact.

"I will forgive you, Yish, but I know now that I need him too."

Lowering his head, Yishay buried his face in my hair as he held me tight. "I can't do this, Kat. The idea of him touching you, it drives me mad."

Inhaling, trembling at what came next, I closed my eyes and took his hand. "Come with me."

Leading Yishay upstairs, I took him into my bedroom. In the lounge, Casimir watched us walk past and followed when I gestured he join us. Yishay narrowed his eyes when all three of us were in the room, and I shut the door. Turning to face them, I pulled my jumper over my head. Both men stood there, watching as I removed all my clothing to stand naked before them. Their need to touch me, to take me, was a lick of flame across my skin, causing me to shiver with mixed excitement and anxiety. Going to Yishay first, I placed my hand on his chest, covering his heart, then I reached out to Casimir and put my hand on his.

"You are both a part of my soul. Separate halves, with only a sliver of me to join you both. You are both good, honorable men, and you both love me. The only way we can move forward and be happy is if you learn to love me for who I am and who we all are to each other."

"Kat, what you are asking..." Yishay warned.

"Is nothing new," I countered.

"It is for longterm."

"I am not saying it will always be three. Maybe it will just be this time, and after this, you are my primary, and Cas has me when you are not home. All I am saying is that if we don't try this, losing one of you will kill me inside."

Glancing at Casimir, Yishay appeared wary and unconvinced.

Casimir lifted his shirt over his head. "She's right, Yishay. If we see each other with her, see that she reacts to each of us the same, perhaps, our bond will allow us to find acceptance with each other."

Gazing back to me, Yishay had his arm already wrapped around my backside possessively. "We are connected through her; I can feel that. I can sense your need for her equalling mine."

"Your fear of losing her is a ball of worms in my gut. It is no different from mine. I also sense your child inside her." Wrapping his arm around me from behind, Casimir rested the palm of his hand gently over my womb. "My future king grows in her, and I will protect them both, and will serve all three of you loyally."

"As long as I share her?" Yishay challenged.

"Loyalty is always to one, for the benefit of others."

Gazing down at me, Yishay held his focus steady, his mind made up. Shaking his head, he stepped away from us, breaking my heart apart.

31

"*You* have to choose, Kat."

As soon as Yishay said those words, Casimir stepped away from me. "No, she doesn't." The pain of giving me up again ripping down our bond like every other time before. Collecting his shirt from the floor, Casimir glared at Yishay. "I am not going to play tug-a-war with her heart and emotions. You are the Král, there is no choice."

My world was bottoming out all over again, making me want to scream and throw myself at Casimir, begging him not to go. The problem was, I wanted to do the same with Yishay, and that made me angry. Raging inside, I grieved and thrashed at being pulled apart inside my soul.

Pulling his shirt over his head, Casimir stepped towards me carefully, like I was a horse that would spook. "You tried, Kat. I will always love you, but you know what happens now."

Cuddled over on myself, I struggled not to lose control and rip the world apart in my pain. Wrapping me in his arms, Casimir kissed me, slowly, allowing the hurt to constrict the beating of our hearts. Casimir and I both choked on the misery that was us. Breaking away panting with a groan of pain, Casimir set his forehead against mine. "I will still do what we agreed to keep you safe." Stepping away, Casimir turned for the door.

"You would give her up? That easily?"

Barely staying upright, I felt like I was being torn in two, and it was killing me.

Focusing on Yishay with hatred in his eyes, Casimir gritted his teeth. "Give her up? Never. I have loved her all my life, and I will love her for the rest of it. Standing here demanding she choose between us when you are Král, and the father of her unborn child is not only cruel to her, it's insanity, and I am not prone to fits of anger or insanity. That is a Halos trait." Opening the door, Casimir left.

Trembling, I knew my legs wouldn't hold me for much longer. Staring at the door confused, Yishay rubbed his chest absently, feeling our pain but not acknowledging it. After a moment, Yishay collected my clothes from the floor and carried them to me. "Get dressed, Kôte. I'll take you home."

Glaring at the bundle of clothing in his arms, I couldn't lift my arms to take it. Stepping backward once, I let my knees buckle under the weight of my loss. Outside, Casimir was soaring through the trees, rage, and loss buoying him above the snow, speeding him away from me before he let his selfishness or my need for him change his mind.

At that moment, I made a choice too. Keeping my face tucked to my chest, arms holding me together, I closed my eyes. "Get out."

"Pardon me?"

"You made your choice. Now, get out."

"You want me to leave? Are you choosing him?"

"Did you not hear him? There is no choice to make. Not between the two of you."

Placing my clothes on the bed beside me, Yishay dropped into a squat to assess me. "Kat, I need to take you home to keep you and my child safe."

Blinking away my tears, I lifted my face enough to meet his gaze, the pain inside tearing me between grief and rage, so chaotic it would be homicidal. "It is unfair, Yishay, for Cas and I to always lose every-thing and for you to lose nothing just because you were born with a crown on your head."

"You were born with that mantle too, Katiana," Yishay snapped.

"And I have sacrificed continuously for that burden. I lost my family and home at age thirteen because of it, so that I could be *'protected.'* My choice of being returned to you was decided by my crown. I get told what to do and am expected to go along with it."

Huffing, Yishay scowled. "No one is taking your free will, Kat. I am your husband, and you carry my child. All I've asked is that you choose between him and me, and you are acting as if I killed him. He walked away, Kat, not me."

Shaking my head, I gritted my teeth as burning hate poured acid into my stomach. "He was ordered the same as I, Yish. Neither of us has a choice. It's always been your choice, and you wouldn't choose me because of jealousy. You decided to be selfish when I offered you the best compromise I could find. You caused *'this.'*" Clenching my fist, I thumped it against my aching heart. "So, get out."

Flinching away from my aggression, Yishay stood to his full height, only a flicker of emotion swimming in the deep blue sea of his eyes. "Let me get this straight. You are leaving me because I asked you to choose your husband and father of your child over the other half of your soul? What about my half, Kat? We can move past this and be happy."

Glaring up at him, I shook my head. How could we be happy when I would always long for a part of me that he forced me to give up? "You told me to choose either. I've chosen neither." Dropping my gaze to my flat stomach, I cupped my womb in my hand. "At least, for tonight." Standing up, I started to dress. My body craved Yishay's affection, the reassurance that he was near. My heart hated him. "Go home, Yish. Go and deal with your warmongering subjects. I want peace while I can have it."

"You want me to leave you here, alone, unprotected?" Yishay pleaded with me to see reason.

"You did that six months ago. I should never have let you get me back."

The moment Casimir didn't come back, I should have run for the free territory and gone far away, where neither of them could feel me anymore and tried to start anew.

Clenching his jaw as my emotions, my grief, and anger froze over to coldness, Yishay gritted his teeth and backed toward the door, fists tight in his seething rage. "I will get my people under control, and then we will have this conversation again, Katiana. Maybe the time alone will help you remember that I was enough once."

"You were never enough; I just made do with what I had." Dressed, I turned my back on him and went to look out the window. Snow fell, Flick and Kenan standing guard in the yeard.

"You don't mean that, Kat. You're emotional and tired, and..." tilting his head, Yishay narrowed his eyes, "hungry."

At the mention of hunger, my stomach rumbled. Rubbing my hand across the flatness, I sobbed, keeping my back to him.

"You starved yourself waiting for me," Yishay crept closer again. "Let me sate you and feed our child before I go."

Shaking my head, I pressed my lips tight over the craving for all he was offering, and the hatred growing the further Casimir went. Despair goaded me. "Get out before I put a bolt in you."

"Our child needs sustenance."

"I need you to leave now!"

Yishay exhaled heavily. "I will leave Kenan to guard you."

Rage breaching the surface, I turned to glare at my husband. "You've got to be kidding me. He fucked me too, remember. He also held me down and drank from me against my will, but you'll let him guard me. You'd let him screw me too, wouldn't you? He's fine because he's a Halos. Anyone is fine but one of my kind, right? You are so hypocritical it isn't funny. Fine, leave Kenan here. He can fuck me and feed me instead of my actual Zápalka."

"I offered!"

"You offer pain, regret, and hate. You abandoned me and expect me to be okay with it, and to trust you again." Frustration pierced my voice until I was screaming at him. Sobbing, I took a breath and met his eyes. "I have tried to forgive you and tried to bridge the chasm you created between us. I have nothing more to offer."

"I created? I didn't bond with another, Kat."

"You caused this when you killed my brother when he came to you under the banner of peace! You brought Casimir back into my life. You abandoned me to him. I tried to resist him, but how could I resist half of my soul, when the other half turned on me? How, Yishay? How was I to resist what the gods made when you turned from me?"

Gritting his teeth and fists clenched tight, Yishay stormed out of the room, every one of his footsteps impacting as if they landed on my back. Curling over in a ball, I tried to protect myself from the hurt. My insides were ripped apart to the point I expected to start coughing up blood any second from the pain.

Rubbing my abdomen as the cramping reached it, I sobbed and struggled to breathe. Keening in pain, I knew I needed to calm down, or the prince of peace inside me would be lost. Sucking in a deep breath, I sobbed on the exhale. Another inhale, I mewled with pain. Again, I sucked in a breath and forced myself to shut it out, to shut them out.

"Kat?" Kenan stepped into the room.

"Please, just leave me be."

"I did. It's been three hours since Yishay left. I've cooked dinner, and Omri called. He said he needs to talk to you urgently. He said it's about the tribond."

Inhaling, I focused my mind and forced myself to get control. "I'll shower and come downstairs. Send Omri directions on how to get here." As Kenan turned to go, my stomach growled. "Wait," I whimpered. Worry etching his face, Kenan observed me. I pounced. My attack so quick Kenan's eyes hadn't even registered I'd moved before I wrapped my body around him, restraining his arms, and my mouth latched onto his neck.

My baby was hungry. Nothing mattered except my child's survival. He would bring our people together, and none of this dark or light, good and evil, Halos and Pálir nonsense would exist anymore. My son would unite a species torn apart by jealousy. His life was all that mattered to me now.

If only he could save me.

32

"*A*re you sure?" I whispered, tears running down my cheeks.

"Are you understanding it any differently?" Omri sympathized.

"Surely, this can't be the only outcome?" Beyond begging, I didn't want this to be true, but my hunger upstairs told me it was.

Bowing his head, Omri sighed. "I'm sorry, Kat. I have done nothing but search the archives for more information. I've gone back a thousand years and found multiple tribond cases. They all had the same outcome."

Placing my face in my hands, I cried. "All of this. Why? Why would the gods put me through all of this?"

"Not all hope is lost, Kat."

"I asked Yishay to allow Casimir to come home with me. He refused. Casimir has left."

Tapping his fingers on the table, Omri considered the polished timber. "If I showed him this, it could change his mind."

"If it doesn't, and this happens, you will have handed him my death sentence."

"Actually, it would be his too because it will only come to pass if he denies your third."

"Which is why none can know, Omri. The Král must be above suspicion." Standing up, I walked to the kitchen window glaring out at the trees. "One thing at a time. The war needs to be dealt with first. If Yishay is going to condemn me out of jealousy, then I can't do anything about it." Taking a deep breath, I made up my mind. "Omri, you will be the captain of my guard. I need you to protect me until my child is born."

"Princess, there are others."

"None that I trust."

"Where is Kenan? I was told he was left to guard you."

Turning just my upper body to meet his eyes, I showed him my hate for what Yishay had made me.

Lowering his gaze, Omri turned his head. "I see. I am too late." Considering the changing light outside, Omri pushed the chair under the table. "I should go. I will return these documents to the archive and secure them away. You understand, if the Král enquires, I must reveal the truth."

"I understand. If he does, could you let me know?"

Bobbing his head, Omri gathered together his documents. Locking the door after he left, I watched the sunrise. Moving upstairs, I knelt by Kenan's body. He was slowly healing, but I'd drained him of every drop of blood. He would be another day yet before he could regain consciousness. Kissing his pale lips, I wiped the tear that escaped and splotched onto his cheek away. "I'm sorry, Kenan."

Changing, I moved out into the light, using the trees to cover my transvecting south. Making my way toward the house I knew was first, I stopped in the tree line out of sight. Casimir approached; the other day walkers with him. When I turned to face Casimir, he hesitated in his step towards me. He studied me. "You can't, Kat. You carry his child. You must choose him."

"I will, after today. But this is my war. They attacked and tried to kill me. I'm ending this personally, and all of you are my soldiers today."

All of the daywalkers went to a knee and thumped their chests as Casimir turned to address them. "For the Princess and the life of our future Král, you will strike in groups of five. No one in the houses survives. Bleed them and burn their hearts. Enrie, you are a group leader, pick your four. You will take the first five addresses on the list."

While Casimir continued giving direction, I walked away to look at the house that held my rage. When everything was set, Casimir set everyone the time for the first attack. The other groups left, and I turned to assess the three left with us. They were all female.

"You look surprised to see female warriors, Princess."

"No, Kolette, I am just surprised to see you here."

"You remember me?" She grinned.

"Of course. I remember all of you."

The three girls I'd trained and played with as a child, were now grown women. All of them stepped forward, and we embraced, greeting each other anew and learning about their lives.

"It's time," Casimir interrupted our catch up. "The first directive is to protect the Princess. Everyone else dies."

"We heard you the first time, Cas," Kolette sassed. "Let's have a party."

Smiling at the wicked grin on my friend's faces, Casimir gave a signal, and all three took to the air for the house. "Ready, Princess?"

"Gods, yes!" Meeting his grin, I took his offered hand. Transvecting quickly, I followed the girls through the broken back door. The screaming had already started.

A man rushed up from the basement. Jumping him, Casimir wrestled him to the ground. Ignoring the others, I made my way to the bedroom that contained my enemy. Abraham's wife was the most vocal person wanting to see me exterminated. From the other side of the door, I could hear her heart pounding as she listened, panicking as her guards and son were slaughtered. Grinning, I lifted my leg and kicked the door hard.

Falling back under the weight of the door, Carlotta scrambled to get out from beneath it. "How are you in daylight?"

"It was right in front of you all these years, and not one of you ignorant Halos ever put it together. The reason the Král was jealous of his brother, my great, great, great grandfather, why he divided a race and painted the Pâlir as evil creatures."

"No, it can't be true," Carlotta crawled back on her hands. Weak and feeble as the Halos made their women, she'd relied on her men to protect her.

"It is true."

"No, you are just bloodthirsty demons!"

"Ha! I never craved blood until your Král ripped my soul in two. I have never been so hungry since he refused to let me be whole." With a leg either side of her, I dropped, thrusting my blade under her ribs at the same time. "I have sacrificed so much. Now, I yearn and starve because of his inability to accept a Pâlir mate." Lowering my face to her neck as she gurgled in death, I caressed her throat with my nose. "I'm so ravenous, Carlotta. I want to bleed the world dry, and it's all his fault."

Sinking my teeth into her neck, I succumbed to the hunger that was driving me, ruling me, demanding me to feed my child. Hating every second of it, every drop of her blood, I cursed Yishay's love in my head. Despite being full to bursting, I couldn't stop drinking. I wasn't dark, I wasn't evil, I walked in the sunlight. I was light, pure and intense. It should shine out of me and burn this bitch to ashes.

Yes, that's what needed to happen. That could stop me from drinking. If Carlotta was ashes, there would be no blood for me to crave. Heat infused my fangs, warming me, filling me with light, and I felt good all of a sudden. All around me was intense heat, and my hunger subsided.

Released from my insatiable need, I stood up and stepped back. Carlotta fitted on the floor, light shining out of the bite on her neck. Bewildered, I watched as that flash spread down her throat, running through her veins, filling her body with a trail of light.

Out of nowhere, Carlotta combusted into pure white flames. The heat and light were so intense, I had to close my eyes and stumble back several steps. A flash grenade and then, nothing. The room returned to darkness, and fine ash floated in the air.

"What the...?"

Standing behind me, Casimir watched on in disbelief. Then his eyes came to me, dilated and full. "Can your brothers do that?"

"I don't know. I didn't know I could do that."

When my stomach gurgled, I covered it and fell back a step. "What's happening to me?"

Taking me in his arms, Casimir held me to him. Relaxing, my hunger momentarily abated. "You have always been special, Kat. Maybe it wasn't the ability to walk in daylight that set your ancestor apart. Maybe it was this power. The ability to destroy his enemies in a flash of light."

"I've become a Ravenor, Cas. It's the curse of the tribond. Without both my mates, I can't control the hunger." Sobbing into his shoulder, I clung to this momentary relief for dear life. If what Omri showed me was right, it was only going to get worse as the fetus grew. Bursting into tears, I held tight to him. "I drained Kenan. This is the first moment of peace I've had since you left."

Tensing, Casimir pulled back and met my eyes, using his thumbs to wipe away my tears. "You will do what you need to survive, Kat. I will teach you what you need, and once that child is out of you, the hunger will ease, and you can find peace."

Without waiting, Casimir took my hand and pulled me back out into the lounge room. The Halos he'd taken down still lie on the floor, a bolt in his heart immobilizing him. "Do it again. Use your inner light to burn him up." Letting go of my hand, Casimir stepped back. "Do it now, Kat. Reduce your enemy to Ash."

Frowning, I was horrified and curious. Kneeling by the man, I turned his neck. Casimir's proximity seemed to have dampened the hunger somewhat, but not entirely. Tentatively, I sank my fangs into his neck, his blood was stagnant from death, and I wanted it over with, wanted him to burn, for my light to vaporize him.

Heat filled my fangs, and again, light and warmth surrounded me. Pulling back, I stood and watched my daylight fill his veins as I backed well away. As the flash grenade ignited, Casimir and I turned away. Afterwards, we stood quietly enthralled as the faint soot floated to the floor.

"There will be no proof of a Ravenor, and there will be no proof of what occurred this day." Taking my hand, Casimir dragged me from room to room, demanding I do it again and again. Swearing the other three to silence, they all watched me kneel by the young man, Abraham's son. He was my age, and I hated that his mother's hate destroyed his life, but I had no doubt he would have hated me the same. He would be my seventh destruction.

Growing tired, I just wanted it over with. Placing my hand on his chest, I started to lower my face. Thinking of the light and heat already, my hand heated before my teeth touched his neck, and that same glow of daylight passed from me to the man.

Standing, I backed away, watching the light radiate faster than before. Not even three steps away, I had to shield myself when he exploded like a solar flare. All of us stood quiet, then I turned to look at the others. "Does this seem right to any of you?"

"It is magnificent, is what it is," Kolette breathed. "If you can do it with touch, you could take out your enemy without a weapon, or having to drink from them. You truly are our Královna."

"Yes, she is," Casimir agreed. "Let's get to the next house and practice some more. "Halidie, grab a vacuum and remove all evidence of the bodies, then meet us at the next location. This is going to be the cleanest war in history." Taking my hand, Casimir led the way to our next enemy. "I want you to walk in, focusing on burning them up. Try to do it without making contact."

Burning them without touching them wasn't possible, but as soon as I did make contact, I could infect them with my fire. Sending word to the others to cease their attacks, and only subdue the enemy, Casimir took me to each and every house on Yishay's list, and I practised my new ability until I could use it without really thinking about it. The new process was for the others to restrain, and me to burn.

Three houses in, we didn't even need to spill a drop of blood to destroy our enemy. The light walkers subdued, I brushed my hand over our enemy's necks, then someone got to vacuum while the rest of us moved on to the next residence. The power relieved the hunger, or maybe it was the excitement or the proximity to Casimir. Whatever did it, I loved it.

Becoming a ravenor, a creature always starving for blood that it went insane and killed innocents, was not on my life-goals list. Humans and Halos alike couldn't be safe around a ravenor. I just had to make it through the pregnancy.

Once the people had their Král and peace was won, I could find calm. Even if it meant having Omri put a bolt through my own heart. Whatever was needed to protect my people and my son from a ravenor, I would do it. Even if it meant dying myself.

33

The cabin was quiet as we landed by the back door. Holding me against him, Casimir addressed the women. "Kolette, check inside. Halidie and Dara, keep watch on the boundary."

My eyes lifted to the sky. There were a few hours left of sunlight, but rain clouds had blotted out the sun. "Will you stay until sunset?"

"No. I will see you safe, and then I need to leave, Kat. I can't stand feeling you and not having you. I don't want to be subjected to his having you and my never being allowed."

It hurt. "Cas, the further you go."

"You have daylight as your shield, and enough enemies left to keep you fed until the child is born."

Closing my eyes, the thought disgusted me. The first drops of rain started to fall. "I don't want this. I don't want to say goodbye to you. I don't want to become...that." Wiping the cold drops of rain from my forehead, I met his eyes, resignation dampening the ethereal blue light that generally shined in them. "At least my heart will be frozen, and I won't feel anymore." It was the only positive outcome.

Exhaling, Casimir stepped into me suddenly, capturing my face. Farewelling me passionately, our souls and hands clinging to one another as his tongue delved into my mouth and told me wordlessly all the ways he would miss me. Growling angrily, Casimir pulled back from me and lifted into the air. "Don't you ever forget how you feel for me, Kat. Don't you dare."

While the first tears trickled down my face disguised as rain, Casimir vanished into the trees. Thunder clapped, scaring me enough to make me jump.

"You're getting wet, Princess."

Speaking over my shoulder, I kept my eyes on the trees. "Am I?"

Coming out the back door to stand beside me, Kolette stared out at the trees. "The Halos upstairs, are you going to kill him?"

Cringing, I shook my head. "No, why?" I couldn't even contemplate killing Kenan.

"I touched him to see if he was alive. He is my zápalka."

The revelation made me instantly jealous. Kolette wouldn't be made to choose between two. Her craving for both her zápalka wouldn't turn her into a crazed monster without reason. "His name is Kenan. He is like a brother to the Král, a member of the first order, and a halfbreed."

"Can I stay until he wakes? I'd like to talk to him."

"Please do." Stepping off the back stairs into the slush of snow and rain, I walked towards the trees. "Give him my apologies."

"Where are you going?" Kolette enquired worriedly.

"Home. My son needs his father."

Lifting into the air, I rode the currents home. I'd done what I could to protect myself. Now, my life, the life of my son, was in Yishay's hands.

Dropping to the ground a kilometer from the house, I walked through the forest slowly. Exhausted, the further south I came, the hungrier I became. Being with Casimir eased the hunger, but it didn't get rid of it. I could only hope that Yishay's presence would do the same.

Stopping by the river, I looked up to the sky. Sitting on a boulder, I watched the water flow over the rocky bed of the river. The sun disappeared, and still, I stayed by the river, getting very cold, but I stayed there.

"Are you deciding if you will come in, or trying to kill yourself through exposure?" Materializing from the shadows, Yishay approached with casual steps.

"We can't kill ourselves by exposure."

"The first answer it is." Taking the boulder next to me, Yishay sighed. "We will work through this, Kat. We will be happy again."

"I doubt it. I'm not here for us. I would never have come back if it was just about us. I'm here for our son."

Taking a deep breath, Yishay gritted his teeth. "I see."

"It's worse, isn't it?"

"What is?"

"It was one thing to lose me to the enemy, to let them kill me for you. But, it's harder to lose me and still have to share a room with me. To know that everything that has happened, you could have prevented."

Yishay's hands gripped his jeans until his knuckles were white.

Standing, I started walking towards the house. "Your son needs feeding."

Standing sentry, Saul, and Yoash would have heard every word. They both bowed their heads and let me pass. As I took the first step onto the wrap around porch, Kenan landed a few meters back. His eyes were hard as they met mine, but when I gazed back with no regret, he swallowed and bowed his head. When Kolette landed beside him, she went to a knee.

"Who is this?" Yishay asked unhappily as he approached Kenan.

"This is Kolette, the first Pálir member of my first order," I answered before Kenan could. "She is also Kenan's zápalka."

When Kenan put out his hand, and Kolette stood straight taking it, Yishay hesitated. "Congratulations to both of you. Why don't you go get settled in at Kenan's, and we can discuss your role in the first order before dawn, Kolette."

Kolette bowed her head. "As the Král wishes."

Not bothering to watch them leave, I walked inside, while Yishay stopped to talk to his first order. With no interest in listening, I headed upstairs. My concern was sex, blood, and sleep, with a shower somewhere in between.

Since Yishay didn't follow me immediately, the shower became the priority. When Yishay finally joined me, I had just finished washing my hair. His naked body pressing against the back of mine was both painful and a welcome relief.

Holding me tight, Yishay kissed the top of my head. "When we married, my greatest fear was that you would learn the truth about what I was and hate me. I held off binding with you and telling you about the Halos because I feared to gaze in your eyes and see that you hate me. I love you so much, Kat, it kills me to see you look at me and know you despise me."

Staying mute, I sobbed as silently as possible. When Yishay lifted his arm in front of me, I licked across the crease of his elbow once. Sinking my teeth, my hunger overwhelmed me.

Hissing, Yishay moved our bodies, so he could press into me. Moaning, I fed. Shifting my hair from my neck, Yishay kissed me once over my pulse, then his fangs were in me, and I was coming hard, the orgasm forcing me to stop feeding to cry out my pleasure.

Holding me to him after we finished, Yishay kissed over my shoulder. Shifting, so my body ejected him, I pulled away despite the comfort his embrace offered because in that comfort was pain and distrust, and a loss he could have saved me from. "I'm exhausted. I'm going to bed."

"When did you last sleep, Kat?"

"It's been a few days since I've had any proper rest."

"When did you last eat?" Frowning, Yishay assessed me as we dried and dressed.

"When I was here. I can't remember."

"That can't be good for the baby."

"Your son is bloodthirsty. He hasn't given me one craving for food since he was conceived. All he wants is blood."

Studying me, worry in his eyes. Yishay licked his lips. "I can get Yoash to bring you something to eat."

Huffing, I slipped into bed. "I just want to sleep. Food can wait until tomorrow."

Though his eyes conveyed his dislike of my refusing to eat, Yishay didn't argue. He stayed until I fell asleep and was gone when I awoke several hours later.

Yawning, I made my way downstairs and fixed myself some breakfast. Sitting down, I lifted the spoon, ready to eat, but the moment I opened my lips to put the food in my mouth, I gagged and couldn't swallow. My stomach churned, and the unquenchable thirst rose like an angry beast within me.

"Princess?" Omri stood watching me concerned.

Shoving the bowl of cereal away, I shook my head. "I can't ingest food. I'm so thirsty."

His brows bunching, Omri walked over to me and offered me his elbow. Blinking up, I met his eyes through my tears. "I can stop you, Princess. Let's take the edge off for now and see if we can get some normal food into you."

"If I can't?"

Omri swallowed. "There is a building, a prison, where only the vilest creatures are kept. It's how the single Halos feed."

"I hate this," I bawled as I took his arm and buried my teeth in the crook of his elbow.

"I know, Princess. It should never be like this."

After a quick feed, Omri made me more breakfast. This time I managed two mouthfuls before my stomach revolted. Omri lowered his head in acceptance. "We have to find a way for you to pretend you are eating. Everyone knows the first sign is to stop eating human food and only feeding."

"Would killing one of them stop this?" I begged.

"From what I read; it would make it worse. Currently, once the baby is born, you will revert. If you killed one of your Zápalka, it would curse you for life."

Exhaling with tears covering my face, I could barely feel them anymore. They'd become commonplace of late.

"Let's go to the prison. We can work the rest out on the way." A plan was made, and Omri showed me how to access the prison.

"How do you choose the inmate?" I asked.

"How bad do you want them?"

"The worst."

"There is a man, we all like to torture him the most. He used to rape and murder children. Little girls," Omri scowled.

My fangs heated with my rage. "Perfect."

As the sun started to rise, Omri drove me home. The car was quiet, the world was tranquil at this time. I'd fed until the killer was dead, and then I'd let my rage incinerate him. It turns out, my light killed Halos and humans alike. Luckily, Omri hadn't followed me into the cell, so he didn't witness my newfound ability. On the way home, he spoke about them finding the body, but there would be none to find.

My stomach curled around itself as I smiled maliciously into the dying night. If he knew, Omri would be terrified and probably try to kill me. He should be. They all should be.

34

"*T*hey can't have just disappeared!"

"Yish, no one has seen or heard of them," Flick repeated. "They just disappeared during the day. No one knows what happened."

Smiling wistfully out of the kitchen window, I rubbed my still flat abdomen.

"Go check the houses. I want to know where they went. If there is any sign of foul play, I need to know."

"Královna," Kolette excused as she accessed the coffee machine. "I think dinner is burning."

Breaking away from my daydream, I quickly turned off the oven and removed dinner before it burned severely. "Thanks, Kolette." I tried not to gag on the smell of the food as I started serving it up for everyone. "Kenan, could you let Yish know dinner is ready, please?" There was no response. Glancing over my shoulder, I found Kenan watching me keenly.

"You look off-color, Kat. Is everything okay?"

"Morning sickness," Kolette interjected as she took the seat next to him. "Both her sister-in-laws suffered it terribly while pregnant. They lost so much weight their husbands worried for their well-being."

Studying me, Kenan frowned. "So, it's a genetic thing?"

Shrugging, Kolette sipped her coffee before answering. "It's different for every female, but it was noted both the Prince's wives suffered severely."

Placing the plates on the table, I tilted my head to the office. "Kenan?"

My stomach revolted at my proximity to the food. Leaving everything, I quickly covered my mouth and ran into the downstairs bathroom, dry heaving over the toilet.

Following me, Kolette turned on the tap, filling her hand with cold water before placing it to my forehead. "He should never have left. He knew his distance would make it worse. He should have stayed, found a place to meet you daily."

Sighing, I leaned into her cold hand. "Yish would have known. He could feel when we were together. He's done what he needs for survival. It would be torture to stay near and feel me with Yish every day."

"Better his psychological torment than what his absence is doing to you."

"I just have to survive the pregnancy."

"And if you can't?"

Lifting my gaze, I met Kolette's eyes in the mirror. "Then you have my permission to tell the Král his selfishness killed his zápalka and child."

Shaking her head unhappy with my answer, Kolette helped me up. "Could taking his brother to you help?"

Thinking about it, I closed my eyes. "His presence doesn't, so I doubt it. Similarities in genetics do not satisfy the needs of the soul."

"Pity," Kolette grumbled.

When we got back out to the kitchen, Kenan was growling under his breath at Omri. For his part, Omri stood arms crossed, just listening to Kenan's tirade. His eyes flicked to me, and he lifted his chin. "Kat, you look unwell. How about you return to bed, and I'll clean up the kitchen."

Cutting-off whatever he was saying, Kenan turned to assess me.

"Thank you, Omri. That seems like a sound idea." Picking up the glass of water I'd been sipping on, I started towards the stairs.

"What's going on?" Yishay enquired as he marched into the room.

"Morning sickness. The smell of the food made Kat ill. I've suggested she go to bed, and I will clean up the kitchen after dinner."

Forehead furrowing, Yishay stepped closer. "I was hoping to discuss your first order with you over dinner."

"What is there to discuss? You rejected my first suggestion, now I have elected Omri captain and Kolette."

Smacking his lips in annoyance, Yishay took a deep breath before replying. "You need more than two. Kolette and Omri can not work every day. You need at least four. Six would be better."

"Fine. Kolette, phone your sisters, and invite them to join you."

Yishay's eyes opened wide. "Females?"

"Yes, because the Pálir trains their women to be warriors too. I will have a first-order I can trust, and you never know, maybe more of your men might find their Zápalka from the arrangement."

Pressing his lips together, Yishay inhaled deeply through his nose. "I want at least one more of my men on your team."

Lifting a brow, I turned to Omri. He would know who to trust better than I. Without hesitating, Omri bowed his head. "Yoash."

"Why not Kenan?" Yishay crossed his arms, waiting for Omri's reasoning.

"The job is to protect our Královna. When our zápalka is in the firing line, we protect them first. Therefore, Kenan can not be on the same team as Kolette."

After he nodded acceptance, I met Yishay's eyes and waited. Huffing, Yishay unfolded his arms. "Fine, Kolette, give me the names, I will call your prince and make the arrangements."

Walking upstairs, I left them to it. Instead of returning to my bedroom, I went to my office and started making a list of what I needed to begin decorating it as the nursery.

An hour later, Yishay came into the room. "I'm worried about you."

"Too late now. You've done everything you can to destroy me. Now, you'll just have to sit back and enjoy the ride."

Grabbing my arm, Yishay turned me to face him. "I never wanted to destroy you, Kat. I love you. I've loved you from the moment we first touched. I don't care that you're Pálir or a princess. I love you for who you are, I always have."

"Who I was," I debated, my hunger growing with my anger. "You loved who I was. Then you abandoned me, and I changed. When I rediscovered my other zápalka, we changed. And after you put your child in me, my body started changing. Finally, you ripped my soul in two by making me give up the other half." Meeting his eyes, torn between hate and love, I just felt even worse. "You loved who I was, then you destroyed me, and that can't be undone."

Turning my back on Yishay, I looked over the list. Despite feeling like I should be crying, the sorrow didn't come. "I need to go out and buy what I need to fix this room up."

Yishay exhaled. "Blue?"

"Green."

"That will be good. Saves redecorating if our second child is a girl."

Swinging around with my eyes wide, I gaped at Yishay. Gods, I wasn't sure I was going to survive the first child, let alone two. "This house isn't big enough to have more than one."

"We can work that out when it's time."

"Why the hell would you think I would stay with you? After everything you've done to me."

"Because you came back, Kat. You put the welfare of our son above your hatred." Yishay took my face in his hands. "Because I won't let you take my son away from me. So, you will stay to be a good mother, and that means the next time you are on heat, I will fuck you repeatedly until you conceive again. Just like I'm going to fuck you until you remember how much I love you and allow me to make love to you again." His hands moved over my neck and shoulders.

Closing my eyes with the way his touch soothed and made me

want him, I whimpered. "I hate how much I want you despite what you've done to destroy us."

"That is the curse of soul mates, Kôte. Even when we cut each other to pieces, we still crave each other," Yishay murmured, his breath rushing across my ear. "It is better to forgive and love, Kat. Hating me is not going to save either of us in the long run."

His lips nipped just below my ear, causing me to sob. "I can't love you with half a soul."

Growling, Yishay threw his fist hard into the wall beside my head. To my credit, all I did was squeeze my eyes shut. I didn't jump, and I didn't flinch.

We were both breathing heavy as we stood there facing off. Opening my eyes, I swallowed hard as Yishay struggled for control. Touching my finger to the inside of his elbow, I licked my lips. "Your son is hungry."

Yishay exhaled hard. "Take what you need, Kat."

There was no chance I could just feed on him; I didn't trust myself to stop. In his presence, I didn't seem as hungry, but I knew what I was, and a Ravenor could never be trusted. Orgasms appeared to be an off switch for my hunger, so I needed to make sex a requirement for feeding on Yishay.

Moving my hands to his lips, I brushed a finger across it. Yishay's eyes flashed up to meet mine, danger swimming within, indicating I wasn't the only one fighting their need for violence and blood. Gods, the idea of us fucking and feeding angry drove me forward.

Kissing him hard, I twined my fingers in his hair and pressed my mouth to his. My teeth bit his lip, the first swell of blood crossed my tongue, and I felt my entire body come to life. Shoving Yishay away from me as I turned us both, I slammed him into the wall retaking possession of his bleeding mouth.

Holding me tight, Yishay dug his fingers into my flesh as he kissed me back just as furiously. Ripping at his shirt, I was desperate to get to his skin. Dismantling my dress just as quickly, Yishay ripped my underwear from my body. Dragging my teeth across his chest, I left twin crimson lines blooming in the wake of my incisors.

Not shying away and seemingly turned on, Yishay grabbed fistfuls of my hair and pressed me down until my face was even with his throbbing manhood. Licking it with my tongue first, I then sucked his head into my mouth. Shoving forward with his hips as he pulled my hair, Yishay rammed to the back of my throat impatiently.

Gagging, I sunk my teeth into his base. Cursing loudly, Yishay cried out in pleasure as his blood filled my mouth. Swallowing repeatedly, I took him down as deep as he could go, drinking my hunger simultaneously. Holding steady, Yishay pulsed in my throat, his hand kneading in my hair until my need for oxygen forced my teeth to disengage and release him.

Withdrawing, Yishay hauled me up and slammed me against the wall. Lifting my thighs to his waist, I cried out as he buried in me as deep as he could go. Feeding at his mouth, I kissed him deeply, sucking on his bleeding lip, mewling as his body pumped mine, driving me closer to satiation.

As I was peaking the edge of climax, Yishay pulled away. Throwing me to the floor, he forced me to my hands and knees before he thrust into me from behind. Holding my hips, Yishay drove so deep into me it hurt. Crying out, I scratched at the timber floors with my nails.

"You want to fuck angry, Kat, I can do that too. You're not the only one hurting. If you are going to make me feel you, you're going to have to take my rage with you," Yishay growled as he pounded into me, making me scream in combined pain and delight.

The heat built inside me. The ravenor smiled, loving the pain, the destruction, the blood still smothering my lips. Gods, I'd bled his dick, and now that was thrusting into me. Knowing that some of the lubrication was provided by his blood had me panting with thirst.

Opening my eyes, I looked across the room at the mirror to where mauve eyes stared back at me. With every thrust of Yishay inside me, every wet slapping sound of his body filling me with cock and blood, my eye color grew darker.

Red eyes were the dead give away of a ravenor. They weren't always red, but when they were in a feeding frenzy, the scarlet of blood blended with our species natural blue irises. That's how you identified them. Unfortunately, you were typically being bled dry before you knew, so it was usually too late.

Pain pierced my soul, but pride lit up the darkness that was eating away at my insides. The eyes of a ravenor were so pretty in my face. It seems, I suited being a monster.

Closing my eyes, I cried out with grief and sorrow for the dark thoughts in my mind. Yishay growled and yelled his enjoyment. Pulling out of me, he put his face between my thighs, licking and sucking, entering his own feeding frenzy on his own blood.

"Give me your cock?" I pleaded.

Flipping me onto my back, Yishay maneuvered his pelvis over me, watching me open my mouth and lick the tip of his blood-drenched hardness. He was so turned on, so hard and big. I'd never seen him like this. His cock was straining with its engorgement, and the veins were standing right out, tempting me to slice them open and drink him dry while he came in my mouth.

"Do it! You want to; I can see it in your eyes, Kôte. The bloodlust is driving you out of your mind. Do it. Satisfy your demon, and I'll satisfy mine."

Blinking, I met his gaze. Yishay's eyes no longer the deep blue of the Halos, but a dark purple, verging on red. When I swallowed in fear, Yishay smiled maliciously. Turning around, he crawled over me slowly, the predatory strength and violence of his body on full display. I'd never seen Yishay like this. It was terrifying, and such a turn on all at once.

"Do you want to know why I never drank from you, Kat? I was terrified you'd die if I lost control. That's why I had to fuck Batyah while I fed on her. Climax stops the bloodlust. Something you have just learned."

"You're...?"

Lowering his face, Yishay covered my mouth with his hand. "Not out loud, Kat. They can't know that you know. My father did it to me. Made me feed by drinking his enemies dry. It is a tradition in the royal family for the last hundred years. The ravenor makes us stronger, faster, and smarter. All of our senses become keener. But we have to learn to control it, not let it control us. That is how we prove strong enough to become king. Controlling the demon within. We are more bonded now than ever before."

Shifting his body, Yishay pushed back into me slowly. My eyes went wide then closed at how wonderful it felt. The ravenor in me purred.

"I'm going to teach you how to control your bloodlust, Kôte, and you are going to love me again. We will be happy together, and if that takes violence and blood to make that happen, I will give it to you." He rammed hard and deep. My back arched with mixed pleasure and pain, his hand still covering my mouth as he thrust again, his strength so much more than I had ever felt.

Picking up speed, Yishay used his hand to turn my head, then he dove forward and sank his teeth deep into my neck. Crying out, I scratched my nails down his back, deep gouges following the wake of my fingers. Moaning as he fed, his throat convulsed in time with his hard-pumping body.

Pleasure filtered through my system, shutting out fear, or sense, or anything not involved in my body cresting climax. My stomach tumbled inside me as Yishay drank more than he should. A little flitter of knowledge shocked my brain back to reality. My instincts kicked in, and I bit Yishay's hand hard. His jaw clenched in my neck, gritting against the pain, then he released my mouth.

"The baby! If you take too much, you'll kill the baby."

Yishay froze. Slowly, his mouth released my throat as he pulled back to look down on me, eyes as red as blood.

Stroking his face tenderly, I appealed to the king and the father. "The baby must be a priority for both of us."

Yishay's eyes darkened a fraction. A smile blooming across his face, genuine in his pride. "Good. You could pull your hunger back for the sake of our child. From now on, when the demon gets control, our child will be the motivation to take it back." His eyes were intent as they returned to dark purple. "Can you do that, Kat? Can you stop feeding to save our child? If you can't, if you can't hide this, then you will be killed with our child still inside you. I won't expose myself to save you. Do you understand?"

Nodding my head, I knew I could do it. I already had.

Rolling to put me on top, Yishay pulled my face to his. "Prove it." Bending his knees up, he took hold of my hips and started thrusting up into me hard and fast. "Prove it, Kat." Turning his head, Yishay offered me his neck.

The ravenor mewled as my mouth latched around his throat. We fucked, I fed, and as the ravenor reached its happy place, Yishay whispered, "Baby." My mouth instantly released from his throat.

Using my hair to pull my head back, Yishay pounded me even harder. His body throbbed violently inside of me as he erupted. Throwing my head back, I came, screaming his name as my body seized so tight I wondered if I could ever relax again. Then I fell limp on his chest, panting and crying, confused and happy and scared.

Wrapping me in his arms, Yishay held me tight, the damage I'd inflicted already healing and vanishing. "You feed with me only from now on. No more running off to the prison with Omri or drinking our enemies without my permission. If you are hungry, you come to me, and I will take care of your needs. Understood?"

"Yes," I whispered, unsure of anything anymore. "Does Omri know about you?"

Yishay took a deep breath. "You wouldn't let me help you, Kat. I needed someone you would trust who could convince you to come back. Within my first order are the blood ring. Have you never heard of them?"

Shaking my head, my tears ran forth to soak his chest. Yishay's arms tightened where they held me pinned to his torso.

"They are my closest soldiers, the ones who swear their lives to protect mine, and we use magic to bind them and their blood to that promise. If I die, they die, so they are very invested in keeping me alive," Yishay explained. "Your brother, Wenceslas, has a blood ring, and your other zápalka, Casimir, is the head of it. That is why I couldn't let him come here, Kat. To have him in our bed, he would need to join my blood ring, and he can not be bound by blood to both your prince and me."

"Can..." I sobbed, "can it be undone or transferred?"

Stroking the hair from my face, Yishay sighed. "Not yet, Kôte. I must be assured of peace and convinced of your love and commitment to me before we discuss such things."

"Are the others...?" I squeezed my eyes shut. Just how far had Yishay manipulated me?

Exhaling, Yishay kissed the top of my head. "You have a long way to go to earn my full trust yet. Let's take one step at a time." Rolling us so he could look down on me, Yishay held his weight above me, his eyes the healthy Halos blue again. "I will love you, protect you, and ensure you get what you need, Kat. All you have to do is love me. If you break my trust, you'll be dead before my secret finishes spilling from your lips. Omri survived the loss of his Zápalka. I'll miss you, dreadfully, but I'll survive."

Pecking my lips, Yishay pulled away, leaving me trembling on the ground. Yet, the ravenor was aroused by the threat. Observing the room and the mess we made, Yishay nodded. "I'll trust your judgment for how you wish to decorate this room. Don't worry about the cost. I've got it covered."

Picking up what was left of our clothes, Yishay held out his other hand to me. The ravenor wanted to jump into his embrace, but I was less sure. Accepting his help, I allowed Yishay to pull me up to standing. Cuddling me to him, Yishay gazed down on my face, eyes happier than our wedding day. "Let's have a shower, and then, I want to make love to you in our bed."

Letting him lead me from the room, I glanced over my shoulder as he led the way and saw a ghost of myself get left behind.

35

"*How* do you eat?"

Standing at the balcony doors drinking his coffee, Yishay was nude and glorious. Turning to face me, he smiled as he took in my naked form beneath the sheets. "It's not new to me. We are only detectable for the first few months when food is unpalatable, and we can't control our needs. But if you are strong enough to overcome the hunger and survive those first few months, then you will be virtually undetectable."

"So, I will be able to stomach food again?"

"Yes. Luckily, your morning sickness will cover that symptom. If you can prevent yourself from draining one of our people dry again, no one should suspect a thing." Finishing his coffee, Yishay put it aside. "You're just lucky Kenan is one of my blood ring."

Sinking back ashamed, I closed my eyes. "He told you?"

"Of course," Yishay dropped back on the bed. "Does Kolette know?"

In answer, I bit my lip.

Yishay exhaled. "She'll need to be bound. I guess you are going to get your own blood ring. What about the sisters?"

"They were all with me when I lost control. That is why I suggested them for my guard."

Pursing his lips, Yishay turned his head. "Will they have told your Prince?"

"No, I don't think so."

"So, you drained others aside from Kenan?" Yishay caressed his fingers across my décolletage.

Meeting his suspicious gaze, I took a breath and confessed I dealt with our enemies. Yishay listened as I explained I just intended to kill them, but I lost control and couldn't stop feeding as my hate and anger dragged me into an uncontrollable rage.

However, I didn't tell him about the heat, or the burning people to dust, or the walking in daylight. He only asked about the feeding. If he wasn't going to trust me with his secrets, I wasn't trusting him with mine.

Avoiding my eyes, Yishay watched his fingers move across my chest. "Where are the bodies? It is not like the Pálir to clean up after themselves."

Rage filled me. Grabbing his wrist, I dragged it down as I sat up, letting the sheet fall and expose myself to Yishay's hungry eyes. "I've never run a kill squad before, Yish, and this wasn't about a Pálir killing Halos. This was the Královna taking out her enemy." When I placed his hand to my mound, Yishay took the invitation to press his fingers inside me. Hanging my head back, my teeth split my lip as my hunger erupted. Blood filled my mouth, causing me to moan in happiness as I gyrated over his hand.

"Gods, Kat, I've never wanted you so much." Fisting my hair with his free hand, Yishay jammed his mouth to mine for a deep tongue-twisting kiss. Suddenly, Yishay fell back. "Sit on my face, Kat."

Shifting my body over his shoulders, I used the wall for support as Yishay guided me to where he wanted me. When his teeth slid into the junction of my thigh and body, I whimpered. Yishay's strong arm held me firmly in place as he drank his fill, his spare hand stroking my sex, sparking my desire like flint striking pyrite.

My breathing was erratic, my sex clenching, my fingers fisting Yishay's hair and pressing his mouth harder against my femoral junction. Moaning, Yishay pressed his thumb to my clit and slid two fingers inside me, stroking over the catalyst of female rapture. My breathing hitched, body seized, and I came, bucking my body against him, pulling his hair and crying out. Teeth releasing me, Yishay licked and sucked the wound. It would heal in a few minutes, but I would lose a good amount of blood from the artery in the meantime.

Sitting back on his chest, I struggled to breathe. Grinning up at me, Yishay urged my body to move lower. "Can you deny how much hotter the sex is, Kôte?"

I couldn't. Things had been great before, but now, all my senses came alive when I fed. As Yishay pressed me over his swollen engorgement, I cringed, still sore from last night.

"See what you have missed out on all these years? It's going to be great between us now, Kat. So. Damn. Good."

Riding him, I was inching towards that second dose of rapture when there was thumping on the door. "The prince is twenty minutes out," Methuselah called.

Grunting in annoyance, Yishay sat up, holding me to him as he stood. "Let's take this to the shower."

The proximity of his neck was too tempting. Licking up the side of his neck, I sank my teeth just as Yishay throbbed inside of me in excitement. Circling my hips as he carried me into the shower, I fed, sighing in happiness as I did.

Part of me was happy that I'd found a way of feeding that wouldn't result in death. Still, something niggled in the back of my head, a concern that I couldn't quite grasp. When my back hit the shower wall, I whimpered and forgot all about niggles as Yishay fucked me into euphoria.

THE CARS PULLED UP NOT LONG AFTER WE SETTLED IN YISHAY'S OFFICE. Rising from his desk, Yishay offered me his hand. We walked hand in hand into the receiving room, the only formal room in the house. Usually, I snuggled up in here to read, but it was where Yishay met with subjects formally.

The door on the other side of the room opened as Saul stepped in, followed by Wenceslas. My brother's face was stern, his pale eyes glinting. Lowering my eyes, I struggled to swallow the cotton wool that filled my throat from the shame of what I had become.

"You are Královna. You outrank him now. Don't you dare lower your gaze in submission," Yishay whispered dangerously. "Remember, they used you as bait, and as a bargaining chip for this peace. Without you, this wouldn't be happening."

Lifting my eyes, my hate for everything I'd been through burned inside me.

Smiling in my peripheral, Yishay nodded. "That's better."

Stopping before us, Wenceslas bowed his head. "Král. Královna. It is with glad tidings that we meet to finally discuss peace between our people."

"It is long overdue," Yishay indicated the lounge.

"Well, we did try several months ago, but apparently our call to talk peace then was not as appealing."

"Your brother threatened my wife. I took appropriate action. You would have done the same."

"Hardly, but I was not so in love with my wife," Wenceslas dismissed. His eyes came to me. "I believe I have you to thank for my widow status, Královna?"

"I doubt your daughter would be so thankful," I argued.

"Perhaps, but her mother's status as a traitor was confirmed, and she must accept that or potentially suffer the same consequence."

The ease of his response saddened me. "She is your daughter!"

"Yes, and I love her, just as I love my sister. But I have a duty to my people, and that duty must always come first," Wenceslas reasoned. "Not long from now, you will be a mother, and I hope you never have to make a choice between love and duty."

"I already have!" That he dared to throw that in my face enraged me.

Yishay's hand squeezed mine. "I believe we are getting off track. We are here to talk about peace, not love. I have taken a Pálir princess as my wife, and she carries a son from both lines of the royal blood. My people are willing to accept peace with the Pálir, and I am willing to acknowledge your bloodline as descendants of the original royal line. We are here to discuss how peace can be achieved."

Bowing his head slightly, Wenceslas opened a leather binder, handing Yishay a sheet of paper. "Our initial requirements for peace, as previously discussed."

Yishay read through the paper, and then the discussions began. After an hour, my stomach was cramping, but thankfully, I wasn't craving blood. In fact, I felt hungry for real food for the first time in days. While I tried to sit through it, my fidgeting became evident to everyone. Turning to consider me, Yishay raised a dangerous brow.

Swallowing hard, I stood. "I apologize, I need some fresh air. I might take the opportunity to organize shifts with my first order now that they are all here."

"You seem unwell, Sestra?"

"Morning sickness has kicked in and has been quite aggressive," Yishay excused.

"I see." Wenceslas studied me. "As long as that's all it is."

Yishay's shoulders rolled back with the offense. "What else could it be? Are you worried I am trying to harm my Zápalka?"

Wenceslas firmed his gaze on Yishay. "I do not believe any of us would harm our Zápalka on purpose, but I know how the future Král is prepared for the throne. If I discovered my sestra was forced to such an existence against her will, I would be very concerned."

Yishay's eyes hardened. "I don't know what you think you know about our ways, but I would never harm Katarina. She is my Zápalka."

"I saw your Zápalka so terrified of you, she shot you in the heart with a black arrow," Wenceslas challenged. "I worry about the relationship you two seem to have."

Keeping my temper on a tight leash, I clenched my fists by my sides. "Enough! I don't think a man who used his own sestra as a bargaining chip should act so high and mighty. You knew sending me back here would hurt me; you didn't care then, so stop pretending to care now the deed is done. Yishay is my husband, my Zápalka, and my Král. The child I carry is his and will be the future Král. I can't tell you if my sickness is morning sickness or a result of having my soul and heart ripped apart. At this point, I don't care. I have suffered all this for peace, so both of you sit down and make it happen. I am going for a walk."

Striding to the door, I stepped out to the foyer, taking a deep breath. Before me stood Yishay's first order on shift, my brother's first order, and my friends who would now become my first order.

"Královna," Halidie and Dara curtsied. Kolette stood beside them, smiling.

"Where is Janeice?" I queried.

"She is outside talking with her Zápalka," a voice that could have melted me spoke from behind me.

A mix of joy and sorrow collided inside me as I turned to face Casimir. It explained why I felt the most like me I had in weeks. Both my Zápalka were in the same building as me. "Who?" I asked tentatively.

"Methuselah. It's a good match."

Closing my eyes, I took a deep breath. "I'm going for a walk. My first order can come with me and get the layout of the area." Stepping outside as quickly as I could, I barely held back the temptation to wrap myself in Casimir's embrace. Being near him and not being able to hold him was torture.

"Královna," Kolette called behind me. "Kat?!"

There was a rush of air as someone landed in front of me. Stopping short, I glared at Yoash, his Halos blue eyes studying me with concern. "Forgive me, Královna. I understand you are hurting, but you can't just rush off like that."

Turning around, I watched the others still approaching. "Did I run?" I asked, confused by how far across the clearing I was.

"I'm not sure what that was. It wasn't running, and it wasn't transvecting, but it was very fast," Yoash informed. "Do you know where you were going?"

Unsure how I'd moved so quickly., I frowned. "The boulder by the river."

Nodding, Yoash waited for the others to catch up before we continued at a reasonable pace to the river. Kolette took my hand as we reminisced on our days as children and the adventures we shared.

The next hour consisted of Omri and Yoash standing watch, bemused looks on their faces, while Kolette, Halidie, Dara, and I relived our spirited youth.

"I guess we should head back, find Janeice, and organize shifts," I sighed eventually.

Rising to stand, I started moving, but as a collective, we froze when we heard a strong breeze approaching. "Take cover," Kolette directed quietly as she pulled me beneath the branches of a tree as twenty or so dark shapes flew overhead.

"Is the Král expecting visitors?" I asked Omri. When Omri shook his head, I closed my eyes and connected with Wenceslas informing him of the incoming group. There was no way to tell if they were hostile, but they were transvecting low to the trees and not coming via the road. That was usually how attacks go.

Once they had passed us, we moved stealthily through the trees following their trail. By the time we reached the clearing, the fighting had started. Rage filled me. "I thought we had dealt with the others?"

"Only the Halos branch," Kolette corrected. "It looks like the Pálir warmongers have chosen to fight alone."

"Well, it looks like I get another outlet for my anger."

The girls all smiled menacingly. "Like with the Halos, we subdue, you incinerate," Dara leered.

"Um, are we missing something?" Yoash queried.

"Just keep up," I warned.

In unison, the girls and I lifted and transvected at speed across the clearing, joining the fight. No one saw us coming, and I think Omri and Yoash were still recovering from females transvecting when we reached the house.

Allowing my rage to pressurize within as I flew across the open ground, I was ready by the time we got to the house. Kolette reached the enemy first, a Pálir fighting Kenan. Grabbing him around the neck, she pulled him back. Breezing past, I stroked my fingers over his face, white glow scaring the flesh I caressed. Letting him go, Kolette moved further into the fray while I touched the men Dara and Halidie had seized.

We moved through the enemy this way. The girls would grab one, hold them long enough for me to touch, and then quickly release and grab another. Some enemy was just in grasp fighting our men, so I reached out for them as I passed.

We were a fair way into the throng when the screaming and swearing started as the enemy combusted where they stood. Immediately, Omri and Yoash joined the girls in subduing the enemy long enough for me to infect them, before moving on to another. We moved inside to where the enemy was already dropping under the skill of the first order.

Still, I infected their dying bodies as I passed, feeling the endless hunger leaving me, the joy of death enlivening me, and peace soothing me. The last man I reached was fighting Yishay. Spinning him in a sweeping fighting maneuver, Yishay ripped his opponent's throat out with his teeth. Floating in, I smiled maliciously at my husband as I caressed the Pálir's forehead, lines of light glowing where my fingers touched him.

Releasing the Pálir, Yishay cocked his head, observing me with curiosity as the cursing and confusion of our men continued in the foyer. Stepping into him, I kissed Yishay's blood-soaked mouth. Taking me in his arms, Yishay kissed me deeply, moaning his joy as we shared his feed.

Then the enemy combusted behind me. Jolting, Yishay pulled free of my hunger to watch. Turning his wide eyes to me, Yishay blinked before he sent a hesitant glance over his shoulder in my brother's direction. "Close your eyes, Kôte. Take ten deep breaths and think of our baby," Yishay whispered.

Smiling mischievously, I did as he requested. There was no need for a mirror to know my eyes betrayed me. While I took several deep breaths, Yishay held me to him and kissed around my head. "You are amazing, Kôte. Once I am done here, I am going to show you just how amazing I think you are."

"Did she do that?" I heard Wenceslas gasp.

"Did you not know how talented your little sister was?"

"I've never seen her do that!"

Kissing my forehead, Yishay tilted his lips upward against my skin. "I've never seen it either, but I've felt her do it through our bond."

My eyes opened in surprise. Yishay hadn't told me he'd felt me do that.

Turning us, Yishay set his bearing so he could look at me but also see my brother behind me. "Though, when I felt it, I wasn't sure what I was feeling, other than uncontrollable burning fury. Now, I know how that manifests. Now, I know just how unique my wife is." Stepping towards me, Yishay caressed his hand over my abdomen. "Is this why my ancestor was jealous of yours, Prince? Is that ability what divided our bloodlines so long ago?"

Staying quiet, Wenceslas studied me, so hard I felt his eyes burning into me.

Considering my brother, Yishay suddenly laughed. "Oh, it's not. This was unknown to you, something new, and now, you are regretting forcing your sister to return to me. Now, you wish you just killed me and used your sister to take the crown for your head."

Clearing his throat, Wenceslas stared past us. "Did you know?"

Craning my neck to see beyond Yishay, I spied Casimir standing just inside the door.

"Yes, but it was only a recent discovery. Like the Král, I felt it manifest and walked in the room in time to see it occur."

"You didn't pass this important information on?" Wenceslas was furious.

"It was too late. Kat was pregnant, in too deep, and her heart already broken. All the pieces were in place, and the queen had to fall to save the future king."

Closing my eyes, I knew he meant the demon. Casimir would have saved me and taken me home, had I not become a ravenor. I'd confessed it to him, so I'd dug my own grave.

"Perhaps, these talks are unnecessary," Yishay decided. My eyes flashed open, danger swimming in my veins. "Now, that I know you would have killed me if you knew you could succeed me, I'm not so keen to grant peace."

"No!" All the men in the room turned towards me, but I kept my face cast down. "I have given everything left of me for peace, for all of our people to coexist without bias, without prejudice, without pain and death haunting them around every turn." Tilting my head, I engaged Yishay with my gaze. "I am here for peace. I have endured for the promise of peace. If you deny me by refusing this treaty, I will make you the sole beneficiary of my fury and be done with this. Am I clear?"

Keeping his face stern, Yishay studied my eyes. He didn't want to agree. He was hungry for violence too. Hesitating as he stared into my eyes, Yishay's gaze cooled, as if remembering his humanity. Taking a breath, Yishay closed his eyes before lifting them to meet Wenceslas. "My wife is right. She has suffered for others to have peace. Our people have languished. It's time we end this war."

"Thank you," I exhaled. "I'm going to rest upstairs."

Choosing to exit the room through the far door, I didn't want to walk past Casimir. Both pieces of my soul existed in that room, so I didn't want to leave it, but if I didn't, I never would.

Waiting in the nursery, I painted patches of the wall with the sample pots Saul bought for me. The Pálir contingent left the house hours later, my soul screaming as the feel of Casimir grew more distant and faded. For a few moments, tears fell down my cheeks. Caressing my abdomen, I breathed through the agony. "For you. I do this for you."

It took another hour for a shadow to fill the doorway. "It's done.

The agreement has been formalized, and copies are being sent out to the community at large."

Stepping into his embrace, I held Yishay, so I could hear his heart. "Tell me I'm going to survive this."

Yishay's arms tightened around me. "I promise you, Kat. You will thrive by my side."

36

"The room looks lovely."

Turning from hanging the mobile, I found Vladimir standing in the doorway. A smile split my face as I waddled towards him. Grinning, Vladimir took too large steps to reach me. He tried to hug me, but the belly between us made it impossible.

Settling for kissing my cheek, he placed his palm on the obstruction. "Soon, you'll never sleep at all," Vladimir cooed.

"The months have flown by."

"In marital bliss?" Vladimir said it with a smile, but the worry was there.

Shrugging, I forced a grin to let it seem like a joke. "The baby keeps us from killing each other." Truthfully, in the bedroom, Yishay and I could quickly kill each other in our lust and hunger for each other. Outside the bedroom, it was still strained. "Did Daneka come with you?"

"Not this visit," Vladimir pointed to the sun shining through the window.

Heart sinking a little, I frowned. "The first order let you in?"

"Dara is on watch duty. She still has her girl's crush on the prince." With a wink, Vladimir observed the room some more.

Peace had been good. While the Pálir were still hesitant coming south, the killing had stopped, and slowly, we were all finding our way in this new world. Most celebrated the treaty. A large party was held on the boundary, former enemies embracing and welcoming each other as kin. Those first few days had been nerve-racking and beautiful.

"The green you've chosen is a lovely color."

"Vlad, why are you here risking being found out and about during daylight?"

Vladimir met my eyes. "I heard you had become a no-nonsense Královna," he smirked. "I still see you as a little girl, not my ruler."

Raising a brow, I leaned on the changing table. My back had been killing me for hours. "I'm not in a good mood today, Vlad. Can we get to whatever is worrying you?"

"It's daylight. Your husband can't take you to the hospital, Katiana. I can."

"Why would I need to go to the hospital?"

While Vlad looked pointedly at my belly, the ache in my back intensified somewhat before releasing. The realization caused me to blink rapidly. "But our babies are always born at night. It's only morning teatime."

Pressing his lips together, Vladimir took a step closer. "Day-walkers are always born in the light. The closer to the peak of the sun, the more powerful they will be," Casimir soothed as he wrapped an arm around my waist to support me and help me towards the door. "I'm sorry, we failed to warn you of so much, Katiana. I begged Wenceslas to warn you of all the pitfalls of carrying a child for the Král, but he worried you would refuse to return if you knew."

"All the pitfalls," I breathed as I turned to assess him. "You knew what would happen to me?"

"It is well documented in history, Kat. I'm sorry. We needed peace."

Breathing through the ache in my back, I shook my head. "I need to tell Yishay."

"He should be able to feel it. Cas was the person who let me know you were in labor."

"Yes, but Cas knows I'm a daywalker. Yishay does not. He probably thinks he can sleep and deal with this at sunset. We need to tell him."

Huffing, Vladimir looked at his watch. "Mind-link him as I help you downstairs."

Letting my brother steer me, I focused on my connection to Yishay. He was only sleeping lightly, already dreaming about holding his child in his arms tonight. From his thoughts, I caught an edge of worry as his eyes fell on me in the dream, his concern I wouldn't be held to him any longer.

The vision tripped me up, Vladimir catching me, stopping me from falling down the stairs. My heart raced with the moment of panic, seeing myself fall down the stairs, landing in agony and causing the baby harm.

"Kat!" Yishay raced out of the bedroom naked, but he exhaled in relief when he saw me standing at the top of the stairs with Vladimir. Confusion crossed his face, followed by suspicion. "What is going on here?"

"I'm in labor. Vlad is taking me to the hospital. You can come now, or come later, it's up to you," I offered.

"There is no point rushing. The baby won't be born until sunset at the earliest," Yishay frowned, eyes watching my brother.

"Actually, Kat was born at midday, just like all our family, are born during daylight," Vladimir educated. "Casimir worried the baby would be born before lunch based on the timing of contractions."

"All of you are born in daylight?" Yishay's brows lowered, his hairline dropping low over his eyes in contemplation.

When I gasped as the ache in my back grew worse, Vladimir eased me forward onto the first stair. "If you are coming, get some clothes and meet us at the car," Vladimir directed.

Downstairs, Dara already had my hospital bag ready and stood by the door waiting. "Kolette is on her way, she should be here momentarily."

Taking a pair of sunglasses from his pocket, Vladimir slid them into place. Stepping outside, I closed my eyes initially but could open them soon after. As I was just settling into the back seat, Yishay came out of the house, a hoodie over his head and his eyes hidden behind dark sunglasses. Ravenors were even less tolerant of daylight. It surprised me I could stand it at all. Before he could get to the car, Yishay stopped to talk to Methuselah.

"I've called ahead to the hospital to let them know we are coming," Dara informed as she slid into the car behind the wheel.

Transvecting across the cleared area, Kolette immediately went for the front passenger seat, Kenan following right behind her.

"You are the Král's guard; travel with him." Kolette shut the door, surprising Kenan. "Let's go."

Blinking rapidly at the change in energy within the car, I noticed everyone was highly stressed around me. "No, wait. Yishay should travel with me."

"No, he should travel amongst his guard," Kolette insisted, her eyes going to my brother.

Glancing between them, I frowned. "What's going on?"

Neither looked at me. "Katiana," Vladimir began, "there is a chance..."

Opening the back door, Yishay bent down and glared at my brother. "Kat can travel with my guard and me."

"She's in the car now, and you should travel with your first order," Vladimir encouraged.

"Vlad," I groaned. Scooting into the center seat, I cringed in discomfort. "Yish, just get in the car. Your guards can follow behind."

Opening his mouth ready to argue, Yishay glared from my brother to me, exhaled, and slid in beside me. As soon as the door closed, Dara hit the accelerator, and Kolette and Vladimir exchanged a look, mouths grim. Wrapping himself around my side, Yishay put his hand on my abdomen. His touch soothed me instantly, the ache in my back retreating to slight discomfort.

"Kôte," Yishay whispered, his face pressed to the side of my head, "I'm scared."

"Of what?" I murmured back, observing and feeling his fear. Yishay's eyes darkened, but I knew it wasn't his hunger feeding the ravenor, it was his fear. Closing my eyes, I opened myself to him and the image of him holding our son while a nurse strips the sheets on an empty bed.

Unsure what his thoughts were, I tried to puzzle it out. Why wasn't I there? Was his fear that I would die? Then it slowly made sense to me why he requested the hospital. We usually did home births. Even the Halos never gave birth in a hospital, but Yishay had insisted. Opening my eyes, I met his. "You're scared of losing me, and of raising our son by yourself."

Yishay pressed a kiss to my forehead. "Terrified." His arms held me tighter. "My mother died giving birth to me."

I knew that. The Král had always been an only child since the divide of brothers because the Královna died in childbirth. My eyes widened as history settled into my reality. Was that why my brother was stressed, why Kolette was too?

Sprinkling kisses over my head, Yishay held me tighter. "I love you, Kôte, and I don't want to lose you. I'm going to do whatever I can to ensure that doesn't happen."

When we arrived at the hospital, Yishay kept his arms around me as I was escorted into the private hospital and its birthing unit. By the time I was admitted, the ache in my back was constant, and while the midwife discussed pain relief, my waters broke. An hour later, I was gritting my teeth, clenching Yishay's hand, and pushing our son into this world.

There wasn't time to worry about Yishay's concerns or the history of Královna's before me. I was single-minded in my focus to get the watermelon forcing itself through my pelvis, out. Really, marsupials had a much better idea about childbirth. So, did bears for that matter.

"One more push, Kat," the obstetrician encouraged.

"I'm so tired!" Suddenly exhausted, I was unable to even hold my head up.

"Come on, Kat. One more push, and you can hold your baby in your arms. Let's make it a big one."

Panting, I sucked in all the air I could, took every bit of energy I had left, and bore down. There was a rush of pain as the obstruction dislodged from my body. It left me feeling relieved, and empty.

Empty of everything, the baby, emotion, energy, and strength, I leaned my head back. Catching a glimpse of the baby being carried away, I closed my eyes. It was done. The future Král was born.

"Well done, Kôte," Yishay murmured against my head.

Holding me, Yishay soothed me with his strength. Devoid of the energy to even open my eyes, I just wanted to sleep.

"Kat?" Yishay turned my face to his. "Kat? Something's wrong. She's not responding."

"Kat?" The doctor called from my other side.

A large dark hole opened beneath the bed, sucking me into it. I wasn't worried, I was too tired to be concerned. Just too tired to care.

"Kat," Casimir whispered in my ear. "Stay with us, Kat."

Jolting at the sound of his voice, I felt Casimir take my hand, Yishay holding my other, and through our bond, I could feel Yishay and Casimir grasping each other's shoulders, sharing their concern for me.

It drew me back; if only because I wanted to witness this was real, that the two men I loved were actually here together with me, working together, touching me together. Finding my last surge of will, I forced my eyes open. Casimir stood there with Yishay on the opposite side of me, both holding me.

"Drink, Kat." Biting his lip, Casimir pressed his mouth to mine, Yishay blocking the nurse's view of us.

Opening my mouth slightly, I tasted Casimir's blood as it filled my mouth. Pinching his lip with mine, I sucked and kissed him. When Casimir pulled back, Yishay followed suit, kissing me, feeding me, making me whole and real.

As they took turns kissing and feeding me, I became more myself, more awake and able to move again. At last, their lips healed, and they retreated from my side to allow the doctor to assess me. She was asking me questions about how I felt, but my eyes were focused on Yishay, as the nurse handed him our son.

Lifting my gaze to Casimir, who stood holding my hand, I sighed. "You knew?"

"Your brother took a gamble that the two of us could bring you back," Casimir enlightened. "He had me wait outside. When I felt you fading from this life, I stepped in." His hand caressed my face. "I would give my life for you, Kat."

Smiling up at him, I would never ask him too. He knew that.

"Kat, meet our son," Yishay approached from the other side.

Taking the bundle of the blue blanket in my arms, I looked down at the precious life I'd created. Lowering my gown, I put him to my breast. The hungry little thing latched on and started sucking. There was no milk yet, but that didn't bother him. After three sucks, his tiny incisors emerged and pierced my skin. He didn't take much, just a sip to soothe his hunger.

Closing my eyes, I sighed content. When I opened my eyes again, Casimir was gone. Frowning, I turned my eyes up to Yishay.

Stroking his son's head lovingly, Yishay met my searching gaze. "He had to go. He's meant to be on duty to the prince."

As my heartbreak began, I was instantly distracted by the lack of bloodlust. Blinking, I bit my lip and searched Yishay's eyes. "It's gone."

Yishay inhaled deeply. "Your bond with Casimir balances it out. It's still there, but you won't lust for it like you did while my son was inside you."

He stood there quietly for a moment, and let me take it in. My hunger would be my own again. How would that affect us?

"It should be like it was before we were blood bound, Kat. You will still get hunger pangs, but you will be able to control it. Our love and my blood will sustain you now."

Absorbing this, I considered him. "Not entirely." My eyes went to the door. No, I would crave the other half of my soul, but at least the ravenor would be more controlled now. That was a relief. That was enough.

37

*a*rms wrapped around me as I watched Donato sleep. "He's a happy child," Yishay murmured against my ear. "How are the feedings going?"

"Good. He's only interested in the milk now." It took two months for Donato to stop sinking his fangs in, but he had. "How was your trip away?" Turning to face him, I stayed in the circle of Yishay's arms.

"Good. The meeting with our people in the free territories was well received, and many agreed to reintegrate back into our society and help teach the Halos how better to interact with humans." Yishay pulled me closer, pressing our bodies together. "Did you miss me?"

Understanding the lustful look in Yishay's eyes, I played coy. "Of course. I am used to having you hold me while I sleep now."

Kissing along my jaw, Yishay growled. "I want to do more than hold you, Kat."

Leaning back a little, I smiled at Yishay and kissed his lips. "I'm ready for more."

Clicking the baby monitor on, Yishay lifted me to his waist. Chuckling, I kissed him as he carried me to our bed. He was gentle and attentive as he made love to me. As he entered my body, I felt us connect with Casimir over the distance. It stung. It must have been so frustrating for him to have had two months reprieve, only to be dragged back in again.

Kissing down my neck, Yishay sank in his teeth to feed; only then did I let the tears fall. The ravenor stopped me caring while pregnant with Donato, but I knew Casimir felt it all those months. Now that my demon was repressed, I yearned for us to be together, all three of us.

"Yish," I panted as his thrusts kept time with his throat swallowing my blood. "Yish, I need to be able to feed our son." His massive body pounded the air out of mine, my voice choked and barely audible. "I can't do that if you drink me dry."

Groaning, Yishay released my throat. When he offered me his mouth, I licked and sucked his blood-covered lips, using my tongue to clean the drips running free. Throwing my head back, I clung to him as he drove my body to climax. As I came down from the rush, raw hunger gripped me. It had been months since I fed the ravenor, and now, she was starving.

Throwing Yishay on his back, I rode him to his own orgasm while I fed on the crook of his arm. As I laid in his arms afterward, I considered our last few months. Human food sustained me again, and my lust for blood had been nonexistent. I thought the ravenor left me after Donato's birth, but now I knew it wasn't about the baby. The baby just revealed the demon in me.

When Yishay's breathing grew heavy, I showered and dressed, then went to the nursery to watch Donato sleep. Like most of our kind, he slept soundly during the day and woke for most of his feeds at night. Daneka assured me that would change. That once he started crawling, he would wake for a play during the day but still want to play all night too.

He was the first daywalker Král. Something I still hadn't spoken to Yishay about. He hadn't queried my brother transvecting here in daylight, nor Casimir's. He hadn't raised my tendency to still get out of bed in the early afternoon to draw, or cook, or anything to fill in my time. Yishay seemed happy to accept it was just who I was.

Donato stirred in his sleep. Ensuring he was covered over, I remembered the ravenor lurking within me. It took my mind back to the last year of my life with Yishay. To the niggle that rose occasionally. I'd thought the ravenor was caused by the splitting of my soul in the double bind. What Omri showed me from the archives suggested that, but something didn't sit right with his account.

Moving out to the walkway, I observed the photos mounted on the wall. The last Král with a young Yishay. The last Královna with Yishay's father. I was the first Královna to survive childbirth since the brothers split our people into two factions. The first Královna to raise her son in centuries.

Frowning, I remembered Yishay's worry for losing me. Everything that occurred between us started flying around in my head, not adding up. Yishay admitted he'd used Omri and the archive material to manipulate me into coming back. He knew that I would need him because he knew I would become a ravenor. But how? I didn't even know until that day, and Omri called Kenan before I drained him dry.

"He knew it was going to happen," I whispered to myself as I studied his family photos. "And they knew it would kill me."

Turning, I stepped down the stairs and went to the first order door. Saul opened it just as I raised my hand to knock. Yoash sat at the table playing cards. "Kat, what's wrong?" Saul asked.

"I want to go to the archives. Now." Turning, not giving anyone a chance to argue, I grabbed up my jacket and stepped outside. Yoash came out and hopped into the driver's seat.

"I need to call another for escort," Yoash said, taking out his phone and pulling up Omri's number.

Mind-linking Kolette, I found her awake. *I need to go out. Be quick.* She was a daywalker, she would be able to transvect in the daylight. Putting my hand on Yoash's shoulder, I stopped him. "I've already called Kolette. She's on her way."

"Oh, okay. But, Omri knows his way around the archives."

"I've spent plenty of time in libraries. I know how to get around one."

We waited five minutes until Kolette arrived, then we drove to the warehouse, which acted as the Halos archive. Inside were rows and rows of books and files. There was a computer terminal that enabled searches, which I typed some key terms into and noted down the locations of papers and files it brought up.

Fidgeting the entire time, Yoash took out his phone at one stage, but Kolette looked at him. "Something wrong?"

"No, I just thought I felt it vibrate," Yoash quickly put it away.

Walking through the archives, I gathered the volumes I wanted, making Yoash carry them to keep his hands full. Once I had every book, I went to the table and started reading through them. Everything I needed was there. The Králs and their wives, and how the Kral's were raised were all there in black and white. It talked about Králs' strength and speed, which was better than any other Halos. About the blood ring and how it originated with our ancestors. The Král, whose jealousy of his brother's ability to walk in daylight, caused the split. Not that it said that here. It wasn't mentioned anywhere about the envy. Only the disgrace of the murderous Pálirs.

Finally, I found the volume I'd been looking for. The history of the tribond. The first recording was two generations after the split, and it was the Král and his Královna. The Královna had met her first Zápalka as a child, and then the king as an adult. The king demanded rights and took his Zápalka from her first love. She died in childbirth.

After that, it was recorded that every second generation of Královna had a tribond. Always, the Král claimed to be the primary, and she died in childbirth. Sitting there, I read the words in fascination. Locating the part Omri showed me to inform me how my soul being ripped apart would affect me, I turned the page.

Reading the entire recount of the Královna, who hadn't been able to hide her ravenor. Had she not died in childbirth, the Král would have needed to kill her after to appease his people. She didn't survive, and he was saved from killing her.

"Královna," Omri's voice interrupted my reading. Lifting my eyes, I watched him emerge from the stacks. "Is there some information I could help you find?"

Standing slowly, I glared at him. "You misled me. You lied. You told me it was because I was a twin. You told me it was because we refused the tribond. It was all lies!"

Omri bowed his head. "I serve my Král with a dutiful heart, Kat. I am sorry you are angry, but it would not have changed a thing by the time you found out."

"Because I was damned the day he forced me to bond with him?" Tears filled my eyes, contradicting my anger. "He infected me through the bond. The only reason I didn't notice in the months after, was because I was away from him, and Casimir's bond held me free from the demon."

Omri shifted. "Actually, he infected you with the bond, but had you never tasted his blood again, the demon would have stayed dormant. It was the mating when you first fed on him again that gave the ravenor life."

My stomach hollowed. Had I never returned, it would never have happened. "I could have been happy with Cas, mated with him, bore children to him, and never have been damned."

We stood in silence. Sinking back into the chair, I looked at the manuscripts. "Yishay knew all this when he took me. He knew it was his turn to be cursed with the tribond, and he made me feel guilty for it."

"He wasn't sure. He hoped he found you before your other Zápalka, but, as with all the tribonds in history, Yish discovered he found you second."

The anguish tore at my soul. "If I went home after school and not held that grudge against my father, this would never have happened to me. I would have married and mated with Cas, and Yishay would have found some Halos woman to breed with."

"I doubt that," Omri objected. "I've studied history, Kat. This was meant to happen. Yishay would have found you somehow. Perhaps, it would have happened at the peace treaty. You would have met and still become the key to peace. However it came about, it was always meant to happen, Kat."

Lifting my watery eyes to his, I heard his passion. "You have a theory?"

Omri took the seat opposite. "The first Král ravenor was not raised to be so. His jealousy of his brother's ability drove him to try and prove himself better. He created the first blood ring to keep his secret. Two generations later, the tribond started happening. I believe the gods have been trying to cure the Král's bloodline of the demon for centuries."

"By having them infect their wives and force their child to their life?"

Omri shook his head. "No, Kat. The infection happened to the first wife. She died in childbirth, just like every ravenor wife after. It is a condition of the infection that the mother must give up her life to produce new life. The Král then raised their child to be like them because how else could they feed the baby?"

The breath rushed out of me. The Král's turned their son's through the negligence of how to balance the feeding of blood and sustenance. While I could well believe it because centuries ago the men didn't help with the baby, so wouldn't have known the blood was only a few drops and the mother's milk did the rest, it still astounded me another woman didn't help.

"The gods created the tribond to counter it. You would have died, Kat, just like every Královna before you. Your brother showing up, his bringing Casimir within close proximity, allowing him to be there with you and Yish when you needed him, that's the only reason you live," Omri confirmed my suspicion. "Every other Král has had the other member of the tribond assassinated out of jealousy, Kat."

"Yishay would have done the same. You talked him out of it."

Omri bowed his head in acknowledgment. "I have studied these texts for years. My theory was we needed Casimir, to save you. In saving you, the future Král would be raised like every other child of our kind. In saving you, our future Král will not only unite the people, but he will not suffer his father's ailment."

Tears fell. "But I wasn't saved. I'm condemned."

Closing his eyes in regret, Omri lowered his face and licked his lips. "Your condemnation saved your son, Kat. The curse will end with Yishay."

"Yes, it will." Standing suddenly, I stormed out.

Yoash and Kolette were waiting by the door. They didn't ask questions, just followed me to the car and drove me home. It needed to end. I couldn't risk Yishay raising my son like him. There was only one solution, one way to ensure that didn't happen.

None of the other Královnas could kill their Zápalka. They would never withstand the pain to cut his heart out. For sure, the first order, especially the blood ring, would prevent them. I understood now why the gods gifted me the ability to kill by fire. Fire cleansed, and that was my fate. To cleanse the royal bloodline of this demon.

38

The sun was setting as we pulled up at the house. Striding inside, I was determined it would end tonight. My anger of Yishay knowingly doing this to me couldn't be smothered. "Where is he?" I demanded of Saul.

"In his office, but the baby is hungry."

"I only need a minute." Moving down the hall before he could stop me, I threw open the door and marched towards Yishay, my rage building ready to consume. "You son of a demon bastard!"

Standing by his desk, his arms folded across his chest, Yishay stood straighter at my entry. "Kat, I was wondering where you went. I have a surprise for you."

"I don't want anything..."

"Katiana."

My feet stopped. Taking a breath, my anger hesitating as I eyed Yishay. The side of his mouth twitched. Pursing my lips, I turned to see Casimir sitting on Yishay's sofa. Eyebrows low, Casimir stood slowly, tilting his head as he observed me. "What are you doing here?" I asked, my voice betraying the torrent of emotions seeing him caused. My rage started to dissipate the moment I met his pale blue eyes.

Stepping forward carefully, eyes watchful, careful, Casimir kept his focus on me. "The Král called me. He has rethought your suggestion and has decided to trial it."

Uncertain I'd heard him right, I blinked. "Suggestion?"

"To have Casimir as the captain of your first order. With your ability to run around in daylight, it makes sense to have one of my blood ring who can run around with you and not be weakened by it."

"Daylight?"

"Did you think I hadn't caught on to your family's uncanny tolerance to sunlight?" Watching me swallow hard, Yishay raised a brow. "I believe that is what caused the rift in our ancestors. Something I expect our son will inherit, and therefore, unite our people truly."

"You are letting Casimir become one of your blood ring?"

"Yes, eventually. We are going to trial the arrangement this week. If it works well, we will solemnize the relationship."

Could I control myself around Casimir? "So, I will need to rewrite the roster?"

Yishay and Casimir both chuckled at this. "No, Kat." Reaching for me, Yishay stroked my cheek. "Casimir will not just be our guard. He will be living with us. More pointedly, he will be sharing our bed with us. We are going to try the tribond how the gods intended it."

This was all very sudden considering how determined Yishay had been for it not to happen, so it made it hard for me to trust it. "What changed your mind?"

Donato started crying, turning my focus to the door. Dropping a kiss to my neck, Yishay then placed another in front of my ear before pulling back. "Why don't you go feed our son, then Casimir and I will meet you in our room for our first trial run."

My stomach flipped and turned excited by the prospect, but wariness lurked beneath. Withdrawing from the room, I wandered upstairs in a cloud of confusion. I'd been so determined, but this changed everything.

Watching from the rocking chair as Yishay gave Casimir a tour of the place, I was still feeling dizzy when both of them stopped in the nursery to admire me feeding my son.

"We should discuss mating as well," Casimir suggested.

"I have my heir. I don't expect you will be able to resist her when she is říje připraven, so it doesn't matter much now. If she bears us more children, it won't change who inherits my title." Yishay stroked Donato's light covering of dark hair on his head, then lifted his hand to caress my cheek. "She's an amazing mother, it would be a crime to deny either of our children her love."

Flattered by his words, I was excited by the prospect, and yet distrust niggled as I met his calculating eyes. "Why did you change your mind?"

"For you, Kat. Because I have always understood what you need. You gave up a part of your soul for our son. Our tribond saved you, but I fear for you if we do not sustain what the gods created. I felt that this morning. I don't want you destroying your life over something so easy to heal. It will make you a better person and mother to have both pieces of your soul."

His words froze me as Yishay turned to smile at Casimir. "Come, I'll show you the bedroom. We can get to know each other while we wait for Kat to be ready."

'*Don't look so nervous, Kat,*' Casimir mind-linked. '*It was your idea.*'

Thirty minutes later, I put Donato back to bed and slowly opened the door to our bedroom. Yishay and Casimir were lying naked talking. Part of me wanted to gush and scream with delight, the other part was nervous as all hell.

"Kat, come join us," Yishay called.

Closing the door, I moved towards them. When I hesitated by the end of the bed, Yishay sat up and advanced towards me. Standing, Yishay smiled down on me as he kissed me, gentle and determined. When I gasped at the hunger of his kiss, he tenderly removed my clothing.

Moving around behind me, Yishay kissed across my shoulder as he did. "Go to our Zápalka, Kat. I want to watch you with him." I hesitated. "It's okay, Kôte. I'm going to enjoy this."

Locking eyes with Casimir, I could tell he'd enjoyed watching Yishay and I kissing. Placing one knee on the bed, I crawled toward him. Casimir's eyes were intense as he watched me approach. Pausing just short of his chest, I looked him over. Biting my lip, I reached a shaking hand out and caressed his hip. Casimir's eyes flared.

Running my hand up to the side to his chest, my trembling eased with the physical contact. Tracing the definition of his torso, I studied his body's reaction, growing hard and long for me.

Casimir caressed my cheek. "It's okay, Kat. He's not teasing you. I'm here to stay." His confidence wavered. "Provided you still want this?"

"I do," I blurted, not giving myself time to think about it.

Smiling, Casimir took my mouth with his. Embracing me, he rubbed his erection against my hip as our tongues danced. A weight settled on the bed behind me, another hard body pressed against the back of me, and then Yishay was kissing around my neck while his hands explored my body.

Gasping, I arched when his hand groped my breast. Thankfully, it was just emptied, and so nothing squirted out. Moaning, Casimir dropped his mouth licking over the nipple, Casimir closed his mouth over it and sucked. Cursing, I threw my entire body at him.

Chuckling, Yishay crawled his hand into the gully of my hips. When his hand brushed against Casimir's erection, he took hold of it and used it to rub my clit. Tensing for a second, Casimir dropped his face to watch. Lifting his gaze to Yishay's, Casimir chuckled. "I always knew you Halos were kinky bastards."

"You are just as much my Zápalka now as hers. The inclination to touch you is just as strong," Yishay admitted. "Trust me, I have never been tempted by a man before."

Casimir smirked. "You know if we do this, it can't be undone."

Yishay kissed my shoulder. "She needs this, and I need her."

Gazing down at me, Casimir smiled gently. "I need her too." Lowering his face, he kissed me slowly.

"You know what we are. Blood exchange will need to happen, and potentially, things will get aggressive at times," Yishay warned as he continued to stroke Casimir against my bud. "Kat doesn't always feed traditionally either."

Casimir moaned. "I fed her first. Trust me, I know. She bites wherever it suits her."

"If you two don't stop talking, I'm going to bite both of you," I threatened. "I think we need to daisy chain."

"What?!" Yishay asked.

Casimir laughed. "She's going to suck me off while you eat her, then we'll swap."

"Not exactly what I was thinking, but good enough," I shrugged, moving down Casimir to access his cock.

Waiting for me to get comfortable before he knelt on the floor, Yishay wrapped his arms around my hips. As I sucked Casimir's tip, Yishay squirmed his tongue along my folds. Moaning, I slowly licked Casimir's length. It was terrific having both of them in the same room.

Sex, since the tribond fused, had been like a threesome every time, but with one guy and a ghost. Now, it was both men touching me, kissing me, licking me. I couldn't even begin to analyze how amazing it felt. Caught up in the moment, I was lost to the intense emotions of completeness, in the overwhelming physical sensation of two men adoring me simultaneously.

Casimir looked to be in absolute bliss as I sucked and licked his hardness, swallowing him down and moaning from the pleasure Yishay was giving me. Never in my life had I been this happy or felt this good. Not just because of physical desire. Having them both naked with me was almost zen-like.

Grabbing my hair, Casimir pulled himself free from my mouth. "Change," he breathed hard.

Rising, Yishay dropped on the bed beside us. Twisting, I took hold of his thick pulsing hard-on. As I lowered my mouth, Yishay grabbed my hair and forced me to look at him. "Remember that first time in the nursery?" He asked, his pupils darkening with his hunger. When I nodded, Yishay smiled and nodded to his cock.

Hesitating, my eyes glanced back to Casimir, who was watching intrigued.

Letting go of my hair, Yishay stroked my cheek. "He needs to see what he has signed on for, Kôte. It's only fair if we find out he can handle you at your worst now."

Swallowing my trepidation, I gave a nod of agreement and wrapped my tongue around his smooth head. Lowering my mouth down his shaft as far as I could go, I dragged my sharp incisors along the base vein as I lifted.

Letting out a sharp hiss, Yishay clenched his fist in my hair. His blood seeped across my tongue - I hadn't cut as deeply this time - and Casimir dived between my thighs, licking and sucking in time with my avid feeding. The ravenor rejoiced, and I vocalized her excitement as I fed on my husband.

Yishay swelled, his excitement and bloodlust engorging him until he couldn't fit comfortably in my mouth anymore. The blood only added to the brilliance of this moment.

Casimir was caught up in our lust, driving fingers inside me, licking and sucking my clit until I could barely breathe. The orgasm ripped through me out of nowhere, pulling me from my feeding frenzy. Chuckling, Yishay encouraged me to crawl along his body and kiss him.

When Casimir laid back down beside us, Yishay directed me to share. Leaning over to Casimir, I kissed him. He moaned as he tasted Yishay's blood in my mouth, and I felt his own hunger rise. Yanking back, I met his eyes. "It won't change him, will it?"

"No." Rising to his knees, Yishay moved my body over Casimir's. "Last chance to bow out for either of you," he warned.

Casimir smiled up at me, his hand caressing my cheek. "There is not a chance I am leaving."

It made my heart swell, and I kissed him again.

Yishay chuckled. "So, be it." He shoved into me from behind, catching me off guard with how hard he hit me. Gasping, eyes wide from the forceful penetration, I took a moment to calm my speeding pulse. The ravenor was chortling.

Staying buried in me, Yishay pushed me forward a little. "Let's do this, Casimir."

Smirking, Casimir aligned his cock using Yishay's penetration as a guiding point. Then slowly, he held my hips and guided me onto him, Yishay helping to impale me.

Cursing, I was so wet, and Yishay still bleeding added more lubrication, so that Casimir just slid in, stretching me open to accommodate both of them simultaneously. It wasn't comfortable, but it wasn't horrible.

"Slow and steady to start," Yishay urged.

We started moving together and apart. Both of them sliding in and out of me, concurrently. The term full to the brim had never had so much meaning in my life, and I knew I'd need to be doubling up on my kegel exercises from here on out.

Pulling me close, Casimir kissed me deeply, matching the thrust of his tongue to that of his cock. Whimpering, I was quickly closing in on my climax. Sensing my nearness, the men picked up their pace, thrusting hard and deep. My body squeezing them both tightly, I cried out.

Casimir swore, Yishay growled, and the pinch of one of their hands on my nipple had me singing my rapture to the heavens. They used that moment to sink their teeth into each side of my neck in unison, feeding on me as they both readied to find their bliss.

While I was in nirvana, the ravenor was beyond that. She was floating so high I don't know if she was ever going to touch down again. Yishay jerked behind me, and Casimir reacted. They came in perfect synchronicity, releasing my neck and voicing their pleasure, albeit crudely.

Collapsing in a heap on the bed, the bond between us pulsed in a way I'd never felt before. Despite Yishay doing this for my benefit to start, I could feel his satisfaction, and I was able to read it for what it was. He wanted this unconventional relationship just as much as I did now.

Panting, we lay with both of them embracing me, and each other for a long time afterward. Eventually, Yishay moved my hair and licked the healing puncture at my neck. "Are you content, Kôte?"

"Beyond!"

Lips lifting on the sides, Yishay kissed my shoulder. "Let's shower."

We did. All three of us. Touching and caressing each other. Yishay and Casimir even caressed each other, all hesitation lost now. The bond had cemented. Sexuality was pushed aside in favor of where our pleasure and happiness would thrive.

Not that it would ever be them having sex with each other, I knew enough to know I would always be the meat in their sandwich, but they could touch each other without finding it awkward.

After the shower, I declared it breakfast time, and we all adjourned to the kitchen to eat. When Yishay excused himself to conduct some business while I cooked, Casimir sidled up to me and wrapped me in his arms. "I've missed you so much. I'm the happiest I've ever been right now."

Understanding what he meant, I smiled. "I never expected this."

"I was just as surprised when Wenceslas called me in to discuss the offer. I still dropped everything to hear him out. Where were you today?"

"Catching up on the royal bloodline history. Deciding how I wanted my son raised." Remembering my determination to kill my husband just a few hours ago, I frowned.

"You were raging when you came home. I thought you were going to lose control and attack your husband. What happened?"

Staring at the frypan, I wondered the same. "I don't know."

Tucking a strand of hair behind my ear, Casimir nodded. "Yishay told me he was worried you would become unstable and dangerous after what you went through to stay alive. He felt that allowing the tribond was the only way to keep you safe."

Lifting my eyes to the window, the dark night allowed me to see Casimir's reflection. "Do you think this will work?"

"Yes, Kat. I wouldn't be here otherwise."

Accepting his judgment, I changed the subject. "I want you to train my son too. He needs to be proficient in both the Halos and Pálir ways. He will unify them eventually, but he needs to learn both to decide the best way forward."

Casimir kissed my cheek. "You are a wise Královna."

"No, I'm just a mother who wants the best for her son."

We sat down to eat, Yishay and the first order on duty joining us. After the meal, Casimir needed to go home and get some clothes and necessities. After I kissed him farewell, I went to check on Donato. He was due for his next feed.

We played together for a little bit before he yawned and cuddled in to go to sleep. Once he was breathing deeply, I placed him in his cot. Yishay came in and cuddled me while we watched him sleep. "Saul woke me to tell me you went to the archive," Yishay sighed. "I knew you finally realized the truth. I know you, Kôte, your sense of right and wrong, so I knew how angry you would be."

"You invited Casimir here to stop me exacting my revenge."

"I told you I would do whatever I needed to do, to make sure I didn't lose you, Kôte," Yishay whispered in my ear. "I meant it."

Closing my eyes, I realized he'd manipulated me again, and I'd fallen into it with no way out. Tears escaped as I acknowledged, deep down, I didn't want to get away from him.

"Just to be sure," Yishay firmed his grip on me. "I have instructed my blood ring, that if anything were to happen to me; if I just suddenly disappear as our enemy did a year ago, they are to rip Casimir's heart out and make you watch."

Anger boiling within me, I swallowed my fear. "I could kill them all in a matter of seconds."

Yishay kissed my shoulder. "True, but you can't protect all your family, Kat. Eventually, they would kill them all. Then they will take our son away from you and burn you as a ravenor."

Just imagining having Donato taken from me was heartache.

"You want to be a good mother. I want a happy wife. Keep your claws sheathed, Kôte, and you will never know the grief of losing your Zápalka and your child. I love you, but I am Král. Don't for a second think I put love above my own mortality."

"A ravenor couldn't," I hissed.

Grinning wickedly in my peripheral, Yishay turned my face to his and kissed my lips. "Everyone is expendable in chess when protecting the king. Even the queen." Moving his mouth to my ear, Yishay sucked my lobe. "It was amazing, wasn't it?"

"What?" Though, I knew.

"Having both of us fuck and feed on you together." Yishay rubbed his nose up my neck, inhaling me. My body squirmed in reaction to the memory. "Forget the past, Kat. Our future is to burn hot in the bedroom, fucking and feeding, and mating. This hate for me will pass, and love will be what lasts."

"Are you sure?"

"No, but I won, Kat. I got my wife, my peace treaty, and my son. I wear the crown; that's all that counts."

GLOSSARY

Běs: Demon
Bohovia: God
Bratr: Brother
Fena and Otrava: Bitch
Hovno: Shit, crap, turd
Jsem pochopil: Am I understood?
Kotě: Kitten
Král: King
Lepeni: Bind
Matka: Mother
Pâlir/Pâlie: Pale one/s
Oběd: Lunch
říje připraven: On heat (lit: Rut ready)
Sakra: Damn it!
Sestra: Sister
Snídaně: Breakfast
Teta: Aunt
Zápalka: Match
Zmařený: Fucked up

JOIN THE BEAUTIFUL AND DEADLY

Join Ebony's Mischief List

Sign up to Ebony's mailing list for the following perks:

- latest news on new releases
- heads up on upcoming promotions
- exclusive freebies like coupons to read Ebony's stories on Radish for free
- first chance at Giveaways
- get a free book

Go to https://ebonyolson.com for more information

SILVER ROGUE

Meeting your soul mate doesn't mean love at first sight.

Anique has spent the last seven years rebuilding her life after leaving her birth pack. Of all the concerns she had about attending her sister's wedding, meeting her true mate was not one of them. This is the last thing she wanted, and she's determined not to let it happen, but the Goddess has other ideas.

Knox is the alpha of the ValleyMorgans. His life is orderly and controlled. Then he receives the Moon's blessing. Knox thought being mated to a headstrong, pampered, alphas-progeny was going to be hell, but its nothing to finding out the Goddess has chosen a fiercely independent rogue to be his mate. Just when he starts to like her, Anique's secrets are exposed; ruined by her own pack, rogue, and living a human existence, could this girl be any more wrong for him?

The Goddess mated them, but that doesn't mean love at first sight, and it sure as hell doesn't mean smooth sailing and a happy-ever-after.

KNOX

Walking into the wedding chapel, my was stride purposeful, knowing I was cutting it fine. My name was murmured in greeting, heads bowing in respect like a Mexican wave through the renovated seating. No wooden pews in this upmarket venue. Marching straight to the front, I met the eyes of the groom and his brother as they turned to acknowledge me. "Alpha, thank you for coming." Dante, my beta, and the groom today, smiled and pulled me into a hug.

"Drop the Alpha crap, there are humans present," I muttered. "Sorry, I'm late. Business as usual."

Dante smiled. "There's a reason you're not in the wedding party."

"That and the groom is meant to be the star of the show. That's why Milton's ugly mug was perfect for the best man," I teased, smacking his brother's shoulder in jest.

Milton was one of my deltas, and anything but ugly if his conquests were anything to go by. Rolling his eyes, Milton grinned. "The best man gets the pick of the best tail, Knox, and you should see the bride's younger sister. You are so going to regret missing the rehearsal dinner last night."

"I was busy being an alpha. Plus, I don't go in for all this hoopla. When I wanted our pack to move with the times, and to become educated, I didn't intend on church weddings," I grumbled, looking around the renovated church.

"Evaline and I both made friends at college. This is how the humans recognize our union," Dante defended for the fifth time.

"All this expense for a man to take his mate. This is where the old way of marking them and mounting them makes more sense."

"Our modern alpha, sprucing the old ways as best?" Dante jested. "Next, you'll tell my wife her place is in the kitchen, bare pawed and heavy with cub."

The image made me smirk. "Evaline is the daughter of an alpha. She already knows her place."

Both Dante and Milton's mouths fell open, then they burst out laughing. When Dante met Evaline, I'd been told that Alpha Stirling had three headstrong daughters, one of whom left the packhouse to make something of herself in the human world, without a man. The scandal that must have caused in an old-style pack like the Beachrunners, I could only imagine. Even in the Valleymorgans pack, I'd only enabled the women so much independence. In a race where women were in high demand, running off to pursue a career was just not allowed. Especially, fertile women who came from a line of alphas, like Evaline and her sisters.

Sobering, Dante lowered his voice. "I heard our stray she-wolves appeared again?"

The reason I was late. If it wasn't for Dante's wedding, he'd have been investigating it all night with me. "A body was found not far from the base. We're not sure if he was just unlucky enough to cross them on a run, or if they hunted him down. Either way, I'd say there are three of them that tore him apart."

"Three?" Milton's eyes went wide. "We've only seen evidence of two before now."

My concern exactly. Each kill, there was a new female's scent on the body. They were gathering numbers, which made them more deadly. "It's been three years since the first stray turned up with the she-wolf's scent on him. They've only killed a handful of times. I'm starting to think we have a wolf recruiting stray she-wolves. He could be offering them protection and letting them deal with strays that enter his new territory."

Milton lifted a brow. "Creating himself a new pack and harem at the same time."

"Either way, they are killing in our territory on occasion," I grumbled. "I don't care if they are taking out stray wolves, but what if they go after one of ours? And why haven't we found them yet?"

"Good morning," a man's voice interrupted to my left. We all turned to see the middle-aged wolf and bowed our heads in respect. "Knox," he greeted, offering his hand.

The alpha of the Beachrunners was a solid man, in his fifties, the silver at his temples spreading further into his short red hair than the last time we met. Taking his hand, I gave it a firm shake. "Stirling. I apologize for not making dinner last night."

"And so you should. If I had to sit through this youthful nonsense, you, as an advocate of modernism, should too." A smile tempted the side of his mouth. "At least, I managed to escape walking Evaline down the aisle."

"How did you manage to escape that?" I liked Alpha Stirling. We'd only met a handful of times, but he was a sincere man. "I was under the understanding that you were wrapped around your daughters' fingers?"

Stirling chuckled. "Since the day they were born. I remember being so proud of their fierce determination, then Evaline turned fourteen, and I realized how mistaken I'd been. I tried to remedy the error of my ways with the younger two. Rhiannon likes tradition, but she wants freedom too. Anique..." Stirling shook his head. "She is worse than the other two combined." Stirling looked around, then to Dante. "Have you seen Anique? Her mother is fretting."

Dante frowned. "She isn't with Evaline?"

Stirling shook his head. "She is not in the bridal party, so no one bothered to worry until now. Rhiannon called her an hour ago and she was nearly here. I know she worked last night, but she should have been here hours ago."

"Maybe she got stuck in traffic getting here from work," Dante reassured.

Stirling shook his head. "That was one child I should not have permitted to leave the packhouse."

"A bit wild, is she?" I asked, amused this was not a problem I suffered in my pack.

Stirling gave me an exasperated look. "I didn't start going grey until Anique became a teenager. Wild isn't the right word. Fiercely independent would be apter. Had she been a boy, she would have made an amazing Alpha." Turning, Stirling went to sit in an empty chair on the bride's side.

Dante chuckled. "What he fails to mention is that Anique is his baby and his favorite. At least that's how Evaline tells it."

"Siblings are always jealous of each other. Wait until you have a few cubs hanging from your tail, then tell me about parental favoritism."

"This from an only child and perpetual bachelor," Milton teased.

"I'm waiting for the woman who can handle me. I'm happy to sniff around until I find her," I winked. While the brothers laughed, I moved to the front row, greeting Dante's mother before I took the seat left free for me.

The Beachrunner Luna walked down the aisle quickly, looking at every face as she did. When she reached her mate, she complained about something, glaring pointedly at the empty seat on her other side. Taking her hand, Alpha Stirling whispered to her. Loud murmurs by the door made me expect to see the bride preparing to walk down the aisle. Instead, Stirling's son and eldest child, Edward, was manhandling a young woman. Gripping her upper arm, Edward scolded her while another of their pack moved forward to take the girl.

On spotting the other man approaching, the she-wolf gritted her teeth and slammed the heel of her stiletto into Edward's ankle. The move forced Edward to release her, and she stepped out of reach. The Beachrunners gasped. Understandably. That was their future alpha, and he was just assaulted by one of their girls.

"I said, no!" The she-wolf growled in defiance as she marched towards Dante. Despite her determined step, she looked terrific, walking down the aisle. She wore a long flowing dress in emerald green that highlighted her tiny waist and made her breasts appear generous. Her cherry hair was hanging the length of her back, in a feminine but straightforward style, and her green eyes were ablaze as she closed on her prey. She could have been walking a catwalk, the way she managed to move with purposeful grace.

"You left this behind last night," the she-wolf announced to Milton, holding out a ring box for him. "Rhiannon called me when I was nearly here, and I had to get the taxi to drive all the way back to the hotel and get it. You owe me fifty for the taxi."

Taking the ring box with wide eyes, Milton patted his breast pocket in surprise. "Shit, I didn't even realize I'd lost them. You're a lifesaver, Anique." When Milton tried to pull the girl into him to kiss her, she pulled away, looking disgusted.

"Gross! I know where your mouth has been."

Laughing, Milton stopped his attempt. Grimacing as Dante kissed her cheek, Anique made her way to Alpha Stirling, where she was scolded anew by the Luna. When Anique explained her lateness, the Luna quieted. Kissing her cheek in greeting, Stirling directed her to sit. Glancing over her shoulder, Anique snapped her teeth at the man who tried to help her brother. Adjusting her seat, she looked poised to escape as soon as the opportunity arrived.

Her green gaze flitted towards Milton, who winked at her. Glaring at him, Anique slid her gaze passed him to meet mine. The instant our gazes met, stars exploded in my vision. The full moon shined down upon her pale face, moonlight radiated out of her, and the need to kneel and howl, forcing her to shift and submit to me, was almost overwhelming.

The bridesmaid walked between us, breaking our eye contact, and snapping me back to the present. "Shit!" Dropping my gaze to the floor for a moment, I then dared another look. Anique was staring at the floor, her eyes wide, chest heaving, fingers griping her chair as if her life depended on staying in that seat.

Blinking, I realized everyone was standing, and the music was playing. Quickly rising up, I turned my eyes down the aisle to watch Evaline make her way towards the groom. She looked beautiful, her auburn hair cut in a short but feminine style, as was the norm for our women. Long hair in human form, meant mangy hair in wolf form. That dragged my eyes back to Evaline's baby sister.

Still sitting in the chair, eyes seeking out the closest exits, Anique kept her focus everywhere but in my direction. It was as if, by avoiding looking at me again, she could pretend it never happened. It also meant she wasn't standing watching the bride come down the aisle, something the bridesmaid, her middle sister, Rhiannon, noticed also.

Taking a step back, Rhiannon whacked her little sister with her bouquet, giving her a meaningful look. Shooting out of her seat, Anique kept her eyes on the ground. Frowning, Rhiannon turned her attention, and smile, back to their older sister. Reaching the front, Edward handed Evaline off to Dante, before taking his seat next to Anique. Edward glaring at his sister, seemed to break Anique out of her thoughts. Lifting her eyes to the front of the church, Anique watched the ceremony, her attention not budging from Evaline.

The celebrant was quick and concise, thankfully, so it was only fifteen minutes later when Dante and Evaline were pronounced man and wife. After waiting for Alpha Stirling and his Luna to congratulate the couple, I stepped forward and did the same. Intending to introduce myself to Anique straight after, I found her chair empty.

"Knox." Sterling approached. "Take care of my eldest and good luck with her."

"She has Dante to keep her in line."

Stirling nodded. "The bonus of a true mating; once a she-wolf submits to her mate, she tends to become more placid." My eyes went to the empty chair where his youngest had sat. Stirling followed my gaze. "Where has that girl gone now? She's acting even more bizarrely than usual today. She didn't even stand for her sister's entrance." Stirling's eyes returned to me with a glint in them. "She seemed very distracted, don't you think?" Realizing he'd witnessed our first glance,

I felt unsettled for the first time in my life. "Maybe I should check on her, see if something happened at work."

"She works in the human world?"

"Yes. Once I let Evaline go to university, I had to let the others." Stirling was searching the church with his eyes.

"Is it normal for Anique to assault her brother?"

Stirling gritted his teeth. "No, but when he tries to assert dominance over her, she does fight back." Stirling met my eyes. "They used to be quite close, but when Anique went away to college, something bitter grew between them."

"Did Edward not get to go to college?"

"Yes, of course. All our males are given the opportunity. We need to earn a living after all. No, the issue is that one of our pack, wanted Anique to be his. Anique has aspirations, ones that required years of dedication, so she refused him. He didn't take the rejection well. Edward thought it was a good match, and his persistent harassment for her to submit to the other wolf drove a wedge between them."

Hissing beneath my breath as if something bit me, I clenched my jaw. Jealousy has sharp teeth. "If Anique is like I've heard, that would not have gone down well."

"They've been at each other ever since. Edward is nearly ten years older than Anique. She was a surprise pregnancy, nearly three years after we'd stopped." Stirling shook his head. "Edward, as the eldest basically took her under his wing. She followed him around, hunting him down when he tried to get away from her. She's never forgiven him for turning on her."

"Alpha Stirling." The man who tried to take Anique from her brother earlier approached confidently. "I was looking for Anique? She was meant to be my date tonight."

Narrowing his eyes, Stirling glared at his pack member. "You and everyone else, Dan. Unfortunately for you, I know you are not Anique's date this evening. You know better than to lie to your alpha."

Instantly, my hackles raised. This was the man who thought to tame my she-wolf.

Stirling indicated to me. "This is Alpha Knox, of the Valleymorgan pack. Knox, this is Dan Strum, my son's best friend. Would you abide one of your pack lying to you?"

"They know better than to try," I growled, not liking the disrespect this wolf was showing.

"But you have a modern pack," Stirling raised a brow to bait me.

"Modern does not mean soft. Modern means being open-minded to new ways of doing things."

"Well, good luck with Evaline, she'll be right at home with your open-minded ways," Dan smiled through the finely veiled insult.

Taking the hand he offered, I squeezed until his smile vanished. "Thank you, we are delighted to gain a she-wolf with such a good lineage. Having heard about Evaline's sisters, I'm thinking perhaps the Valleymorgans should take them off your hands also."

Tilting his head to appraise me, Stirling eyed the power challenge occurring in front of him. Stiffening, Dan tried to crush my hand back, but while not a weak wolf, he didn't possess my strength or training. Wincing, he relaxed his grip. Only then did I release his hand. "Good luck getting the girls to go along with that," Dan grumbled and left.

Watching him walk away, I couldn't resist my smile.

"Are you serious about taking on my daughters, Knox? I didn't think you allowed new wolves unless they were mates?"

"I don't, but how are we to meet potential mates if we don't allow single she-wolves to visit? It might also benefit Evaline if her sisters visited for a few weeks, to help her settle in." Looking over to where Rhiannon was flirting with Milton, I chuckled. "I think at least one of your daughters might be happy to visit."

Stirling smirked. "Don't read into that too much, Knox. Rhiannon is not saving herself for her true-mate. She quite enjoys having her tail chased."

"And, Anique?" I couldn't help but ask.

"This conversation is very reminiscent of one I had with Shona's father, the day before I marked her." When I hesitated, Stirling nodded. "Be careful, Knox. The one you have your eye on will rip a wolf's throat out before she submits to him."

The challenge warmed my insides, my wolf grinning in anticipation. "She would be the first to refuse me."

"I don't doubt that for a second, Knox," Stirling smirked.

"Excuse me, Alphas, it's time for the family photos," Rhiannon interrupted politely.

Stirling groaned. "Have you seen Anique?"

"She's outside, hiding from Dan and Edward," Rhiannon informed her father. "She texted me where to find her when she was needed."

Nodding, Stirling pursed his lips at me. "Knox, could you find Anique and keep her free from being harassed for the rest of the wedding? If you can do that, I'll consider your request regarding my girls visiting with their sister." Eyebrows jumping, Rhiannon opened her mouth to talk. "No!" Stirling cut in, "He has to find her, Rhiannon. We can delay the full family photos by ten minutes." Stirling smirked as he walked off. Studying me with curiosity, Rhiannon gave a quick bow of her head and followed her father.

Stirling was testing me, or he was providing privacy for his daughter to reject me, I wasn't sure. Either way, a challenge had been issued. Taking a deep breath to clear my nose, I exhaled it away. Going to the chair Anique had been sitting on, I breathed in deep. Her scent was a mixture of herbs, almost free of the usual she-wolf scent, but also free of the perfumes human women liked to wear. It puzzled me for a moment, then I remembered that this girl was trying to avoid being found.

"How clever. She used an anise base." Taking another deep breath, I tried to catch the combination. The anise hid her wolf scent, the other herbs hid the aroma of the anise, but not quite. Waiting a moment to cement the smell, I moved towards the side door. Following the herbal trail, I wandered through the gardens where people were smiling and chatting, and down a path that seemed to lead into a paddock. Turning just before the fence, I almost doubled back around the back of the building, until I found a willow tree hanging over a pond.

Sweeping back the fronds, I found Anique sitting by the edge of the pond, watching the fish swim. She almost appeared cat-like, the way her head tilted as she watched the fish.

"I don't want a mate. I don't care what the Goddess says, I won't submit to you." Keeping her eyes on the fish, Anique snapped her arm out quickly, then back, water falling from it. Gently, she unfolded her hand to reveal the suffocating fish. She plopped it back in the pond just as quickly.

Impressed by her reflexes, I smiled as I edged closer. "A mate was not on my agenda either," I informed her, coming to stand by her. "At least, not yet. I have plans that being mated would get in the way of." Becoming qualified as a trainer would take months away from home to study and to clock up the teaching hours. Before I could do that, I had to train up Dante to fill in for me at work. With he and Evaline about to embark on their honeymoon, taking a mate of my own would put my ambitions on hold permanently.

Rising up, Anique brushed the grass and leaves from her dress. "Then we are agreed. We will ignore the first phase and go back to our lives unaffected."

Removing a leaf from her hair, I lifted a brow. "I didn't agree with that."

Anique frowned. "But-"

"I agreed I don't want a mate right now. However, we are true-mates, and we have already seen the first phase of the moon. It would be impossible to forget each other. My proposal is that we get to know each other; become friends. That way, when we are ready, it's is just a matter of completing the other three phases."

Clasping her hands together, Anique looked at me through her brows, refusing to meet my eyes again. "And how would the Valley-morgan Alpha, and a rogue she-wolf of the Beachrunners, account for spending time together?"

A what?! When I rocked back like she'd elbowed me in the chest, Anique's eyes sparkled. "Oh, no one told you I'm rogue?" She stepped away from the pond. "I turned human. I live with and date humans. I've never returned to the packhouse since I left for college. It's why I'm going to have to spend this entire farce avoiding my brother and his friends, or they are going to drag me home, tie me up, and force me to shift," Anique growled. "And that would kill me."

Assessing her, I saw the ferocity her father described in her forest eyes. "Because Dan would mark you and force you to submit."

"He'd try," Anique frowned.

Now, I understood why she stayed away. If Dan marked her, she'd have to rip his throat out to avoid submitting to him. It's what Stirling was warning me about. That didn't explain why she was rogue, but I'd find that out soon enough. "Well, avoid no more." I offered her my arm. "Your Alpha has asked me to be your escort tonight, to keep the wolves at bay," I winked.

Studying me, the side of Anique's mouth twitched, giving an edge of a smile to her lips. "Really?"

"Really," I acknowledged the real question. Has my father asked you, an outsider, to protect me? "Really," I assured. Stepping closer, I was tempted to put my nose to her neck and breathe her scent. "Now, it's time for the family photos."

Placing her arm in mine tentatively, Anique allowed me to walk her to the makeshift photoshoot. Dan was there waiting with Edward, but we ignored them and walked up to the wedding party. "Stirling, your daughter, as requested." Grinning, I delivered her to her father.

Taking his daughter's hand, Stirling pulled her into his nook protectively, his eyes lighting up. There was no hiding that this wolf adored his daughter, and wanted her to be happy. Starting to suspect he'd been protecting her all these years, I puzzled out what I knew. Anique was the first to be allowed to move out of the packhouse. What happened that forced an Alpha to take such drastic action to protect a she-wolf?

DARK FANTASY / PARANORMAL ROMANCE / FANTASY BY EBONY OLSON

STANDALONES

Of Shadow and Light

Boundary

Silver Rogue

HIERARCH SERIES
(Radish Fiction Exclusive)

Succumb

Numinous

Masked

Exodus (Coming 2020/21)

RAVEN'S WING TRILOGY
(Radish Fiction Exclusive)

Phased

ROMANCE SUSPENSE BY EBONY OLSON

Hotel Series

HOLLY CLAIRE TRILOGY

Henderson

Cassidy

Holmes

Holly's Trilogy: Books 1-3 Hotel Series (Compilation)

JESS BUTLER TRILOGY

Best Man

Eleri Royals Series

Calypso

Standalones

Black Mark: The Complete Saga

Rain: A Dark Past Romance

Protective Instinct (December 2020)

ABOUT THE AUTHOR

Ebony lives in Sydney, Australia, with her husband, daughter, and six rescue cats. She loves to read fantasy, thrillers, and paranormal romance, spending most of her free time with her nose in a book or writing.

Having always possessed an over-active imagination Ebony spent her younger years regaling friends with fantastic stories, holding her audience captive with the passion and suspense of her characters plights. In adulthood, she shows no signs of stopping her imagination from spreading across as many pages as it can find.

Website: http://ebonyolson.com/
Ebony's Mischief & Mayhem Peeps

 facebook.com/EbonyOlson.Author

twitter.com/Ebony_Olson

instagram.com/ebony_olson

amazon.com/author/ebonyolson

bookbub.com/authors/Ebony_Olson

goodreads.com/Ebony_Olson